Queen of Spades:
The Complete Collection

Jewel Geffen

ISBN: 9781798864845

CONTENTS

BOOK ONE: THE BLACK AND WHITE CLUB

Percy

"Are you sure this is the place?"

Percy Brice stared up at the glowing facade of the mansion. Huge marble pillars lined the front of the vast house. Everything looked golden and gleaming and expensive. It was almost tacky, but the overall effect of the place was so stunning that it didn't really bother him. He glanced down his phone, checking the GPS. "That's what it says, hon."

"Wow."

"I know."

"Percy... this is incredible."

"Pays to be the boss, I guess."

"No kidding."

His wife Jennifer was shaking her head. She seemed hardly able to believe what she was seeing. He didn't blame her. They started up the long stone walk leading to the ornate door, and Percy tapped the knocker. He gave it a gentle clack, worried he might damage it if he banged on it too hard. Like everything else, it looked expensive.

He'd been blown away by the house they were setting him up in. Even now, filled up with packing boxes and junk as it was, it was still by far the nicest place they'd ever lived. They kept asking each other how they'd ever gotten so lucky. But *this* place was on another level. The house they'd given him, though magnificent, was like a shack next to this palace. He thanked his lucky stars again that he'd taken Tommy's advice and applied at the firm. Clearly, there was a lot of money to be made here.

It was a big deal, moving from Minnesota to Florida, and every single step of the way he'd felt sure that he was making a huge mistake. But now they were here, their first night in town, and it was like some incredible dream come true. His new boss Jonas Harrington had insisted that Percy and his wife come to the so-called "little party" he was throwing. One look at the mansion, however, gave Percy the idea that Mr.

Harrington didn't actually do anything that could reasonably be called "little."

"I feel a bit under-dressed..." Jennifer fretted, patting at her perfectly sensible but by-no-means glamorous outfit.

"You look great, honey." He gave her a peck on the cheek.

In truth, she looked beautiful. At least, she looked beautiful to him, and always had. She was a tall and shapely woman of almost forty years, with long brown hair and soft dark green eyes. They'd been married for fifteen years now. In all that time, he'd never laid eyes on a woman he thought was more attractive.

The door opened. The lights were dim, and there was a low throbbing music coming from somewhere deep inside. A woman stood before them, slender and elfin and very tan. She wore a slinky red party dress and her crimson lipstick seemed to pop off her mouth when she smiled. Jen fretted again at her outfit reflexively.

"You must be Percy. And your lovely wife. Please come in." Her smile was enormous, almost unnervingly so. She stepped back and ushered them inside. "I'm Matilda Harrington, and I'm so *thrilled* to meet you. Jonas has told me nothing but good things."

"Great, glad to hear that. I'm, uh, it's a pleasure to meet you too." Percy and Jennifer stepped inside, walking gingerly on the immaculate tile mosaic floor.

They came in from the walkway and went down a long hall. Jennifer gasped at one of the paintings on the wall, but Percy didn't recognize it. "Is that real?" she asked.

Matilda just laughed, leading them on into a parlor. It was crowded, the lights low and the atmosphere intensely sensual. Matilda smiled, "I'll let you mingle. A lot of these fine people are Percy's new coworkers, so please make nice. The mini-bar is over there, and I'm just a tootle away if you need anything."

"Um, thank you."

"Yes, thank you," Jennifer added, eyeing the assembled guests with something like horror. There were maybe thirty thirty people at the party, and of course they were all incredibly dressed. Lots of low-cut tops and silky material and dazzling jewelry. She groaned, and muttered under her breath in Percy's ear, "I feel like a farmer's housewife in this."

"You look great, really," he murmured back, though he was starting to feel a bit out of place himself in his rumpled suit-coat and baggy trousers. The men were all younger and trimmer and better dressed than him, and he couldn't pretend that it wasn't obvious. He felt a warm tingle of embarrassment worming up his spine.

"Tilly baby," he heard a deep and resonant voice from somewhere behind him. Matilda Harrington lit up, turning at once. Percy looked.

There was a man coming in the door behind him. Tall, six foot five easily, and built like a fitness guru, with muscles you could see rippling beneath his trim-fitting suit. His head was bald and so smooth that it shone in the moody lights, and a single gold earring flashed in the right lobe. He had a neatly trimmed black beard and piercing eyes. His skin was a rich and chocolate brown, a sort of burnt mocha hue. He met Percy's eyes briefly and flashed a startlingly bright and toothy grin at him. "My man," he said, placing a hand on his shoulder as he stepped neatly passed the flustered Percy.

"Percy darling, you're blocking the door..." Jennifer muttered.

"Right, sorry..."

Matilda went right to him, resting her hand on the man's bicep and standing actually quite a bit closer to him than two people normally did, even at sultry parties like this. Especially if one of those people is married. Because this guy was certainly *not* Jonas Harrington.

"This the champagne you looking for, Tilly?" he rumbled, lifting a coke green bottle in his large hands.

"It is," she practically cooed, sliding the bottle from his hands, "exactly what I wanted." She turned briefly to Percy and Jennifer. "Percy dear, this is Marquis. Marquis, this is Jonas' new associate and his wife."

Marquis smiled softly. He plainly wasn't much interested in either Percy or Jennifer. His eyes hardly left Matilda Hamilton's as he gave Percy and firm handshake and greeting. And her eyes hardly left his.

"Are, um, I mean, do you work at the firm as well?" Percy asked, struggling to make some kind of conversation. He was tired and jet-lagged and he'd been moving boxes and furniture all day, but damn it if he wasn't going to at least *attempt* to not make an idiot of himself.

The tall black man laughed softly. "Me? A lawyer? Naw, man, not me." He didn't offer anything else.

Matilda pulled at his arm. "Come pour me a drink, would you?"

He nodded, a little grin tugging at the side of his mouth, and he took her by the hand to lead her towards the mini-bar.

Percy patted his pockets absently, feeling like he'd forgotten something. He felt flustered and a little overheated, and he wasn't sure exactly why. He turned to his wife. "So, uh... shall we mingle?"

* * *

They did their best, but they never got exactly comfortable at the party. Everyone there seemed a good ten years younger than them, and they had only a vague understanding of most of the subjects being discussed. Percy's new coworkers seemed like a decent bunch, as decent as a gang of young lawyers could be, anyway. Eventually, after an hour of slightly strained small talk, they slipped out into the hall.

Jennifer let out a deep breath and leaned against the wall. "Yikes," was all she said.

"Yeah."

They looked at each other, and they burst out laughing. They couldn't help it, they were so tired and so out of their element, there was nothing else to do but laugh about it.

Jennifer wiped a tear from the corner of her eyes. "Good luck guessing who the couple from Minnesota are."

Percy scoffed, grinning. "Nah. Just give me a few months hitting the gym and the tanning booth and I'll looks just like those guys."

She snorted. "You at the gym. *Right.* Anyway, I'll never be mistaken for one of those women. God, I couldn't believe what they were *wearing.*"

"You're the prettiest one in the room, honey."

She rolled her eyes, but blushed faintly. "Oh please."

"I mean it. I could see them looking at you." It wasn't just flattery; he had caught more than one admiring look cast in his wife's direction. To be honest, it had given him a bit of a thrill, seeing the fit young men eyeing her with such obvious interest.

She waved him off, taking a moment to study the art hanging in the hall. It was good stuff. Jonas clearly hadn't skimped on the decor. He had a clear preference for classical nudes. There was something strange about standing in a hallway full of naked women and acting like there was nothing particular about it. "It's all..." she searched for the words, "It's a very... well, *sexual* vibe in there. Or am I imagining it?" Her voice dropped to a whisper when she said the word. *Sexual,* like a murmured secret.

Percy shrugged. "Oh, I don't know. Something maybe. They're young, and this *is* Florida, after all. People cut loose down here. More than they do up north, anyway."

"I guess."

The door burst open, and Jonas Harrington crashing into the hall. He'd tripped on the door-frame, and come tumbling into Percy's arms, just avoiding landing flat on his face.

The head of the law firm, and Percy's new employer, had been curiously absent up to the point of his dramatic entrance. It wasn't *exactly* the way Percy had planned to great him.

The rotund little lawyer disentangled himself, apologizing profusely. "Jesus *Christ*! God, I swear I haven't been drinking. Not too much, anyway. Not *yet*, anyway." He laughed, brushing his shirt back down and straightening his wire-rimmed glasses. "Percival Brice! My god, there you are at last! Skulking by the look of it."

He felt his cheeks color. "Not at all, Mr. Harrington, we just-"

Jonas waved him off. "Don't think of it, Brice. We old fogies have to stick together. Listen, I just want to say what a pleasure it is to have you in our clutches at last. Glad we were able to lure you away from that frozen wasteland. A talented litigator like yourself shouldn't be wasting his talents in Duluth!"

"Well, thank you very much, sir, it's an honor to-"

"I think you're just what this place needs, Brice. Some gravitas, some *experience*. These young pups need an old hand to look up to. That's what I'm counting on. The job you did on the Masterson case? Brilliant. I'm looking for more work like that."

"Of course, Mr. Harrington."

"And this is your beautiful wife? Genevieve?"

"Jennifer," she said, taking his offered hand and giving it a gentle shake.

He smacked his forehead. "Of course, my apologies. You've met Tilly, I hope?"

"Yes, she-"

"What a peach, am I right? I'm a lucky guy, I know, I know. But you've obviously done alright for yourself, eh, Brice?" He winked at Percy, eyeing Jennifer with obvious admiration. She had a good eight inches on him, and looked very statuesque indeed leaning against the wall beside a Rubenesque nude.

"Um, thank you, sir. I guess I have."

"He *guesses*," Jonas laughed. "Well, don't mind me. You two enjoy the party, alright? And Brice," another firm handshake, "welcome aboard." And he was gone.

Jennifer gave Percy a long and meaningful look, her eyebrow quirked.

Percy shrugged. "He's the boss."

* * *

Around eleven o'clock the party started to wind down. They were both dead tired after their long day of moving and were about ready to call it a night. Percy excused himself to find a bathroom, leaving Jennifer yawning beside the punch bowl while a bunch of lawyer's wives tittered about their country club memberships.

He got lost, of course, and found himself wandering cluelessly through the halls of the enormous house. He finally found a restroom, well away from the party and quite likely one of the Harrington's private washrooms. Would he get in trouble for wandering off and invading their privacy? Never mind, it was late and he was tired and there was no one around. He'd just pop in quick and be on his way. The door swung open soundlessly - a far cry from their place in Minnesota with its creaky hinges and groaning floorboards.

He did his bit and washed up at the immaculate sink. The basin looked like real ivory, the handles and faucet seemed to be gold-plated. He dried his hands on a fluffy white linen towel and spent a good four or five minutes obsessively going over the place to make sure he'd left nothing amiss.

He cracked the door, noiseless still, and peeked out into the hall. His heart leaped in his chest. There was someone right outside, just across the hall! He shrank back, pulling the door with him so that it was barely open, no more than a hair. He saw a man's broad shoulders, the back of a smooth dark head, and a pair of slender white hands reaching around to cup the man's taut buttocks. He heard soft wet sounds, and a faint moaning.

"Mm... that's right baby. Do it how daddy likes."

"Yes, daddy..."

Percy felt his eyes widening. He recognized the voices. The deep male timbre of Marquis' rumbling voice, and the breathy trill of Mildred Harrington. They were locked in a deep and passionate embrace, kissing fiercely. Percy swore wordlessly, shaping the words. God, he didn't want to see this! This was the last thing he needed, to get tangled up in his new employer's personal life. And yet he could not take his eyes off them.

He saw Mildred's leg rise, sliding along the black man's flank. His large dark hand moved smoothly up the thigh, following the deep slit in her cocktail dress. He could see the petite woman visibly trembling. He heard her voice, soft and shaking, murmuring something.

"Do it, daddy, do it."

A low chuckled. "You know how Imma do it to you, baby-girl."

"Yes..."

Marquis bent low, and Percy saw him slip his hand down the front of Mildred's low cut dress, cupping the small breast inside, then sliding the shoulder-strap down to expose the pert white swell of her naked bosom. His dark fingers teased expertly at the small pink nipple.

"Take me, daddy."

Marquis chuckled again, and lifted the slender women easily off her feet. He tossed her bodily over his broad shoulder and turned about with a swagger. Percy felt his heart skip a beat. They weren't coming here, were they? He recoiled, clutching at the knob. But no, they turned and went down the hall in the other direction, Tilly giggling madly.

Percy let out a breath he hadn't been aware of holding, and rested his head heavily against the door frame. Christ, that had been a close one. What had he seen? An affair? They certainly weren't being especially discreet about it, it was obvious almost from the moment he'd entered the house that something was going on. He could hardly believe that they would be that bold about it, however. Carrying on practically under Jonas's nose!

He slipped silently into the hallway when he thought that enough time had passed. He felt a rather desperate urge to get far away, and back to the relative safety of the party.

"Enjoy the show?"

Percy stopped dead in his tracks, no more than a dozen paces from the bathroom door.

Jonas Harrington stepped quietly out of a shadowy doorway, his wire-frames glinting. The little man seemed to be attempting - and not entirely successfully - to hide a grin.

"Sir, I... well, I mean. I was just looking for a bathroom," he stuttered lamely, feeling like an idiot. His head was spinning.

"Quite a peach, isn't she. My little Tilly-mouse."

"I..."

"Oh, don't be so nervous, Percival. I know all about her and the gentleman."

"You... know?"

"More than that, my boy, a great deal more. I have no issues with our man Marquis. No issues at all. Quite the stallion, isn't he?"

"I'm not sure I understand, sir."

Jonas Harrington patted Percy's arm. "I think you understand more than you think. If you have questions, well... you just drop by sometime." A card was suddenly in the little lawyer's hand, and then pressed quickly into Percy's.

Percy tucked it into his shirt pocket in a kind of daze, not even reading it. "Thank you, sir," he said, not exactly sure for what he was thanking the other man. It just seemed appropriate somehow.

"You're quite welcome, Brice. Now then, I'm afraid you're going to have to excuse me. I don't want to miss the performance."

Jonas patted Percy's arm once more and moved quietly after his wife and her lover - there was little doubt in Percy's mind now that Marquis *was* quite plainly Matilda's lover, though he didn't entirely understand it. He watched his new employer for a moment, then hurried back the way he'd come, towards the slow hum of music still throbbing from the party room.

* * *

He was exceptionally quiet on the ride home. Jennifer kept giving him sidelong glances as he drove.

"Something on your mind, Percy?"

He stared out the window. Palm trees swaying in the starlight. The Florida night was cool and still. To think the snow had been ankle deep in Minnesota when they'd left. That had been less than twenty-four hours ago, and here he was actually getting overheated without so much as a jacket on. Somewhere in the far distance, glimpsed occasionally through the gleaming towers and twinkling streetlights, he could see the glitter of moonlight on the ocean.

"Percy?"

"Hm?"

"I asked if there was anything on your mind."

"No. No, not really. Just... you know."

"Tired?"

"*Dead* tired." He forced a grin. He still had not yet read the card in his jacket pocket, but he could feel it there, weighing on him.

"Did you have a good time?"

"I guess so. Not really our scene though, is it?"

She shook her head ruefully. "Not exactly, no."

He reached over and gave her hand a squeeze. She smiled at him. He looked at her for a moment, their eyes meeting. The shifting lights of the beachfront city played across her features, neon and pale. Her long chestnut hair curled about her face, full and dark, and her green eyes sparkled. "It's a lot to get used to."

"It certainly is," she said, sighing softly.

"We'll be okay," he said.

"I know."

The thrum of the car on the highway lulled them back into a comfortable silence. Beneath the quiet, however,

Percy's mind was working furiously. What had he seen, really? And what did it *mean*? Something was going on with Jonas Harrington and his wife, something more than just an affair or an open marriage. He was sure of it, and he was going to find out.

* * *

They collapsed into bed almost as soon as they got home. There were moving boxes stacked against the walls and the TV lay on its side. They'd not even had a chance to make the bed properly, but lay atop the bare mattress and tangled blankets.

It kept replaying over and over again in his mind, the pale and slender white hands caressing the black man's strong back. The dark hands cupping the smooth white breast. The sounds of their mouths, their lips open and tongues intertwined. The glint of Jonas's glasses from the shadows. Take me Daddy...

He rolled over. Jennifer lay beside him on her side with her back to him, breathing softly, not yet sleeping. He touched her, a bit tentatively, running his hand over the curve of her hip.

She stirred, murmuring sleepily. "Love you, baby."

He slid himself gently against her, pressing himself to her, feeling the warmth of her, the silky smoothness of her nightdress against his bare chest. His hand gripped her, squeezing her hip. She wriggled gently, letting a contented moan slip out. He pushed against her, pressing his whole body against hers. His chin on her shoulder, his arm wrapped over her, his feet tangling with hers. Her full rump against his crotch.

She turned back a little, looking in the darkness. "What's up, babe?"

"Do you want to try?" he asked, moving subtly against her, grinding on her soft body.

"Tonight? Aren't you too tired, baby?"

"No, I want to try. If you're up for it."

She smiled sleeping, rubbing at her eyes. "You know I am."

He slipped his hand up under her nightdress. Her skin was so soft on his hand; it sent tingles rushing through him. His fingertips brushed over the soft cotton hem of her panties.

She turned back and kissed him, smiling against her lips and wriggling back against him. She pushed her butt on him, working it, grinding slowly.

He kissed her back, and their mouths opened. She tasted clean and fresh. He could taste the minty mouthwash on her tongue. Her tongue darted inside his mouth, exploring tentatively. Her hand dipped down below his waist.

"Is he awake?" she asked, touching his privates through the cloth of his underwear.

"Give me a sec."

"Okay, hon." Her tone was cautious, reserved. She was trying not to pressure him, he could tell. Didn't want to get her hopes up.

He squeezed his eyes shut. God, not again. Not this *again*. Come *on*. He willed himself to perform. It had been this way since the Masterson trial. The stress of it had been crushing. For three years he'd been in crunch mode, grinding himself down to nothing. He hadn't had a hard-on in so long, he could hardly remember the last time. And from the looks of things... tonight wasn't going to be the night.

God, he was such a goddamn failure... Jen had been a trooper through it all, supporting him every step of the way, never blaming him. It didn't matter though. It *was* him, his inadequacy. If he couldn't even please his wife, what did it matter if he'd won the case? What did it matter if he got the great new job? He'd hoped, and he knew that she did too, that the end of the trial would fix things. It hadn't. But maybe the move would do it; maybe the change of scenery would help him. Now it seemed that not even that would help him.

Jennifer reached into his underpants, her hand sliding under the tight waistband and the tight white cotton. She stroked him, gently, eagerly, expertly.

They were both holding their breath, waiting for the response. Anything, any twitch.

He sighed heavily and took hold of her hand. He pulled it gently away. "Never mind, honey. Just too tired tonight after all."

"Okay," she said, and he felt a lump fill his throat at the sound of her soft sad voice. She'd wanted this. She'd wanted it bad, had been holding out hope for so long, waiting on him so patiently. But she was tired of waiting, he could tell. He cursed himself for having gotten her hopes up only to disappoint her once again.

God. He was such a fuck-up.

"I, uh... just have to brush my teeth," he said, fighting back tears.

"Alright, babe." She lay back down, pulling the covers back up over herself. Of course she knew he'd already brushed them, she'd been standing right beside him at the time. He slipped on his slippers and shuffled to the bathroom.

He stood there before the mirror. A rumpled tired looking man now a few good years past forty, over-worked, overweight and over the hill. *Christ*, what had become of him? He didn't care for himself, but Jen deserved better. After everything she'd done for him, all she'd sacrificed, she *deserved* so much more. He put down the toilet seat cover and sat there, his head in his hands.

He pulled down his briefs and looked at himself, at his flaccid little cock. He felt like swearing out loud. He was broken and useless. Done for. He grasped hold of himself, giving it a few swift experimental strokes. Maybe?

No. If Jennifer couldn't do it, there was no way he was gonna get there on his own. He imagined her, pictured her naked body, the way her face looked when they were doing it.

As close as he could remember it, anyway. He thought of Matilda and Marquis, and he thought he felt a twinge, but no. Nothing.

His suit was draped over the towel rack. He'd been too exhausted to even hang it up properly. He got up tiredly and put it on a hanger, trying in vain to smooth out some of the wrinkles. It was bad enough already, he didn't need to make it worse. He'd need to have it pressed, or maybe he'd just buy a new one with his signing bonus. He wasn't sure his dependable old Minnesota clothing would fly down here in the sunny south.

He was about to go back to bed and try and sleep off the memory of his failure when the thought occurred to him that he'd not yet looked at the card Jonas Harrington had given him. He fished it out of the jacket pocket and took a long hard look at it. The card was completely midnight black on one side, the corners sharp and crisp and the paper elegantly thick. He turned it over. There was writing on the front in embossed silver letters. *The Black and White Club.* Beneath that, an address and the words *by invitation only.*

He turned it over again, studying it curiously. He felt slightly disappointing. That was all it was? An exclusive bar or something? He shrugged, tucked it back into his jacket pocket, and went back to bed. Jennifer was already asleep, breathing softly. He brushed the hair off her face and looked at her for a long time. "Sorry, honey," he murmured finally, and lay down beside her. It was only seconds before he was fast asleep.

* * *

Their first few weeks in Florida went by in a blur. Between moving into the new house and starting the new job, they hardly had a chance to catch their breath. The disastrous first night was not mentioned, and they didn't even discuss trying again. Better not to get her hopes up, Percy kept telling himself. He tried on his own, hoping he might be able to make something happen, but of course it was to no avail. Maybe it was time to see a doctor, not that there was much hope of it helping.

Back when his problems had first started he'd tried to get on Viagra. Why not? It was embarrassing, but he could swallow his pride. It could be a lot worse, after all. Then came the bad news. It turned out that a certain rare type of heart disorder ran in Percy's family, nothing too serious, but the doc had strongly recommended not taking any chances with the little blue helpers. He told Jennifer that he was willing to roll the dice, but she said that it wasn't worth the risk, and that was that.

Maybe it was time for a second opinion. And who knew what might have changed since then? Medical science was advancing at leaps and bounds, maybe there had been a new development which might make his problem go away.

Yeah right. He should be so lucky.

He was driving home on a calm Friday night after a grueling second week of work. It was almost nine o'clock. They certainly weren't taking it easy on him on account of being new. If anything, he thought they might be gently hazing him. See if the old guy can keep up. He'd kept up, but the effort was tremendous. He hoped it wasn't going to always be like this, it was almost as bad as it had been during the Masterson trial. And *that* had almost driven him to the breaking point.

He reached absently into his jacket pocket for a mint. They'd served garlic bread with lunch and his breath was going to knock Jennifer over when he got home if he didn't do something about it.

That's when he felt the card again. The little monochrome card from Jonas Harrington. *The Black and White Club.* He glanced at it for a moment, holding it awkwardly against the wheel while he popped the mint into his mouth. He came to a stoplight.

The red light seemed to flood over the car. There had been a sprinkling of rain that afternoon and the city streets were gleaming. He hesitated for just a moment, then he picked up his phone and typed the address on the card into his GPS. Only four miles away, just turn right and head straight along on the nearly empty street.

Come on, Percy. Don't be stupid. Don't waste your time.

The light turned, and the silver lettering on the card in his hand went from red to green. Without thinking on it for a second longer, he turned the wheel hard to the right, shifted into the turning lane and off he went.

It was crazy. *He* was crazy. What the hell was he thinking? He needed to get home. Jennifer had waited for him long enough, whatever dinner she'd fixed was probably cold. Again.

He wouldn't stay. He wouldn't even get out of the car, he decided. He'd just take a quick look. Just drive by the place, have a quick peek. That was all.

Percy drove automatically, allowing the GPS to guide him. The antiseptic uptown district faded, slowly shifting character as he went. There were fewer doctor's offices and public buildings now, and more nightclubs and strange little hole-in-the-wall restaurants. He saw girls standing on the street corners, girls of all types and colors in tiny tight little outfits, leaning out to show themselves off and beckoning at the passing cars. He drove on.

You have arrived at your destination.

He pulled over, keeping the blinker on and the car running, and he leaned over to look out the passenger window. At first, he thought the GPS must have made some kind of mistake. This couldn't be it, there was nothing there. Then he saw it, a plain door lit by a dull purple glow under a dark awning. A small sign card beside the door - he had to squint to make it out it - read *The Black and White Club.*

He pulled ahead a little, letting the car drive a few feet forward. On the other side of the door there were three men resting casually in the mouth of the alley. Three tall and muscular African-American men dressed in a casual sort of formal-wear. Black slacks and white shirts, with velvet black jackets or vests on. No ties, their top buttons undone. They stood there with an easy sort of grace. The one in the middle was smoking something. A blunt? He blew pale smoke into the warm night. One of them spotted Percy's card idling and pointed to it. He looked like he was laughing. The others joined in, one of them flashing a peace sign in Percy's direction.

Percy waved back awkwardly, blushing deeply. Why was he embarrassed? He hadn't done anything wrong. But his cheeks were still flaming. He tucked his head down and pulled the turn signal down the other way, and drove back out onto the rain-slicked streets.

* * *

"Have you ever been with a black guy?"

Jennifer laughed. "*What*?"

"You know. Like sex. Had sex with a black guy."

"I know what you *meant*, Percy, I just..." She shook her head, totally bemused. "I can't say that I have, no. You do realize that I grew up in the sticks, right? I don't even remember *seeing* a black person until after you and I were married."

"You ever think about it?"

"Have I ever thought about having sex with a black man? I don't know. Jesus, Percy, where is this coming from?"

He shrugged.

"Do... Do you think I cheated on you? Is this some kind of test?" She crossed her arms, glowering. "Is this... what? Some transparent attempt to trick me into admitting something? Because there isn't anything, Percy, I-"

"Jen, Jen," he cut her off, crossing the room and putting his arms around her stiff body. "I'm not trying to *do* anything. I was just curious. We've been married a long time and, well, I mean. We've never really talked that much about our, you know. Our fantasies and things. I just want to know what *you* want. Even if it's only in your wildest dreams or your subconscious or whatever. It was only an innocent question, I promise."

She relaxed a little, leaning against him slightly. "Well... I mean. I have thought about it before, I'll admit that, Who hasn't? It's such a... I mean, there's this *mystique*, right?"

Percy felt a thrilling sort of charge running through his belly. "Yeah? So what's the appeal? I mean, in all honesty."

"Honestly?" She hesitated. "I'm not racist, you know that."

"Of course."

"I mean, I get that it's a stereotype, but... It just seems so *raw*, you know? Almost bestial. Being just... ravaged by this totally dominant man, completely in control of you. With black guys... it's weird. It's like, they don't really care about satisfying you, but they're just so good it happens anyway. They just *use* you, and you want to fight it but you can't because it feels too good and your body just takes over. Just being at the mercy of something so big and powerful and relentless. Being totally dominated, but... still having a kind of power over them... I don't know. It's complicated."

There was a silence between them for a long moment. "Wow," Percy said.

She blushed. "It's just a fantasy right? I mean, I know that might sound... offensive, when you come out and say it but... I mean, I can't help what I feel, right? It's not about reality, it's just sex and fantasy. So it's okay, right?"

"Yeah. Yeah, it's okay." He held her tight against him. His brain was swimming with a thousand contradictory thoughts. He wasn't sure if he was upset or turned on or jealous or eager, but he was feeling *something*. Something deep within himself was stirring, and had begun to awaken.

* * *

Percy sat in his office, staring at the black and silver card in his hands. He thought of the mysterious door beneath the dark awning, of the three lithe young men standing in the purple neon light.

His phone chirped. A text from Jennifer. He thumbed the notification and brought it up. *-It's Sunday tomorrow, baby. Do u finally get the day off?*

They'd been working him mercilessness for almost two months solid now. In those eight weeks, he'd managed just a half a dozen days off, and those had been in the first couple weeks. He brought up his schedule on the PC. Booked, two appointments in the morning and a conference all afternoon. Damn it. He texted back. *-Short day on Sunday, I promise. We'll get dinner somewhere.*

-U owe me, Percy Brice.

-I know. Sorry honey. Make it up to you. We'll go somewhere nice.

-How nice? :P

-Go out today, buy something pretty. One of those sexy Florida dresses maybe.

-Sure u can handle it? ;)

-I think so, hon. I'm sure you'll knock their socks off.

-Who's they?

Percy stared at the phone in his hand. Who *had* he meant? Wires crossed, that was all. He'd been thinking of the three young black men in formal wear. But why? He glanced at the card again. *The Black and White Club.* He could be adventurous. They weren't like all the other boring people who never went anywhere more exciting than the Olive Garden. They could dare the underground. And after all, it came recommended by Jonas Harrington himself, who hardly seemed the type to frequent an establishment that was anything less than lavish and tasteful.

-Knock MY socks off, I mean. He texted back.

-Okay, baby. See u tonight.

He thought of that brief conversation he'd had with Jonas in the hallway. "*If you have questions, drop by sometime.*" That's what he had said, wasn't it? Obviously he had some kind of arrangement with his wife, an open marriage. Percy had heard of it, but never seen such a thing back home. Things were different here. Freer. Whatever floats your boat, and all that. Obviously Matilda had met her lover at the restaurant. Why not?

He couldn't deny a certain... desire. He wanted to see what the place was like, to get a look inside it for himself. The mystery of it seemed to call to him, summoning his interest. He knew he wouldn't be able to get it out of his head until he actually ventured to go there for himself.

Percy looked at the card again. *By invitation only.* Well... Jonas had invited him, hadn't he? Would something more than that be required to gain entrance? He flushed preemptively at the thought of taking Jennifer there and being turned away at the door. After promising something grand, too. Perhaps he should speak with Jonas about it once more just to confirm?

But no. Something told him that he'd rather keep it to himself. He had a strange feeling of doing something illicit, though it was hard to say what prompted the feeling. It was just the atmosphere around here. Spring had come, and you couldn't go three blocks without seeing someone in a bikini or a Speedo. He was still adjusting, that was all. He'd had no luck in the bedroom department, and it had opened up the strain between Jennifer and he all over again. He had really hoped that the move might take care of his problem...

Things had been alright otherwise. He'd settled into the job quiet well, even if they were keeping him crushingly busy. The house was looking fantastic; Jen had done an incredible job making it feel homey, as usual. She was a deft hand at that sort of thing, and had considered taking a job as an interior decorator at one point, before Percy's career had made the idea of her having a job redundant. There were a lot of things Jennifer could have done, and Percy was sure that there was at least some part of her which regretted being stuck at home. He sometimes wondered what she got up to all day, though could never quiet work up the courage to ask.

He tossed his phone on the desk and went back to work with a heavy sigh.

* * *

She did go out and buy a dress that night, but she refused to show it to him. She'd blushed a little when she said it, which he decided to take as a good sign. The thought of her in some slinky little form-fitting number made his stomach do flip-flops. They'd been married a long time, and he'd become quite intimately familiar with her body, as one did during a long relationship. But he hadn't really seen her done-up before. There had been little occasion for it back in Minnesota.

He managed to get out of work at the promised time on Sunday. Of course they tried to rope him back in with more stacks of briefs, but he begged off and managed to sneak out the back before they could chain him to his desk again.

She was ready to go and waiting at the top of the driveway when he arrived at the house. She wore a long coat, light enough not to overheat in, but big enough to hide the dress beneath. He smiled. He didn't get the full effect until after she'd opened the door and slipped into the seat beside him. He just stared at first.

"Wow."

"What?" she blushed, touching her face.

"You look amazing." He gave a low whistle.

She laughed. "God. It's nothing."

But she really did look incredible. Her face was lightly rouged so that her cheeks glowed a warm pink. Her eyes were lined with a striking black and shaded with cool blue. Her red lipstick popped. She'd had her hair done. He didn't really know much about styles or fashion or anything, but it looked amazing to him, full and rich and curling artfully about her features. She'd never been much for makeup before. It had been ages since they'd gone to a formal event which had called for it, and she wasn't one to get done up just to go about the house. He'd seen pictures of her in her younger days looking very sleek, but this was something else. She'd matured into the look, and it was truly stunning.

"It's not too much, is it?"

"It's perfect, honey."

"Well. I don't get a chance to dress up much."

"Maybe that's going to change now," he said, and put the car in drive.

She sat in silence, looking out the window and enjoying the warm evening. "So where are we going, anyway?"

"There's this place downtown Jonas recommended to me."

She laughed. "Can we afford it?"

"Honey," he said, "we can't afford to miss it," and he flashed her a grin.

"You're being very mysterious, Percy."

"No I'm not."

"Yes," she said, "you are. What's the big secret?"

"Nothing. I'm just glad to be getting out, finally."

"Even if I did have to beg you."

"Come on, you know it's not like that. They're working me to bone over there."

She sighed. "I know, I know. I just... hoped things might be different here. Seems like they're almost worse. I get so lonely, you know..."

He reached over and gave her shoulder a little squeeze. She nuzzled at his hand, her eyes shut.

It wasn't fair. He *knew* it wasn't. She deserved better, deserved more time, deserved someone who'd be able to get it up for her at the very least. Maybe he just wasn't man enough for her. The thoughts were heavy and dark in his mind. He tried to clear them out, tried to be cheerful. He wasn't going to screw up their first dinner date in weeks by getting in his head about things. He couldn't fix it all, had to go one step at a time.

They parked a half a block down from the club. Jennifer had been eyeing the neighborhood as they drove.

She looked at him with an eyebrow skeptically lifted. "My my, aren't we being adventurous."

"You ready?"

She popped open the door and hopped out. "Always."

The nondescript door glowed violet under the dark awning. Jennifer gave it a look. "It's fine," he said reassuringly, stepping up to the door with what he hoped looked like easy confidence and giving it a hard rap with his knuckles.

He shifted from foot to foot. He cleared his throat. Just as he raised his hand to knock again a little window at eye-level slid open with a rasp. A dark face pressed up against the window. "Yeah? What's up, man?"

"I, uh... I'm here to visit the club."

"You don't get in alone, white boy. Where your woman at?"

He hoped Jennifer wasn't overhearing this. What *was* he getting himself into? He leaned back a little, clearing his throat again, and nodded in Jennifer's direction.

The man at the window arched his neck to get a look at her, and smiled. His white teeth shown like pearls in the darkness. "Very nice, my man. You have an invitation, I'm sure?"

He held the black card up to the slot. "Um, Jonas Harring-"

"Shh shh shh. We don't use names here, white boy." He eyed the card. "Yeah, okay. Mr. J said you might be coming by." Another broad smile. "Lucky your woman's looking so fine though. Guess I can let you in."

"Ah... thank you."

"It's all good, my man."

The heavy door opened with a harsh grating sound, like a dungeon door being cracked open after years of disuse. Percy was starting to get a bad feeling about things. He hesitated at the threshold. Jennifer came up behind him. He could feel the question forming on her tongue, *is everything alright?* He took her hand and set it on his arm and he stepped boldly inside.

The doorman smiled at Jennifer, and it was an altogether different sort of smile than the one he'd given Percy. "Welcome to the Black and White Club, ma'am," he said, all elegance and easy grace. "May I take your coat?"

"Um... Thank you. Yes, please." She loosed the outer belt and undid the oversize buttons. The doorman stepped up behind her, reaching up to take the jacket. He almost, but not quite, seemed to caress her shoulders as he took it and laid it over his arm with the slightest of bows. She turned with a slight blush.

Percy had to force himself not to gawp at her. She looked gorgeous. The dress was midnight black, and hugged her every curve. Her wide hips and full rump and lush breasts were on full display in the slinky dress. The top was cut low, so he could see the soft swell of her pale bosom. Her shiny black pumps gave her already impressive height an extra boost, giving her a good three inches on Percy and putting her almost on a level with the doorman.

"Just down this hall and through the door, Ma'am. Sir," he added, nodding to Percy almost as an afterthought.

The hall was bare and a bit grim, to be perfectly honest. Little better than naked concrete, with no ornamentation but a long carpet with a swirling black and white pattern which led up to the doorway. Percy followed his wife to the door, feeling no small amount of trepidation. This wasn't some kind of twisted joke on Jonas's part, was it? It couldn't be. While the head of the firm clearly had some eccentricities, he'd struck Percy as being a decent enough sort.

That fear vanished when they went through the door, and was replaced with another worry entirely. The club was lavishly and exquisitely appointed. The color-scheme was of a rich dark crimson, velvet smooth and lush. A copper-gold chandelier turned slowly in the dimness of the high ceiling. There was an array of tables in the center of the large room, and a number of couches and settees along the walls. At the back there was a long bar, behind which dark bottles glittered and shone. The atmosphere was close and sexual, with low light and a throb of quiet jazz. There were perhaps a dozen couples seated throughout the room. There was an immediately apparent diversity within the room. All of the women, every single one of them regardless of their age, from early twenties to well into middle age, was white. They were all dressed in close-fitting and revealing garments. One woman near the door, who Percy couldn't help but notice, was wearing sheer black lace and nothing underneath, with little if anything left to the imagination. Something like a quarter of the men were white, usually older. The rest were black, most of them young and all of them impressively virile.

Several couples were getting quite intimate, cozy and close on the couches and kissing with their arms around each other. Some seemed to be going a good deal further than that. Nobody was naked or anything, but there was clearly some stimulation going on, hands caressing erogenous areas through cloth. A petite woman sat on a man's lap with her legs spread and her head thrown back on his shoulder while his hand circled her lower belly. All of the couples engaged in this sort of activity were, invariably, mixed.

"Um... here's a table," Percy said, and pulled out a chair for his wife. She sat, with some trepidation, and folded her hands in front of her. She wriggled a little in her seat, crossing her arms over her full breasts.

"What sort of place is this, Percy?"

He tried to play it off casually. "A dining club. At least that's what I was told." It was a bit of a stretch.

"Dining and what else?" she asked, eyebrow raised.

He shrugged. "Socializing, I'd imagine."

A couple, a woman of about forty-five and a large black man who couldn't have been half her age, came in through the beaded curtain at the back of the room. She had the flushed and contented looked of a woman who had been very well satisfied indeed, and he the swaggering walk of someone who'd been hard at work. She was laughing, and couldn't seem to keep her hands off him for longer than a moment at a time. They went to the bar and he ordered her a drink.

Their waiter appeared before Jen could comment on the scene. He handed them each a menu and a wine list. Percy ordered them a white wine and an appetizer and they settled in, taking stock of the activity around them.

"Well," said Jennifer wryly, "when I said we were being adventurous. I had no idea that we were getting quite *this* adventurous."

"I, um," Percy cleared his throat, "I didn't know it would be quite-"

"I'm proud of you, Percy. I wouldn't have thought you had it in you. Thank you for this." She raised her glass to him, then downed the whole thing in one long drink. She tapped her empty glass on the bottle, nodding her head for him to pour her another.

"You didn't? I mean, thank you. I mean, you're welcome."

"Still," she said, giving him a reproachful look, "you could have warned me first. This isn't generally the sort of thing couples surprise each other with on their anniversary."

Anniversary? He felt himself pale. Fuck. Fuck fuck fuck. How had he forgotten? He'd *never* forgotten, not for fifteen years. Fuck! He coughed, trying to hide his shock. "Well, you know. Thought it might be an experience."

"So *this* is why you were asking if I've ever been with a black man before. I get it now... Yikes, Percy. I don't know about this. This is... it's a *big* step."

"Well, you know... I just figured we'd check the place out."

"You said Jonas told you about this place? I suppose it's where Matilda and Marquis hooked up."

He blanched. "You knew about that? That they're together? How did you find out?"

She snorted. "*Please.* It was obvious from the first second I saw them together. I just wasn't sure how it got started. I guess I have my answer now. That's it, isn't it? This is a place where white couples find black men to have sex with their wives."

Percy felt his throat go dry and his bowels tighten. It seemed obvious to him now, and he felt like something of an idiot for not realizing it right away. He supposed that he had known, deep down, but hadn't quite been prepared to admit it to himself. Was that what he wanted? Jennifer to have sex with someone else? A man like Marquis? The thought of it... Well, he wasn't entirely sure what to make of it. He wasn't sure how he felt, but it wasn't necessarily a bad feeling. "Well," he said, "we don't have to decide anything right away. We're just here for dinner."

"Right," she winked, smirking and shaking her head. "I really can't believe this, Percy. I didn't think you could still surprise me, after all this time. I don't know though. I just don't know." But she was already scanning the room, eyeing the various men with obvious interest, and something like hunger.

"Well," he said, "it's your call, honey."

She blushed. "Thank you, baby. Just for the thought, even if nothing's going to come of it."

He couldn't believe that he'd forgotten it was their anniversary. She deserved better. More. He was so strung out from the job; he didn't know how he was going to make it work. Maybe this wasn't such a bad idea. How did he really feel about it, now that he was here? Would he be able to handle thinking of her doing it with another man? Was he like Jonas after all?

He wasn't sure. A person could never be completely sure until they were in the moment. But he was starting to think that maybe, just maybe, he would be into it. He thought of Marquis and Matilda, and he tried to imagine Jennifer in Tilly's place. It was... well, to be perfectly honest with himself, it seemed really hot. She deserved to have a lover that could satisfy her.

Even before his problem, he'd never been able to keep up with her. Once a week was enough for him, or even once a month. He'd never had that insatiable feeling that the boys and later men around him had seemed to demonstrate, with all their talk of nightly conquests and up-at-all-hours carousing. She was the kind of girl they would have gone wild over, someone who was always ready to go and would ride you until dawn if you let her. She was sexually voracious and adventurous and he'd been holding her back for a long time. He knew it, and it hurt. She'd never once complained, never once tried to make him feel bad about it. And he believed her when she'd said the other day that she had never cheated on him. Jennifer was truthful to a fault, and if she was going to screw somebody, he knew that she would have just come out and said so. She'd been patient with him, and generous, and what possible reason was there to keep holding her back? Why deny her something just because he couldn't provide it himself? It wasn't as if she was forbidden to get a back-rub from someone just because he wasn't a masseuse. He didn't have it in him to be everything for her, and if he needed to, well... call in for backup, that hardly made him less of a man, now did it? Maybe, in some way, he owed it to her to give her this opportunity.

"Hello? Earth to Percy Brice?"

He blinked. "Hm?"

"You've been staring into space for five minutes. What's on your mind?"

"Oh, you know, just..." He was spared a longer answer, as the waiter returned just then with their meals. It was good, better than he'd expected, to be honest. They ate, shooting sly glances at the couples kissing in the booths and trading giddy looks with each other. He was starting to feel comfortable, like this thing might actually not be such a bad idea, when the waiter came back. He set a drink in front of Jennifer and stepped back with a slight bow. It was a showy margarita, with a slice of lime and a salted rim. It seemed to glow green.

"Oh, I'm sorry," Jennifer said, "I didn't order this."

The waiter smiled, and nodded at the bar. "Compliments of the gentleman."

There was a young black man sitting with his back to them. He was tall and sleek, with very short hair and thick muscles almost bursting out of his short sleeved shirt. He was more casually dressed than many of the others, with crisp black pants and a tight white shirt hugging the contours of his sculpted body. He seemed to sense their eyes on him and turned. He looked at them for a moment, his soft brown eyes passing swiftly over Percy and the waiter to settle on Jennifer and the drink in her hand. She quirked an eyebrow and lifted the drink to him slightly, then took a long slow sip, not breaking eye contact as she did so. His expression was unsure for a moment, then he grinned, shaking his head ruefully, and lifted his bottle to her.

"Perhaps madam would like to take her drink to the bar?"

Jennifer looked at Percy, the question not vocalized but obvious. He looked at her, and he looked at the man. God... Was he ready for this? Could he handle it? *Christ.* He shrugged, smiling indistinctly. Jennifer took it for a yes and slid out of her seat.

He watched her go, watched her crossing the room with her hips rolling and her backside twitching. She looked arch and lithe and luscious and hungry. She spoke to the man. Percy couldn't hear a thing over the soft jazz music. She reached out and touched his bicep, leaning close to say something softly in his ear. Very close. He seemed amused, chuckling quietly, and he grinned.

The waiter cleared his throat. "Anything else I can bring you, sir?"

He thought for a long moment as he watched his wife get up on the bar stool. The man leaned over and said something to her, his thick black lips so close to her ear that it almost looked like he was kissing her. Percy felt something stirring, a hot and tingling sensation that started in the bottom of his gut and moved up and down his spine. For the first time in almost three years, he felt his cock getting hard.

"No," he said, waving off the server, "I think I'm just fine."

Jennifer

"Oh, I'm sorry," she said, holding up her hand to refuse the drink being placed before her, "I didn't order this."

The waiter pointed towards the bar. "Compliments of the gentleman."

She turned and looked. The man sitting there was gorgeous. Actually *gorgeous*, and that wasn't a word she often applied to men. There was just something so breathtaking about him. He was tall and muscular and yet there seemed to be something gentle about him, something warm. When he turned to look over his shoulder at them his eyes locked with hers, she felt something inside her chest get tight. Those eyes... Soft and deep and full of hurt, but hopeful. He looked like he could have picked up Percy and hurled him across the room if he took a mind to, but the tenderness in his eyes just made her want to cradle his head in her lap.

She was immediately attracted to him in a way that didn't really happen to her. She was sensible and practical and level-headed. She'd never been the sort to be swept off her feet, she'd much rather keep them both planted firmly on the ground. Maybe it was just because she was giving herself permission to be attracted. This plan of Percy's was absurd. Absurd, and so very like him. He wasn't the kind of husband who would insist that he could repair the burnt-out wiring or fix the plumbing or figure out the route on his own. He would call the electrification, or the plumber, or stop for directions. He'd never been one to let his ego get in the way, and that was one of the things she loved about him. But calling for back-up to fix their broken sex-life, well... that was something else.

She'd been so surprised when they first entered the club that she had hardly known how to react. It had seemed in turn horrifying, ridiculous, thrilling, pathetic, exciting and downright funny. She'd thought of herself as playing along. This was just a game, a joke really! She could laugh at herself as well as anyone else, and going to bed with Percy had always been the sort of situation where you had to pick between laughing and crying.

But now... now that she was looking at this man, this beautiful young man who had somehow picked her out, a thirty-eight year old woman in a room full of younger and no doubt more inviting targets. Now her eyes were locked with his and she was starting to think that maybe this wasn't such a ridiculous idea which Percy had come upon, even if it was only for one night, for one hour even! It had been a long long time since she'd really been with a man. Even before Percy's problem had arisen, it wasn't as if he was rocking her world or anything.

She loved him, truly and deeply, but there was a part of her, one which she kept hidden deep down inside her, that wanted more. The love she had with Percy was the sort of love you might hope to have when you were old and gray and just wanted someone kind and dependable and sweet to sit beside in the park while you watched the birds. She did want that someday, and wanted to have it with Percy. They were forever, as far as she was concerned, which is why she had never pushed him on his, well... his failings. But she couldn't deny that she wanted more, no matter how long she'd spent trying to convince herself that she could live without it. She was still young, really, and she wanted to *fuck*.

She looked across the table at her husband, and he seemed to give her an encouraging nod. Then the waiter spoke up again, "Perhaps madam would like to take her drink to the bar?" and it seemed like a very fine idea indeed.

Jennifer pushed her chair back, picked up her margarita, tossed her hair, and strode across the room. Her heels clacked on the floor in a way that made her feel sexy and powerful. God, what was she doing? She hadn't done this sort of thing, approaching a strange man in a bar, since she was twenty years old. What the hell did she know about it? She was going to make a fool of herself, but at least nobody would know about it. None of her friends from Minnesota were here to watch her embarrass in front of this gorgeous black man. She stood there for a second, drink in one hand and the other hand on her hip. He'd turned away from her again, and was nursing his beverage with the quiet determination of a person hoping to get properly drunk. She cleared her throat, and he nodded, "You wanna sit down?"

Oh God, what was she *doing*? What business did she have chatting up this beautiful brooding black man? She almost turned and walked away, but she'd come too far now to give up so quickly. She pulled out the chair and sat beside him. She had to focus to keep her hands from trembling.

"Thanks for the drink," she said, lifting the glass and taking a little sip.

He looked surprised for a moment, then amused. "My pleasure," he said. His voice was as rich and smooth as butter, creamy deep and soft. She couldn't help but feel a little chill, a kind of tingle in her tummy.

She leaned in close to him. "Are you buying for all the girls in here tonight, or am I special?"

He shook his head, grinning. "I guess you're just special." He lifted his drink, "Here's to you."

She drank. "I'm Jennifer Brice."

"Tyrone Jackson."

She smiled. "Nice to meet you, Tyrone Jackson."

He nodded, looking down a little shyly, she thought. "Nice to meet you too." And a little smile twitched in the corner of his mouth.

She felt her heart do a little flip inside her. God, he was *shy*. Somehow, just the idea that this incredible specimen of a man could feel somehow intimidated by her of all people made gave her an unbelievable thrill. A little piece of her actually fell in love with him right then.

"Kiss me," she said. Oh *God*. Was this really happening? What was *wrong* with her?

He blinked, his smile growing, incredulous. "Excuse me?"

"Would you please just kiss me? On my cheek here."

"Why do you want me to do that?"

"Do you want to ask questions all night?"

"No ma'am." He leaned forward and gave her a little peck on the cheek, just brushing his soft lips against her.

"There," she said, feeling a swimming feeling inside herself, "now we're friends."

"Glad to hear it," he said, looking at her a like she was crazy.

Well, she supposed that she was a little bit crazy. At least she felt that way tonight. "Why don't you tell me about yourself, Tyrone Jackson."

He stretched out, taking a moment to look her properly up and down now that she was at close range. She felt a sickening thrill as his eyes wandered slowly over her body. The dress had been a good idea, she'd come so close to leaving it in the shop, had actually picked it up and put it back on and off the rack three or four times before finally taking it to the counter. She knew she looked good, and she could tell that he appreciated what he was seeing. She stretched a little, trying to be subtle about it, pushing out her assets and giving him a good show of her legs.

He looked up at her, and their eyes locked again, falling into one another as they had from across the room. He blinked slowly, and looked at her from under unusually long lashes. "Why don't you have that drink, ma'am, and I'll tell you anything you wanna know."

She picked up the drink, never breaking eye contact, and she tossed back the margarita in one long swallow. She set the glass down with a little clink on the counter, and licked her lips slowly. "So where are you from, Tyrone Jackson?"

He grinned, turning to the bartender. "Another drink for the lady, man." Then back to her, "I'm from Maryland."

"What brings you to Florida?"

"School."

"You on a sports scholarship?"

"You think that because I'm black I'm not smart enough to get into a good school without one?" The words could have been harsh, but he was smiling as he said it. He was teasing her, she realized, and laughed.

"God, of course not. You look so athletic, that's all."

He grinned. "Football."

"Ooo, impressive."

"Yeah, I guess."

"And what are you studying?"

"This really what you want to talk about?"

"Not really."

"Me neither. You come here a lot?"

"No," she said, taking the fresh drink and having a long sip, "my first time. You?"

"Mine too," he said.

"Really?"

"Yeah. More or less."

"So what brings you here?"

"I got this friend. Sorta friend. Hooked me up, said I'd meet tons of hot white ladies hungry for some action." He turned suddenly, looking at her again, and his gentle eyes seemed now piercing with interest. "That why you're here?"

She leaned back, smiling, biting her lower lip. Jesus. She could feel her husband watching her from across the room. What did he think of all this? Did she really care? Of course she cared. It had been his idea though, dammit, and he'd forgotten their fucking anniversary, she had been able to see it on his face. "I... suppose that I am," she said, chuckling softly and burying her face in her drink. She could feel her cheeks flushing."

"You suppose you am *what*?" he pressed, this little smirk tugging at his mouth.

"What, you're going to make me say it?"

"Well, after I kissed you and all, seeing as we're such good friends now. Yeah, I wanna hear you say it."

She stared at him for a long moment. Was this amusing or annoying? She wasn't sure yet. "I. Want. Cock."

"What kind? You looking for just anything? Because you don't need to come here for that."

"I want a *black* cock. Okay?" She felt her cheeks flush red.

"That's what I'm talking about. Okay girl, slow down, slow down. You don't have to shout about it, girl."

"You *made* me say it."

"You wanted to say it. You like it, I can tell." He finished his drink with a long swallow and set the glass down. He turned in his chair, legs casually apart and heels on the footrest. She couldn't help but see the bulge in the front of his pants, a heavy, thick, and very full bulge. It seemed to be stuffed into his clothing, down the right pant leg like an anaconda waiting. It wasn't the poky little jut of the erections she'd seen before either, but a huge lazy thing. He wasn't even hard, she realized, and it was twice the size of anything she'd ever seen before.

She felt her breath catch in her throat just a little bit. Oh *my*.

He grinned. "Yeah. You like that the look of that, don't you?"

"I... god... Yes. Yes I do... Is that... *real*?"

He snorted. "Fuck ya, it's real! Shit, you think I'm gonna stuff a soda bottle in my pants or something?" He leaned back a little, preening slightly, clearly loving the attention. "You wanna touch it?"

She recoiled, blinking fast. "Do I *what*?"

He repeated himself, slowly and plainly. "Do you wanna touch it? I know you do, I just wanna make you say it."

"I..." And he was right. She *did* very much want to touch it. She'd never seen a cock like that before, it was almost making her dizzy just to think about what she might do with something like that. What she might *try* to do, she honestly wasn't sure if she could even handle it, or what she might attempt.

"Come on, I know your boy's watching. You show him how you treat a real man's dick. Go ahead and rub that big black cock."

She leaned forward, hesitantly. He reclined against the bar, gesturing lazily to the bartender for a refill. She felt like everyone in the room was watching her, though she supposed that logically nobody really was - except Percy, of course - but she didn't dare check. She'd lose her nerve if she checked, she was quite sure of that. She got closer, lifting her hand slightly. Her throat felt dry. Nobody had ever done this to her before. She was used to guys coming after her, handsy clumsy guys trying to sneak a squeeze of her ass or brush the side of her breast, always with the out of being able to protest that it had only been an accident. When things went further some might shamefully press themselves against her, waggling their stiff cocks at her like a kid chasing someone with a hot dog. Some would silently take her hand and place it on themselves, as if they couldn't bring themselves to say the words out loud, or thought she needed to be told where the matter of interest lay.

Tyrone wasn't like that. He just waited. He just watched her, with a knowing sort of smile, his legs a bit apart and that monster in his pants beckoning to her. He wasn't going to sneak around or try and petition his way to her interest. He knew that she wanted what he had, and he knew that she wanted it more than he wanted her. With equipment like that, and his looks, he could have probably anybody he wanted. Now she knew what those trembling hesitant boys felt like when they stared at the mysterious swells under her shirt.

She realized then that she wanted to see it, wanted to see it very badly indeed. She felt like a child standing in front of the Christmas tree, gazing in awe at the biggest most magnificent box in the most beautiful wrapping paper. You never knew was going to be underneath, only that it would be amazing and that it was probably something you'd always wanted.

She reached out, forcing herself to steady her hand, and she touched it.

It was hot and firm and *big.* Just looking at it didn't really get across how much there was too it. Even just feeling the shape of it through his pants, the size of it was dazzling. It felt like her brain was shorting out. Her hand, she was fairly sure, wouldn't even be able to wrap all the way around it. Her gentle grasp moved slowly up and down, not to stimulate it exactly, but just exploring its shape. It seemed to go on forever. God, just the thought of having something like that *inside* her... it was almost too much to contemplate.

"Oh my god..." she whispered.

He laughed, but she wasn't joking. Not even a little bit. This was a serious cock.

"Is this... this is all real."

"Shit. Yeah, it's real, you know it is."

"Oh my *god.*"

"You going to do something about it, or what?"

She looked up at him, biting down on her lower lip, only dimly aware that she still had her hand on his crotch in a room full of people. "I..."

Something chirped. His phone? He groaned under his breath and dug it out of his pocket. He looked at the screen for a long moment, then sighed heavily.

"What's wrong?"

"Nothing, I just... Shit. I gotta go."

"Go?"

"I'm sorry." And he was already getting up.

Her head swam. Just like that, it was over, and he was on his feet and turning to the door. "Wait!" she caught his sleeve. "Can I have your number?"

He seemed taken aback, then he smiled. "Yeah. Yeah, of course you can." He grabbed a pen out of his pocket and started scribbling on a bar napkin. He slid it over to her.

She picked it up slowly, looking at the digits scribbled there. "Am I going to see you again, Tyrone Jackson?"

His grin widened. "Well now. That's up to you, isn't it, Jennifer?" And he started for the door.

She sat there, watching him leave, and had a sensation of slowly returning to herself, of coming back down to earth. And she was decidedly, very much, almost unbearably turned on. She felt warm between her thighs, a moist heat that spread outward from that special place. She wanted him. If he'd asked, she would have gone with him tonight.

Well... that wasn't meant to be, it seemed. She looked at the number again, then entered it into her phone. She felt the bartender drifting towards her, and slid her glass in his direction. "Give me one more," she said, her eyes never leaving the doorway through which Tyrone had gone back out into the night.

* * *

Percy flopped down beside her on the bed, red faced and panting and breathing heavily. "Oh god," he kept saying, his voice husky and almost choked.

She laughed. "You like that, baby?"

"Oh yeah," he said, "I liked that a lot."

She smiled, reaching down to touch herself, feel the warmth down there, the still open sensation. "Me too," she said.

"You were thinking about him, weren't you?" he asked, not accusing but curious.

She nodded in the darkness. "Yes I was."

She gone home with Percy not long after Tyrone had made his sudden exit. He'd been all over her; they hardly made it to the car before he was touching her. To her amazement, he'd actually had an erection. For a moment she was so delighted that she actually forgot about everything else that had just happened. She'd plunged her hand into his pants, grasping hold of the lovely little thing and giving it a nice firm squeeze, as if to reassure herself that it was really truly there. They made out hard and heavy right there in the car, hiding behind the tinted windows as the traffic slid by in the rainy evening amber light. They went at each other like teenagers, groping clumsily and hotly at each other. Of course even at his highest state of attention he didn't have anything on the monster she'd caressed inside the club, but she would take what she could get. She sucked him right there in the front seat of the car, bending awkwardly over the gearshift to take his tiny little penis in her mouth. He'd moaned, stroking her hair gently and quivering.

She came up licking her lips, not having finished him off, but having given him a good start anyway. "You liked watching that, didn't you?"

He nodded, moaning pleasurably.

"Take me home, Percy. I need something inside me. Now."

He had the car in gear before she'd so much as finished speaking. They tumbled into bed as soon as they were through the door, tearing at each other's clothing. His mouth closed over her nipple, suckling it gently, almost timidly before she pulled him tight against her and told him to bite it. He did, not as hard as she wanted, but enough to get her going. She felt creamy and eager down there, and his little thing slipped in like it was nothing. It didn't measure up to how Tyrone's would have been by any means, but it felt good to feel something other than her own fingers for once. She'd ridden him hard, bouncing up and down and digging her fingernails into his chest and shoulders.

"Are you thinking about it too, baby?"

"What?" he'd asked, with the flushed face of a man trying very hard to focus on something and not entirely succeeding.

"Thinking about the huge black cock opening me up, sliding in there and stretching out my pussy lips. Me creaming all over it and taking him inside me. Fucking him, fucking that black dick."

He'd moaned, shuddering, and spurted inside her. She supposed she could take that as a yes.

She lay beside him, breathing hard. She wasn't exactly satisfied, but it had felt good. It felt like it was new again, though maybe that was just because it had been such a long time. Tyrone had been the thing that made it work. It had done it for Percy, for whatever reason, and it had done it for her. She wasn't going to let it go this easily.

Jennifer rolled over, feeling through her purse in the dark, and dug her phone out of her purse. She checked the number again. He hadn't given her a fake, had he? What if he just wasn't into her, and was trying to dodge her? There was been an edge of strangeness to the whole thing, his odd initial reticence, her bold to the point of particular behavior, his sudden exit. Maybe it was just because of the oddity of the situation. They were meeting in an exclusive interracial sex club, after all. Not exactly a recipe for calm normality.

She'd come this far though, what was one more gamble? She wrote him a text.

-This is Jennifer from the club. Sad that u had to run away.

She sat there, staring at the screen, feeling Percy's cum leaking out and drying between her thighs, waiting for an answer. A cool breeze came in through the window, tickling her skin. Suddenly, after maybe three minutes that felt like half-an-hour, a ding and a notification.

-Sorry. Dog got hit by a car. My roommate texted me.

She frowned. Was it just an excuse? God, she hoped he wasn't the sort to make up a story like that just to get out of an awkward date.

-O my god! Is he (or she?) okay?

-She's alright. Wasn't too serious.

A long pause, then a picture came through. It was Tyrone sitting in the waiting room of what she assumed was a veterinary clinic. He looked tired, but happy, and had his arm thrown around a border collie with a cast on her front paw.

-Oooo, so cute! Glad she is okay. What's her name?

-Beyonce.

-R *u serious?*

-lol, I let my little sister name her before I went to college.

-Haha! She's beautiful.

-Thanks.

-I was sorry I didn't get to see more of you tonight.

-I'll bet ;)

-I mean it. That thing in your pants is amazing. I can't imagine how beautiful it must look.

-You can see it now if you want.

-I can?

-You just have to ask.

-Can I see it?

-You know better than that. You have to ask right.

She grinned. She could feel herself getting warm again between her legs, a low tingling heat that went right to her fingertips and made her tremble a little. *-May I please look at your black cock, sir?*

-Good girl.

There was a long delay. She found one hand idly moving down her belly, tracing the curve of her hip and settling very gently over her pubic bone. She didn't do anything, just waited, holding herself. Finally, the promised image came through. He must have been back in his apartment, lying on a narrow bed with burgundy sheets, his pants down around his knees and his shit pulled up. His legs were slightly parted - incredibly lithe and well-muscled; she had no problem now believing that he was a football player. She could see one arm raised, holding the phone is the classic selfie posture, and the other gripped his cock at the base of the shaft. He was harder now than he had been at the bar, and it stood up at attention, though still not fully erect she was sure.

It was incredible. Long and girthy and smooth, ebony dark, and midnight black at the head. She felt her mouth drop open, and her hand involuntarily begin to move between her legs.

Percy stirred beside her. "You still awake, honey?"

"I'm just talking to someone."

"Who?" he asked sleepily.

"The man from the club."

"Oh?" he sounded somewhat more awake now.

"He sent me a picture of his penis."

"Why?"

"I asked him to."

He was quiet for a long moment, then said, "Wow," in a kind of awed tone that said he couldn't believe she'd actually had the nerve to do it. She was a bit impressed with herself, to be honest, though not nearly as impressed as she was by the picture on her phone.

"Look," she said, turning the screen.

"Holy shit," he murmured, "guess it's true what they say."

"I guess so."

"Send him one back."

"What?"

"Send him one back."

"A picture of a penis?"

"Oh my god. Honey. Send him a picture of yourself."

She sat upright. "What? God, I can't do that! I don't even know him."

"You know him well enough to ask to see his nudes."

"Well, yeah, but that's..." she trailed off. She'd heard so many horror stories on the news on the net. People's intimate photos being stolen or hacked or shared or whatever. "I don't want to end up on some sleazy porn site," she protested.

"I doubt he does either," Percy commented dryly. "Just don't show your face."

"Why would he even want that?"

He laughed softly. "He's a guy, Jen. Believe me, he wants to see you. He wouldn't have sent that if he didn't." With that, he turned around, pulled the covers up to his chin, and seemed to doze back off.

Jennifer thought on it for a long moment, gnawing her lower lip and playing idly with herself. Then, throwing caution to the wind, she hopped up out of bed and hurried across the carpet to the bathroom and shut the door.

She looked at herself in the mirror, really looked. Surely he wasn't going to be excited by this. She was in good shape, and she was pretty, she knew that. She had a good body. But would it be enough to arouse the interest of someone like Tyrone? She wasn't sure. She cupped her breasts, pulling faces in the mirror, pouting her lips and sticking out her tongue. She tried pushing them together, crossing an arm shyly across them, letting them free with her hands on her hips.

God. What was she doing?

Finally she screwed her eyes shut and lifted the phone and snapped a picture. It was blurry, of course, and she missed most of her body. Okay. She held the phone up, lining up the shot carefully, keeping her chin just over the top of the frame. She tapped the screen, then checked the picture. Her body from neck to knees. It was all there. The lighting was okay, didn't make any unsightly shapes or anything like that. She swore under her breath and hit send.

Her nakedness at that moment seemed too much for her. She yanked her bathrobe off the towel-rack and swept it over her shoulders, wrapping herself tight and belting it snugly. She hurried out of the bathroom and downstairs to the den.

She couldn't sleep, not now! She turned on the TV and tried to go as long as possible without checking her phone, never managing more than a minute at a time between looking. She sat there in the darkness watching infomercials and feeling like she'd gone crazy.

Finally she couldn't take it anymore, and set the phone on the coffee table. Forget it. He'd probably gone to bed already. It was, after all, almost two o'clock in the morning. Who would but up at this time except someone as off their rocker as she was?

Ding!

She leaped off the couch, glad there was no one there to see what an idiot she was being, and swiped the screen. One word text from Tyrone. -*Wow!*

-Good wow or bad wow? She texted back.

-Definitely a good wow. Your so fucking hot.

-Haha. Come on.

-I mean it. You're looking fine as hell.

-What would you do to this body of mine if you had the chance?

-Do I?

-Do you what?

-Am I going to get the chance, or are you just playing with me?

-Free tomorrow?

-Yeah.

-At my house? Afternoon?

She waited, her breath quickening.

-I'll be there.

She shut her eyes, a strange shudder running through her body, a tingle of fear and excitement and dreadful anticipation. She texted him her address, send a kiss smiley, and tossed the phone aside. She didn't how she was going to be able to sleep with this much jittery energy running through her, but she was going to have to try and get some rest. It was looking like tomorrow was going to be a big day.

* * *

Jennifer slept in late. No surprise there. Percy was already gone. He was always going in early these days, six o'clock in the morning most of the time, and usually stayed late. These law firms and their hours. She didn't know how any of them survived it.

She sat, bleary and yawning, and pushed her hands through her hair. It was a mess, of course, she'd fallen asleep without even thinking of putting it up. Hadn't showered either, and she still smelled faintly of sex.

First order of business: coffee.

The espresso machine was already going as she stumbled out into the kitchen. Good old Percy. She sat at the table in her bathrobe, sipping slowly and pretending to read the newspaper while doing little more than idly flipping the pages over.

Had last night been real? Had Percy - her meek little Percy! - actually taken her out to a sex club? Had she really flirted with a stranger half her age? Some young black man? And those texts, the pictures! They couldn't be real. She went out to the den and dug her phone out of the seat cushions.

Nope, there it was. Oh god, it had all been real, hadn't it? All actually happened. Every message, and one new one:

-Looking forward to it.

She scrolled up idly and looked once more at the picture he'd sent her. It gave her a little rush of pleasure. God, here she was standing there in her bathrobe, coffee in hand, and she was looking at pictures of strange men's genitalia at ten-thirty in the morning. What was *wrong* with her?

There was another text, from her friend Patty. *-Hey there, Jenny! Hope you're enjoying the Florida sun. The gals at the book club all miss you dreadfully. Hopefully now that you've settled in you'll remember to give me a call sometime. Love, Patricia*

Very Patty, tacking on a little dig there. And who *signed* a text message? But of course she was right, Jennifer should have done a better job staying in touch. The move had been such a whirlwind and all, but it had been over two months now and she really didn't have an excuse at this point. She supposed that, on some subconscious level, she had been trying to cut ties with the old Minnesota crowd. More as a way of putting herself out there in her new town than to get rid of them. She wasn't going to make any new friends if she was stuck inside reliving the past all day long. Of course, she thought ruefully, she hadn't exactly had much luck finding new friends regardless. Not that she'd been exactly putting in the effort. She took a cue from Patty's text and resolved to go to the book club here in town. She'd seen a flier and had been planning to check it out, but never gotten around it. She would this time. It was coming up in just a few days.

She couldn't think about that today, though. She had a date to get ready for.

* * *

The doorbell rang a little after four. God, already? The day had seemed to drag on, and she'd spent hours bouncing around the house unable to focus on anything, changing her outfit over and over again. But now that it was here it seemed the time had vanished in a blink. She wasn't ready for this. She didn't think she'd *ever* be ready for this.

Jennifer too a very deep breath. Then she took another. Then she opened the door.

He was leaning casually against the rail, hands in his pockets and an expression of calm boredom on his face. He was wearing cargo pants, slung low and loosely belted, and an old college hoodie. "You gonna invite me in or what? People like me get shot for hanging around in this sort of neighborhood."

She blushed, stepping back and ushering him inside.

He wandered in, looking around, eyes roving about the place, looking everything up and down. He didn't say anything at first, just moved about the room. He almost seemed like he was casing the place. Was that the word? God, she couldn't think that, it was profiling, or something. She couldn't help it, though, it had just popped into her brain. The fault of the media, most likely. She'd just seen too many stereotypical movies.

"Nice place," he said, still not paying her any particular attention.

"Can I get you a drink?"

"Sure. Whiskey," he said, picking up a picture of Percy and she at their wedding.

"Alright, just a moment."

She beat a quick retreat to the kitchen, her cheeks burning. It seemed paradoxical, but she had felt more comfortable in the club. She'd been anonymous there, here her whole life was laid bare. She felt naked, and she was still fully dressed. What would it be like to actually take her clothes off in front of him. She couldn't quite get a handle on Tyrone, there was something about him. He was different from anyone she'd ever met. Or was it just her? It could be her imagination, really.

She came back with a bottle and glasses. He'd seated himself in Percy's chair, the big leather one which he liked so much to come home and sit in while reading the detective novels he loved so much. Tyrone looked very different in it. The big chair seemed to swallow little Percy, but Tyrone owned it, seating himself as if on a throne. She poured him a glass and set the bottle down beside him. "Help yourself."

He looked her up and down. "I think I'll do that."

She felt a shiver go through her. Okay, she had to get a hold of herself. She needed to know what his deal was. "Why are you here, Tyrone?"

He leaned back in the chair, sipping his drink. "You invited me, didn't you?"

"Yes yes. But why did you come?"

He grinned. "I haven't come just yet. Believe me, you'll know when that happens."

She blushed. "I'm just trying to understand you."

"Look, you know why I'm here. You're a good looking woman. I want you. And... I feel like there might have been some kind of connection at the club. I wanna know if I'm crazy or not, or if there might be something between us that's more... *real*, I guess, then some of what goes on there."

"What is it that happens there?"

"You know exactly what goes down. Women like yourself with boring little white boy husbands," he held up the wedding photo, "wanna get a taste of something. They recognize that a black dick is the only thing that will satisfy."

She chewed her lip, faintly aware that she was rubbing her thighs together and moving a little from foot to foot, pressing her legs rhythmically together on her throbbing sex. God, did he have to keep talking about his thing? She couldn't get the image of it out of her head, or the way it had felt in her hand...

Tyrone downed his glass of whiskey. "Ain't no reason for us to waste time here. I know what you need." He reached down and tugged his sweatpants down a bit. He wore loose black silk boxers. She could see it beneath the material, thick and ready, just waiting for her. "Now come over here and get a taste."

She took a step forward, but he tutted, raising a hand.

"Not so fast girl. You coming on just like this? Shit, you gotta get a man going first. Get these clothes off."

Jennifer hesitated for a moment. Was she really going to do this? It seemed like he'd just come in the door, were they getting right down to it like this already? She'd expected... she didn't know, more pleasantries? It sounded stupid. He was here for sex. That was why she wanted him here. She reached back and undid the strap of her dress, letting it fall in a single sultry motion to reveal her lingerie beneath. Black and scarlet, lace and velvet, hugging her breasts and pubis and ass and hips. She looked good and she knew it, the black lace framing her pale white skin perfectly, and the crimson velvet inviting one to look closer...

She turned a little, posing for him, sliding her hands down her hips, bending over at the waist. She wondered if she looked silly. *Think sexy, Jen!* She cast a sultry look back over one shoulder, a hand on her ass and another tracing her collarbone. There was something going on over there in Percy's chair, that was for sure. She could already see the action happening beneath his boxers. Something stirring.

"That's more like it..." he said softly, nodding with approval. "Now come on over here and do something about this. But don't come over like that. I don't like a white woman looming over me like that."

She blinked. Looming? "What do you mean?"

He smiled slowly, and reached up to lace his fingers together behind his head. "Get on all fours. I want to see how you move. Come over here sexy for me, and I might let you suck this black dick."

She blanched. Could she do that? It had been a long time since someone had told her to be sexy. Percy wasn't exactly the sort to ask for anything. She was lucky if she could convince him to be on top every once in a while. She got down slowly on her knees. The carpet was soft on her skin and on her palms as she lowered her hands. She looked up at him through a wave of chestnut brown hair, her bottom up in the air and her breasts low. She went to him, as seductively as she could manage.

He nodded approvingly. "Okay, baby. You go ahead and take it out. You earned a good look at it."

She wasn't sure yet if she was turned on or annoyed, but she knew that she wanted what he had. She wanted to feel it again, but for real this time. Touch her skin to his. She undid the single button on the front of his boxers and reached inside. It was like uncoiling a snake, she had to maneuver it up and out through the opening of his underwear. It thumped down on his lap with an actually audible sound.

She felt dizzy, her eyes going wide. She'd thought she was ready, after all she *had* touched it before, and seen the photo he'd sent. But somehow neither of those things had truly prepared her for this.

His cock was enormous. It was heavy and long and as thick as her forearm. She hardly knew what she'd be able to do with the thing. She held it up gingerly, grasping it with both hands. For an instant she was acutely aware of the fact that she was down on her knees in lingerie with a near stranger's penis right in her face, but it passed. All that mattered were the butterflies in her stomach and the warmth filling her and the heavy sticky feeling in her panties. Her mouth was watering. She slid her hands slowly and gently up and down the shaft, just testing the size of the thing, seeing how it reacted. It got harder in her hands, standing up somewhat. Surely there wasn't a man alive with the blood to get a monster like this actually a hundred percent rigid, but he seemed to be quiet satisfactorily erect.

"How do you like it?" she asked, licking her lips.

"Make it wet for me, girl. Nice and sloppy."

She leaned forward and closed her pink lips over the ebony head.

"Hm, yeah girl..." he leaned his head back, hands gripping the leather armrests of Percy's chair.

She would have smiled had her mouth not been otherwise occupied. He tasted good. A bit salty and warm and very very alive. She sucked gently, teasing the underside of the head with her tongue as her lips sealed around the soft flesh. She suckled it gently, running the tip of her tongue in small circles. She had her hands on his knees, holding herself carefully away so that she wasn't leaning against his legs.

Wow! Just the head, and she was already feeling like it was more than she could handle.

"Come on now, you can do better than that." He took her hands and moved them, placing one on his inner thigh and the other down at the base of his shaft. Then he put his own hands on the back of her head, pushing his fingers deep into her hair. She felt like a toy being used, and a sexy dirty nasty lovely feeling rose up inside her. She opened her mouth as wide as she could, letting him slide deeper inside, taking as much of him as she could. Her hand strayed down a little, cupping his heavy balls in her palm.

"That's more like it... Come on now, make it sloppy like I said. Get that spit going."

She pushed a little deeper, and let herself salivate, the juices gathering and spilling over her lips to run down the length of his shaft and down her chin. She put her other hand on his shaft, holding it up and squeezing firmly.

She was starting to feel almost dizzy. She'd *never* done anything like this before. The blowjobs she had given in high school were very different, more of a timid and secretive wordless suck, usually in the backseat of a car while the guy glanced nervously around for approaching cars. It had been fun because of the risk, but that was about it, the way stealing a six-pack of cheap beers from the drug store was fun even if the stuff was awful. This was something different. Not that it didn't feel risky. Even here in the safety of her own home, it seemed like anything could happen. God, what about her friend Patty? What would she say if she saw Jennifer doing something like this? The shock would probably kill her right then and there.

And Percy. She hadn't told Percy that anything like this would be going on. Would he be angry? Turned on? Indifferent, or hurt? She wasn't sure, but she wasn't going to stop. If anybody walked in, Percy, Patty, or the whole goddamn neighborhood, she was going to keep at it.

She couldn't believe how *good* his cock was! It wasn't just the size, but the warmth, the feel, the softness of it. It was like a great big teddy bear, she could imagine snuggling up beside it at night and holding it tight while she slept. She wanted nothing more than to make it feel good.

He was slowly but surely, inexorably but gently, applying pressure to the back of her head. She felt the cock filling her mouth and throat more and more until it seemed to blot out everything else. There was nothing except the black dick, and there was nothing she had to think about except how she could please it. She worked hard, slobbering and sucking and rubbing, caressing his shaft and testicles.

She let it fall from her mouth and found that she was breathing hard, almost gasping. The massive dark snake glistened with precum and saliva, gleaming like a great ebony tusk. She grasped it with both hands, holding it up before her like an idol. She licked it contentedly up and down the shaft, exploring it from tip to base, then she went lower, taking his balls in her mouth, first one then the other, then both together, which was almost more than she could handle.

She didn't want to stop, but she wasn't sure how much longer her jaw could handle him. An ache was starting to come alive in her head and neck. Fortunately it seemed like things were progressing on his end. He was leaning his head back and moaning deeply, his hands tugging and clenching in her hair as his hips started to roll a bit, pushing deeper towards her.

Finally he pulled her away from him. "Fuck, baby, that's so damn good. You better at this than I thought you'd be."

She smiled shyly, wiping her chin. "Thank you..." She couldn't help but be a little confused. What was going on? He hadn't... well, he hadn't gone all the way. Was he planning to finish himself off? She'd seem guys do that before, take over and jerk themselves the rest of the way. She couldn't help but be a little disappointed in him, however, as she'd certainly not expected that he would take the quick way out. She was a bit relieved that he was giving her a respite, but how could this be the end?

He looked down at her, and reached to take her chin in his hands. His big fingers were soft, but his hold was firm. He lifted her face up to him as he stood. His cock hung heavy and glistening and ready, bobbing slightly up and down as the force of his erection struggled against the sheer weight of the thing. He grinned. "You got a nice pretty little face, Jennifer," he said, grasping his cock with one hand at the base of the shaft, "And you suck so good." He slapped his cock against her, laying it down on her upturned features.

She couldn't help laughing, brushing him away and rubbing her eyes. "Hey!"

He laughed back, giving himself a quick one-two stroke. "Where's your bedroom?" he asked, glancing around.

She cocked her head to one side, frowning. "What do you mean?"

"You don't have a bed? Come on girl, keep up."

"It's, uh... it's there, that room. But why?"

"You rather I fuck you on the floor here?"

She felt herself turn pale. God. That thing. *Inside her?* She'd essentially written it off as impossible as soon as he was out of his pants. Sure, she'd fantasized about it, but... she couldn't *really*. Not something that big, that powerful. She just wasn't equipped for it.

He caught her change of expression and grinned. "What, you thought I was gonna let you off that easy? This dick wants your little pink pussy. Wants it *bad*. You gonna tell him that he can't have his pussy?"

"I..."

He held her chin again, and slapped his cock on her face. This time, he wasn't joking. He was owning her, claiming possession of her body. "Whose pussy is that? Is this my pussy?"

She felt her mouth go dry. This was it, this was the moment. She could either say no, and he would probably get pissed and leave and it would be the end of it. Her little adventure. Maybe she'd had enough. It was already more than she'd bargained for. Or, she could say yes and... Well, to be honest she wasn't entirely sure what came after yes.

He lifted her to her feet, bringing her up with one strong pull, and he moved close to her. His fingers held her body, caressing her naked lower back, pressing the lacy and very full cups of her brassier against his chest. He slid one hand around to her front, and slowly, agonizingly slowly, he lowered it, slipping it beneath the hem of her frilly black panties. She stiffened, going absolutely rigid. His fingers moved slowly over her soft mound, brushing through the little tuft of soft brown hair, and his long middle finger went lower, teasing open the cleft of her. She gasped as his finger touched her there, opening her slightly, filling the space between her outer lips, teasing her opening.

She was unbelievably wet, wetter than she could ever remember being. Somehow she hadn't noticed it as it was happening, but it was now very much undeniable. She was soaking for him, her panties sopping and her lips overflowing with a juicy inviting warmth. He teased at her labia with the pad of his fingertip, and he leaned in closer, pressing his body tight against her. His lips were right against her ear, opening, tasting the lobe, nipping gently at it. She felt her eyes roll back and her legs give out, but she didn't fall. He had her crushed against him, held tight, his finger slipping easily - so *incredibly* easily! - into her wet and welcoming hole.

"Now," he said, his voice a soft murmur in her ear, "whose pussy is this?"

"Yours..." her voice was soft, alien to her ears. Was it her? Had she really said *that*? She didn't think she could have, but the words were there, hanging in the air.

She felt herself being lifted, carried the fifteen steps across the room, and felt herself laid down on her bed. Not just hers, Percy's bed too.

Her eyes were half-shut as she writhed with desire. She was dimly aware of their bodies separating for a moment, and of him undressing, then she felt him again, his huge powerful body now completely naked, pressing down on her. She hissed, and her arms and legs wrapped tight around him involuntarily, crushing him close against her.

She needed this, she realized. She needed *him*. Somehow, she was going to take that huge cock. She didn't know if she could, but she needed to. She reached down and pulled her panties to the side, revealing her opening for him. She felt the weight of his shaft laying over it, the head up around her belly, batting wetly on her skin.

"Put it in me, please, put it inside."

"That's my girl," he moaned softly, his voice deep and calm as he reached down, "you gonna take it so good, baby."

"Please, I want it."

"Here I go, baby." He reached for it, and put the fat head of his black cock between her lips.

She reached down suddenly and grabbed hold of his hips. "Wait!"

"What?"

"Are you... are you going to put on a condom, or..."

He chuckled, and he wrapped his huge hands around her waist. "I gonna fuck you right now, baby. I'm gonna fuck you with this raw black cock and fill you up with my black seed. If you want me to stop, you just say the word, and I'll be on my way. You can call your white-boy husband to come take care of this pussy, if that's how you want it."

"But... but I..."

"Just say the word. Say you don't want my seed. If you don't, I'm going to bust this nut so deep that you'll be feeling it inside for days."

She stared up at him. His face was calm, almost expressionless. Was he putting on an act, or did he genuinely not care? She imagined what it would be like if he left now, if she didn't feel him inside her right now. It was too much, too awful to think about. To come this far, to be brought to this place and not be satisfied... she couldn't handle that.

"I ain't hearing a no," he said, reaching down to slid his cock slowly up and down over her wet lips.

Each motion sent a tingle of ecstasy flooding through her, a harsh shiver of joy almost too intense to handle. She rolled her head back, biting hard on her lip and tensing her whole body. God, she had never been so wet in her whole life! Was this a safe day? Could she risk it? Jesus, what if he got her pregnant?

She'd tried before with Percy, years ago when they'd both been younger and it had seemed like a good time to start a family. They tried and tired, and nothing happened. The doctor finally spilled the bad news: low sperm count. Nothing wrong with Jennifer, but Percy just wasn't up to the task. She'd comforted him, and been privately relieved. She hadn't been ready then, and Percy didn't really seem like he was... well, man enough for the task, to be honest.

But this? This was something else. She didn't even *know* Tyrone, and here he was talking about cumming inside her. She hadn't ever let her high school boyfriends put it in there even *with* a rubber. Too risky, and high school Jennifer hadn't been interested. They'd been disappointed, but it was her body and their little white cocks hadn't been worth taking the chance.

She blinked. Had she really just thought that? Was that it all along? They just hadn't been good enough? Not manly enough, not virile enough? Not *black* enough? Maybe this was what she had been waiting for all along...

Tyrone leaned back, lifting his cock. It slapped against his chest. "Okay, now I'm getting pissed off. Shit, you gonna make me wait all day?"

"Okay," she said, "okay, you can."

"Naw, that shit ain't good enough anymore, girl. You gotta ask for it now."

"*What?*"

He smirked, a cocky grin that lifted one side of his mouth. "You gotta tell me that you want this. And you gotta say it right. Now, I'm already annoyed that you're holding me up here, so you better say it right the first time, okay?"

She stared at him, her lips open, her mouth dry. *Say it?* God, could she do that? Well, she'd already done a hundred things today that she would have never thought herself capable of doing, so what was one more? She wasn't going to let it end like this, without being satisfied. She swallowed hard. "Please," she said, "please fuck my little white pussy with your big black monster. Shoot it inside me, please."

He smiled. "That's better, girl. That's a whole lot better. Okay, you just lay back and let me fuck you good."

She let her head flop back and her thighs fall wide open. She squeezed her eyes shut. Was she really *doing* this? Was it really *happening*?

She felt the huge cock press once more between her soft and sopping lips. Oh God. This was it. His grasp on her hips tightened, and he drew her down a little on the bed, pulling her towards him, *onto* him.

She gasped as his massive cock parted her lips, and she threw her head back, moaning and digging her hands into the sheets. Everything was blotted out in that moment, vanishing in a cascade of brilliant blue stars. There was nothing in the whole universe except the bed beneath her and the cock pushing slowly into her. She felt herself stretching, opening in a way she never had before. He pushed open her inner walls, filling her completely. He must have been four times Percy's size at least.

"Oh... *God...*" she heard herself moaning, "Oh God, it's so big..."

He laughed. "Girl, I barely started." Then he pushed his hips forward.

Jennifer screamed. It wasn't a cry of pain exactly, though it did hurt in a dull and distant sort of way. She screamed because nothing she had ever before experienced had prepared her for this moment. She flopped back, laying limp as he pushed himself fully into her. Her hands started to trembled violently, and her teeth clenched. He kept pushing until his balls were lying against her body, his cock sunk fully into her. Then he pulled back. Before he'd got halfway out he shoved it forward again, driving it hard into her.

She felt like she was changing inside, her body shifting form to accommodate his size and power. She was his now, and this was all she needed to be: a place for him, a well of pleasure for his mighty phallus.

"Yeah," he groaned, pushing her legs up and slapping her thigh, "Hm *hm*, you're taking this black cock so *good*, girl."

"T-thank you, b-baby!" she squealed through her teeth, feeling her body going limp under the weight of his assault. The pleasure was immense, she could feel it in pulsing waves, rushing through her entire body in great spasms of ecstasy.

He thrust into her six times, great pumping thrusts that seemed to assault the very foundations of her being. He grabbed her ankles tight, pushing her legs back. She felt her legs bending, folding over so that they were almost down beside her. She lay on her back with her legs folded back, her wet and wanting sex hungry for that massive thing being fed into it. She looked down, and saw herself, utterly exposed and naked, broken with lust. And she saw him, his hard black body taking possession of her. His hands grasped her ankles tight, and his dark black shaft was buried in her pink folds, plunging in again and again.

"Fuck..." he moaned, throwing his head back, "I'm gonna cum..."

"Yes," she moaned, "cum in this pussy. Cum inside my white pussy, baby, I need it."

She hadn't planned to say the words. She never would have planned to say something like that, it just wasn't her, no way. That wasn't how she talked. It wasn't her speaking though, it wasn't Jennifer Bryce, devoted wife of Percy Bryce. This was Jen, a cock-hungry slut for black dick, it was all Jen, and she hadn't even know that this person existed inside her, but she was coming out now, and she would *not* be silenced.

"Yeah baby," he said, increasing his pace, thrusting harder and harder, "this is it, this is how it happens."

"Do it to me, baby! Fuck me fuck me fuck me!"

She was lost. There was nothing outside of him and the feelings he was giving her. She felt the first thrashing waves of orgasm flood through her, who'd never had a vaginal orgasm in her life. She'd become so used to rolling over and putting a hand between her legs while Percy lay spent beside her. She could get herself there. Men didn't really give women orgasms through intercourse, that was basically a myth, she'd accepted that as a fact.

And yet here she was. He hadn't done anything for her, hardly touched per pussy and ignored her clit completely. He hadn't returned her oral pleasuring, hadn't gotten her warmed up, hadn't done anything except plow his massive cock into her again and again. It wasn't supposed to work this way, that wasn't supposed to be enough to make a woman feel good.

But it did.

Oh *God* it did. This beautiful magical black cock was working miracles in her. She was vaguely aware of thrashing in agonized ecstasy as he held her firmly down and pounded into her over and over and over and over again. She started screaming, this time they were fully cries of pleasure, with no doubt whatsoever. She was having an orgasm. It rippled through her, flashing behind her eyes like a fireworks show. This was the first time a man had ever made her cum without her having to do anything, without having to guide or assist him in any way.

She was his, her body belong to him, and it was telling both of them that simple fact without any room for confusion.

All her doubt vanished, all her hesitation. She was his. She belonged to this dick.

He shuddered, and gave one finally massive thrust that she was amazed didn't split her open, and with a moan he started to cum. She felt his huge cock pulsing and pumping hot white jizz deep inside of her, flooding her fertile womb with his powerful seed.

She cried out once more, thrashing and moaning as he filled her. She felt the room go dark around her, and for some time after, she knew no more.

Tyrone

Tyrone was breathing hard, chest rising and falling. The woman lay before him, lost in some kind of orgasmic trance. She looked almost like she'd fainted. He couldn't help grinning to himself with satisfaction. *Another happy customer.*

That thought gave him a moment's pause. Customer. Like he was just some whore she'd picked up. No. It hadn't been like that. There was something, a spark between them. He'd felt it from the moment their eyes had met in the club. There was something real here. He... liked her. This wasn't just a lay, it had been *good.* She fucked a lot better than he'd expected. He was used to women not being able to handle his girth, begging off at the last minute and offering halfhearted handies as a substitution. It seemed like everybody thought a big dick was nothing but a blessing, but for him, for all his life, it had been more like a curse.

He felt like an attraction sometimes, like people wanted to have sex with him just to get a look at the fabled monster, and then balked at actually doing anything with it. How many girlfriends had he had in high school that were all too happy to get head from him only to scoff and turn their nosed up when he asked for reciprocity? All white girls, of course, trying to make themselves look cool or rebellious or enlightened by dating a black guy. Or just trying to piss off their parents.

It wasn't his preference, exactly, but it had just been the only option at the time. He'd grown up in an aggressively white neighborhood and hardly known any other black people as a kid, much less available attractive black girls around his own age. So it had always been white girls, and he'd gotten used to it, had adapted his tastes. He wasn't sure anymore if he was even interested in fucking a black woman, which was a thought that made him feel just a little bit ashamed.

Whatever, he wasn't hung up anymore on how it looked or what other people thought. He did what he wanted when he could, because goodness knows those opportunities were few and far between.

He looked down at her again, laying spread out on the bed in a rumpled heap. There was a thick white bead forming between her pink lips, and slowly starting to drip down. He grinned. Man, it had felt good to bust a nut in there. The white lady had a good pussy, that was for sure. He thought that he would actually be down to have another go at her sometime, if she hadn't been too traumatized. He'd been hard on her, no doubt of that, but she'd taken it well. More than that, she'd seemed to love it.

"You alright there, baby?"

She moaned, smiling and grabbing a pillow. She pushed her face up against the soft cotton and gave a long groan of pleasure. "Oh God, yes," she said, tossing the cushion aside and smiling at him.

He laughed. She was cute. It was easy to forget she was almost twice his age. She looked good, full and plump and sexy, not skinny or bony like a lot of white girls. She was more filled out, with a nice plump ass and heavy ripe breasts. He reached down and gave her perky pink nipples a tweak. She yelped and covered her breasts with her hands, giggling.

"You look real good with your pussy filled," he said.

She flopped her head back, shoving her hands into her hair. "Oh *God*, I can't believe you came inside me!"

"What, regrets?" he teased, pinching again at the once-more uncovered tips of her breasts.

"No!" she laughed, swatting him away, "no, it was *amazing*. God, it was incredible."

"You too, baby."

"You liked it?" she smiled coyly.

"Yeah. Yeah, I did." And he really had, which wasn't always the case. To tell the truth, it wasn't altogether often that he was really satisfied by sex. He was just too much for most women to handle, and he ended up holding back so much that his own pleasure was hardly a concern.

"You like how I feel?"

"You know I do."

"You want more?"

He felt his eyebrows shoot up. "You serious?" The last time a girl had asked him to keep going had been... well, he didn't think that had *ever* happened. The few times he'd been able to get all the way they had been so relieved that they usually couldn't wait to run to the kitchen to find an ice pack to stick between their thighs, and usually moaned about their aching pussies for days afterwards until he felt too guilty to try again, even if they were up for it, which they usually weren't.

"Yeah I'm serious," she cooed, reaching down and sliding her long middle finger between her pussy lips. A strand of thick cum pooled around her knuckle, gushing up over her lips and spilled over the diamond of her wedding ring on the next finger over. "What, you thought you could get away with just fucking me once and you'd be done? That felt so good, I'm just getting *started*, baby."

"Uh, well, you'll have to gimme a sec," he said, reaching down and stroking his spent cock.

"Hm, come on... you need encouragement?" She slipped two fingers inside herself, coming out creamy and dripping. She brought her cum-slick fingers slowly upwards, dripping across her pale tummy and breasts and them slipping them in her mouth. She sucked his seed off her fingers, slow and sensuously lingering on it, her tongue working skillfully. She sucked off the diamond stud last, and he felt himself getting hard again.

"Gimme your phone."

"Excuse me?"

"I said gimme you phone for a second."

She looked up at him for a moment, seeming quite confused, then she reached awkwardly behind her and grabbed it off the bedside table. "What are you going to do?"

He clicked it on. No password, cool. He switched on the camera and pointed it at her. "Smile, baby."

She laughed. "Oh, God, what are you *doing*?"

He grabbed his hardening cock with his free hand and stuffed it back into her sloppy pussy without warning. She gasped, throwing her head back and grabbing at the sheets. He snapped the picture button three or four times. "Hm, that's good," he said, not looking at her as he scanned through the pics. Blurry, blurry... there it was: a perfect shot of his thick black cock burying itself deep in her creamy snatch. "There we go..."

"Are... you... taking... pictures?" she panted out.

"Gotta let hubby know what you're getting up to, baby. Which one is he? Percy, right? Yeah, that's it."

"*What*!? Give me that!" She reached up, flailing awkwardly at the phone in his hand. She didn't get far, impaled as she was on eleven inches of dark meat.

He hit send and tossed the phone down beside her.

"Oh my *God*..." she moaned, scrabbling for the device, checking that he hadn't been bluffing. Tyrone grinned. He didn't bluff. "You really did it..." she said, her voice somewhere between amazement and outrage.

He slapped her thigh. "Come on, girl, I'm doing all the work here. How about you turn over. Show me how you move that ass."

She stared at the phone screen, obeying automatically, twisting around and lifting her rump towards him. He grabbed hold of her juicy ass and pulled her back towards him, sinking in deep. She grunted, her head flopping down to the bed as he filled her. Oh yeah, she was his now.

"Come on!" he smacked her pale ass hard, three times in quick succession until it glowed pink. "Come on, fuck me, baby."

"Yes, sir..." she moaned, working herself back and forth on him.

He grinned. This looked like it could be the start of a truly beautiful relationship.

* * *

"Yo, Tyrone!"

He looked up from his burger, chewing absently and flipping through a sports magazine someone had left on the cafe table. Marquis was crossing the courtyard, a newspaper under one arm and a dazzling smile under his huge reflective shades. He was wearing a sweater of some kind, the sort you usually only saw in fashion magazines. Didn't seem to bother him that it was about eighty-five degrees out. Nothing was more important than looks to Marquis, at least that was the impression that Tyrone had gotten.

"My man," Marquis said, still smirking. Showing off those pearly whites.

"What up?"

"I hear you did the deed, brother. Roped yourself in a good little heifer."

Tyrone snorted. Marquis had been the one to recruit him, a couple weeks back. He worked as an assistant football coach, which was saying something considering the size and pedigree of the college's team. He wasn't sure if it was a six-figure kinda deal or up to seven, but the guy was a high roller. Tyrone didn't know if Marquis owned the black and white club outright, or if he just ran the place for someone else, but he was the face of the place. He'd been recruiting for some time from the football and basketball teams, and had only recently branched out into the track sports, at least that was what the rumors had led him to believe.

Nobody on the outside really knew what it was that Marquis got up to, or why he was always spotted chatting up guys who could only be described as especially virile - and always black. If Marquis wasn't so aggressively and publicly heterosexual, there might have been rumors of a different sort. So, it was with some amount of trepidation that Tyrone had first accepted the assistant coach's offer to "meet him for lunch sometime," but he'd accepted. Marquis took him across town in a sparkling new sports car and bought him a steak at a fancy restaurant - the sort of place Tyrone could only dream of going as a poor college student - and asked him if he'd ever fucked a white woman before.

Tyrone had just about choked on his sirloin.

Marquis laughed at his reaction, but the question hadn't been a joke.

Tyrone had felt his cheeks warm, and he'd shrugged offhandedly. "Yeah, I mean. I dated a couple. We fooled around, whatever." What the hell kind of question was that more a football coach to be asking a student?

"How'd you like it? You like getting that white ass?" He held his hands up in front of him and pantomimed a little squeeze, still grinning madly. Tyrone saw his jaw drop open in the reflected image in the other man's glasses.

"Um, coach, I..."

Marquis waved away whatever he'd been about to say, suddenly getting quite serious. "Look, Tyrone, here' the thing. I run a club downtown, a place of class and sophistication. The Black and White Club, you ever hear of it?"

"No sir, I don't think I have."

Another dazzling grin. "That's right. You don't hear about it unless you're a part of it. We're exclusive and we're discreet. Those two things are extremely important to the sort of people we're looking for. Now, if you decide to join us, I know you'll uphold that. Likewise, if you want to pass on all this, I'm counting on your keeping the conversation to yourself."

This was getting too weird. What was this, some sort of secret society? He got enough of that from the smirking frat boys wandering around in their silk jackets looking like the cat that caught the canary. He started to ease up out of his seat, "Coach, I don't know what this is all about, but I-"

Marquis cut him off. "There are a lot of rich white married couples in this city, Tyrone. A *lot* of them. And when I say rich, I mean the kinda dough that makes my ass look cheap. These are the kind of people who got everything they ever wanted, except the one thing that matters most."

Tyrone felt himself settle back down into his chair. "What's that?"

Marquis smiled. "That's what *we* got, Tyrone. Right here, baby." He reached down under the table and grabbed at himself casually. "There is a whole city of rich white women out there looking for a real man to treat them good in bed, and a whole lotta brothers like yourself whose services they so desperately want. And it can be extremely... let's say lucrative."

Tyrone felt his brow furrow, "Wait, so you..."

"Hold up. This isn't about anything illegal. It's a dating service, essentially. We don't condone anything transnational. Just putting those in need in touch with the goods. But I think you'll find that they can be extremely generous after they'd had a good dicking from someone who actually knows what they're about."

"So what about these husbands, man? Sounds like a good way to get shot or something."

Marquis' grin only widened. "I ain't talking about cheating, boy. Hubby's in on it too."

"Whoa," Tyrone laughed, shaking his head, "what, this some kind of kinky threeway, man? I don't know about *that* shit."

"It depends. A lot just wanna watch, some want to hear about it afterwards. A couple want to take part. Depends on the person. It's your call, you the man here. They gotta respect what you say, that's what this whole thing is about. You're the bull, she's the pussy, and he's just the limp-dick motherfucker gotta get outta the way so his woman can take a good nut for once."

"So... what, I just show up at this club of yours and wait for some hungry white ho to pick me up?"

Marquis laughed. "There's more to it than that, maybe, but essentially yeah."

"Why you talking to me about this, man?"

Marquis sat back in his chair. He seemed to ponder for a moment if he was going to say something, then he leaned forward and knitted his fingers together. "We don't let just anybody in the club, man. I gotta keep the place to certain standards. These women are looking for an experience like they never had before, and not every brother is capable of it. But, ah... I seen you in the showers, Tyrone, after practice ya know. And, uh... You got it going on, brother."

"You been looking at my cock, coach?"

Marquis lowered his sunglasses, his eyes were serious behind them. "Boy, the *whole* team been looking at that monster from day one, they can't help it. You an elephant-dick motherfucker, my man. And that's the kind of monster I want in my club."

Tyrone sat back in his chair, his mind whirling with confusion.

Marquis shrugged, dropping a pile of bills on the table. "It's a lot to think on, I know. But you do think about it. Let me know what you decide. But let's just keep this between the two of us, I know I can count on your for that."

In the end, of course, Tyrone had decided to give it a shot. Screw a bunch of rich white bitches? Why not, wasn't like he had better ways to spend his time. Couldn't play Xbox every night, man. He'd taken the offer. Marquis had all kinds of rules about what he had to wear there and shit, which had been a bit intimidating, to be honest.

The night he met Jennifer had been his fourth night hanging at the club, and he'd never gone further than momentary flirtation, just didn't feel comfortable with it for whatever reason. He'd felt a bit like he was being pimped out or something, and it shut him down hard. But then he'd seen this lady, sitting there in her slinky gown with her nervous little white-boy husband wringing his hands and her looking like a sculpted goddess and just eating him up with her eyes and it was like something had clicked.

Marquis grinned, his smile as radiant as ever. "She was a good one, I hope."

"Yeah, yeah. It was good. Guess I have you to thank for sending her that drink?"

"Guilty. Just giving you a bit of a push out the door. She worth it though, right?"

Tyrone couldn't repress the grin. "Yeah, she was good, coach."

"Alright. You went all the way with it then?"

He nodded.

"Good boy."

"Yeah, thanks."

Marquis got right back up, gave him a smack on the shoulder, and was on his way already with a parting, "Keep it up, brother. And remember. Talk to me if you need anything."

Tyrone just shook his head and went back to his lunch. Before he could take more than a couple bites, his phone dinged. He thought about ignoring it, but you never knew. A text. From her. Jennifer. He found that he was grinning before he'd even read it.

-U asshole.

He frowned. Okay, that wasn't what he'd expected. *-What?*

-I can't believe u sent that picture lol. My husband has been lecturing me all day.

-Let me talk to him.

-What would u say?

-Tell him to stop being such a bitch.

-Lol. I'm going to tell him u said that.

-Good. Marquis had filled him in on what sort of husband he might expect to find coming into the Black and White Club. Rich, of course, and there was always a level of snobby privilege that came with that. But these were guys who got their rocks off on being slapped down, humiliated. The more you told them they were pitiful and inadequate, the more they'd be into it. Tyrone didn't think he'd ever really understand white people, but whatever.

-He wants to fuck me.

-Too bad. That pussy is mine. Tell him to wait his turn.

-Are you serious?

-Gimme his number.

A moment later, she'd done it. He leaned back in his chair, looking across the sunny cafe. It was Sunday, not a cloud in the sky. No work, no classes. He had nothing better to do than mess with the guy. Anyway, he was enjoying this, a lot more than he'd expected. It felt good to be bossing around a mature and sophisticated white couple. He'd been so nervous with all his white high school girlfriends, afraid of what they'd think or what they would tell others if he was too assertive or aggressive. He had always left it to them to take charge, and it had felt wrong to him. This though, this felt so right. She was his by right of conquest, basically, and the twerpy little boy she'd married would just have to deal with it.

-Yo man, this is Tyrone, the dude attached to that cock you saw fucking your wife. You got something to say?

-Hello Tyrone. This is Percy Bryce. I'm very pleased that you and my Jennifer had a good time together. I'm very grateful for your services - far more than I'd expected to be, to be totally honest. I'm glad to hear that you and Jennifer have both expressed interest in extending your engagement beyond a single encounter. As such, however, I think it would be beneficial to all parties, yourself included, if we could go over some ground rules.

Tyrone rolled his eyes. Jesus, what a tool! He texted Jennifer quickly: *-Wow, your husband's a real dork. He sounds like a textbook.*

-Lol. He's a lawyer.

Figured. He texted the guy back. *-Sure, sounds smart. What you got in mind?*

-Well, as I'm rather inexperience with this whole situation, I was rather hoping that you might be able to provide me with some sort of guidelines for how this sort of thing is generally done, and we could work something out together from there which would be mutually satisfactory.

Experienced? That was a good one. Still, it didn't hurt to play the role. He was the one calling the shots now, so he might as well call 'em good. It wasn't every day you got an opportunity like this, after all.

-Okay, first thing you gotta understand is that her pussy belongs to me now. You want to play with that shit, you gotta come through me first, understood?

-I understand, and I accept.

-Good. Second, your not in charge of shit here, okay? You want to watch me fuck her, you gotta ask. You want to lick my cum out of her pussy, you gonna beg for permission first. She belongs to me, and you belong to her. If I say you can do it, and she says you can do it, that's the only way your doing anything. If I come over and want to fuck her without you hanging around, you better clear out. If I want you to warm her up first, you better get in there and lick her out good for me. My cock is the only thing you have to worry about anymore. Keep it happy, and it'll keep your wife happy, you got it?

-I understand completely.

Tyrone switched his phone off. Well, that was that. Good talk.

* * *

"Dude, where do you *go* every night?"

"Every night? What the hell are you talking about?"

Barry sat up in bed, tossing his tablet down on the mattress. "Okay okay, not *every* night. Just practically every night. You got something going on, dude, and I want *in* on it."

Tyrone grinned. Beyoncé was hopping around happily, licking Tyrone's ankles and panting. He gave her a scratch behind the ears. His roommate had clearly been wanting to ask this question for a long time now. Barry was a skinny black nerd with an afro and a collection of comic books about four feet high piled up in the corner, and he had some intimacy issues.

"No issue with *me*," he'd say, puffing out his chest, "the ladies just can't handle this Barry's juice." He said that a lot, and seemed to think it was incredibly clever.

"I don't have anything going on, man."

"Bull*shit.* You always texting somebody, always creeping out. I would think you have a girl on the side, but I know don't."

"Yeah? How you know that?"

He started counting off the reasons on his fingers, mock-thoughtfully. "You black, you poor, you got *no* game, you got no car... and if you had a girl I *know* you'd be telling your pal Barry about it, bro, so don't *even*."

Tyrone grinned. "Yeah, guess so."

"Don't *play* with me, man! I know *something* is up!"

"Don't worry about it, Barry."

"Don't worry about it, don't worry about it. *Shit.* You pulling some *Batman* shit up in here, dude."

Things had been going on with Jennifer and her husband for a couple weeks now. He'd been back there fucking her at least a dozen times now, and each time was better than the last. She was made for black cock, there was no way around it. So far he'd only gone over in the late afternoon, after classes were over and the buses were still running. He'd hike down to the bus stop across the quad and take it up to their neighborhood, fuck her senseless, and get the bus back in time to cram through his homework and drop off to sleep.

Tonight, however, things were going to be a little bit different. Tonight was gonna be an actual date, or something. *Dinner*, they'd said. Dinner with both of them.

He hadn't really seen or heard much of Percy in the time he'd been with Jennifer. They'd exchanged a couple text messages, more of the same as that first time, really. He knew that she kept him well in the loop though, often sending him messages *while* he was fucking her. She took pictures and videos of his cock hammering her, or the pools of cum in her mouth and pussy or spangled across her boobs or her ass, and she sent it all dutifully off to Percy. He assumed the guy was just madly jacking it in the office bathroom, or something, but he was never around when Tyrone was there doing his thing. That had suited him just fine so far.

But now things were going to change, apparently. He wasn't sure what was going on, and he wasn't sure that he liked it. He'd gone to fancy dinners with the parents of his white high school girls before, and it was always terminally awkward. He hoped this wasn't going to be anything like that. He was just going to have to keep up a tough front. After all, he was the bull. Didn't need to let on to them that he felt like a kid sometimes, brushing up against their middle-aged life. It was like a football game. Just keep your head down and do the thing like you own that field, and nobody will be able to stop you. You had to sell yourself the myth of your own invincibility if you wanted to stand a chance.

They were meeting him for dinner at six, down at the Black and White Club. That was a bit more of a trip, as the bus route kinda wound around the city before heading downtown, so he'd need to leave early. And he'd need to dress up. Marquis was insistent on that point almost above everything else. Motherfuckers gotta look dapper as fuck if they coming in *my* club, he'd say. Dandy that shit up.

Of course that gave Barry a whole new angle to get worked up over, but whatever.

His phone chimed. -*U still coming tonight, stud?*

Jennifer. He grinned and texted back. -*I think so. Show me those pretty lips one more time, remind me what you look like.*

She sent him a picture of her pouted lips, all done in red lipstick and sexy as hell. -*Or were these not the lips you meant?* she teased.

-*I'll see the others later, I hope.*

-*You better believe it, stud.*

He stuck his phone in his pocket and shrugged his jacket on over the button-down suit. He felt like a fucking waiter or something, but Jen said he looked, quote: snazzy as fuck, so whatever. Snazzy. Now *there* was a white person word, but he'd take it.

He headed out, dodging Barry's insistent questions, and headed towards the bus stop.

* * *

It was a quiet night at the club. It was usually pretty sedate here on weeknights, so no big change there. He got arrived at about 5:30, and ordered a drink.

"Hey there, champ. What's this, drinking alone?"

Marquis.

"What are you doing here?"

He laughed. "Well, it's my club, isn't it?"

"Is it? I've been meaning to ask."

"Fifty percent stake, if you wanna split hairs. I'm the one who manages the place, though, so it's more like seventy-five / twenty-five, in reality."

"Who's the silent partner?"

"Not something you need to worry about, my man. And you're changing the subject."

"They're coming. Be here in a quarter of an hour, I guess."

"Good, good." The older man slapped him on the shoulder. He didn't leave though, but stood there, seeming to be deep in thought.

"You wanna sit, or...?"

Marquis leaned against the bar. "Look man, this is my side gig. I'm a coach, and a good coach knows that there's more to being a coach than just the sport. I'm here for you, if you ever need anything. Seems like you been getting on with your folks real good, but if something ever comes up. Anything. You come talk to me, okay? I've seen it all, kid, and I got your back."

Tyrone took a long swallow of his drink. "Thanks, man. I appreciate that."

"No problem."

"You got something going on tonight, or what?"

Marquis grinned. "A gentlemen never tells."

"You seeing that little Tilly chick again, aren't you?"

Marquis clicked his tongue and tapped the side of his nose. "You take care. Anyway, looks like you got your own filly to take care of."

Tyrone twisted to look towards the door. Jennifer and her husband were coming in, the little man looking as nervous and out of place as always, the woman looking stunning. She was wearing a little red jacket and a wispy black dress. He grinned, recognizing it right away. She had shown it to him once a couple days ago in an online catalog and he had told her to buy it. So, she'd actually done it. She slipped off her jacket and handed it to her husband, and her cheeks reddened as she did. The top of the dress was sheer, and did almost nothing in the club light to disguise what was underneath. He could see the perfect swell of her pale breasts, and the pink tips of her nipples pointed out, visible to all. The place was pretty empty, but she was already turning more than a few heads. A black guy drinking at the end of the bar shook his head, whistling softly under his breath and muttering a low *damn*. Tyrone grinned. Back off, guys, this one's mine.

He got up from the bar, drink in hand, and he crossed the floor of the club.

She smiled at him when she saw him coming, and made an awkward little flutter of her hands as she had to force herself mid-motion not reach up to cover her breasts. *Don't even bother, girl, I've seen 'em closer up than that.* "Hey there, beautiful," he said, sliding his free hand around her waist and pulling her tight against him to put a kiss on her cheek, "you look amazing."

"Hello, Ty," she said softly. She was a good deal more shy here in the club than he was used to. But of course, he realized, they'd been in her home most of the times they were together. She was probably pretty buttoned-up in her normal life, and didn't usually let out the side of herself that he'd gotten used to. She'd started calling him Ty a little while ago, not asking or checking or anything, just started doing it. It had been in a post-coital moment, her limbs wrapped around him and her body flushed with sex. She could probably have called him anything and he'd have been cool with it. He'd never liked being called Ty, and had always told people not to, but her... he let her get away with it. Was even kinda starting to like it.

He gave the husband a nod. "Hey man, how's it going?"

Percy nodded excitedly. "Very well, very well. Thank you. Yourself?"

"It's all good, bro."

"Shall we take a seat? I'll order us appetizers."

"Yeah, sounds good."

They crossed the club and headed for a dimly lit booth in the corner. The seats were velvet soft and the table marble smooth. Tyrone slid in first, spreading his stance wide so he almost took up the whole side of the booth. He patted his lap. "Hop on, Jen."

"Oh my *God*," she said, blushing and looking away, not making a motion to do so.

He grinned and grabbed her by the waist, pulling her firmly over. God, he loved how that ripe ass felt sliding over his thigh, settling in over his cock. He slipped a hand around her midsection, holding her body against his. "You feel that, baby? You feel what you're waking up down there?"

She blushed deeper. "God... not *yet*, settle down, mister."

He laughed.

Percy cleared his throat and got into the booth across from them. He took care of the ordering - Tyrone mentioned offhandedly that he'd have the salmon and how about a sample platter to start. It gave him a weird thrill, spending the guy's money. Alright, he was already fucking the shit out of his wife, but the money was a nice touch. He wondered if Percy Brice realized how much time it would have taken Tyrone to save up the cash to afford a dinner like that at a place like this. Probably not. Rich people, he'd found, were usually pretty ignorant of what life was like for those less fortunate than themselves. That was just how it went. Some people were born lucky, had more opportunities, whatever. You had to make do with what you had, 'cause there wasn't anybody waiting to give you shit just for showing up. Now Tyrone, he had something. A unique skill - an attribute, you could say - and he was going to use it for everything it was worth.

Jennifer shifted, and he felt his cock settle between her cheeks, thick and powerful and very very obvious even through his pants. He grinned as she shifted a little more, trying to get away without being obvious to her husband what she was doing, then giving up and settling in.

"Jennifer tells me you play sports. Football, wasn't it?"

"Yeah, that's right. You should come to a game sometime."

Jennifer brightened up. "Oh my, yes. Could we? That would be great. I would really really love to watch you play." Her hand strayed to his bicep. He saw the husband's eyes follow his wife's motion, and the little guy started squirming a little in his seat. Discomfort, or something else?

"What, uh, what position do you play?"

"Tight end." He slipped a hand down Jennifer's side as he said it, sliding over the hip to cup her juicy ass and give it a good squeeze. She yelped a little, and tried to disguise it with a flurry of coughing that fooled nobody.

"What... um... what does that entail?"

Tyrone laughed. "You don't know your football, huh?"

"Oh *God* no," Jennifer interrupted Percy's stammering replay, "poor Percy's useless at the whole sports things. We went to his brother's place the other year for the Super Bowl and he kept interrupting to ask these dumb questions, until Charles - that's his brother, Charles - finally told him to go to the kitchen and help the girls make snacks."

Percy blushed, "Well, I'm better with that sort of thing anyway. I know a few good recipes, and-"

Tyrone cut him off. "Don't sweat it, bro, it's cool. I dig it. You're not a sports guy, that's fine. Talents lie in another field, that's all."

The older guy grinned, looking absurdly pleased. "Well yes. I mean, I'd hardly expect Chuck to know how to file a disposition or... well, you know."

Tyrone leaned back in the booth. His hand still hadn't left Jennifer's ample backside, and he was working it without missing a beat, squeezing and pinching mercilessly. As Percy babbled about the complexities of modern legalese, Tyrone brought his other hand up and placed it on Jennifer's side. Slowly, he moved it up. The feel of the skin-tight lace send shivers of delight right down to his crotch. He could feel himself getting bigger. And he felt her breath getting shorter and more urgent. He cupped her breast, feeling the soft shape of it in his hand through material no thicker than a negligee. He moved casually, finding the bud of the nipple and pinning it between the knuckles of his middle and ring fingers. He heard her gasp softly, wriggling in his lap.

"You wear this just for me, baby?" he murmured in her ear.

"Do you like it, Ty?" she whispered back, her voice feathery and shuddering.

"Yeah," he said, giving her ripe breast a good squeeze, "yeah, I like it."

Percy was still droning on, but he'd reached a hand surreptitiously into his pocket, and he was watching the two of them with feverish intensity. Sweat prickled his brow, and the hand on the tabletop drummed nervously. Or excitedly.

The food started to come out, and he let up on her. He didn't let her off his lap, but he let go of her for the moment. Everything tasted incredible. He fed Jennifer fruits from the platter, little cubes of melon and strawberries and grapes. She licked the juices from his fingers. He slid his middle finger between her lips, caressing the tip of her tongue. She sucked sensuously on him for just a moment before he slid it free. A tiny clear strand of saliva webbed between her lower lip and the tip of his finger, then broke off and hung from her mouth. For a second she just stared at him, her eyes cloudy with building lust, her mouth open and her cheeks flushed. God, she looked so damn fuckable. He felt himself getting really hard now, a proper erection rising.

She blushed and wiped her mouth on the back of her hand, clearing her throat softly.

They brought the main course, and Percy ordered another bottle of wine. He poured for all three of them when it arrived, his eyes darting back and forth between his wife and her lover. His hand as he poured was far from steady.

"So, like," Tyrone took a bite of salmon. It was exquisite, flaky and moist with a crispy skin in a sort of tangy sweet sauce. "Tell me about yourself, man. What kinda lawyer are you anyway?"

"Corporate. Our firm represents a variety of business interests across the... um... what was I saying?" he trailed off, his dinner untouched, and he stared longingly across the table.

Jennifer had started rocking back and forth a little, shifting her hips to grind herself against Tyrone's cock. Her face was flushed red with some combination of embarrassment and desire. Tyrone had his hands on her hips, and was guiding her movements. There were people watching now, a good handful of them from all around the club.

Percy glanced nervously about. "Jennifer, are, um... are you sure you should? In front of everyone?"

She moaned softly, almost sobbing. "I can't help it, Percy... I need it so bad..."

"Jennifer!" Percy hissed, sounding somewhere between appalled and impressed. However mortified he may have been, however, Tyrone couldn't help but notice that the guy's hand was doing a little dance inside his pocket. He grinned. They were both wrapped right around his finger.

He leaned in close and murmured in her ear. "Your boy looks like he's about to pop over there. Why don't you do something about it?"

"Like what?" she breathed.

"Take off your shoe," he said.

"Huh?" But she figured it out quick enough. She slipped her heels off and lifted a stockinged foot to place it none-too-gently between her husband's legs. Tyrone couldn't see much of what was going on under there, but if Percy's expression was anything to go by, she knew what she was doing. He could hear the little *whisk whisk* of her hosiery-clad toes on the front of his pants.

"Yeah, like I said," Tyrone went on, sipping his wine, "you should all come to a game sometime. I'm sure Jennifer could fill you in on the finer points, Percy. Afterwards, maybe you should come on down to the locker room. I've got some friends on the team that I'm sure would love to meet you, Jen."

"What?" Percy squeaked, his glasses slipping off the tip of his nose and clattering to the table beside his soup bowl. He picked them up and started cleaning nervously.

"You know, a lot of the guys here at the club were, I don't know, recruited, I guess, from the team, so they have experience. Know just how a sexy white bitch like this wants to be treated."

"Uh huh?" Jennifer panted, her motions increasing in speed slightly. Her rocking back and forth was starting to have an effect on him as well. He could feel that warm damp spot soaking right through her panties and into the flimsy material of the dress.

"That's right. Bunch of big ass niggas with a taste for white girl pussy. How would you like that, get passed around the locker room by a bunch of sweaty football players all juiced up after a big game? That sound like your jam?"

She just moaned low in her throat.

"I think that might be a bit much," Percy laughed awkwardly, his eyelids fluttering as he tried to keep his composure.

Tyrone gave Jennifer's breast a squeeze, "You think so, man? But what would you say if you were there watching it? I think you might change your mind. Which makes you harder, thinking about us all pounding her one after the other, or three of us taking her all at once and filling up these pretty pink holes with our black cocks."

"Oh my God," Jennifer moaned, her breath rasping, "oh my God, oh my God."

"You hear that, man? She's soaking over here. Just thinking about it got her creaming her panties. This bitch needs *dick*, and bad. You do, don't you?"

"Uh hm," she groaned.

"Tell your husband what you want, baby."

"I want cock..."

"Yeah? You want his dinky little white-boy dick?"

"No..."

"What do you want?"

"I want your big black cock..."

"Tell me you wanna big nigga dick in you."

She bit her lip. "I want it..."

"Say it, baby, it's cool. Look your boy here in the eyes and tell him."

She sat up a little, panting with desire, and she planted both hands on the table. She was grinding very obviously now, rocking her hips aggressively back and forth on Tyrone's erection. Her cheeks were flushed and her nipples were rock hard under her sheer top. She stared at Percy, who seemed practically knocked against the back of the booth with his eyes open in horrified ecstasy. She looked her husband right in the eyes and spoke, her voice trembling but intense. "I want this big black cock in my pussy right now, honey."

Tyrone grinned. It gave him a weird thrill, hearing that. Her pretty little prissy white mouth forming those words right out here in the open for everybody to see. Yeah, he was ready.

Percy swallowed hard. "Oh..." he murmured very softly, and swallowed again. "Oh." He stared for a long moment, then he flagged the nearest waiter, who came over right away.

"Sir?" the waiter asked, his eyes taking in the scene, brows climbing.

"Is there, ah, well, I mean to say, ahem." He cleared his throat, swallowed hard, and said quietly, "is there a room here that we might make use of?"

The waiter nodded, lowering his voice discreetly. "Of course, sir. Suite number four is available, just through there, sir. The key," he presented an elegant, almost ornamental key from on his person and gave it to Percy. "The room will be charged to sir's bill."

"That's fine, thank you." Percy took the key. He held it gently in his fingertips, rubbing it softly. He seemed to steady himself, and looked up. "Shall we?"

* * *

Tyrone whistled admiringly as they stepped through the door. The suite was really something else. The bed was massive and soft, crimson velvet bedding and cushions piled high. There were mirrors everywhere, one of them opposite the bed that went right from the floor to the ceiling. There was a Jacuzzi and hot tub in an adjoining room, and a huge stately walnut dresser well stocked with more types of sex toys and lubricants that he ever could have imagined. The walls were hung with a half-a-dozen impressively rendered works of exquisite art, all of it relating to one particular subject matter: black men and white women in the act of love. Well, that was the nice way to put it. What was actually going on, depicted in lush oils and expressive watercolors, was filthy and explicit fucking.

Percy turned the lock in the door and slipped the key into his jacket pocket. His eyes bugged out a little when he turned around, and he forced a nervous chuckle. "Oh my."

Jennifer slunk into the room, hugging the walls and writhing seductively. She looked around, acting very coy and mysterious, as if she hadn't just been practically dry humping him a few minutes ago.

Tyrone slipped off his jacket. He felt cool and in control, powerful. This was his playground right now, and they'd do anything he wanted. He could feel it.

He went to the foot of the bed and turned around. They were both staring at him, Percy from the door, Jennifer against the wall opposite him. He reached down and grasped the zipper of his slacks. Slowly, their eyes following his every motion, he drew it downwards, and undid the button. He reached in, grinning slightly to himself, and he pulled out his massive erection.

Jennifer groaned softly, and Percy gasped a little.

Tyrone grabbed himself by the base of the shaft and gave it a little shake. The fat purple head was slick with precum. "Come here, girl," he said, nodding at Jennifer. "Show your boy what you do with this."

She came to him at once, dropping to her knees before him and taking it deep in her mouth, sucking and slurping hungrily, the way he'd carefully trained her. Percy was swallowing and blushing at the door while his wife gave Tyrone what was almost certainly the sloppiest, wettest, most enthusiastic hold nothing back no holds barred blowjob the guy had ever seen before in his life.

"Fuck yeah," Tyrone moaned, lifting his shirt and running his fingers through her hair, "Aw, that's *it*, baby. You do it good for me. You suck the shit outta that black dick."

"Yes, sir," she moaned, dropping it from her mouth just long enough to speak before he grabbed the back of her head and pushed her back onto it.

Drool already cascaded down her mouth and chin, sliding sloppily down his balls and thighs. She grabbed his pants, dragging them down as she sucked, then reaching up to grasp his buttocks, taking hold of him so that she could pull herself deeper down on him.

"She ever suck your balls, man?" he asked her husband, grinning lazily.

Percy just shook his head. He seemed frozen in a kind of shock, but the little bulge in his pants spoke volumes.

Tyrone grabbed his dick and held it up against his chest. "Show your husband how you do it, baby."

She groaned gratefully, wrapping her tongue around his testicles, suckling at them gently and firmly, working at them with her fingers. She went at them sloppy and hard. Tyrone looked down. His ball-sack looked midnight black slapping against her pretty pale white face.

"Stand up, baby, turn around, look at the man over there."

She did as instructed, wiping her mouth and rising unsteadily to her feet. He held her against him, his cock jutting out beside her, just resting on the swell of her shapely hip. She looked at her husband, and Tyrone saw in the wall length mirror a mixture of defiance, shame, excitement, and giddy lust swirling on her features. Her hand fell to his cock instinctively, grasping it like a drowning swimmer holding their life preserver. She didn't even seem aware of it as she gently tugged at it, insistent and needy as a baby at a bottle.

"Take off your clothes, man," he said, nodded at Percy.

The other man disrobed slowly, slipping his jacket and pants off with exaggerated care. He stood there against the wall, plump and pale and a bit splotchy, his glasses glimmering and his hands opening and closing nervously. His little cock was quiet erect under the potbelly swell of his stomach.

"You want that little cock, baby?"

She shook her head. "No. I want *your* cock, Ty. I need it, sir."

"Yeah, that's what I thought." Tyrone reached around and grabbed the sheer front of Jennifer's dress with both hands. He closed his fists and he yanked hard. The incredibly expensive material ripped like tissue paper in his hands, and her pale breasts spilled out. She shrieked a little with surprise and excitement and a flash of erotic fear, and reached up to cover herself. He grabbed her hands by the wrists and put them back at her sides, then reached up and clutched her breasts in his hands. They filled his large palms nicely, full and ripe, so white between his black fingers that the skin seemed almost translucent. Her hand went back to his cock, working it slowly, and her head fell back against his strong chest, her eyes closing in delight as he handled her.

"You've never seen her like this, have you man?"

Percy shook his head.

"Why do you think that is, brother?"

"B-because, ahem," he cleared his throat, swallowing hard and fighting for the words. "B-because she... she needs a... a real man's cock."

Tyrone grinned wolfishly, pinching Jennifer's nipples hard enough to make her squeal and writhe in his arms. "That's right, man. That's exactly right."

He took Jennifer by the arm and led her up onto the bed. She crawled up on all fours. He turned her around so that she was facing her husband and herself in the mirror. He got up behind her and pushed her dress up over her hips, revealing the sweet pale white cheeks of her ass, so beautifully framed by the sheer black of her dress and the shocking red of her lacy little panties. He hooked his finger under the band of her underwear and pulled down slowly. She was so juicy and ready that the material actually stuck to her sopping pussy, and had to be peeled away. He slid the panties down around her knees, where they held her legs together. Her sweet pink pussy looked so good when she was bend over like this, that little pink slit between her creamy thighs, the puffy lips pushed beautifully together, just waiting to be spread open.

And the neat little pink hole above, pinched so tightly shut. Her breasts hung low, framed by the tatters of her ripped top.

He put his hand on her smooth back, and he pushed her face gently down until her cheek was touching the soft crimson duvet cover and her ripe tits were squished onto the bed. He wound his fingers through her hair, gathering the long chestnut locks up into a ponytail and gripping hard. He tilted her head up so that she was looking right at her husband. She didn't say a word through the whole process, just moaned softly and eagerly, her hips still shifting with a desperate fluid motion of enticement. She stared at Percy, her eyes clouded with overwhelming lust, and she whimpered softly.

Tyrone leaned forward, and he whispered in her ear. He spoke, very low and soft, for a good two minutes at least, then he leaned back. "You got that, baby?"

"Yes sir..."

He settled in behind her, keeping a grip on her gathered hair with one hand and smacking her soft pale ass with the other. She winced, and writhed. He reached down and grabbed his cock, slowly lifting it and placing the fat black head just there against her puffy lips, not yet parting them.

"Percy, honey?" she spoke softly but clearly.

"Ah... yes, dear?"

She looked at him, looking him right in the eye, and she said the words she had been instructed to impart, and a good few more besides. "You're never going to have this pussy again, honey. Your little white cock couldn't possibly satisfy me, and I can't waste my time screwing a pitiful thing like that. My cunt belongs to big blacks cocks only from now on. It belongs to Tyrone, and anybody he wants to share it with."

As she spoke, he rocked his hips forward, ever so slowly entering her. Her soaking wet lips parted incredibly easily, buttery smooth over his slippery head, and opened for him. He pushed in, shutting his eyes with pleasure as her tight pink walls closed over him like a warm and snug sleeve. He felt everything so clearly, every little ripple and fold inside. So smooth it was as if his whole body was sinking into a bath of warm honey. She kept talking, and she was going beyond what he'd instructed her to say now, her voice raw and ragged and frequently interrupted by moans and squeals of pleasure.

"I want his black cock so bad, it's all I can think about. I've always wanted it, even if I didn't realize it. I need black dicks, not just his but as many as I can, all the time. I need my holes filled, and I need their strong black seed deep inside my fertile body. You're going to have to watch your wife fuck dozens and dozens of fat black cocks and love it. You're going to have to jerk your little think while you watch me get pounded over and over and over again, and know that your inferior sperm isn't ever going inside me again."

By the end they could hardly understand what she was saying, it was all lost in her cries of agonized ecstasy. After he'd gone fully inside, Tyrone had held there for just a moment, then pulled slowly back out. He'd gone back until there was nothing but the tip inside, beautiful and dark parting her creamy pink slit like a deep sea diver's heavy rubber glove opening a clam shell after pearls. Then he'd shoved it back in. Hard. He'd grabbed her ass and her hair and he'd rammed her with everything he had, pounding her again and again like a piston engine operating at max capacity. She could hardly get a word out between the squeals. Finally it was too much, and she had to give up, abandon all rational thought and give herself over fully. He doubted she was even capable of *thinking* a complete sentence right then, must less expressing it. He was hitting it harder than he'd ever hit it before. The angle was perfect, her body opening its deepest doors to him. He was eleven inches deep in her, slamming all the way to the balls.

"You ready for the nut, baby?" he grunted.

"Give it to me, give it to me, *give it to me*!" she cried, her eyes almost rolling back in her head.

He grinned, and pushed her off him. She slumped down, limp as a doll, twitching and shivering with agony, orgasmic delight shuddering through her. She looked back, eyes wide with confusion and naked desire.

"Wha?" was all she could manage.

He laughed. "You gonna get it, baby, *trust me*, you gonna get it. I just want your boy her to see what's going on here. Come here, man."

Percy's eyes were owl wide. "M-me?"

"Yeah, you. Come here and lay down on your back."

He did as instructed, shaking little a leaf. Some combination of uncontrollable desire and shredded nerves.

Tyrone reached down and slapped the guy's stomach. "Look at that little piggy tummy, man, what's up with that? Damn, boy, bet you can hardly see your cock when you piss." He slapped Jennifer's ass. "Get up on there, baby. Give him a taste of my cock."

She mounted him, squeezing his head between her thighs. Her dripping wet cunt sopped all over his face and mouth. He moaned, his tongue fluttering.

"Yeah, he likes that," Tyrone chuckled. "Suck his dick, baby."

She made a face. "I don't want to."

"When I tell you to suck a cock, baby, I'm not asking." He grabbed her back the neck and pushed her down, her full breasts on his rounded stomach. Her husband's little pink cock slipped into her mouth, and he groaned. "That's *better*. You look beautiful, you two, just fucking right. Only one thing missing now."

He slid into position, straddling the little guy's head and lifting her ass up just enough to let his cock back into her pussy. She squealed, coming up off his dick. Tyrone's hand clamped on the back of her head, pushing her back onto it.

"You keep sucking, girl. I tell you when you done. And you keep licking that clit, boy, lick it fucking good."

He grabbed her ass tight with both hands and started fucking again. His balls, still sloppy from Jennifer's mouth, slapped against Percy's forehead.

"*Shit.* Shit, that's a good pussy. I know you gonna miss this, boy, but you just do your job and lick it good, I might let you fuck her mouth sometimes, okay? Yeah, that's right. Fuck, it's so tight on my fat nigga dick, I think I'm gonna cum soon. Gonna fill this bitch right up, and I want you to keep these sheets clean, you hear me, man? I don't wanna see one drop of this nigga's pearly white cum on this bed. You lick that shit up like a good boy."

Percy moaned his acceptance, licking sloppily and hungrily at his wife's clit. Her juices ran down his chin and cheeks.

Tyrone groaned. "Fuck, I'm gonna cum, I'm cumming baby!" He snarled, thrusting powerfully, so hard that Jennifer gasped and let her suction on her husband's cock slip. He pushed her head down until she gagged. Then he came.

He could feel it, the sensation of power and control and pure joy surging through him. God, she felt good. His cock twitched as his thrusts slowed. His cum pumped into her, felt like buckets of it. Shit, she was taking it. He was buried eleven inches deep in her perfect pink pussy, and he was dumping his cum deep into her fertile womb.

She was breathing so hard and so raggedly that it sounded like sobbing, a combination of exhaustion and amazement. Her pale thighs shook. "Oh my God..." she moaned.

Slowly, as his cock let up and the last few spurts of his seed gushed into her, he started to withdraw. He slid out slowly, and his black cock slapped down on Percy's face, going messily across his cheek. He leaned back against the pillows with a heavy sigh, putting his hands behind his head and feeling about as good as he could ever remember feeling before in his life.

There was a beautiful bead of cum right there between Jennifer's still-gaped pussy lips, like a fat pearl. It started to roll downward. She'd lifted herself up a little on her haunches, shaking and gasping still, and her pussy was a couple inches above Percy's mouth.

"You know what to do, man," Tyrone said lazily, giving himself a few final strokes as he started to get soft again.

Percy opened his mouth wide, his eyes shut. The perfect bead of cum slid down, turning teardrop shaped as it hung, then fell onto his waiting tongue.

Percy swallowed, gagging softly.

Jennifer groaned throaTilly, still working patiently at her husband's little cock.

Tyrone grinned.

This really was the start of something beautiful.

* * *

They were quiet when they left the club. It was late, something like two thirty in the morning, and the moon was dusky blue bright above. The streets seemed to glow with a pale light.

They didn't talk much. What was there to say? They were excited still, suffused with a kind of giddiness that came from having done something none of them considered possible. Percy muttered that he needed to swing by the office for something. Jennifer offered to drop him off but he said he'd take a cab. She offered Tyrone a ride, but he shrugged and said he'd catch the late bus. Somehow he felt like he needed to be alone. She kissed them each softly on the cheek, one after the other, and then they left her, standing there with her car keys in her hand on the side of the road in blue moonlight.

It wasn't a long walk to the bus stop, but as he strolled it seemed to him that the quiet streets seemed to go on forever. He sat on the bench at the stop, and he watched the sparse traffic sliding through the night. The bus came to a stop with a hiss and a grind. It was practically empty. He sat alone way in the back, staring out the window and thinking long and hard about what had happened.

He'd gone further tonight than he had ever thought possible. He figured they probably all had, yet they'd gone there together, and that had counted for a lot. Everyone had seemed to slide so comfortably into their role, seemed to fit there.

He wondered if this was the sort of thing he could actually do again, and he thought that maybe it was. He'd felt something strange, a sensation of almost belonging. It had felt right somehow. He'd gotten into this whole thing on a whim, just looking for an experience and an easy lay, really. He wasn't sure exactly what it was becoming, but it was something.

He wondered what Jennifer was doing at that exact minute. Sitting in her expensive SUV, driving alone towards her big house on the swanky side of town. Driving so casually into a place where he sometimes felt half afraid of going, a place where he was not entirely welcome. But there was a part of him going in with her. His seed pearly and warm inside her pink folds, was traveling through the gate.

Tyrone smiled, and he lay his head back and shut his eyes. The bus rumbled and clattered as he rolled on into the warm Florida night.

Book Two: Her Black Master

Percy

"Here's the thing, Brice. Here's the thing."

"What's that, sir?"

"In the end, it's all about her."

Percy frowned. "I think I understand, but how do you mean?"

Jonas Harrington leaned back in his seat. He sipped at his white wine, and seemed deep in thought for a long moment. "Let me try to explain. She's the focal point of everything. Sure, it's hot watching him get his rocks off, and god knows that I enjoy seeing her squirm around like that. But his enjoyment and my enjoyment are not what make me want to do it. It's her. Seeing her like that. Knowing how she's feeling, watching her move beyond performance, access something deeply primal. I see her fuck him, and I know that she's doing it for herself, because it's more pleasurable than anything. She's not trying to seduce him, because, in the end, she doesn't care about him. Not really. And she's not doing it for me, to impress me or turn me on. It doesn't even matter to her if I'm in the room or not. She's doing it for *herself.*"

Percy wasn't too sure about that whole *not caring about him* bit. After all, he'd seen Jonas's wife Matilda, and he'd seen the way she doted on Marquis, her black lover. He'd seen the way she looked at him. Worshipful. Like she would do anything to please him. He wondered if Jonas might be deceiving himself to a certain extent.

And what did that say about his own wife? Jennifer looked at Tyrone the same way sometimes. She didn't just want the younger man; she *loved* him. Percy was jealous, of course, but it was a sweet jealousy, an erotic lustful feeling with no bitterness or fear. It was a strange sensation. But he knew that she loved him too, albeit in a very different context. He certainly didn't begrudge her her affection for the other man. After all, Tyrone was able to offer her something that he couldn't.

The whole adventure had in fact all started with none other than Jonas and Matilda Harrington. It had been quite a few months now since Percy and his wife had moved to Florida from their old home in Minnesota so that Percy could take a job at Jonas's law firm. The very first night they were in town they'd come to a party at Jonas's house, and Percy stumbled upon a very odd scene: Matilda and Marquis brazenly making love in the hallway of Jonas's mansion, while Jonas himself looked on from a distance. By way of explanation, he'd given Percy an invitation to the exclusive interracial cuckold club where they were even now meeting for dinner: The Black and White Club. It had been quite a journey, but Percy had finally worked up the courage to bring his wife there, and she had very quickly hit it off with a young black man named Tyrone.

For months afterwards the two of them had been in a state of constant passion. Percy himself had made love with them three or four times, but that was certainly the exception. Tyrone fucked Percy's wife with a kind of raw power and aggression which Percy himself never could have managed, and Jennifer had responded to it with an almost animal-like lust. When she wasn't meeting with him, she was texting him. Always lewd and sexual conversations, to be sure. She shared many of these conversations with him, and took quite a few pictures and even videos of her exploits.

As for Percy, he was content with physical contact on a very infrequent basis. For himself, he had found that masturbating to Jennifer's photos once or twice a week was an almost orgiastic bacchanal, by the standards of his own modest sex drive. Before he'd seen her fuck Tyrone, Percy had been impotent. That problem had cleared right up. He was happy, and Jennifer was happy. He never thought he would have even been interested in something like this, but you couldn't argue with the results.

These long summer months, however, had been quite torturous for all three of them. Tyrone was still in school, a junior in college, and he had gone home for the summer.

Jennifer had gone from almost daily sex back to something like celibacy, and it had been driving her crazy. She even flew up to see him once, but it was apparently been extremely awkward with Tyrone's family around and neither of them wanting to offer any awkward explanations. Jennifer had pretended to be a teacher of his just passing through town, but the pretense had been, in her words, exhausting to maintain, and they had only been able to sneak away for a motel room quickie once or twice, so they'd reluctantly decided that it wasn't an idea worth repeating.

But now the drought came to an end. The fall semester had begun, at long last, and he'd gotten back into town not three hours ago. Which was why Percy found himself dinning alone on a Sunday night. Jennifer had more or less kicked him out of the house that afternoon, saying she had a great deal to prepare for and didn't want him messing about and getting in the way. She had a date tonight, she said, and she was planning to get fucked on every single piece of furniture in the house and didn't need him hanging around, thank you very much.

"Not my *desk*!" Percy had exclaimed, coming in to find her dusting off the grand oak desk in his study.

"Percy," she had said, arching her eyebrow, "Do I need to ask Tyrone about this?"

"No, no," he'd muttered, scurrying in to gather his papers and pack them safely away. He had little hope that the alpha male bull would be much interested in the sanctity of Percy's work space. That was the point at which she'd lost patience and firmly suggested he go out for a while. Overnight, maybe, in a nice hotel room. Give himself a little vacation.

He hadn't been left with much of a choice. She kissed him at the door and promised to keep him well supplied with updates and pictures throughout the night, if she could manage it. The last next she'd sent him, almost an hour ago, read simply -*he's here*. And none had followed since.

Percy had found himself drawn to the club downtown. He'd wandered in and ordered dinner. That was where Jonas found him.

Matilda and Jonas had come there for dinner together, but Tilly's lover Marquis had spotted her there and the two of them had stolen away to one of the rooms upstairs, leaving Jonas on his own.

"You don't want to watch?" Percy had said, a small part of him looking for an excuse. He liked the other man well enough, but he hadn't planned on spending his evening with Jonas Harrington.

"No no," he'd said, "let the little love-birds have their fun. Come on then, let's you and I talk."

And so they had talked. Or, to put it more accurately, Jonas had talked and Percy had listened. The other man had been in the game, so to speak, for quite some time. Tilly wasn't his first wife, and she wasn't the first he'd shared either. He had quite a few stories to say the least, and wasn't shy about telling them. As they'd moved through the appetizers and the main course, however, the discussion had become almost philosophical. Now, their dinner finished some time ago, Jonas was working on his four glass of wine and elucidating on the finer points of the cuckold relationship experience.

"The sort of women that marry men like you and I, Brice, they're buttoned up. Even the free spirited ones, even the wild ones. They've still been trained to restrain themselves. All their lives, they had to hold back. They want to please their parents, their teachers, their bosses, their husbands. It's what they're *conditioned* for. But, given the chance, if you can break through the conditioning, give them access to something that revolves entirely around their own pleasure, well... then you get something magnificent."

"What's that, sir?"

"You get an explosion, Brice. A veritable explosion of sexual energy. They've been building it up their entire life and then it gets unlocked all in one furious burst. It's incredible to see."

Percy supposed that he couldn't disagree with that. He'd been married to Jennifer for sixteen years and before Tyrone had come along he had never seen the wild and intense side of her which had since emerged. She'd done things he never could have imagined her capable of.

"Have I ever told you about my first wife, Brice?"

"No sir, I don't think so."

"She was something, I can tell you that. A real firecracker. But not at first. No, definitely not a first. She was a quiet little mouse when I married her, just eighteen years old. A virgin, believe it or not, that rarest of species. Let me tell you something, Brice, I never fucked her."

"Never?"

"Not once. Our wedding night, there we were, her in this silly lace night gown, lying in bed. I came into the room naked. And quite eager, let me tell you. Oh, I'd fooled around a little, but I was hardly what you'd call experienced. I came in there hard and ready. She screamed. Shrieked like she'd seen a ghost. I didn't even understand it at first, until she covered up her eyes and hid under the covers. Let me tell you, I didn't get any action that night."

"My god."

"It was a different time, Brice. She'd never had it explained to her, never told what was expected of her. She was terrified. I tried to explain it to her. She agreed to try, seemed intrigued. Eventually I starting to think that she actually wanted it. But no matter how we tried I couldn't do it. For weeks I tried, and never got anywhere. She was closed up tight."

Percy frowned. "How do you mean?"

"I couldn't put it in, Brice! She was sealed. That pussy was locked up tighter than Fort Knox. Rare condition called vaginismus, but of course I only found that out much later. To put it in layman's terms, she was so afraid of sex that she squeezed herself shut. Today of course they have ways of solving the issue, physical therapy and all that, but we were in the dark. Eventually I just had to content myself with a sexless relationship. Of course it was torture at first; I was a young man after all. But I adapted. I learned to live with it."

"So what happened?"

Jonas smiled widely. He took a long slow drink of his wine, then poured himself another glass. He savored the moment, luxuriating.

Percy found himself feeling a little bit irritated by the other man. He hadn't come here to listen to his boss's entire life story. He pulled out his phone and checked it surreptitiously. Still no texts from Jennifer. He typed a quick message and sent it. -*Having a good time, sweetie?*

All around him there were couples coming and going. Black men prowling the club looking white women to borrow from their husbands. Soft background music played, classical and stylish. The lighting was low and moody. Somewhere up on the second floor Tilly was getting her brains fucked out, while Jennifer was no doubt doing the same at home.

He felt a rare flush of desire. Why should he be left out of the fun? He *was* her husband, after all. Was it really so much to ask that she send him a quick photograph or update?

"Well," Jonas went on, "years pass. Two years, no change. I've given up trying. She made an effort, did everything she could, but nothing. By that time she'd grown as frustrated by it as I was. It's a mental thing, you know, a psychological block. Anyway, we'd given up.

"But there was this man. His name was Henry Lewis. He worked in the mail room at my firm. A black man, about my age. The two of us became friends. We used to eat lunch together, shoot the shit. Both liked the same sports team, you understand, the only two fans in the building. Not the home team, so we were on our own. Over time, we struck up quite a friendship. Eventually, I tell him about my problem. Our problem, my wife and I. He acts like it's nothing, he says he's known plenty of girls like that, and he knows how to take care of it. Easy, no big deal. I was annoyed, I thought he was making fun of me, or talking some macho bullshit. Almost lost it at him. But no, he tells me, he's for real. He can help. I left without another word."

"You were upset."

"That's right. But I thought about it. I thought long and hard. What did I have to lose, anyway? I'd been married to years and never so much as consummated it. So, eventually I worked up the courage to talk to her about it. Ask her what she thinks. She was even more dubious than I was, but she agrees. I couldn't believe it. I guess it goes to show that she'd become even more desperate than me by that point."

"So, did it work?"

Jonas smiled, and took another drink. "Patience, Brice, patience. So, the big day finally arrives. He shows up at my door, and I'm expecting to see... something. A doctor's bag, I don't know. I ask him what he's planning to do, and he just grins at me and says that he's going to solve my wife's problem. Of course I'm skeptical, but I'm at my wit's end. My wife comes out and he tells her that they need to be alone. She's terribly embarrassed about the whole thing, naturally. I tell him that there's no way I'm letting him be alone with her. He just shrugs and says that it's not a problem with him, but he's not sure that I can handle it. I told him that I would be fine."

"And then what?" Almost against his will, Percy found himself being drawn into the man's story.

"He asks my wife to bring him to her bedroom. Says he needs her to lie down and take off her underthings. You know, looking back on this, I can hardly believe that any of it happened. We weren't exactly kinky back then, Brice. Just normal people, didn't do anything perverse or unnatural, wouldn't have even known how. We weren't the sort to do anything untoward, but there we were, letting a man, practically a stranger, undress my wife right in front of me. I suppose it shows just how desperate we were."

"Or maybe that you had in inclination in that direction all along without knowing it."

Jonas smiled. "Maybe so, Brice, maybe so. Chicken and the egg, isn't it? Anyway. She's lying there on the bed with her skirt up over her head, she's hiding under it because she's so embarrassed. And my friend unzips his pants and just pulls his penis out, right there in front of me. I almost clocked him. 'That's your big idea?' I shouted at him, 'You're just going to screw her? Don't you think I tried that?' And he just smiles at me, and he says that I've never tried it with *his* dick. I was furious, but my wife speaks up from under her skirt, says to just let him try. We've both nearly given up hope at this point, so why not? It's not going to work anyway, he's going to try and she'll be closed up and that will be that. So he moves in and he slides his cock against her furry little pussy. He starts rubbing her with it, massaging the big black head on her little pale pink lips. She just lies there, stiff as a board, not moving, not saying anything. I'm just sitting there in my chair, practically ripping the armrests off as I twist around in the seat. Nothing seems to be happening, and I was about to leap up and throw him out, give him a beating for good measure, if I can manage it. Then I hear a sound I've never heard before."

"What?" Percy found he was leaning across the table, quite rapt.

"I hear a moan. A soft and low moan... of pleasure."

"Pleasure?"

"That's right. Somehow, he's done it. He's inside her. Her tiny little virgin pussy, that I'd been trying to get my own little white soldier into for years with no success, has opened up for this big black stallion. At first he just slides in, just stays there, stretching her, easing into her. Then she starts to move. That's right, *she* starts, she's rocking her hips against him, responding automatically. She's fucking *him*. As soon as he feels that he knows that she's ready, and he grabs her hips and pulls her down, and he starts going to town. He fucks her like a beast, pounding her mercilessly. There are quite a few times that I want to intervene. I'm ready for it, just waiting to hear her moans turn to screams, but they never do, only get more and more intense, more desirous. She can't get enough of it. I'm sitting there at the foot of the bed, just watching his ass as he goes at her. Finally she starts to scream, but it's very much not the sort of scream where she wants me to stop him. Very much the opposite. He pulls out and puts his thing away and tips his hat at me, and off he goes. She never had a problem again. It was the first time I'd ever seen a female orgasm, and the first time I'd witnessed the awesome power of a black man's cock."

Jonas took a long drink of wine. He seemed distant, lost in a kind of reverie, as if he were reliving the moment right then and there.

Percy leaned back, and swallowed hard. He hadn't even realized it, but his throat was dry.

His phone dinged, snapping him out of the trance he hadn't even realized he'd been in.

-Sorry hon, can't talk now, busy. Don't worry, taking pictures.

He sighed.

Jonas grinned. "Oh, don't worry about it, Percy. She'll have lots to tell you about in the morning."

Percy blushed. "You know she's..."

"Oh, I'd recognize that look anywhere. Take my advice, Brice: put your phone away. Live in the moment." He got up from the table, picking up the still half-full bottle of wine. "Care to join me?"

"Sir?"

"Come along, Tilly doesn't mind an audience, Brice. Now that you've heard all about the former Mrs. Harrington, it seems only right to end the night by having a look at the new model."

Percy blanched. "Oh, sir, I couldn't, I-"

"What's the matter, Brice, not interested? Oh, but don't even try. Remember, I caught you that night at my house, all those months ago. I remember seeing the little bulge in your pants."

"Excuse me?" he felt himself pale. The way he remembered it, he'd been too terrified to have possible gotten it up, not to mention he'd been feeling rather impotent at the time. But maybe he had been.

"Don't worry about it, Brice. My treat. Trust me, they put on quite a show."

"Well... if you're sure they won't mind."

"Of course not. Let's go, let's go."

Percy got slowly up out of his seat. Was this alright, would Jennifer mind? He doubted she'd answer him if he put the question to her. She was occupied. But why shouldn't he? It was only looking, after all...

As Jonas led him through the dark curtain at the back of the room and up the stairs to the rooms above, Percy thought back over the spring. It had been like nothing he'd ever experience before in his life, that was for sure.

Percy had never been very comfortable with girls, not when they were right there in front of him, anyway. He felt safer with pictures. Pictures didn't judge you, or notice your inadequacies, they were just there, and he was safe on the other side. He still remembered the first picture Jennifer had sent him. They started dating in the summer, and it had been amazing. They'd gone on long walks in the park, strolling together hand in hand. He pointed out all the different types of trees that he knew, and she pointed out the birds darting from branch to branch. It had seemed so simple, and so beautiful.

After a few months though, she'd started pressuring him to take things further. It was subtle, she wasn't pushy. But he could sense it, he could feel her desire. The way her eyes would linger on him, the way she would touch him a little longer than usual. They'd become best friends, and there had been a part of Percy which had wanted it to stay that way forever. But it didn't really work like that, did it? A man and a woman, both young and single, it wouldn't have seemed right to just be friends. If he didn't make a move then he knew that he'd lose her. Some other man would come along, more virile and aggressive, and he'd sweep her off her feet. She would promise to stay friends, promise they'd always be together and her new relationship didn't mean they couldn't stay on good terms...

But it wouldn't last that way. He was going away to law school soon, and she still had her senior year to finish. The distance would grow, and their friendship would fade. Her new man would take more and more of her attention, until there was no room left for Percy. He'd be cut out eventually, and he'd lose his best friend. Lose the woman he loved so deeply. So he did the only thing he could do: he had sex with her.

It had been like something out of a romantic movie. They'd done it outside on a gorgeous sunny August day, alone in lonely glade far away from the bustling campus, under a canopy of sycamore trees. They'd just finished eating the picnic he'd made and they were lying back on the blanket staring up at the sunlight flickering between the leaves. He'd turned on his side and they had looked at each other for a long moment. Then, summoning every ounce of courage he had, he leaned over and kissed her. She kissed him back. "Do you want to?" she asked him. He just nodded, his throat too dry to speak. She stood up and she undressed, striping naked in the dappling light. She was so beautiful. He couldn't believe that she was here with him, actually couldn't believe it. He was sure that he'd fallen asleep in the sunshine and was dreaming, that he would wake at any moment and find himself alone. That thought was what gave him the nerve to go on: the thought that it might not be real.

He sat up, and she unbuttoned his shirt, kissing his chest. She undid his pants and slid them off. He trembled in a sudden cool breeze, or maybe he was just shivering. She'd swung her leg over him. "Don't worry," she had whispered, "today's a safe day." Then she lowered herself onto him, her hands on his chest.

Three weeks later he went away to law school, but they were officially a couple then. He wrote or telephoned her almost every day. Of course this was a long time before email and text messages. For her birthday he bought her a Polaroid camera and asked her to take pictures of herself to send to him. In all honesty, he'd meant the gift innocently. Jennifer, however, wasn't the innocent type. It wasn't long before she started sending him photos of all sorts of things, at first just teasing, a leg here and ankle there, and escalating. Pictures of Jennifer in her underwear, pictures up her skirt, pictures with her top pulled down. Pictures of her naked in her dorm room bed with her legs spread.

He opened each new letter with trembling hands, shaking with anticipation and desire. He would lie on his back and look at the photos, just stare at them loss in bliss while he touched himself under the covers.

Then something had happened. She'd started talking about a new friend of hers. Obliquely at first, not mentioning a name or any detail, then more often. She started talking about the friend in their phone calls, and he didn't think anything of it. Then it came out that, he didn't know if she decided it was time he knew or if it had just slipped out accidentally, but she admitted that her new friend was a man, a junior one grade below her. Benjamin. That was his name. Or Ben, usually. She was helping him study, she said, that was all. But she kept talking about him.

He remembered the conversation with absolute clarity. It was a snowy night in November. He was at the library studying when he'd looked up at the clock. They talked on the phone every night at eight o'clock, that was the arrangement. He'd never missed a call. She had, once or twice, but he didn't mind. He wasn't going to miss it though. He'd gathered up his things in a rush, checking his books out and dashing across the snowy campus. He'd yanked the phone off the hook, still panting from the run, and he'd punched in her number. Four minutes after eight, no big deal, that clock was fast anyway.

It rang a couple times before she picked up. Rang longer than usual. "Hello?" she sounded different, strained somehow. A bit out of breath herself.

"Hey baby, how's it going? Sorry I'm calling late."

"No, it's okay. I was just going to call you."

Something in her voice told him that she was lying, but he didn't press it. She'd often admitted to feeling guilty about not being as good at keeping in touch as she thought she should be.

"Are you alright, babe?"

"Yeah, I'm fine..."

"Jen. What's going on?"

She'd cleared her throat. "Um. Well, Ben's here. We were just finishing studying. He was about to leave."

"Oh. He's still there now then?"

"Yeah. But, uh, he's leaving."

"Do you want me to call back another time?" He was a little bit annoyed. Of course it was Ben. Lately it seemed like he was all she wanted to talk about. He'd done this, he'd done that, she was so proud of him. He had to fight the urge to roll his eyes.

"No, it's okay."

But he could hear the pull in her voice. She wanted to go. He felt his heart sink. He was going to lose her. It was happening, the sex hadn't saved him, it had only delayed the inevitable. How did he keep her if she wanted someone else?

"Is, um, did your day go okay down there, Percy?"

"Yeah yeah. It was fine. Look... Jen. You and Ben..."

She was quiet for a long time. "Percy, I... you know I would never cheat on you."

He didn't know that, for a fact, but he was willing to accept her word on it. "But you want to?"

"He... he kissed me. I didn't ask him to, he just did it."

"Did you like it?"

"Percy, don't. Please, I didn't-"

"Jen, Jen, it's alright."

"What?"

"It's alright. I don't mind. It was nothing. Just a misunderstanding."

"Percy, he... he brought condoms... I saw one fall out of his pocket when he was getting his lighter."

"So... are you going to screw him?"

"Percy! Of course not! I'm not some sort of... whatever."

The line had been quiet between them a long time. Neither of them spoke. Percy felt something, a heaviness inside, a fear. He was going to lose her. At the same time, however, there was something beneath the worry: an excitement. Somewhere across the country his girlfriend was being pursued by another man. He imagined her naked body in the man's hands. Imagined her moaning and twisting for him, imagined her opening herself for him. He was afraid of losing her, but the thought of her screwing another person only made him excited.

"Look, Jen... if you want... I know it's been a long time since we've been together. Physically, I mean. If you want, just for tonight..."

"What are you saying, Percy?" she sounded hesitant, guarded, like she was waiting for a trap to be sprung.

"I'm saying, if you want to do it with him, just for tonight. Do what you need to. I won't ask about it, won't try to find out anything else about it. It's just for tonight. Okay? Just do what you want to, and it's alright with me. I won't ask."

For a long time, so long that he thought she'd hung up or that the connection had dropped, she didn't say anything. His heart was pounding in his chest.

"Okay," she'd finally said, and that was all. They'd talked for another few minutes, trying to keep things casual. Then she told him that she loved him. He told her the same, and hung up.

True to his word, he never asked her what happened.

She stopped talking about Ben after that. A few months later she graduated and moved to the city where he was going to school and got a job. The year he finished law school they got married. Nothing like that had ever happened again. He'd chalked it up to wild oats, just a college dalliance. But he kept every photo, and he still looked at them sometimes, reliving those moments.

There was one picture, a picture he received about a week after that phone call which was different from the others. It didn't seem any different at first. It was Jennifer, naked on her bed, holding her breasts up, one hand holding each sizable boob as she smiled at the camera. It took him a long time to realize what was bothering him about the picture, and when he figured it out he felt like an idiot, of course, for not seeing it sooner. The camera he'd gotten here was a basic model, no frills. It didn't have a time delay. Somebody had to press the little button to take the picture. Every single photo she'd sent him had that same tell-tall feature: one arm raised up and holding the camera to point it at herself. Every photo except this one.

So, the question was then: who had taken *this* picture?

Percy looked at that photo more than any of the others, especially when he wanted to touch himself. He'd never thought too hard on it, never tried to mentally recreate the situation, never drew the obvious conclusion in his head. But a part of him knew. And that part loved it.

Jonas paused with his hand on the door knob. He turned to Percy and grinned. "Can you hear that, Brice?"

Percy leaned in a little. He blushed. Yes, he certainly could hear it.

On the other side of the door he heard the frantic creaking of bed springs, a rhythmic tap tap of the headboard knocking against the wall, and a series of shrieking cries of pleasure coming quite recognizably from none other than Matilda Harrington.

Jonas put a finger against his lips. "Shall we?" he murmured, twisting the handle and opening the door.

Percy was rather taken aback when he stepped through the door. He'd had his own experience here at the club once before - quite a memorable night, to be sure. The room he'd been in had been elegant and stately, class and sensuality in harmony. This space was nothing like that. The floor was bare hardwood, worn and scuffed. The walls were quite undecorated, unless you counted the sizable collection of whips, paddles, chains, dildos, harnesses and other devices - which Percy frankly hadn't a chance of identifying that were hanging on the far wall.

Matilda was bent over a low leather bench in the center of the room. Her hands and feet were securely strapped down, forcing her into a bent-over position with her rump pushed up in the air. She was naked except for a heavy black collar secured around her delicate neck. The room was dark except for a

Marquis was walking calmly around her, quite naked with a many-headed short leather whip wrapped around his hand. He smiled widely at Jonas and Percy as they came in, his white teeth bright in the gloom. Jonas grinned back, pointing Percy towards a pair of chairs in the corner of the room. They sat quietly, and Jonas poured Percy a drink. The door swung shut with a clack. It occurred to Percy that Matilda must know that somebody had come inside the room, but couldn't possibly see who it was from her current position. She didn't say anything, she was just panting and moaning.

Marquis slapped the whip casually down on the smooth curve of her pale bottom. The black leather straps smacked down, and came slowly sliding off as he withdrew. Matilda yelped, then giggled softly. "Ooo, Daddy..." she cooed.

Marquis stepped up behind her, lifting his thick cock and slapping it against her. "You ready for more of this, baby-girl?" he rumbled, his deep voice echoing in the little room.

"Please, Daddy, you know I want it!" she wailed, wriggling her bottom at him.

He grinned, stepping closer.

Matilda's tiny little pussy was soft and pink and smooth. Percy could see it perfectly from where he sat, bathed in light with the little lips already parted. She couldn't have been more than five feet tall, and looked like a toy next to Marquis and his monstrous erection. How could she possibly hope to take such a beast, given her tiny frame? He supposed it couldn't be the first time.

"Look at that then," Jonas said, leaning over and clinking his glass against Percy's, "we've arrive just in time for the best part of the show."

Marquis slipped his cock up and between Matilda's pussy lips, parting her little pink cleft. Her grasped hold of her ass, squeezing each cheek tightly with one hand. His skin seemed impossibly black against her lily white flesh. "You tell me how much you want this, baby-girl."

"I want it, Daddy, I want it *so* bad! Please, fuck meeee!"

Marquis grinned, and he granted her request.

Percy watched, feeling a little dazed, as she was pounded impossibly hard against the frame by her enormous black lover. She took it with ease, opening for his humongous cock like it was nothing at all. Percy wondered if she'd even notice being penetrated by someone like himself.

"Fuck me, Daddy! Oh, you fuck me so much better than my husband! You're my Daddy, you're my Daddy!" she squealed.

Percy turned away, cheeks glowing a little. He knew that this was the sort of thing Jonas liked to hear, and he'd certainly heard more intense things said, and by his own wife no less. Still, it was an odd feeling sitting there next to your employer while you watched their spouse getting fucked quite so thoroughly.

Even after all this time, there was very much a part of him that wasn't sure if he was ready for all this. Things had moved fast. He tried to imagine how he would have reacted to any of this six or seven months ago.

The door opened, and a couple came inside. A white man and woman, his wife, Percy thought. They were older than anybody he'd seen there before, even older than Jonas. They must have been sixty-five or seventy at least, though they certainly looked quite fit for their age. They both very white hair, the woman's in a tight bun and the man cut short with a long beard. He was dressed in an immaculate suit and she in a rather fancy gown that left very little of her still-impressive bust to the imagination. The man smiled at Jonas and gave a little bow before the two of them went and sat at the seats on the far wall.

"You know them?" Percy whispered, in what he hoped was a quiet enough voice.

Jonas waved his hand vaguely. "Oh, I think I've seen them about the club before. No doubt they're admirers of Tilly's. She's quite the star here, you know."

Percy looked back at the little woman, bucking and thrashing as she started to orgasm. Marquis' cock was coming out sticky with a thick white cream, but the man clearly hadn't cum himself. She was starting to cream herself on his dick, Percy realized. He blinked. "I believe it," he whispered back to Jonas.

The other man refreshed his drink and settled in, watching the show with obvious reverence.

Across the room, the old woman was sliding off her long glove and reaching into her husband's pants.

What have I gotten myself into? Percy thought, almost amused at the absurdity of the situation. He could hardly imagine what all his friends from back home in Minnesota might have said if they saw him now in a place like this. He glanced once more at his phone. No messages.

Percy took a deep drink of Jonas's wine and he settled in to enjoy the rest of the show.

* * *

The old man held his hand out, almost regally. "Reginald G. Mason."

Percy shook it tentatively. The old man had a firm grip.

The man's wife stepped forward to shake his hand as well. She'd put her glove back on, Percy was grateful to see. "Oh, don't. You can call him Reggie, everybody does. And I'm Penelope."

The old man scoffed. "Oh, *everybody* calls me that, eh? Well, we'll see. Fine, fine. Reggie will do."

"Alright, Reggie," Percy smiled. Penelope patted fondly him on the shoulder.

"And you are?" the old man asked, stepping into the silence before it could turn awkward.

"Oh, God. Sorry. I'm Percy. Percival Brice."

"Lovely. Good to meet you, Percy. And no need for apologies. I know the look of a man who's just watched our man Marquis have his way with some little bit. Quite a heart-stopping experience, isn't it?"

"It's... quite something to see," Percy admitted, clutching his drink close and swallowing. It had indeed. He hadn't expected the show to go on for long after arriving. Surely the man would simply orgasm and that would be that. It turned out to be quite an elaborate display, however, and he'd found himself sitting there watching in bug-eyed wonder for almost an hour of the most athletic and acrobatic screwing he'd ever witnessed. By the end of it there were almost a dozen couples watching, many of them playing on the sidelines. They'd all burst into spontaneous applause at the end. Jonas had lifted his glass to the crowd. "My wife!" he'd said, grinning from ear to ear as Tilly was unstrapped and helped down from the harness, trembling and smiling. Someone brought Marquis a drink and he'd toasted the whole room. Afterwards, Percy had wondered out into the hall, where he'd found himself cornered by the older couple who'd first come in to join them.

The old man laughed. "But what in the world are you doing here by yourself, my good man? Don't you have a wife about someplace?"

"Oh, yes... well. She's at home. With her, well... her lover."

Reggie tapped the side of his nose and gave Percy a conspiratorial wink. "Say no more. One of our boys, I do hope?"

"They met here, yes."

He laughed. "*Excellent.* Good to know we're still bringing lovers together after all these years."

"We?"

"Well, this is club, isn't it? Mine and Penny's. And Marquis as well, though it was Penny and I who started the thing, all those years ago."

"Oh?"

"Yes, yes. We've been around for quite some time now. Since the end of the seventies, I think. God, how the times flies. Why, Penny and I were about your age at the time, and it occurred to us that surely there must be a better method of finding good young bucks to have a time with than newspaper personals and magazine ads. Not reliable in the least. Had a few rather ghastly experiences, I don't mind telling you. Of course that was part of the fun back then. The danger, the adventure."

"Is that so?"

Reginald G. Mason took Percy by the arm and led him on down the hall, talking all the way. His wife Penelope gave a long-suffering sigh and followed after. Percy recognized the sound. Clearly, she'd heard Reggie tell the whole story quite a few times before, and long since accepted it as one of her husband's unavoidable idiosyncrasies.

"That's right. Different world back then, Percy, different world. People weren't quite as understanding of the whole thing as they are now. Of course, even now it's quite a taboo. Imagine thirty years ago! Thus the secrecy of the place. But of course that's also for fun, don't you know."

"Naturally," Penelope added dryly. Percy glanced back at her, the regal elderly lady looked like a queen or duchess or something. He found it hard to imagine her in her thirties meeting black men with newspaper ads and bringing them back to her house. He wondered if she was still active on the scene, or if she and her husband just drifted through on inspections like this one.

"The club was Penny's idea. Indirectly hers, at any rate. She said to me, Reggie, why can't we just have a place where we can meet? Why not? And I thought to myself, why not indeed? It seemed like a fine idea. By the end of the year we had the place up and running. Oh, it was a good deal more modest back then, but it served its purpose, I should say. Of course the damned internet has gone and made us a bit obsolete now, hasn't it? Ah, oh well. Everything has its time. And we've still some life in us left, I suppose. Nice to see the place with a good crowd in it again, like the old times..."

"Well," Percy said, feeling he had to say something, as Reggie had begun to drift off a bit there at the end. "I've been quite pleased with the experience. This place is lovely. We never would have... you know, gone down this road if not for the club."

"Ah, that's lovely to hear," Reggie said, smiling broadly and seeming to cheer up quite a bit.

"I do hope we see you here again, Percy," Penelope added, touching him gently on the arm, "and I hope we get a chance to meet your lovely wife someday."

Reggie laughed. "Indeed. Who knows, maybe we'll see her in Tilly's place one of these days, eh?"

Percy blanched. "Oh, I don't know about that. M-maybe someday." He forced a nervous laugh.

God, he couldn't even imagine that. All those people watching? It gave him a shiver of dreadful excitement. No, no he didn't think he could handle that. He started down the steps, pulling out his phone and glancing at it as he went. Still no messages. He shook his head and sighed. Well, he guessed he'd had enough of the club for one night. Time to go out and find a hotel for the night. Something in walking distance, as Jonas had kept him steadily plied with glass after glass. He'd hardly realized how much he was drinking at the time, as his attention had been elsewhere at the time.

He strolled out into the warm summer night, his head swimming and his mind full.

* * *

The night seemed to swallow him. The sidewalk was warm under his feet with the heat of the afternoon sun. He could feel it rising through his shoes as he stood beneath the street lamp. He stared out at the beach, at the water beyond. There were still a few people out there on the sand, even now after ten o'clock at night they were still there, walking through the blue half-light beneath the moon and the stars and the electric light. He saw the dark figures of people dipping in and out of the shallows, their laughter carrying across the distance.

"What's going on, baby? Why you all alone?"

He looked up, a bit startled. There was a woman standing against the lamppost. She was tall and thick, her skin dark. She wore tight red vinyl that seemed to squeeze her voluptuous body, pushing out her breasts and backside. She had large gold hoop earrings and her fingers were heavy with jewelry. He pointed to himself, miming a quizzical expression.

"That's right, I'm talking to you, baby." The woman laughed, a deep husky chuckle, and she came towards him. He saw that she was wearing very tall high heels, spiked stilettos that looked like they could double as deadly weapons in a pinch. She draped herself over the back of the bench. "You looking for a good time, honey?"

"Oh," he said, and blushed, "Oh, um... well, I'm married."

She laughed again. "Shit, baby, I know *that*."

"You do? How's that?"

"Well why else would you be sitting out here waiting for Saffron to come rescue you?" She smiled, blinking slowly at him. "Look, honey, if not for married men I'd be out of a job. They're the ones who need me the most."

Percy grinned ruefully. "Is that so?"

"You better believe it. I mean, a lotta guys get married, but not a lotta girls can give a man what Saffron can."

"And what's that?"

She leaned close, almost pressing herself against him. "You looking to find out, baby?"

"I could be." He turned awkwardly on the bench, bending back to try and look at her. What was he *doing*? He wasn't going to have sex with some prostitute. That just wasn't him, in so many ways. He was only going to piss her off by leading her own, and he didn't want to end up on the wrong end of her spiked heels.

She looked at him, studying him. Then she laughed again. "Naw, naw, you ain't. I can tell you ain't the type."

He frowned. "Why do you say that?"

She shrugged. "Been doing this a long time, I know 'em when I see 'em. You ain't ready. But come back when you is, Saffron'll be here. Unless my prince charming come find me before then." She laughed again, but it sounded more forced this time. Almost sad.

"How long?"

"How long I been walking the streets? Shit, why you wanna know that, baby?"

"Just curious, I guess."

She sighed, slipping one leg then the other over the top of the low bench and sliding gently down to side beside him. "Oh, shit, I dunno. Since I was seventeen years old. So four years, I guess. Seems like a long time."

"Wow."

She gave him a look, eyebrows raised. "But don't be thinking Saffron some busted ass ho or nothing. This baby's fresh as the day she born."

"I d-didn't-" he started to stammer, but she laughed again, interrupting him.

"I'm messing with you, baby, just messing with you. Naw, it's alright. I get by. Anyway, it is what it is."

"I suppose so."

The two of them looked out at the moonlit ocean together, watching the midnight swimmers dipping down beneath the black surface, popping up again a few feet away, wet bodies shining in the starlight.

Saffron nudged him a little with her elbow. "So what you out here for if you married and not looking to get some."

Percy laughed softly. "Oh... it's a long story."

"Ohhhh, you have a fight with the misses, that it? She kick you out, baby?"

"Not exactly... She's, well... she's entertaining someone at the house."

She frowned at him for a moment, then her mouth opened and she leaned back, a kind of realization crossing her features. "Oh... you from that freaky club, ain't you? Some big black buck got your lady at home right now, don't he?"

He chuckled. "Guilty as charged. How'd you know?"

She scoffed. "Baby, I work right down the *street* from that place, you think you the only white man I seen wandering around out here by himself while his wife getting her freak on? *Please.*"

"Fair enough."

"So what's in it for you, honey? I mean, what do you *get* out of that?"

"It's... complicated."

"No shit."

"I just... like to watch."

"So why ain't you there *watching*? That's what I wanna know. Seems like you got the short end of the stick, baby."

He sighed. "Well... I suppose."

"Having second thoughts, baby?"

"Some. Maybe. I'm not sure."

"Well... I got work to be doing, baby. You ever feel like you need something more than watching, you look me up. Saffron will take care of you. You know where to find me."

He grinned. "Thanks. I appreciate that. Wait, here," he dug into his pocket and pulled out a twenty dollar bill.

"Uh uh," she said, "I'm not here to beg, baby, I work for my money."

"Please," he said, "for listening. It meant a lot."

She cocked an eyebrow at him. "If you gonna insist, guess I can't say no, baby."

"Thanks."

She rose from the bench and went back down the sidewalk, her wide hips swaying with every step. He couldn't help admiring her body, and wondered if maybe he should have taken her up on her offer. But... no, that wasn't him. Not yet. He didn't need that. He took out his phone, checked it. Nothing.

He started down the street in the opposite direction that Saffron had gone. The moon glowed above.

* * *

"Room for one, please. No. Just for tonight. Thanks."

The elevator was out, so he took the stairs. His room was on the eighth floor; it was quite a hike and he was very much out of breath when he finally made it to his room. It was nice enough, he supposed. He flopped down on the bed and grabbed the remote. Maybe watch some television to pass the time? Maybe even a dirty pay-per-view movie...

No. He wasn't in the mood.

Percy lay back and stared up at the ceiling. What was he *doing?*

Ding!

He sat up. His phone. It was in his coat, draped over the back of the chair. Probably just another one of those spam texts he'd been getting. He really should talk to someone about blocking them someday.

-Hey hon, sorry I haven't been in touch with U. It's been a crazy night.

Jennifer! He rushed back to the bed. *-No problem. What have you been getting up to?*

-Why don't I let the pictures do the talking for me ;)

-Okay! He could feel his fingers trembling as he typed. Finally!

And then they started to come in, one after the other, picture after glorious picture, every detail of the very busy night captured in highly explicit detail. He reached down and until his belt, then the button and zipper, struggling to get his pants down without dropping his phone or accidentally sending a message of random gibberish. He managed to slip them down to his knees, then picked the phone back up. More and more pictures were pouring in.

He smiled and reached down to take hold of himself.

Maybe things weren't so bad after all.

Jennifer

Today was the day. Ty was coming back today. After being gone all summer long, he was finally coming back to her.

She'd shooed Percy out of the house and been cleaning all day. She supposed that was silly. Ty wasn't the sort, after all, to care overly much about the decor. Besides, she planned on keeping him much too busy to notice anything except her.

The summer had been torture. Waiting for him to return, wishing he was there with her. She'd even gone to visit him once, but it hadn't really worked out, to say the least. His parents had been quite rightly curious about the middle-aged white woman who was suddenly so interested in their son, and neither Jennifer nor Ty felt much like explaining it.

She supposed that she was just a little bit crazy, falling for a man so much younger than she was, but she couldn't help it. Ever since that first moment when their eyes had met across the club, she'd known that there was something between them. It was stronger than just pure lust, though it was that as well. There was a true connection. She felt like she would do anything for him, anything to be his.

She dreamed almost every night of his body, his arms around her and his lips against hers. She dreamed of undressing him, taking his clothes off one article at a time, her hands caressing his beautiful black skin, feeling his sculpted muscles and strong frame. She was a big girl, not overweight but certainly large. Tall and thick, plump in the right places. She'd gotten used to overpowering men; half her boyfriends had been shorter than her and most of them smaller.

But not Ty. Definitely not Ty. He was the only man who made her feel little. He would pick her up and his arms and hold her without batting an eye; he made her feel safe and small in a way she'd never experienced before.

They'd gone wild in the spring, fucking like teenagers every chance they got, doing it all sorts of ways, for hours upon hours. Sometimes Percy was there, but more often than not she just filled him in after the fact. She liked including her husband, but she had to admit to herself that she preferred to have Ty all to herself. Just the two of them in a room with no clothes on and nothing to do but make love. He was continually finding new ways to push her beyond her limits and expand her mind - not to mention other things!

All the while she had given him everything, let him do whatever he liked with her body. So far, he hadn't stopped amazing her. He took her and used her in ways she didn't think possible, and she loved every second of it. She kept waiting for him to get bored of her, move on to someone else, someone closer to his own age, maybe. It was the secret fear gnawing away in the back of her mind: that she would lose him.

Those fears had a way of evaporating when he held her, however. She hoped that it would happen tonight, because the fear had had a long time to grow since she'd seen him last. Was it going to be the same, now that he was back? How *could* it be? Oh, but she hoped it would. She hoped it more than anything.

She was straightening the pictures in the hall when she got to the calendar that hung beside them. She stared at it, frowning. There was something in the corner of her mind, what was it? Then it hit her. She gasped out loud and rushed across the house, hurrying to her bedroom and digging in the bedside table drawer for her little planner. She checked the marked day in the little calendar there and counted forward. *One two three... fifteen sixteen... twenty-five twenty-six...*

Uh oh.

Today was very much not a safe day for her. She shut her eyes and flopped back on the bed, biting back a curse. She clutched the little book to her chest, and she stared up at the ceiling.

The sex with Ty had been incredible. Mind-blowing, amazing, orgasmic in every way! But he wouldn't wear a condom. And she wouldn't ask him to. There was a part of her, a powerful almost overwhelming part of her that simply could not ask. It wasn't that she was afraid, or timid about the subject. She'd been quite ruthless with all of her boyfriends in the past, before Percy. Rubber or nothing, she used to say, and she'd meant it.

But Ty was different. Putting a condom on that cock... it would have been a kind of sacrilege. She had never in her life felt more complete than when his seed was flooding her insides. She felt like a woman when he came in her, it was just *right* in a fundamental way. She simply couldn't deny it. It would have been like asking him not to breathe.

But today wasn't safe...

They'd been lucky in the past, not that either of them had shown much concern about it. When he was right there in front of her, ready to take her, it didn't much matter to her if it was safe or not. They'd simply been lucky that the timing worked out.

She groaned, then smiled wryly. Another decade or so and it wouldn't be a concern any longer, she could do whatever she pleased.

But what about *tonight*? He was coming over. He was going to fuck her; there was no way the night could go otherwise. She wasn't going to be able to resist him, as soon as she saw his face, as soon as his hands touched her body she would be his.

She'd tried going on birth control in the past, before she and Percy had started trying unsuccessfully for a child. Unfortunately, something about the pill didn't agree with her. Some sort of hormonal imbalance, the doctor said, so she'd gotten off them. Percy's low sperm count had made it redundant to try going back, so she'd never asked. She supposed there were other options. A diaphragm or even an IUD. But the truth was that she didn't want any of that. She... wasn't sure exactly what she wanted.

Never mind. She'd cross that bridge when she came to it, she supposed, for now she just had to get ready.

Her phone rang. Of course. She picked it up with a sigh. Sure, they had an answering machine, but it had been drilled into Jennifer over and over again when she was younger that it was extremely impolite not to pick up the phone. Within three rings! her mother used to say, and her father would grunt in wordless agreement. They'd been very posh, in their own way.

"Hello, Brice residence," she said, and she could hear her voice go up an octave or two. She had one of those fake-cheery phone voices, she'd been told. And even now that she noticed it every time she still couldn't help herself from doing it.

"Jennifer. *Darling.* My word, it *has* been a long time."

She felt herself break into a wide smile. "Oh my *God*... is that you, Cathy?"

"You bet your Floridian tush it is! Jennifer, it has been *so* long since I heard from you. After all this time, I'm almost surprised you still recognize my *voice*."

"Oh God, Cathy, I am so sorry. It's just been crazy down here. Busy busy busy, you know me."

"Hm, yes, well you always were an active little one, weren't you?" There was a note of recrimination in her voice, not wholly undeserved.

Jennifer had been pretty bad at keeping in touch with the old crowd. She had talked to Cathy once or twice over the last few months, but with someone like Cathy that might as well have been not at all.

"Look, Jennifer, I've been saying to myself, what am I going to have to do to talk to my friend again? And it occurs to me that the only to make sure is to just come on down there myself. So, Brian has a week of vacation, and he says he wants to go to Florida and hit the beaches, so I think to myself, what a coincidence..."

"Oh my God, Cathy, that's perfect! You're coming here? When?"

"Well darling, I didn't want to give you the chance to go to ground again, so I'm giving you as little warning as possible. My little revenge. We'll be there tomorrow."

"Tomorrow! Are you serious? Oh my goodness... Well, I can't wait!"

"Hm, yes. Well, I expect to see rather a lot of you, darling, to make up for all the time we've missed. And you will, I hope, be able to show me around your new town. I'm sure you've had *plenty* of time to acclimate yourself."

"Yes, yes! That would be lovely. Oh Cathy, I can't wait! Oh, I know, I'll take you to the book-club meeting here on Wednesday, if you like. It will be just like home. Only warmer." She'd started going to the book club during the summer mainly just to give herself something to do so that she didn't go completely insane. Anyway, she loved books, even if the crowd down here was a bit on the stuffy side. Of course, they'd been stuffy back in Minnesota, Cathy included, but they'd been *her kind* of stuffy, so it hadn't bothered her.

"That sounds like a plan, darling, a lovely plan. I do *so* look forward to finally seeing what's become of you down there. I imagine I'll find you tanning yourself in a bikini on some spring break party beach."

Jennifer laughed. "Oh my *God*, Cathy, no! Look, you'll just have to see for yourself."

"I will, won't I? Well, it won't be long now. See you soon, darling. Ta ta."

The doorbell rang.

"Cathy, I gotta go. Love you. See you soon, I can't wait!"

She hung up and rushed to the door. Goddamn, Cathy, she hadn't even had a chance to do her makeup! She glanced at herself in the mirror on her way to the door. God, she didn't look *old*, did she? Crap, nothing for it. She looked good, she thought. She was dressed casually, but sexy, she thought, with a tight little top and cut-off shorts that showed off her legs very well. She finally understood why all the girls were wearing them. Before Ty it had seemed so silly, but last time she'd found herself at the clothing store she'd gravitated right to them, imagining her man's hands touching her while she wore them, his eyes glued to her. Her hair was pack in a loose ponytail. She looked sporty and young, but not like one of those child pageant moms or anything. She looked hot, she decided. The bell rang again.

"I'm coming, I'm coming," she muttered, hurrying across the house. She sent Percy a quick text to let him know that Tyrone had arrived. Because it *was* Ty, it had to be. If this was the damn mail man again with another package she was going to wring his neck...

She swung the door open without even bothering to glance through the peephole. It was him. He stood there, very casual, leaning against the rail. He looked beautiful. He wore a tight white t-shirt that showed off his arms and fit snugly over his abs and pecs. His muscles seemed like they might burst the sleeves if he flexed too hard. He wore a silver stud in one ear, and he'd grown a neatly trimmed beard since she'd last seen him. It made him look years older, not to mention *very* sexy.

She felt her breath catch in her throat. Just looking at him, seeing him here in front of her for the first time in so long, she felt completely tongue-tied. She stood there like an idiot, her mouth opening and closing and not a sound emerging.

"You know, I think I'm gonna need to get a key if you're planning to keep me standing on the porch all day long, Jen." His voice was cool and smooth, sounding faintly amused.

"Sorry! Sorry, come on in, please, come in, Ty." The words came stumbling out in a rush as she blushed, stepping back and waving him in. She immediately felt silly in the outfit which had seemed oh-so-cute just a moment before. Stupid, what had she been *thinking*?

She rushed away deeper into the house, babbling as she went. She'd been speechless a second ago and now she didn't think she could *stop* talking. "Come on, I'll get you a drink. Do you want a drink? I'll get you a drink. Or... do you need something to eat? I can make something, I've got all sorts of things I could make. What are you hungry for? It must have been a long trip, it was, wasn't it? Have you been to the dorm yet? Did you come straight here? I could order out something, I could do that."

"Hey, Jen?" His voice was low and calm.

"Yes, Ty?" She turned around, flustered, blinking rapidly and patting her sides as if there was something in one of her pockets which might repair the situation. He was leaning against the wall in the living room, watching her flutter back and forth.

"Come here."

"Okay," she said, her voice very small and quiet. She went to him, feeling a bit like a scolded child, cringing a little. She'd made such a fool of herself. Could it be that she'd completely forgotten how to behave around a man? She hadn't been like this since she was fourteen years old, and even then she didn't think she'd ever been *this* frazzled by the sight of a cute boy. Of course, back then she'd never known anybody quite like Ty.

He gathered her in his arms, hugging her close, pulling her body against his. She let out a long slow breath, settling against his chest. He stroked her hair, caressing it gently as his arms closed around her body, enveloping her. She pressed her nose against his shirt, breathing in the scent of him, sweat and skin and a sweet tang of aftershave or cologne. "It good to see you again, baby," he said softly, kissing the top of her hair.

She felt herself smile. "It's good to see you too, Ty."

"I would love something to drink, babe. And, yeah, I'm hungry. Whatever you wanna make, I'm in, or we can order out. But there's something I gotta do first."

She looked up at him and he looked back, his big brown eyes soft and deep. "What's that?"

He just grinned, and his hands slid down her back, pulling her close against him, then moving a little lower to cup the swell of her firm backside. His hands slipped into the back pockets of her little booty shorts, and squeezed.

* * *

She poured him a tall glass of bourbon.

Ty grinned. "Gotta say this for the man, Percy always has good shit in the liquor cabinet."

She smiled back. "Oh, he's quite the connoisseur. One of his many passions."

"Well. My compliments."

"I'll be sure to pass them along."

"My compliments on his wife, too. She's really something."

She laughed. "Oh, better than the bourbon?"

He smirked. "I mean, I don't know if I'd say *better...*"

She pouted and tossed a cork across the counter at him. He dodged to the side, laughing.

Jennifer sighed and stretched out. She felt like she'd been making love for the past week. The clock on the wall said it was eleven o'clock. Tyrone had arrived at, what? Five, maybe? Six solid hours of passion. God, she was tired. She tried to fight back a yawn and failed.

"What's this? You gonna quit on me already?"

"Jesus, you still want to go? Fine, fine. Just lie me down on the bed and have your way with me."

"I might just do that," he said, cocking one eyebrow and taking a sip.

"You wouldn't."

"I would, but you wouldn't be just lying there for long, I know you."

"Okay, Mr. Football Star, we're not *all* trained athletes. I think this is the most exercise I've had in a month."

"Oh, I'll whip you into shape in no time, you best believe that."

She grinned, leaning in close across the counter. She felt her breasts escaping from the loosely tied fluffy bathroom. "You promise?" she said softly.

He gave her a long look, then nodded. "Got my word on that."

Tyrone was wearing a pair of loose boxers and nothing else. God, she loved looking at him. His body was like a statue come alive, some large than life Greek deity sprung from the marble. They sat on either side of the long marble kitchen counter, several bottles of various sorts of alcohol between them, along with the remains of their thoroughly demolished Chinese takeout.

The woman at the restaurant had been quite nonplussed to take their order. It had taken a couple tries to communicate exactly what it was she wanted. No doubt it would have been easier if Ty hadn't been fucking her mercilessly doggy style at the time. Suffice to say she hadn't had time to do any cooking of her own.

They would probably have just eaten in bed if they'd been there when the food arrived, but they had, by coincidence, been in the kitchen anyway. Jennifer had been bent over the counter on her tiptoes when the doorbell rang. She said that she'd better get dressed, but Ty said not to bother. He gave her a clean dish towel to cover herself with and told her to bring the food in. Of course the towel was only about one foot by two feet. The delivery guy got quite an eyeful. Jennifer didn't think she'd ever blushed that red in her life. It certainly wasn't something she'd have done before this, but he'd pushed in in all sorts of way. She was doing things she never would have dared to do before, and she was loving it.

Now they were relaxing into a sort of post-coital bliss. Post-post-post-post-coital, to be more accurate.

She was fairly sure that they had, in fact, made good on her promise to screw in every single room in the house. Including going at it on Percy's desk. She didn't say anything about it, but she'd been careful of where and when he orgasmed. Once in her mouth, once on her breasts. The third time had been tricky, and led Jennifer to an experience which she had never before dreamed she might attempt.

As a matter of fact, that had been the time they'd done it in Percy's study, she thought ruefully. She might have to hold off on sending him *those* pictures. Just for now, anyway. She had been lying on her back on the big oak desk, which turned out to be just the right height for Ty to take her from a standing position. She was staring up at the ceiling, her arms wrapped around her knees to hold them all the way back, when she'd felt something.

He was fucking her slow, long full strokes, almost teasing her, just relaxing himself into her body. Then she'd felt his hands reach down to cup her ass, sliding around to caress her butt-cheeks. His thumbs had moved gradually lower, until they were resting just below her pussy. And then he did it. On thumb started circling her little hole down there, slick with the juices dripping from her pussy, it had moved like silk over the little opening, then pressed in a little.

She'd gasped, lifting her head to look up at him. "What are you doing?" she panted.

"You don't like that?" he had asked, slipping it in a little deeper.

"No, I... I do..." she'd been surprised to realize that she actually did.

"You want a little more?"

She'd nodded, biting her lip, not willing to say it out loud. Now *this* was something she'd never even considered before. Of course she'd heard of it, anal sex was very much in vogue with the young people today. It seemed like everybody was trying it. But Jennifer had never considered it for herself. It seemed too dirty, too kinky, too *strange*.

But now that she felt him inside her there, it sent a shiver running up her spine, straight to the pleasure center. It felt... well, it felt really good. And why not, after all? There had to be *some* reason so many people were doing it. He slipped his thumb out and replaced it with the first to fingers of his right hand. She trembled again. Oh wow. He went slow, very slow, letting her ease into it, stretch and loosen to accommodate him comfortably before even trying to move his hand. He'd stopped thrusting, but she could feel his cock was rock hard inside her still.

"Think you can take the real deal, baby?"

Her eyes had widened at that. His cock? In her ass? *Jesus.*

Back when they had first had sex, she hadn't believed that Ty penis could fit inside her pussy, but it had turned out to be so right. He filled her perfectly. She wasn't so sure the same magic would work again. Of course, if they did anal, she wouldn't have to worry about him cumming inside her...

She nodded slowly.

He grinned. He reached up and slipped himself out of her pussy, sliding himself down so that the head of his cock was against her lower hole. "You trust me, baby."

She laid her head back. She felt her cheeks flush. "Yes, Ty. I trust you."

Then he'd pushed forward, and entered her.

Even now, two hours later, she could still feel it. She was sitting rather lightly on the kitchen stool. It had been amazing, but she was pretty sure that she was going to be feeling it for a while.

Ty leaned forward and stuck his fork in the last piece of Sesame Chicken. He looked up at her and his eyes were so soft and beautiful that she felt a kind of dizzy happiness swoop through her.

She smiled. "You know... I really missed you."

"Yeah," he said, "I figured that out by about the fourth round or so."

"Not just the sex... I missed *you.*"

He looked down, a little smile playing across his lips. "Missed you too, babe."

* * *

An hour later, after one final languid session, they'd both tumbled into bed. He fell asleep almost at once, but she stayed away, curled up in his arms. It felt so good to be there...

So good, in fact, that she'd very nearly forgotten about everything else, the whole outside world had faded way. An outside world which included Percy. She felt a flash of guilt. Fortunately her phone was still just in reach.

She dimmed the screen as low as it would go and took a quick look through her photos. She'd gotten some good ones, and taken quite a few. That was a relief, for a moment she'd been worried that she might have forgotten to take any pictures at all, having been in such a state all evening. But no, she had a good bunch for him. She sent off a quick text apologizing for not having gotten back sooner, then selected the best thirty or so photos and hit send. One by one they flickered out into the either, transmitting from her device to her husband's.

She switched off the phone and lay her head back down on Ty's chest. Her eyes closed, and she left sleep take her, confident that the memories of her night of passion would get where they were supposed to go on their own.

Ty was gone when she woke up, quite late actually, almost eleven o'clock. There was a little note on the pillow, scribbled in a back page of her planner which he'd torn out. *See you soon, beautiful. -Tyrone*

She smiled and went back to sleep.

* * *

"So... all is well with our friend?"

Jennifer blushed. "Oh, yes, I suppose."

"Good, good, glad to hear it." Percy whistled casually, strolling across the green to where his ball sat waiting. He grabbed a putter from the bag in the cart, lined up his shot and gave it a tap. The white ball rolled across the pale vermilion of the green and, with a plop and a clonk, went right into the hole. Percy grinned.

"Fine shot, Brice!"

"Thank you, Bryan, thank you."

Cathy lowered her sunglasses and gave Jennifer a piercing look. "Friend? My goodness, what friend are we talking about?"

Jennifer felt her blush deepen. She wanted to glower in Percy's direction, but had to settle for sending angry thoughts in his direction. "Oh, just a friend of ours. He got back into town yesterday, but Percy didn't have a chance to see him yet."

Cathy laughed, a single sharp barked *ha* that conveyed very little in the way of actual amusement. "Naughty Percy. And naughty Jennifer, entertaining gentleman callers without her husband."

"Oh, come on now, Cathy! It's the twenty-first century. Nobody's bothered about that sort of thing anymore."

Brian gave a humph to indicate his total lack of interest in the subject at hand. "Off to the next one, shall we?"

"Of course," Jennifer agreed, "good idea."

The four of them all piled aboard the golf cart, Percy at the wheel, and they started off towards the next hole.

Cathy and Brian had gotten into town at about two in the afternoon, only an hour or so after Percy arrived back at the house. Jennifer, who'd ended up sleeping in practically until one o'clock, had had scarcely a moment to even say hello to him before Cathy was on the phone. Their hotel was already booked and their bags were being sent over by a courier service. Brian, it seemed, was quite eager to hit the links as soon as possible. Percy said that he had the day off from work, and he'd love to take them out. Jennifer had been pleading silently for him to say no, but no such luck.

Her entire body ached. She felt like she'd just played in one of Tyrone's football games - with *her* as the ball. Just getting into her golf attire had been quite the adventure. Percy had helpfully advised that she might consider taking up yoga, which earning him a dirty pair of pants hurled at his head. She was lucky she noticed the hicky on her shoulder just before heading out the door; she'd changed quickly into a shirt with a higher collar. Cathy never would have shut up about that if she'd seen it.

Of course, even Cathy wouldn't have been able to imagine how it was that Jennifer had come by the mark, or what sort of evening she'd just had. For her part, Jennifer planned to keep it that way. But then Percy had decided to start with the sly remarks...

The course was beautiful, and it was a gorgeous late summer day, not a cloud in the azure sky and only a handful of other golfers on the course. Cathy had been her usual nose self, and immediately started peppering them both with questions, though she often supplied her own hypothetical answer instead of waiting for hear what they might have to say. Brian mostly grunted, his attention entirely focused on the game at hand.

Cathy and Jennifer shared the backseat of the golf cart. The other woman nudged her not-too-gently. "So, this *friend.* A young man?"

"I suppose so... yes."

"Quite young," Percy chirped helpfully, "What is it hon, twenty? Twenty-two?"

Jennifer ground her teeth. "Something like that."

Cathy leaned back, her eyebrows climbing so high you could see them peaking over the tops of her bug-eyed sunglasses. "Oh my. I don't know if I'd trust myself around a young man like that. You must be made of stronger stuff than I am, Jennifer."

Brian grunted.

"Oh, it's nothing like that, Cathy. Please!"

Cathy laughed. "Oh, I'm sorry if I've offended your delicate sensibilities, darling. I know you and Percy are a pair of old fashioned ducks and all, but like the man said, it's the twenty-first century..."

Jennifer had to suppress a grin. *If you only knew.*

"Now, this is a friend of Percy's?"

Percy piped up again. "Oh no, he's really more Jennifer's pal. I've met him a couple times, of course. Seems like a nice young man."

Cathy scoffed. "Oh, Percy, *watch out*, darling."

Jennifer frowned, "What, you don't think a middle-aged woman can be friends with a young man?"

"Oh, Jen, all this time I thought you were such a Charlotte, and now you're starting to go all *Samantha* on me!" She cackled with laughter.

"Oh, I am *not*," Jennifer pretended to pout. Not even Samantha had ever gone as far as she had, at least not on any Sex and the City episode *she'd* ever seen. "Drop it, Cathy, it's nothing."

"Alright, alright! I can take a hint. You have your little secrets for all I care! I won't say a word about it."

"Thank you."

The silence lasted about four seconds until Cathy started in on the golf course topiary sculptures, which really were a bit shaggy, don't you think?

Fortunately the ride to the next hole didn't last much longer. The other three hopped right out, trotting over to set up their shots. Jennifer came last, and couldn't keep herself from moaning when she got out, her whole crotch aching in protest as she lifted her leg up to step out of the gold card.

Cathy turned back and gave her another arch look. "Are you entirely alright there, darling?"

Jennifer forced a grin. "Oh, I think I just pulled a muscle."

"Heavens, doing what?"

"Uh..." she stared, open-mouthed, her mind suddenly going blank.

"Yoga," Percy supplied, fighting back a smirk. "Jen's taking it up, you know."

"Well, I'm not sure it's helping," Cathy said, watching Jennifer's stiff almost bow-legged walk.

"Oh, you know," Percy said, "Just gotta break it in, you know how it goes."

This time Jennifer did glare at him, and she didn't much care who saw it.

* * *

-Last night was amazing. I'm still feeling it :P

-Haha, I bet. You were incredible. Didn't know you were such a kinky little girl.

-Who are U calling a little girl, Mr?

-Just you, baby.

-Oh okay then.

-What are you doing today?

Jennifer looked up from her phone. They were on hole sixteen of the eighteen hole course. Almost there. She didn't know if she was going to hold up for those last two holes. Her entire body was screaming at her to get itself back into bed.

-Golfing with friends from Minnesota. It's torture.

-Haha, why?

-U know why :P I need to be on bed rest after what U did to me, U monster.

-You seemed to enjoy it at the time :)

-Okay fine. Just not sure I'm going to make it through these next two holes.

-You can do it. You made it through all the holes last night.

-OMG your the worst.

-Haha.

-When can I see you again?

-This week is a little crazy. Start of the semester and stuff, football practice starting back up. But soon. Maybe a week or so.

-A week! I can't last a week... :(

-Okay okay, maybe I can see you sooner.

-yay! :)

-I'm free on Wednesday afternoon, I think.

-I made plans :(told my friend I would take her to the book club.

-Where?

-At the library downtown.

-Okay.

-Sorry.

-No problem. We'll figure something out. See you soon.

-Kisses!

* * *

She did survive the golf course, in the end, but it seemed to her like it had been a near thing. They dropped Cathy and Brian off at their hotel, Cathy still jabbering and Brian still silent. Jennifer promised to meet Cathy at the beach the next day and then off they were.

Jennifer slumped down in the seat. "Oh my *God*, I need a nap, Percy."

He smiled. "Yay, I'll bet. You seemed a little out of it today."

"God, I was lucky to be able to stand, after the night I had."

"Pretty rough, was it?"

She smiled. "You saw the pictures, baby, you tell me."

"You looked incredible," he said, and pulled out of the drop-off lane. It was a twenty minute drive back to the house.

"Which one did you like best?" she asked, feeling a little spark of mischievousness creep through the weariness.

"Oh... I couldn't pick."

She leaned over in her seat, sliding her hand down between his thighs. "What if I... made you pick?"

He laughed, a kind of strained and awkward chuckle, and he swallowed.

She leaned in close, so close that he would be able to feel her breath on his ear. The car hummed beneath them, and her seat belt strained as she leaned over. "I know you to see his cum on me..."

He swallowed again, harder this time, and his hands tightened on the wheel. He cleared his throat a little.

"Which did you like better? The one where it's on my tits..." she lifted her free hand to touched her breasts while her other hand held him a little tighter. "Or did you prefer the one where it's in my mouth..." she licked the side of his ear, very slightly, just the tip of her tongue.

He cleared his throat again. "Y-your, ahem, um... I, I liked the, uh... the mouth one."

"Hm, I knew you would." She could feel him getting worked up, getting into quite a tizzy. Was this dangerous to do while he was driving, sure. But then again, you could get killed going to get the morning paper, so what was life without a little risk. "You know," she said, shifting her weight a little so that she could feel him better. God, it was good to feel him hard again, after so many years of him being flaccid, "I didn't get to take a picture of it, but he came three times last night..."

"O-oh?"

"Hm hm... that's right." Her voice was a husky whisper, still so close to his ear.

"Um, where... where was the third time."

"Guess."

He blushed deep red. "Jen! I..."

"Oh no," she said, "don't play shy with me. After your little performance out there, teasing me in front of Cathy and Brian. Oh no. I want you to guess."

He cleared his throat one more time. "Y-your... in your pussy?"

She shook her head, giving his balls a little squeeze. "Nope."

"Was it... on your back?"

She squeezed a little harder. "No. It was inside me, Percy."

He frowned, perplexed for a moment, then, like a light switch had been flipped on, his expression changed. "You... you're not talking about..."

"In my ass, Percy."

He looked at her, staring and blinking.

"Percy! Watch where you're going!"

He yelped, looking back to the road. A big black SUV was barreling towards them; they'd drifted out of their lane a little. It honked. He swerved the wheel, getting them back in their own lane. Jennifer laughed. Percy swallowed. His grip on the wheel was so tight that his knuckles were turning white.

"Oh my God, honey, be *careful.*"

"Right, right. Sorry, I... did you really take it up the ass?"

"God, why do you think I'm so sore today? He went *hard*, Percy. That boy has *no* mercy."

"Jesus, are you okay?"

"It was amazing."

"Wow."

"Yeah."

He glanced at her, "But no pictures?"

"Sorry. I was a bit in the moment."

"Damn," he said, softly under his breath.

"Oh my God, do you like that, Percy? You like seeing that sort of thing?"

He blushed. "Hey, you're the one who did it!"

"I just never knew."

"All guys like it. Well, most of them, I guess."

"Well, I guess I'll have to make sure and bring back evidence next time it happens."

"Next time?"

She just smiled, and gave his little cock another squeeze. She leaned back in her seat, feeling tired again. God, she was worn out. Last night she'd had about a year's worth of sex. A year in her old life, anyway. Maybe she *should* take up yoga, like Percy had said. She could imagine the expression on Ty's face if she showed off one of those fancy flexible poses to him...

"What about you, Percy, what did you get up to?"

"Ah, not much. I met Jonas at the club, saw a couple people there?"

"People?"

"Matilda and Marquis. They were, uh... sort of putting on a show."

"Oh my."

"Yeah, bunch of people there. Actually, I met somebody interesting. The original founder of the club was there with his wife. Guy named Reggie. And Penelope, that was his wife's name. Seemed nice enough."

"Interesting."

"Yeah, I guess. We had a good talk, I suppose. Then I just, I dunno, wandered around town a little. Found a motel, and got those pictures from you finally. Thanks for those, by the way, really made my night."

"No problem, sweetie. You know how much I like showing off for you."

"Yeah," he grinned, shaking his head. "You're really something, you know that, honey?"

She smiled sleepily. "I know. Thanks, Percy."

By the time they got home she was already asleep.

* * *

Cathy moaned sensuously, stretching her arms skyward and fluttering her fingers. She dug her toes into the sand, wriggling contentedly on her beach chair. "My *God*, Jennifer, this is the life. I can't believe you're not out here every day."

Jennifer shaded her eyes and looked out across the shimmer white beach. The ocean beyond was glittering topaz. "Me neither. I've been missing out. This place is so beautiful."

Cathy lowered her sunglasses, eyeing the firm backsides of a group of young men walking past. "It certainly is," she said, licking her lips.

Jennifer laughed. "God, Cathy."

"What? You're telling me you *don't* look? Please."

"I... I mean, I *look*, but I don't make such a *show* of it. I mean, my goodness."

"What can I say, I like to look! No harm in looking. God knows men have been looking at us for long enough, I'd say it's high time for a little payback."

Jennifer rolled her eyes dramatically.

Cathy swung her feet around, sitting sideways on the chair so that she was facing Jennifer straight on. "Look, girlfriend, the boys aren't around anymore. We have to talk."

Jennifer felt her eyes narrow a little. "What about...?"

"About this 'friend' of yours." She hooked her fingers into little quote gestures.

"Oh." Jennifer sank a little deeper into her beach chair. She'd known they were going get there eventually, as soon as she saw that Brian wasn't coming along. A part of her was actually surprised it had taken this long to come up.

"Look, Jen, I've told you everything there is to know about myself. I mean, I told you about *my affair*, didn't I?" her voice lowered to a conspiratorial hiss at that. She had indeed told Jennifer about her "affair," as often as she could, it seemed sometimes.

As far as Jennifer had been able to figure, the so-called affair, which had been with local boy who mowed their lawn in the summer, hadn't gone any further than a furtive kiss and a grope before he'd gone and moved to another town to get a job at his uncle's pharmacy. To hear Cathy tell it, however, it had been quite a torrid romance, the stuff of cheap Harlequin paperbacks and bad Lifetime movies.

"Now I now you pretty darn well, Jennifer, and I can tell when you're hiding something. And Percy, oblivious as can be, chattering away like there's nothing happening! Who is this friend of yours, and what's really going on between you two?"

For a moment Jennifer really didn't know what to say. She'd been expecting this confrontation, but somehow hadn't thought ahead to the part where she needed to explain herself. She couldn't think of anything to say that didn't sound like complete and utter rubbish. Cathy was a chatterbox and quite prone to exaggeration, that was for sure, but she wasn't stupid. She'd know if Jennifer told her a stupid lie and she'd know if Jennifer didn't say anything at all.

She could feel the seconds ticking away.

But why not? Minnesota felt like a world away and, to be completely honest, she didn't have that many ties left to the place. Cathy was the closest friend she'd had there, and nobody in Minnesota had any real connection to Jennifer's family, who all lived in Maine. So why not tell her? Even if Cathy did blab it around it wouldn't effect Jennifer any. But how much to tell?

"Alright, alright. There might be *something* going on. Maybe."

"Oh my *God*, I knew it! Spill, girl, spill. Tell me everything."

"Look, Cathy, it's... well, it's complicated."

"Well of *course* it's complicated, Jennifer, Darling, this sort of thing always is, believe me, I know." And there she was, back to the affair again. Jennifer wondered if Brian actually knew about it and just couldn't be bothered to care. "What about your Percy, my God!"

"Percy... knows about it. It was sort of his idea."

That actually managed to shut her up for a moment. She sat there in her beach chair, mouth open, just staring.

"Look, Cathy, the thing is, well... we have an arrangement."

"Oh my *God*, Jennifer, an arrangement? What kind of frickin' arrangement could you possibly have?"

Maybe this hadn't been such a good idea after all. Cathy sounded like she was on the verge of hysterics. Her voice had gone up several octaves, and she was practically shouting now. They were far from alone on the beach. Jennifer squirmed in her one-piece suit, feeling naked and exposed. She wished she were buried neck-deep in the sand with a big sun hat on her head. "Cathy, please do calm down."

"Calm? I'm *calm*, Jennifer, I'm very calm! It's fine, it's fine," she took several long deep breaths, holding her hands out as if to steady herself.

"Percy and I have become... distant, in that way. Not emotionally or anything like that. We're still very happily married."

Cathy scoffed.

Jennifer frowned and carried on. "*Very* happily married. We just decided that it would be alright if I... explored, a bit. That's all."

Cathy looked over the tops of her sunglasses. "Jennifer, isn't thirty-five a little *young* for a midlife crisis?"

"Thirty-eight, Cathy."

"Whatever."

"It's not a crisis, Cathy, it's just... sex."

And there was the open mouth again. Cathy was certainly getting out her quota of scandalized outrage today. "Just *sex*? Darling, you have no idea. How are you really this naive? It's never *just* sex. Oh sure, you think it's all fun and games now, but honey it doesn't work like that."

"Oh, is that so?" Jennifer felt a grin of amusement tugging at her lips.

"Don't smirk at me, darling. You just wait. You might think it's all very casual, but it'll happen."

"What's that? What's going to happen, Cathy?"

"It will explode in your face, darling. And not in the way you're thinking, you dirty bird. In the *bad* way. You just make sure you're ready for it."

"If you say so, Cathy."

"I *do* say so, and more besides. This is dangerous, Jennifer. Sex and love go together, where there's one the other always follows. It's a frickin' law of nature, darling. You can love Percy and not have sex with him, and you can screw this friend of yours and claim you don't love him... but it can't stay that way forever. Eventually things will fall apart and you'll probably end up losing them both. Take it from me, *I* know. I knew that if I didn't break things off then Brian would find out and leave me. It was only a matter of time. It... it still hurts, Jennifer," she put her hand over her heart, sniffing dramatically, "but I made a choice."

"You didn't choose, Cathy, he *moved away*, I remember."

"But I could have followed him! I almost *did* for God's sake. But never mind that. Just remember, someday you'll have to make a choice. That's it, I've said my piece!" She threw up her hands and lay back. If it was possible to make lying in the sun an aggressive activity, then it could only be said that Cathy was aggressively tanning, as if the activity call upon great force of will.

Jennifer shook her head and lay back in her beach chair. Cathy could go on all she wanted, but this sort of situation was hardly in her area of expertise. Everything was going to be perfectly fine.

* * *

The downtown library was impressively large, and largely empty. On Wednesday mornings from ten to one, the conference room and lounge upstairs were turned over to the book-club. Although they seemed to consider themselves quite unique, the club really wasn't any different from the one she'd gone to in Minnesota.

It was the usually assemblage of chatty ladies, among whom Jennifer was one of the youngest. The oldest were positively octogenarian. There was occasionally a man or two, and an actual young person from time to time, but such occurrences were rare to say the least, and such people rarely made repeat appearances.

The Florida book club, much like its spiritual partner in Minnesota, often seemed only partially concerned with books, and often functioned like more of a spinsters gathering than literary discussion circle, but Jennifer didn't especially mind that. It was as good as any soap opera, listening to the grannies go off about their ungrateful children or useless husbands. The books which they were supposed to talk about were usually only read by about half the group, if that. Jennifer herself was a fairly voracious reader, but there had been times back home when she'd turned up to the meeting and had to ask the person sitting next to each other what book it was again which everybody was talking about.

Cathy wasn't much of a reader, but she was a talker. She always bought the books, not content to simply check them out from the library like most of the others, but she rarely seemed to read further than the first few chapters. Jennifer suspected that she skimmed the plot synopses online with her smart phone during the meetings.

She wasted little time insinuating herself with the Florida crowd, most of whom Jennifer was only slightly familiar with even after coming to the group half a dozen times. Before they'd even made it past the coffee and bagels phase of the meeting and moved to sit down for the discussion, Cathy was already chattering away and laughing with several others.

Jennifer envied the other woman her easy way with people sometimes. Although she supposed it was the trade off to having no sense of restraint or self-awareness, so there was that.

They were just about to sit down when the door of the conference room swung open, and a young man walked into the room. For a moment there was a hush that fell over the gathering. The man was tall and muscular, clearly athletic. He had soft brown eyes, strong hands and rich dark skin.

Jennifer felt her eyes almost bug out of her head. She had to bite back a cry of surprise.

Tyrone.

Her mind raced. Those texts, when she'd told him that she wanted to see him, that she was going to the book-club, that it was at the downtown library... So, he'd come. He'd looked up the time and place of the meeting, and he'd come. She didn't know if she was furious or delighted, but her stomach began at once to twist itself into a knot.

Kendra Whitehead, the de facto leader of the book club, cleared her throat officiously. "I'm sorry," she said primly, "I think you're in the wrong place."

"This is the book club?" he asked, stepping smoothly into the room, his hands casually in the pockets of his sports jacket.

"That's right..." she said, somewhat hesitantly.

"Cool, this is the place then," he said, sidling over to the refreshments table and helping himself to a donut, not a care in the world.

Kendra stared at him for a moment, then sat down, cheeks flushed and tongue-tied.

Jennifer hurried over to the table, pouring herself a cup of coffee that she didn't especially want and trying to act as casual as possible. "What are you *doing* here?" she hissed under her breath.

Tyrone grinned, taking a big bite of the pastry and chewing it thoughtfully for a long moment before answering. "I'm here for the literature, Jennifer. Didn't realize you came to this book club too."

She frowned, whispering sharply, "That's not true!"

"What, you don't think I read? Typical." His manner was quite breezy and off-handed; he seemed hardly aware of the fact that every set of eyes in the room was watching him with intense curiosity. He was the one young black male in a room full of older white women, and he seemed as comfortable as ever.

"Typ- What? What do you mean *typical*? Do you really expect me to believe that this is some kind of coincidence?"

"Where you sitting?" He asked, stuffing the rest of the donut in his mouth.

She blushed and hurried back to the table, blowing on her coffee and trying to keep her head down. He sauntered after her, nosing casually about the room before circling back around and sitting just to her left.

Cathy scooted right in and sat on her right. She leaned in close. "Oh my *God*, Jennifer... is this *him*?"

"Him who?" Jennifer hissed back. She hoped the ambient sounds of conversation still fluttering through the room were enough to mask her words from the general crowd. She had this sickening feeling that everybody could hear every word that was coming out of her mouth.

"Your so-called friend, mister arrangement."

"What? That's ridiculous, Cathy."

"He *is*, isn't he!" Cathy leaned even closer, practically talking right in Jennifer's ear now. "My God, Jennifer, he's *black*."

"Oh thanks, Cathy, I hadn't noticed," Jennifer whispered back, her teeth grinding.

Kendra cleared her throat again. "Okay. Alright, everyone, let's all gather around now, everybody have a seat... thank you. The book this week was Midnight Sun, by Indigo Willis." She lifted her copy, like a lawyer swearing something into evidence.

It was quite the trendy pick for the book club, and had been seem as something of a daring choice when it was selected at the end of last week's meeting. The novel, which Jennifer had in fact read this week, was something of a literary romance, which as far as she could tell was distinguished from a regular romance by the fact that none of the sex in it was especially hot, and had been largely replaced by a great many scene of people poetically gazing out across fields and thinking about their ancestors.

The story concerned a woman of color torn between two men, a young jazz musician who she had grown up with and the rich white man who owned the tenement building in which she lived. It had been rather well-written, Jennifer thought, though she hadn't considered quite how close to home it was for herself until she was here sitting beside Ty with the book in her hand.

"Oh, I don't know," one of the women said, breaking the silence, "I didn't like all that moping around. I mean, we get it, you're *oppressed*, just move past it already!"

Several women chattered their agreement, tut-tutting the book as having been somewhat miserable to read, a far cry from the Agatha Christie mystery they'd previous enjoyed.

"It's another of those *Oprah* books, isn't it?" another commented, "very dour."

"And I didn't see what was so bad about Chester!" one piped up. "He seemed like a lovely gentlemen to me."

One woman nodded in agreement, a rather elderly lady with spiny pink reading glasses and curly gray hair. "Oh, well you know, those *mixed* things never work out, that's what it was." There was a low chorus of agreement then, almost as an afterthought, she leaned towards Ty, waving a hand dismissively, "No offense, of course."

He raised his eyebrows. "None taking."

She couldn't tell if he was simmering with rage or quivering with suppressed laughter, but either way it was making her squirm.

"Well, look, I mean, what does Jamal *really* have to offer her? I mean, *I* don't even *like* jazz very much..."

"Oh, me neither. All that messing around. Just play the notes normally! Enough with all the craziness."

Ty leaned back in his seat. "Well," he said, "I think that Jamal does offer some advantages over the other guy, Chester."

The whole room turned simultaneously to look at him. He smiled calmly, crossing his arms across his chest.

"Like what?" the older lady asked, laughing a little bit. "He's poor, he's a bum, he plays that awful music. Chester owns the whole city block, and he's obviously from a good family. What could Jamal possibly offer her that he can't?"

"Hm," Ty stroked his chin thoughtfully. He turned suddenly to Jennifer, and he smiled. "What do you think?"

She felt her throat go dry. Oh God. And now everybody was looking at her, just perfect. Then she felt something. Ty's hand, moving slowly under the table out of sight - please oh please let it be out of sight! - along her thigh. His finger found the hem of her skirt and hooked under it, slowly pulling it back. He rested his warm hand on the inside of her leg, and started sliding it slowly upwards, ever so slowly, agonizingly slowly.

"Um... well..." she said, trying to focus her mind despite the attention of the room and the hand moving gradually closer to her privates. "Jamal has, uh... he has... passion."

"Passion?" Kendra asked, looking over the tops of her glasses with a rather dubious expression on her features.

"T-that's right," she said, struggling to go on. He was touching her panties now, his fingers moving in slow and methodical circles against the cotton of her underwear. She could feel herself beginning to tingle down there, something awakening inside her. "Jamal gives her something Chester never could. He makes her feel... excited, and alive and... *sensual.*"

Some of the older women made faces at that word, frowning and wincing as if they'd just heard something both preposterous and rude. Jennifer didn't much care at that point, as she was beginning to slip away into her own little world. Everything was shrinking, the whole room fading as the feeling of Ty's fingers against her panties intensified. He was still sitting there, just watching her, his face perfectly calm and ordered, giving away nothing. She could feel herself crumbling, and she desired more and more just to gasp and moan and slap her palms down on the table, to shout out that Chester could never compete with Jamal because of Jamal's beautiful big black cock.

She restrained herself, but only just. Jennifer cleared her throat, blinking slowly. Her thighs were squeezing tight on Ty's hand, clenching rhythmically. "Chester could never satisfy her. He doesn't have what it takes. It's obvious that Jamal is the only one for her."

Kendra seemed to be fighting the urge to roll her eyes. "Well, that's very romantic, Jennifer, but let's try and stick to what's actually in the text."

One of the grannies spoke up, "My great niece is dating a Negro, you know. Oh my, her parents are beside themselves. Not that I'm against them, certainly, but back in my day, oh my goodness..."

Kendra blushed, glancing quickly up at Tyrone, whose expression remained placid. "Yes, well, let's focus our discussion on the book itself. I think we should talk about chapter four, there were several very interesting passages."

"*Yes*!" Jennifer cried out, gripping the edge of the table. Ty's fingertips had just slipped into her, pulling her panties aside a little and parting the folds of her sex to touch her there.

The whole room turned to look at her. Cathy looked both appalled and impressed, everybody else just looked confused.

Jennifer blushed. "Yes, that, uh... that seems like a very good idea, yes."

Kendra blinked. "Thank you, Jennifer. I appreciate your enthusiasm. Alright, let's see... page forty-eight..."

Jennifer gripped the edge of the table and shut her eyes and tried very very *very* hard not to make another outburst. Ty wasn't especially helpful.

* * *

The week passed in a blur. She saw Cathy several more times, but the other woman seemed determined not to speak of anything which had transpired. They ended up having rather a lovely time. Cathy could be obnoxious, but she was a lot of fun to be around when she wasn't prying. They went to the beach and the shopping center almost every day. It was nice to be back together with one of her old friends. She still hadn't made any deep connections in Florida and she'd forgotten how much she missed the easy banter between Cathy and she.

She didn't see much of Ty, only the occasional flirty text. His senior year, apparently, was going to be a lot more academically aggressive. She was afraid that she wouldn't see as much of him as she'd hoped.

Today was Saturday, and it was Cathy's last day in town. Jennifer met her at the hotel just before their taxi was due to pick them up for the trip to the airport.

Cathy embraced her gingerly, holding her fingers splayed out. "Of course I decided to paint my nails right before I started packing," she stuck out her tongue, waving her hands.

Jennifer laughed. "*Cathy*! Why?"

"Well, Darling, I was chipped and my nails looked a fright. I simply had to do something. I know most people don't dress up to go on planes any more, but I'm certainly *not* most people." Cathy lowered her sunglasses and gave Jennifer a hard look, as if daring her to offer some sort of contradiction.

Jennifer shook her head, grinning. "You certainly aren't, Cathy, you certainly aren't."

"I'm going to assume that's a compliment, darling."

"Of course."

"Well then. Give me another hug, and come visit me in the frozen north sometime."

"I will Cathy, promise." She wasn't sure she'd be following through with that, but in the moment, at least, she meant it. They embraced briefly, until Brian started coughing and grumbling. Cathy rolled her eyes. She paused for one last moment before pulling away. "Jennifer," she said, giving her rather an intense look, "be *careful.* Remember what I told you."

Jennifer nodded. "Okay. And it was good to see you."

"Of course it was. Ciao, darling."

She waved an elaborate farewell and trotted across the lobby. A moment later she was ducking into the taxi, and she was gone.

Jennifer turned away, shaking her head.

Bing!

She jumped a little, and dug her phone out of her purse. There was a message from Ty. -*Are you free, baby?*

-Yes. What's up?
-I'm downtown, you wanna meet me?
-Sure! Just tell me where.

* * *

Jennifer looked up and down the street. She felt the hair on the back of her neck stand up, and she shivered and checked yet again that the car doors were locked.

She didn't have much experience in these sorts of things, but it seemed to her like this was something of a rough neighborhood. The walls were scrawled with lewd graffiti and strange symbols which she suspected might be gang signs. Strange dark men lounged about the dirty shopfronts, eyeing her and her shining black SUV with obvious interest. Half the stores seemed closed, and, as for the other half, she could hardly make out what services they even provided. There were a few pawn shops and laundromats, but the rest seemed to be a hodge-podge of junk shops and curio dealers that made no effort to disguise the suspicious origins of the goods they were peddling.

She glanced at her phone, double checking the address which Ty had sent her and the location showing on the directions app. This was the place, alright.

Jennifer, she thought, *what have you gotten yourself into*? She hoped this wasn't Ty's idea of a practical joke.

Jennifer took a deep breath and stepped into the darkness of a long low alleyway between two head shops, and shuffled her way gingerly down the gloomy path, being very careful not to smudge her rather expensive clothes on either side of the narrow ally.

She found the door right where the app had promised, about halfway down the alley with a little sign glowing above the door. *Lynette's Art and Ink*. She shook her head, marveling at herself for having the nerve to have made it this far, and she pushed open the door and stepped inside.

The shop was actually quite nice. She passed through a jangling beaded curtain and into a roomy sort of boudoir. There were chairs and couches and throw pillows about, little tables with bottles of wine and ornate pewter goblets set up on them, shelves with odd miniature sculptures of everything from peace signs to and intricately detailed reproduction of female genitalia. Every single open space on the walls had been filled in with a picture. They weren't hanging there, but actually painted directly onto the plaster. At least a hundred little paintings, each in a different style and of a wide variety of subject matters. It was an odd place, for sure, but it was clean and charming and seemed to have been very well tended to. Soothing eastern music flitted in from an adjoining room. Jennifer felt herself relax at once.

-I'm here. She messaged him.

He didn't reply right away, so she sent another. *-Are U here? I don't see U?*

She bit her lip, wandering a little further into the shop. There was a cork board with about forty 4x6 photos tacked up on it, each of them showing a person's tattoo. The ink work was fine and delicate, all black, no colors, but rich and textures and finely done. Jennifer didn't know anything about tattoos, but they looked very good to her. She'd always been drawn to the large colorful sort, a friend of hers in Minnesota got a lovely bluebird tattooed on her calf and she thought it actually looked rather nice.

But these tattoos were different. They weren't exactly pretty, but were all very striking. Particularly on the white patrons - although they seemed to be about half and half black and white - the rich black lines seemed very powerful on pale skin. Ty had a tattoo, just a little one on his shoulder. It was the school team's logo, and a date written beneath it. The first day he'd started, he explained to her. The black ink had been almost invisible on his dark skin, and she'd had to lean close to decipher the fine workmanship.

She was about to leave the cork-board when something caught her eye. A face she knew.

It was Matilda Harrington. She was covering her face, rather halfheartedly and with a cheeky grin playing across her face. Her dress was unbuttoned down to her waist, and was open, revealing her pert little breasts. The skin of her right breast was a little pink, and the black tattoo ink stood out brilliantly on her pale skin. It was a little shape with a letter inside it. Jennifer frowned, and leaned closer.

"Queen of Spades." A raspy female voice spoke right next to her.

Jennifer started; she gasped a little, and jerked back.

The woman laughed a little. She was young, no more than twenty-eight, Jennifer guessed. Her skin was dusky and her features Asiatic. She wore heavy makeup, especially around her eyes, which seemed to pop. She wore violet contacts that seemed almost to glow. Her lips were painted black. Her clothing was loose and skimpy, supplemented by what seemed like hundreds of dangling necklaces and bracelets.

"I'm sorry."

"A queen of spades tattoo. It's a symbol."

"A symbol of what?" Jennifer asked.

The women lifted a smoldering cigarette to her dark lips and took a long drag. "White woman who only screws blacks. Usually a swinger. Tattoo's a kind of initiation. Marks her for everybody to see. So they know which way she goes."

"Oh."

The woman smiled. She the features of a snake, charming, intoxicating... deadly. "You looking to get one?"

"Um... not today."

Her smile only widened. She held out one jewelry encrusted hand, almost as if she expected Jennifer to kiss her rings. She gave it an awkward shake instead. "I'm Lynette," she said, her voice cool and knowing. "I suppose you're looking for Tyrone. He said you'd be here."

"Uh... that's right..."

Lynette drifted away, waving a hand airily for Jennifer to follow. "He's back this way. I suppose you'd better come along."

Jennifer glanced once more at the picture of Matilda Harrington. *Queen of Spades...*

Then she tore her gaze away and followed.

The back of the placed looked very different from the front, antiseptic white and very clean, almost like a hospital. Ty was lying down in a big padded chair, a bit like you sat in in a dentist's office. He had his shirt off and was lying back with his hands behind his head, looking very relaxed.

"I found your lady eyeing my Queen of Spades work," Lynette laughed, taking a quick drag on her cigarette before snuffing it in the ashtray.

"Oh *really*."

Jennifer blushed. "I wasn't *eyeing* it... I just saw it."

"Sure, sure," he said, "I believe you."

She rolled her eyes and crossed her arms.

"Why don't you come over here and kiss me," he said.

She liked that a lot better, and went to him at once. She leaned over him, her hair falling to brush against his bared chest. He smiled softly up at her. She bent down and touched her lips to his, softly at first, but then deeper. Her mouth opened to his, and she tasted him. She kissed him for rather a long time, caressing the side of his face.

"You sure about that tattoo?" Lynette asked, eyebrows arched.

"Maybe next time," Jennifer shot back, tossing her hair as she straightened back up.

Ty grinned.

"So..." she said, looking around the room, eyeing the tattoo needles and little ink containers. "What's going on, Ty? You're getting some work done?"

"Yeah." He reached down and touched his chest, the powerful muscles of his chest. "Getting something done right here."

On his heart. She felt a flutter in her chest. "What... um... what are you getting done?"

"I want your initials here. JB, right here. So I always have you with me. Couldn't stand going so long without this summer. Now I'll have you everywhere." He grinned, his soft brown eyes shining up at her.

She felt like her heart was expanding, growing in her chest and feeling as if it might burst. "Oh my God, Ty... that's beautiful." She leaned down and kissed him again. "I love it. I'm yours."

She leaned back, moving to sit in the chair across the room as Lynette turned on the tattoo machine and started to work. She was touched, more than touched, she was *moved.* And yet, as she sat there watching, she couldn't help but hear Cathy's words in her head.

Love follows sex. You'll have to choose, and you'll lose them both. Be careful.

But then he looked at her and all her fears vanished again, like mist disappearing in the light of the midday sun.

Tyrone

Lynette leaned down, frowning as she squinted at his chest.

Tyrone tried to get a look at what himself without moving too much "What, you mess up or something?"

She sent a glower in his direction, snorting dismissively at that notion. Her purple eyes glowed eerily in the pale light of the tattoo room. "I don't mess up, big boy. Just looking at your scar," she rasped.

"Scar?" asked Jennifer, leaning over to get a closer look.

"Oh boy, all these pretty ladies fussing over me," he laughed.

Jennifer blushed a little. Lynette just rolled her eyes. "Sorry, Tyrone, I'm not a cradle robber like this one here."

Jennifer gawped. "Cradle robber! What? That's not-"

Lynette chuckled dryly. "Just teasing. Hm, must have hit a soft spot."

"Do you have a rest room," Jennifer asked, rather icily.

Lynette lifted the tattoo needle for a moment to point in the direction of the little bathroom adjacent to the work space. Jennifer went off in a bit of a subdued huff, and Lynette bent back down to go to work.

"So that's your fair lady, eh?"

He was about to shrug, and forced himself to remain still instead. "I guess so."

"She's a pretty one."

"I noticed that too."

"Bit older than you."

"So are you, Lynette. And I've heard the stories about you."

She laughed, sticking her tongue out to fiddle at the piercing in her lower lip. "You do like to talk. All you black boys in Marquis' little gang. Don't believe everything you hear. And don't believe everything she tells you."

He frowned. "What's that supposed to mean?"

"You're an experience, Tyrone. Her little fantasy. I don't see her in here getting your initials inked on her chest."

He shook his head slowly. "That's not what it's about. I'm not marrying the woman. I have my team's logo, and I'll never play for them again after my senior year is over. It's about the memory, that's all."

She cocked one eyebrow at him. "Is it really? Well... don't get your heart broken, Tyrone. I hate having to ink over my own work."

"I'll keep that in mind."

* * *

"Well... *that* was certainly an interesting experience." Jennifer sat back in the driver's seat of her SUV and breathed a heavy sigh. She'd seemed to relax immediately as soon as the door closed, like she'd just set down a heavy weight off her shoulders.

"You like it?"

"The tattoo? Oh my God, Ty, it's lovely. I can't believe you did that. It's... a lot."

"Too much? Because, like I was telling Lynette, it's not-"

She leaned over, touching one finger against his lips. "It's perfect, Ty. Thank you." She smiled then, a slow and wicket sort of smile. "I just don't know how I'm ever going to replay you, is all."

He grinned back. "I'll bet you can think of a few ways."

"Hm, I'll bet." She tapped the wheel, her fingers dancing on the leather cover. "You... uh, you know how to drive, right?"

He rolled his eyes. "Yeah, I can drive, baby. Shit." He decided it would be better not to mention that he'd learned by stealing cars with his cousin Leroy, and didn't actually have a license, as such...

"Sorry, sorry, sorry! Just checking." She took her hands off the wheel, raising them defensively for a moment. Then she reached down and undid her seat-belt. "Come on," she said, "hop out and come around. You're driving."

"Oh yeah?"

"That's right. You wanted a lift back to the dorm, right? So you drive."

He pulled a face. "I... guess I could do that." He felt a brief twinge of nervousness, but he thought that he managed to keep it off his voice and expression. He'd certainly never driven anything like this monster of an SUV, but hey... he could give it a shot. What could go wrong?

He'd been impressed that Jennifer had made it to the tattoo parlor. It wasn't exactly the sort of place he expected she often found herself. Even for him this seemed like a pretty rough part of town.

He stepped out and walked around to the driver's seat and got behind the wheel. She scooted over while he went outside. She held the keys out, dangling them in front of him and nodding when he took them. "Okay then," she said, turning to face the road.

He hadn't driven in a while, but it came back to him quick. The car handled smooth and easy, almost too easy, given its bulk. He got up to ten miles over the speed limit before he even realized how fast he was going, and choked it back a little. The cars he was used to driving made you work for every bit of speed you squeezed out of them.

"So... do you guys all bring your women here?"

He laughed. "You guys?"

"You know. The bulls from the club. I saw a lot of those Queen tattoos or whatever they are on her board."

He shrugged. "Yeah, I guess so. Marquis and Lynette go way back. He points the guys here when they need ink. It's cheap, but you can trust her. Some of these places will fuck you over good. Dirty needles and shit like that. What'd you think of Lynette?"

"I'm not sure if I like her or not," Jennifer answered, rather tactfully.

"Yeah. Me neither."

"Hm."

They drove a little while that way in silence. Jennifer was watching the road signs very attentively. She seemed to be waiting for something. Or maybe she just didn't entirely trust his driving.

They had to take the highway between downtown and the campus. As soon as they hit the on ramp she took out her phone and snapped a selfie.

By this time he knew what that meant. The before picture. "What's up?" he asked, his hands sliding easily over the leather grip as he turned.

He could feel her looking at him. He saw her licking her lips out of the corner of his eye. "Just a little payback for your surprise visit to the book club." She reached over and felt the front of his jeans. He could feel himself responding immediately to her touch, and starting to stiffen a little.

He laughed, shaking his head. "Oh no," he said, "no no no, no way."

"Why not?" she moaned, sliding over a little bit and slipping the top part of her seat belt behind herself so that she could bend over and lean across the wide cabin of the SUV.

"I'm trying to drive, baby! Gotta, you know, watch the road..."

"You know," she said, ignoring his protests and pulling his zipper slowly down, "I tried something like this with Percy just a few days ago. He couldn't handle it. I thought maybe... you would be..." She reached inside, her slender fingers navigating the button of his boxers and opening the fly to reach inside.

He felt a low shudder move through him as her hand reached around his shaft. Shit. He took one hand off the wheel to grasp the back of her head as she lowered her mouth down towards him and pulled his cock out through his open fly.

"Hm..." she moaned, that beautiful gentle moan that he'd come to love so much, and she took him in her mouth.

He leaned back a little, shifting his one-handed grip on the wheel and struggling to focus his attention on the road. Well, if he had to die, he supposed there were worse ways to go.

* * *

"Tyrone! My *man*! Come on, hold your friend Barry tight in a loving embrace." Tyrone's scrawny roommate launched himself across the room, arms spread wide and a big dumb grin on his face. There was a batman bobble-head sticking out of his big afro and a pair of comic books sticking out of his back pocket.

"Uh, hey Barry," Tyrone deflected a little, turning to the side and letting the other guy grab his arm and give it a big comical squeeze.

"Man, I didn't even know if you were here or not. Had me worried there."

"Barry, school started last week. I thought you dropped out or something."

Barry frowned. "Last week? Are you sure? Shit, dude. Uh... I dunno, gonna have to check with my adviser about that. Whatever, it'll work out. The important thing is that we're together again."

"Right."

"And Tyrone," Barry leaned in close. His breath smelled like he'd just eaten an entire pack of chewing gum, so minty that it almost knocked him over. "I, uh... brought a friend."

"Oh yeah?"

Just then, as if on cue, a heavyset white girl emerged from the other room. She had on a bulky sweater with a big picture of an anime style cartoon girl on the front. Tyrone's border collie trotted happily after her, wagging her tail furiously. "I love your dog," she said, giving Tyrone a tentative little wave.

"Tyrone, this is Becky. Becky, this is my man, my roommate. Tyrone." He held a hand up and whispered in Tyrone's direction. "Could use some wingman shit here, dude. Becky and I are, uh... looking to be something of an item, yeah?"

"Gotcha," he whispered back. He had to fight the urge to laugh. Barry's style of seduction was, to say the least, rather unorthodox. He wasn't sure exactly how much help he was going to be to the other guy.

"Barry told me you're on the football team," the girl said, rocking awkwardly back and forth on the balls of her feet. She laughed oddly, staring at him. "That's cool."

"Uh... thanks."

"Becky and I met at the club," Barry chirped happily.

Tyrone started. "The Club? Really?" He tried to picture Barry and Becky in the Black and White Club, but couldn't quite conjure the image.

"Yeah, the comics club and the anime club switched rooms this year, I went to the wrong one by mistake. Becky's the president, we ended up, you know... hanging out." Barry grinned smugly. Becky smiled and slid over towards him, wrapping her arms around him and pulling him close. His tiny little figure seemed in danger of being absorbed by her bulk and swallowed whole. She gazed adoringly at him, her eyes glowing and looking almost as big and wide as those belonging to the girl on her shirt.

"Barry's really cool..." she said. She had a low and sort of dull voice, kind of monotone and flat. It made Tyrone sleepy in a weird way.

"Aw, you too, dude," Barry said, nuzzling his nose in her hair, which was blonde with streaks of red which had begun to fade to pink. His glasses slipped down his nose and he had to break their embrace to push them back up.

Tyrone's dog came trotting up and sat at his feet, panting and whimpering softly. He dug a treat out of his pocket and tossed it to her. She devoured it happily, curling up on the carpet at his feet to slobber all over his shoes while she ate.

"I didn't think you could have dogs in the dorms?" Becky asked.

"Yeah, Beyoncé's a service animal," Barry explained, quite incorrectly.

"Beyoncé?"

Tyrone rolled his eyes. "My sister named her. And she's not a service animal."

"Huh? Really?" Barry scratched his head. "So, uh, how'd you get her, dude? I always just assumed, I guess."

Tyrone grinned. "Well, I mean, I just didn't tell anybody."

Becky laughed flatly. "Ha ha. That's so awesome. Your secret is safe with me."

"See?" Barry said, beaming from ear to ear, "Didn't I say she was cool?"

"Very cool, Barry. Very cool."

The other guy just nodded, and pulled her closer. She allowed him to hug her, but her eyes were fixed on Tyrone the entire time.

* * *

-I miss U, Ty...

-Miss you too, Baby. I'm hoping to see you soon. Been crazy though. Coach is driving us really hard this season.

-I feel like it's been so long. I need to feel your cock inside me again. I want it so bad.

Tyrone lifted his head. The locker room was a bustle of activity as his teammates got undressed and hit the showers. The whole placed smelled of cleaning chemicals and body sweat.

Marquis stood at the far end of the room, arms crossed and reflective silver shades over his eyes. Tyrone wondered if he was scoping the team out for more recruits for the Club. He caught Tyrone looking at him and grinned, nodding slightly. Tyrone nodded back.

Marquis had made quite a habit of collecting players, his position as assistant coach made it easy for him to scope out possible recruits and approach them. It had worked on Tyrone, anyway. He'd actually run into two other players on the team at the Club before, when he'd been hanging out there. Before he'd met Jennifer. They'd avoided making any kind of contact with him for the most part. No reason to mix business and pleasure, though between the Club and the football team he wasn't actually entirely sure which one was which.

He could see them right now. They looked like anybody else, just two more players. You never would have known it. Hank Johnson the linebacker and DeShaun Roberts the wide receiver. They had little in common besides the fact that they were both black. Hank was beefy and thick and built like a brick house, while DeShaun was more lithe and slender.

Tyrone found himself wondering idly just how many people had been recruited from the team over the years. Every couple years the students would graduate and Marquis would have to start all over again. What was he going to do at the end of the year when he graduated and moved on? He supposed it wasn't likely he'd ever see Jennifer again. That was a strange thought. Not bad, exactly. This wasn't some romance, he wasn't here to sweep her off her feet. She was already married after all. He automatically reached down and touched the spot on his chest where were initials were no permanently etched. Was she going to be only another memory? A passing shadow of college days gone by?

He watched Hank strip down and head for the shower. DeShaun followed him a moment later. Okay, there was something else they had in common: they were both endowed well above average.

He shook his head, turning away and typing another message to Jennifer. He was going to end up just like Marquis if he didn't watch himself.

-I'll see you soon, babe. Promise. You'll get all the dick you can handle.

* * *

He kept his promise to Jennifer. He'd caught the bus uptown right after football practice and surprised her at home. They'd fucked fast and hard, not even bothering to fully undress. He just pushed up her skirt and pulled her panties to the side and bent her over the dining room table and screwed her until she screamed and pounded the hardwood and curled her toes.

By the time he made it back to the dorm it was already dusk and he was dead tired, hardly able to keep himself upright. Beyoncé rushed up to him as soon as he was through the door, yipping and licking his ankles.

"Hey girl, hey... good dog." He scratched her behind the ears and she rubbed happily up against him. She flopped down on her back, gazing up at him pitifully with her tongue lolling out of her mouth. He groaned. "You too? Girl, I'm too fuckin' tired."

She cocked her head to the side and whimpered.

"Oh fine. Jesus." He knelt down and rubbed her tummy.

The room was still dark. Barry must be out, who knew where. Tyrone got up with a yawn and a groan, his back and legs aching. Between the unusually intense football practice, the full day's load of coursework, and screwing Jennifer, his body was begging for rest. He thought he would probably just drop unconscious right there on the floor if he shut his eyes.

He forced himself up, much to Beyoncé's chagrin, and stumbled to the mini-fridge. He pulled out a couple things and slapped together a sandwich. It wasn't bad for being thrown together by the light of the microwave clock. God, when was the last time he'd eaten? His stomach felt like it was chewing on his spine.

He finished eating and stumbled back to the bedroom. He didn't bother turning on the lights. He wasn't planning on staying awake long enough to need them. It was a hot August day, and he felt sticky and hot. He started stripping in the gloom, and staggered to his dresser to dig out a clean pair of boxer shorts.

All of a sudden he heard movement behind him, a heavy step that couldn't possibly belong to the scrawny Barry. He whipped around, his boxers clutched in his hand. Shit, who the fuck could have broken into his dorm room? A burglar or something? He lifted his hands defensively, eyes still not fully adjusted to the dark. He was too slow, and the large figure wrapped their arms around him, pulling his naked body close against theirs.

Then the intruder started kissing him. He felt hot wet lips pressing against his, and the warmth of bare skin brushing against his chest and legs. A hand fumbled between his legs, groping awkwardly at his genitals.

"Hey. Hey! *Hey*!" He broke away from the kiss and embrace, tripping on the night stand as he scrambled for the lamp switch. He clicked it on, blinked in the sudden glare, and looked.

A large and pale woman stood before him. She had very wide hips, a huge rump and surprisingly small breasts, which she slowly brought her hands up to cover. She had a tattoo of a slender anime boy on her hip. It was Becky.

She pulled a face, grabbing a blanket off Barry's bed and wrapping it around herself. "Uh... oops. Sorry, Tyrone. It's Tyrone, right?"

"What the *fuck*?" he spat, struggling to get his boxers on and salvage the tattered remains of his dignity.

"I was waiting for Barry..." she mumbled.

He felt his eyebrows draw together in a suspicious glower. Surely she was familiar enough with Barry to have felt the difference between him and Tyrone. After all, Tyrone had at least six inches and fifty pounds of muscle on his skinny nerdy roommate. It could have been an honest mistake, but surely she would have known before she'd fondled his junk and kissed him for such a long time.

She sat on the edge of Barry's bed, eyeing Tyrone's penis with a raised eyebrow. "Wow," she said flatly, "I guess it's true what they say about black guys..."

"Yeah," he snarled, yanking his underwear up and pulling a pair of jeans on, "what do they say?"

"Uh... you know."

"Yeah yeah, I know. Just stick to Barry's black dick from now on, okay?"

"He's not as big as you."

"I'm sure he can get the job done."

She blushed. "You smell like sex."

"*What*?"

"You smell like you've been having sex with someone. I can tell."

He grabbed shirt that had been draped on the edge of the bed and started buttoning it up. "Are you for real?"

She wrapped the blanket tighter about herself. "Sorry. I've been told that I'm socially inappropriate at times. Should I not have said that?"

"I think most people probably would have left it alone, yeah."

"Sorry."

Jesus that had scared him. For a second there he'd been expecting to get a knife in the guts. His hands were shaking as he did up the last button and sat down on the bed across from her. Why was she still here? And still naked? Why wasn't she getting dressed and leaving? He felt a prickle on the back of his neck. What if Barry came back right now? It wouldn't look good.

"Who were you having sex with?"

He groaned. "Nobody. A friend, alright?"

"Barry thinks you're having sex with a teacher."

"What? I'm not having sex with a teacher, what the fuck?"

She shifted on the bed, her weight causing the springs to creak and moan in protest. The blanket slipped off her chest, flashing her breasts at him for another moment before she pulled it back up again. He couldn't help but notice that her nipples were pierced. "Barry says you're always sneaking out and that he's seen you sexting with a mature woman in secret."

"If it's so secret, how does Barry know about it?" Tyrone asked, gritting his teeth.

"He can see your screen from the bed here." She lay on her back to demonstrate, pulling out her phone and holding it at a slight angle. Tyrone could indeed get a decent glimpse of the screen from where he sat. He blushed, thinking of all the pictures Jennifer had sent him that his roommate might have seen.

"She's not a teacher, okay?"

"So how'd you meet?"

"What do you mean?" He narrowed his eyes.

"How did you start having sex with an old white lady?"

"She's not *old*, okay? Older, but not old."

"Sorry."

"We just met, alright?"

"You're in that Club, aren't you? I've heard about it."

He felt his throat tighten. God, whatever happened to secrecy? "I don't know what you're talking about."

"There's this secret Club. I've heard about it though. A bunch of sports guys and stuff are in it. Black guys who have sex with older white women."

He swallowed. "I don't know anything about that."

"Yeah, okay," she rolled her eyes a little. She clearly wasn't convinced. Christ, if she knew about it then she was sure to tell Barry sooner or later. And Barry was already suspicious enough of Tyrone's extracurricular activities.

"Look... let's just keep this between ourselves, alright."

"Sure. It'll be our little secret. I won't tell Barry what happened, either."

"*Nothing* happened."

"Okay, if you say so." She wrapped the blanket tight around herself and swept out of the room, padding off to the bathroom and exposing most of her backside as she went.

Tyrone waiting until he heard her leave the dorm room before he allowed himself to lie down. Good thing too, as he feel fast asleep just about the second his head hit the pillow.

* * *

-Hello sir. This is Percy. I was hoping we could discuss something when you have a moment.

-I'm good now, what's up?

-Well, I'm not sure if you know this or not, but Jennifer's birthday is coming up in just a few days.

-I didn't know that. That's great. Did you have something in mind?

-Not exactly, but I'd like to do something special. Maybe something to take things a little further.

-Further? Like what? Are you thinking of what we did in the club that night?

-No no, I'd rather not participate, though I would like to watch.

-Okay, cool. We can figure something out. When is it?

-September 25th.

-Shit.

-What is it?

-We have a game. First football game of the season. I can't get out of it, coach will kick me off the team if I'm a no show.

-Well, maybe we could go and see the game together. That could be an alternative. Even if we can't work out something more kinky, I'm sure she'd enjoy seeing you play.

-Yeah. I'll make sure you guys get tickets.

-Alright, that sounds like a plan.

-I'll see if I can come up with something special afterwards.

-Wonderful. Let me know if there's anything I can do to help. And I'd like to make it a surprise for Jennifer, if that's alright.

-Cool. I'll make sure birthday girl has a good time, don't worry about it.

-I'm sure you will. Already looking forward to it.

* * *

The next day Tyrone had an idea. He was sitting in the locker room watching the players come in off the field when it struck him.

He talked to Marquis first. The assistant coach was hesitant about it, but he agreed to give Tyrone the go ahead, conditional on his promise to keep things very very quiet.

"Ah... shit. Fine, fine. I'll make it happen. Just keep a low profile, kid. And I don't ever wanna hear about this. Since you came to me, I guess I'll let you go for it. I'll make sure the place doesn't get disturbed, tell the janitorial staff not to come by until later. Just make sure you're out of there by nine, alright. No later."

Tyrone grinned. "No problem."

"Alright. Have fun, my man. Have fun."

That taken care of, Tyrone went looking for Hank and DeShaun. He found them hanging out together, a little apart from the crowd of players going in and out. He'd found out a little while ago that they'd been friends from high school and that Marquis had recruited them as a package deal.

"Hey guys," he swung his leg over the bench, "can I ask you a question?"

Hank looked up at him, blinking slowly and working on a nub of chewing gum. "You just did, buddy."

DeShaun licked his lips and narrowed his eyes. "This about the, you know... The place?"

"Yeah. Something like that." And he told them his plan.

Hank looked doubtful. "I dunno, man. Marquis is down with that?"

"Yeah, I cleared it with him. He's gonna make sure things are quiet."

"Lemme see what we're talking about here," DeShaun said, snapping his fingers and holding out his hand.

Tyrone grinned and pulled out his phone. One picture was all it took.

"I'm in," Hank rumbled.

"Yeah man, I'm game. No question," DeShaun agreed, "long as you're sure it's been cleared with the man."

"We're all good to go, buddy."

They both nodded. "Then I guess we're in," DeShaun said, grinning lopsidedly, holding out his fist.

Tyrone bumped it, then Hank's, and got up to send Percy a message about the change in plans.

* * *

It was a big crowd. Tyrone felt it wash over him the moment he stepped out onto the field. The sound and the energy of it washed over him. He felt it surge through his body like an electric current. Across the field the other team was coming out, their red and gold uniforms gleaming in the pouring of artificial light.

He felt light and loose and limber and ready to play. It was good to be back on the field after the long summer away. He glanced up at the stands. Jennifer was in there somewhere, she'd sent him a message before he'd stuffed his phone in his locker and come out. He felt his new tattoo tingling under his uniform.

The announcer's voice came cutting through the roaring crowd. The smells of clean cut grass and sizzling concession stand foods and rubber shoes and the tang of antiperspirants filled the air. He breathed in deep, and hustled out to take his position on the green field.

* * *

The team came bursting back into the locker room, everybody shouting and cheering and jostling together. Someone popped a champagne bottle and sprayed it over the crowd. Totally against school policy, of course, but who cared? They'd won.

The team had been on fire, racking up touchdown after touchdown. Tyrone felt a fierce hot ebullience surging through his chest as the players started jumping up and down and chanting the team's cheer.

The coaches came bustling through, trying to look grim and professional but unable to keep the smiles from tugging at the corners of their down-turned mouths.

It had been a damn good game.

Tyrone spotted Hank and DeShaun, inseparable as always, from across the room. DeShaun gave him a wink and tapped the side of his nose.

Tyrone grinned. For them, the night was only just starting.

* * *

"Oh my *God*, Ty! You were *amazing*. God, that was a great game! Wow!" Jennifer came clattering across the locker room floor, running pretty damn well considering the high heels she was wearing.

Ty grinned as she threw herself at him, wrapping her arms around his neck and beaming up at him. Who the heck wore high heels to watch a football game? He didn't care though, she looked incredible. Under her long jacket she had on a slinky black dress the clung to the curves of her body tight as a glove. Her makeup was spectacular, and made her eyes and mouth pop gorgeously. He leaned down low and kissed her deeply there in the middle of the empty locker room.

The place had cleared out pretty quick as everybody went their separate ways to this victory celebration or that one. Tonight, everybody was partying. Except the other team, of course. No doubt spirits were lower on the buses heading back out of town with the losers sitting on board. That was the way it went though. Today wasn't there day, tomorrow might be.

The locker room wasn't anything like the grubby dirty naked halls of Tyrone's high school. The college football team's locker room was state of the art and almost luxurious. There were hot tubs and a fully appointed exercise room packed with the most of advanced equipment available. There was a lounge and a theater for studying plays and game footage... just about anything you could want. The main room was a long area with nicely padded benches running along the length of the blue painted locker doors, with one hall leading to the showers, one to the other rooms and one on the other side heading towards the field.

Even so, it looked a little drab with Jennifer standing in it, resplendent and beautiful and smiling her megawatt smile.

He hugged her tight. "Happy birthday, babe."

She kissed him again. "Thank you, Ty..." She gazed up at him for a long moment, then broke away to look around. "So, am I going to get a tour, or what?"

"Yeah, sure. Why not? You ever been in a football team's locker before?"

"Well, I was a cheerleader in high school, so..." she giggled, pretending to blush. "Nothing like this though. It's amazing! God, it's like something an NFL team would have."

He laughed. "Not quite that nice, but yeah. It's pretty tight. You might have noticed they take their ball pretty serious around here."

"Yeah, I picked up on that." She stuck a finger in one ear for comic effect. "I think I almost went deaf after the cheering when you guys first scored."

Percy came tentatively down the steps, his hands in his pockets. Tyrone gave him an affable punch on the shoulder. Percy rocked back a little, but he grinned, nodding a greeting.

"How's it going, man?"

"Going well, thank you."

"Enjoy the game? I mean, I know football's not really your thing..."

"It was an experience. Jennifer kept me filled in on the particulars. You seemed to play very well."

"Hey, thanks man. Good to hear. So. You guys want a tour?"

Jennifer nodded excitedly, hopping a little bit on the tips of her toes and clapping her hands.

"Okay then, let's go take a look."

He gave them the full five-star tour of the place, even letting them take a peek in the coach's lounge, which was technically off limits to students, but what the hell. The whole place was technically off limits to Percy and Jennifer, but here they were anyway. Had to break the rules sometimes. Of course Percy had been hesitant at first once he found out that they'd be doing a little unauthorized exploring, but Tyrone had been able to convince him without too much trouble when he let the guy know what he had in mind for Jennifer tonight.

Her smile hadn't faltered for a moment as they'd looked around. Now, at the end of the tour, just outside the one room they hadn't gone in yet - the showers - she turned to him and grabbed his hand, clutching with in both of her own. "Wow, just *wow*! This is really frickin' cool, Ty, thank you so much for letting us come down here and see everything. It's really a good birthday present."

He grinned. "What, you thought this was your birthday present? Nah, babe. *This* is your birthday present." He wrapped his knuckles on the door frame of the showers.

Right on cue, Hank and DeShaun came out from the shower room, stripped out of their uniforms and dressed in nothing but big clean fluffy towels wrapped around their waists. He could see Jennifer's eyes widen as she took in their appearance. She glanced quickly from Tyrone to Percy to the two new arrivals and then back around once more, her mouth open and her face lighting up with a slowly dawning realization.

"No... no, you can't be serious... No, no way, this isn't..." she whirled around, looking at Percy, then at Tyrone. "You two *planned* this whole thing out, didn't you? Right?"

Percy grinned. "You said you wanted to go further, so... it was Tyrone's idea." He shrugged, "Happy birthday, hon."

"Oh my God, this is... wow." She cleared her throat, turning to Hank and DeShaun, her face flushed and pink. "Um... I'm Jennifer." She held her hand out to shake their hands, first one then the other.

"This is Hank. This is DeShaun. You saw them both play tonight. They're, uh, they're friends of mine from the Club. I asked 'em if they could do me a favor and make tonight a little special for you."

"Oh my God," she said, laughing and hiding her face behind her hands.

"I wasn't sure they'd be interested, but I gave them one look at your picture and they were both on board right away."

"Yeah man," DeShaun said, smiling as he moved in close, his hand sliding around behind Jennifer to hold the small of her back. "You looked so fine, ma'am, Hank and I couldn't wait to meet you in person."

"That's right," Hank grunted, moving around behind her, his huge hands settling down on her shoulders and giving them a surprisingly tender caress.

"Oh my God." She was smiling so wide that she couldn't hide it even with both hands on her face.

"You said that already," Tyrone said, reaching out to grab the zipper of her dress and slowly begin to draw it downward.

Behind him he heard Percy taking out his phone. Jennifer's husband stood silently by, phone held up to make a video recording of the scene unfolding before him.

Hank leaned in close to start kissing her neck, his big lips planting wet smooches on her shoulders. Tyrone slipped the zipper all the way down and started sliding the dress down off her body. DeShaun unhooked her bra and slipped it off, he leaned in and started licking her nipples, tongue flapping as his hand cupped and squeezed the other breast.

"W-what... I don't even know what to do..." she moaned.

"You don't have to do anything. Just lay back and leave it to us, birthday girl." Tyrone slipped his uniform off. Hank and DeShaun dropped their towels. They were already hard. Jennifer's hands found their cocks, moving automatically to grasp the thick black shafts. Hank was shorter and thicker, DeShaun longer but a bit more narrow. Tyrone stepped up to her, kissing her full on the mouth. He felt his own erection slip between her thighs, pushing in to nestle in the cleft of her legs.

She moaned against him, reaching out to stroke his back.

He picked her up, hands slipping down to grip her buttocks. He lifted her easily and laid her down on her back on the long bench. DeShaun and Hank stood one on either side of her head, stroking their cocks and moving up towards her open mouth.

She took one in her mouth first, then the other in turn, sucking the ebony tips and playing with their balls, one cock in each hand.

Hank groaned. He reached down to grab her head and turn her in his direction, stuffing his thick cock deep into her mouth. She opened wide, stretching her law open to take the whole thick shaft until his balls were caressing her cheek. DeShaun slapped his cock against her tits, one then the other. He swung his leg up and over her so that he was straddling her, and reached down to push her breasts together. He let a long dangling strand of warm spit fall from his mouth and rubbed it along his cock, then slipped it between her boobs.

Tyrone leaned down low. He grabbed the waistband of her black lace panties and slowly, very slowly, peeled them off and pulled them down. He left them looped around one ankle, and spread her legs wide. He sifted himself forward and entered her pussy, slipping it easily between the wet folds.

She moaned wordlessly, her mouth stuffed full, her tits fucked and her pussy pounded simultaneously. No more than two minutes ago she'd been fully dressed, standing there and talking to them. The three of them had moved in unison, with the same speed and precision as in any of the complex plays they'd executed on the field earlier.

Percy circled the activity, seeming somehow removed from the activity at hand, hidden behind the camera lens. "Wow... that looks amazing, honey. God, you're so hot right now..."

"Keep fucking me," she moaned, taking a deep breath, "keep fucking me, keep fucking me."

Hank stuffed his cock back in her mouth. "Don't talk, beautiful, just suck that big black dick. Just suck it."

Tyrone leaned forward, slowly letting himself fill her deeply, stretching her out inside. She shifted her hips to meet him, taking him fully inside her.

They moved in unison, all three men and the woman.

"These titties are so pretty," DeShaun said, grunting softly. "God*damn*, girl, you feel good."

Hank moved away, stroking himself and grinning. DeShaun got up, licking his lips and playing with her breasts.

"Okay guys," Tyrone said, "everybody get in line."

They fucked her pussy one after the other, first Tyrone then DeShaun and finally Hank. She gasped, her eyes flying open as his fat cock pushed into her, stretching her a little further than ever before.

"Oh God... oh God, that's a big cock." She flopped down on the bench, her pale legs splayed wide and her hands tangling in her hair.

Percy moved up closer to her, still holding the camera. He slid along the bench until he was looking down at her. "How big is that dick in you, baby?"

"It's so big..." she moaned, "Oh my *God*, honey, it's so *big*." She reached up, feeling at the front of his pants, stroking idly at his clothed little dick as she was used by the three black men in turn.

"You like it?" Percy asked. "Tell the camera."

She blinked, a little bleary and confused, then she reached up and took hold of the phone, not removing it from Percy's hands but pulling to down so that she was looking right up into it. Tyrone could see her face in the screen. She spoke slowly, emphasizing each and every word. "I. Love. It. I love black cock inside me. I love being used by three black cocks."

"Good girl," Tyrone grinned, stroking her flank with the back of his hand.

She lifted her head and smiled at him. "This is... the best birthday present..." she panted out before flopping her head back down.

"Shit!" Hank grunted, "I'm cumming!"

"Cum on those pretty titties," DeShaun said, pushing them together for his friend.

Hanks pearly white seed shot out in thick spurts, painting Jennifer's breasts with iridescent streaks that rolled slowly down the smooth white flesh. One thick drop dangled like a teardrop jewel from the perky tip of her pink nipple before falling and landing on her taut stomach.

DeShaun slapped her thigh, "Okay, beautiful. No me, go ahead and turn over for me."

Jennifer obeyed enthusiastically, turning over so that she was on her hands and knees on the bench. DeShaun stood behind her, slipping his long dick into her sloppy wet hole and fucking her fast and hard. He came quick, pulling out to spray his cum over her back.

"Oh my God," she said, laughing and rolling slightly from side to side. "You got me all over... I'm so covered in cum..."

"Do you like that cum, sweetie?"

She smiled once more into the camera. "I love it." She took a deep breath, and looked around the locker room. "Well, he came on my front and he came on my back... where do you want to go, Ty?"

He bent his head close, pressing his forehead against hers. He kissed her softly. Their eyes were open, his soft brown and hers cool blue. They looked not at each other but into one another. "You know," he said.

"You want to cum inside me?" she asked, her voice soft and breathy.

He just nodded.

She smiled. "Good. I need your seed in me, Ty, I need it so bad."

He just nodded, and lifted her up off the bench. He carried her down the hall a few feet and into the showers. Her legs wrapped around his waist and her arms around his neck. She kissed him softly as he carried her. Her long silky blonde hair fell like a shower of pale goldenrod about him. It felt like they were alone in the world, even if there were three other men watching them intently. She reached down, lifting her hips a little away from him, and she slipped his cock into herself, moaning against his neck as he filled her up.

"That's right," she murmured, "that's just where you should be. Just there inside me."

He nodded. "I know. That's right where I wanna be, baby."

She started to rock against him, grinding herself on his cock.

He carried her into the showers and turned on the water. It rained down on them, steaming hot and clean. He felt the sweat running off his body. Her damp hair clung to them both, surrounding them.

"This right here... this is what I need."

Tyrone growled. He'd never felt this turned on, enveloped by her body like this, living inside her as the steam rose about them in pale clouds. He caught a glimpse of himself in the mirror at the far end of the room. His black skin, her white skin, her hands on his back, her ankles crossed as she rocked herself back and forth.

He stepped forward, pressing her back against the wall of the showers. He pushed her against the wet tile, and he fucked her hard.

She started to breath fast and shallow, her hands closing and opening, her fingernails raking down his back. "Yes, yes, yes... fuck me like this, Ty, fuck me so good. Fill me up, fill me up, cum inside me, cum... cum... cum... cum..." She whispered that last work over and over in his ear, murmuring it again and again as he pounded her.

Finally, he obeyed. He felt his whole body shake as he emptied himself into her body, flooding her womb with his gushing seed. He almost dropped her, but tightened his grip, leaning against her as he came.

"Hm..." she moaned softly, stroking the back of his head, holding him close against her. "Thank you... thank you..."

He looked up once he'd regained control of himself, and he grinned shakily. "No problem."

She smiled, and reached down to hold his face in her hands, one slender palm on each cheek as she stared into his face. "Hey, Ty?"

"Yeah?"

"Do you think you could give me one last birthday present?"

"What's that, babe?"

She just smiled.

* * *

"You're really sure you want to do this?" he asked, a couple hours later, his hands wrapped around hers.

She nodded, and leaned her head back against the cushion. "I'm sure, Ty. I want everybody to see how I feel. Want them to know that I belong to you."

He grinned. "Okay, baby. Okay." He looked up and nodded at Lynette.

"You ready, darling?" the mixed race artist asked, tugging at her lip piercing and watching Jennifer's face. She held the tattoo needle poised in her hand.

Jennifer nodded. "I'm ready."

"Alright then," Lynette said, leaning down, "let's get started. This may hurt a little."

Jennifer turned to look at Tyrone. She winced a little and squeezed his hand tight as the needle first pricked the skin of her calf.

On the table was a drawing of the tattoo she wanted. A black spade with a white space left inside it in the shape of the letter Q.

The Queen of Spades.

Book Three: Crown for the Queen

Chapter One

Welcome to Miami.

Percy Brice stepped out of the sleek company car and looked up at the imposing glass and steel facade of the hotel in which he would be spending the foreseeable future. He groaned, and slung his bag over his shoulder. Hotel living had long since lost its glamour for him. Too many dreary nights away from home while on a case. It wasn't quite as bad in the glorious Florida heat as it had been back home in wintry Minnesota, but he still felt a pang to be back home with his wife.

Jennifer had promised to stay in touch with him frequently, as she always did. And he knew she would. She knew how hard it was for him to be away, and she'd always paid special attention to his low moods when he was away. She was very gracious that way, very kind. He still wasn't sure what he'd ever done to deserve such a woman, and still woke up pinching himself every morning. He didn't even mind the fact that he had to share her...

And then, all of sudden coming unbidden into his head, a picture of Jennifer laying on her back in the College Football team's locker room, three black men taking turns with their cocks in her mouth. And not just her mouth either...

He shook his head, trying to clear away the image. Not because he didn't like thinking about it - he most certainly did, and had watched the video tape of the event dozens of times since it had taken place - but because he needed to focus. This was the first big case he was taking on for his new Firm, and he would need all his focus. It wasn't often Percy went to court, most of his lawyerly skills were applied in meeting rooms and conference calls rather than in front of a jury. This case was different, however, and he'd need his A game.

He wouldn't be alone in the courtroom, however. Jonas Harrington, the eccentric head of the firm, had informed him that he would be serving as co-council for someone from the

Miami office, a young up-and-coming attorney. James, he thought the name was. It was in the file he'd been provided with, but Percy had hardly had a chance to look it over yet. There would be plenty of time for that later, plenty of long lonely hotel room nights for pursuing boring paperwork. He had wanted to make his last few nights with Jennifer as pleasurable as possible.

"Oh, God... Oh God, Daddy..." she'd moaned, laying on her back right there on the kitchen table, her legs spread wide and her hands cupping her own breasts, fingers circling and pinching her puffy nipples. Tyrone, her African-American bull, had been deep inside her, his every thrust making her quiver and groan and clutch the sides of the table for support. She'd leaned her head back, and looked up at Percy, who had been standing opposite the table from Tyrone. She had smiled at him, the most beautiful smile he could imagine, and she'd opened her mouth, putting out her tongue and gesturing for him to take off his pants. Percy had glanced up at Tyrone, who'd given his permission with a grin and a nod, and Percy had pulled out his hard little erection, right there in his own kitchen. Jennifer had leaned her head back towards him, her mouth open wide, and she'd-

But no, no! This wasn't the time for that. *There you go again, Percy.* He resisted the impulse to slap himself. He had to *focus.* He pushed through the swinging glass doors and walking into the lobby. It was a ritzy looking place, he had to give it that. Probably the nicest looking hotel he'd ever stayed in. But of course Jonas was very much of the opinion that image counted for a great deal, and that no image was better to project than that of wealth and prestige.

He looked around the lobby. James was supposed to be here, he was sure of it. He didn't see anybody who looked like a lawyer, however. Just great. He set his bag down and took a seat in the lounge area. He glanced at his watch. Well, he was on time, anyway.

He felt a shadow fall across feet, and looked up.

A pair of cherry red high heels, lacquered and shining. Black pantyhose over shapely legs, a tight but professional goldenrod yellow pencil skirt and suite coat. Bright red lipstick, smoky eye-shadow, a stern expression. A woman stood over him, her arms folded and her brows arched. Her skin was perfect ebony black of dark marble, and her dark eyes flashed. "Percy Brice, I assume?" her voice was mannered and her tone clipped. An English accent, he thought, or traces of one at any rate.

He leaped to his feet, patting down his flyaway hair and pulling at his rumpled suit. "Yes, ahem, um, yes indeed. Thank you."

She gave him a look of cool dismissal and held out her hand. "Natasha James."

"N-Natasha, of course," Percy laughed awkwardly, reaching for her hand. She gave him quite a firm handshake, her delicate dark fingers with their crimson polish belying the strength of her grip. "Jonas didn't tell me you were a, uh, a woman. I heard 'James' and well, oh but never mind..." He trailed off, withering under her unimpressed gaze.

She turned away, crooking a finger after for him to follow. He grabbed up his bags and scuttled behind her. She spoke as she walked without missing a step, "There are a great many things which Jonas neglects to mention. I think you'll find that he can be quite secretive, in his way. For example, I'm sure he declined to inform you that I was strongly opposed to the idea of having another lawyer on this case."

Percy adjusted his glasses and cleared his throat. "He, um, he didn't, no."

She whirled on him, and he had to stop dead in his tracks to avoid running right into her. "I didn't ask for you, Mr. Brice, and I don't especially need you. Jonas seems to be under the impression that you'll be helpful, however. All I ask is that you keep out of my way and let me win this case. Do we understand each other?"

He blinked rapidly. "Perfectly," he said, his voice timid and subdued.

Her eyebrows arched even further, something he'd not thought possible, and she whirled back around and kept walking. "Hm. I trust you are *at least* up to speed on the case, Mr. Brice?"

He flushed. "Ah, well, I have the file here and I'll be sure to-"

She turned and shot him a steely look. "Yes," she said, "please do." Then she handed him a plastic keycard. "The elevator is there, Mr. Brice. You are in room 377. I will be in the Jefferson Conference room at 6:00 tomorrow morning. Please do acquaint yourself with the particulars before then. We have a great deal of work to do."

He took the card, stammering, "I, uh, I'll do that, to be sure. Of course. See you then. I'm very pleased to be working with you!" his voice rose in volume towards the end there, as she'd turned and started walking away long before then. He shook his head and stepped into the elevator. He jabbed the button for the third floor. The moment the doors were closed he let out a deep and heavy sigh and slumped against the wall.

This was going to be quite an adventure after all.

* * *

-Are U doing alright, honey?

-I don't know. It's a tough case, and the other attorney seems like she's going to be on my ass. Not literally, of course.

-Haha. U should be so lucky ;)

-I don't know what I'm going to do, Jen. I don't like it here. I miss you.

-Aw, that's so sweet, baby. I miss U too. Sure U can't come back?

-I wish. Jonas would kill me. He seemed quite insisted that I be here. Said something about being a moderating influence. I guess I know what he means now. The other attorney is a bit of a ball-buster. Might not play well in court.

-Is she that bad?

-Not bad. Just intense. Real shark, if you know what I mean.

-Ugh, I hate lawyers! Present company not included :P

-I know the feeling. Sometimes I wonder if I'm in the wrong profession.

-Just stay strong. I'll see U soon enough.

-I know. A month just feels like a really long time. Are you seeing our friend tonight?

-No :(

-How come? I thought it was your night?

-He says he has a big assignment due. Can't make it. He says I'll distract him from his studies too much.

-Which is true.

-Haha, yes.

-I love you, honey.

-Aw, now you're leaving me too?

-Sorry. I have a ton of paperwork to get through before morning. Going to be a crazy night as it is.

-Okay... goodnight, Percy.

-Goodnight, sweetheart.

* * *

Jennifer Brice tossed her smart phone onto the bed with a groan and flopped back down onto her pillow.

She looked at the lingerie hanging up just inside the closet door and pouted. Not that it did any good, with nobody there to appreciate her moping. She hated being home alone. And Percy was going to gone for an *entire month*. She'd been hoping to at least see Ty, but he was so busy with school. His senior year of college was going to be intense and difficult, he'd told her, but he would make as much time as possible for her, he'd promised. Well, it was looking like "as much time as possible" wasn't going to be enough to keep her satisfied.

Miami wasn't so far away, just a two hour drive. Maybe she could go and see him sometime, just to break up the monotony of being by herself. Not that he would have much time for her. She knew how these big cases were, they sucked up lawyer's hours like nothing else.

She got up and pulled open her underwear drawer and started digging into the piles of bras and panties and mismatched socks. Finally she found it, her little savior: an inch long silver bullet vibrator. It was the only thing that had gotten her through the long nights and business trips and years of suffering through Percy's sexual deficiencies. She hadn't needed it for a long time now, not since Ty had come into her life.

Looked like she was on her own again for tonight though. She'd been so ready for Ty, had been expecting him all day long, and then at the last minute he'd bailed. *Ty,* she thought to herself, *you've driven me to this.*

She got under her covers and snuggled up and slipped her hand down between her thighs. She pushed the little rubber button with her thumb and moved the bullet into position, and she waited. It hummed away in her finger, buzzing pleasantly.

Nothing.

She frowned, shifting her hips, scooting down a little bit, pressing it more firmly against her clitoris. It felt alright, and gave her a nice little tickle, but it wasn't making her feel *good.* Not the way it used to.

She groaned, reaching one hand out and feeling around on the bedside table for her phone. She scrolled through her pictures, found an image of Ty's cock. That was more like it. She felt herself getting more receptive already, feeling that swooping loosening flutter down there, the gradual moistening starting to happen. *Come on, little guy, don't let me down.*

She scrolled through the pictures. God, it was beautiful. That huge black cock, so thick and juicy and full. She loved having it in her hands, in her mouth, everywhere. She'd never felt this way about somebody's body part before, had always considered herself above all that. When guys talked about girl's butts or breasts she had always laughed, shaking her head, thinking that they were immature and silly. She understood a little better now.

Ty was more than just a cock, though. He was everything. She closed her eyes and she tried to recall the exact feel of his hands on her body, his lips brushing against her neck, his deep brown eyes gazing into hers.

"Ugh..." a soft moan slipped out from between her lips. She needed him, needed him so bad right now.

The loneliness was no longer the most pressing issue for her. She needed a particular kind of companionship, and she needed it right now, or she was going to lose her mind. The phone screen glowed. She stared at it, extremely tempted to send Ty a text. Come over and fuck me, please please please please.

No. No, she was better than that. She was going to respect his needs, his life. He had more going on than just pleasing her. She was an adult woman, not some desperate schoolgirl. She could be patient. He would see her soon, she was sure of that.

The vibrator buzzed.

She groaned, smacking her head against the pillow. "Come *on*!" she instructed the little device, "come on..." She could already tell that it wasn't going to get her where she wanted to go.

She reached down, touching a finger experimentally between her pussy lips. Still a bit dry. She didn't think it would feel that good right now to put her fingers inside herself. And besides, her slender little digits couldn't possibly hope to compare to the sensation of his big cock filling her up, stretching her out so fully...

No, she wasn't going to text him. Not tonight.

She reached down and touched her ankle. It had finally stopped itching. Her tattoo looked amazing, the little black spade with the letter Q. Nobody had seen it yet except Percy and Ty and the artist. Queen of Spades. Owned by black cock. Percy's eyes had just about bugged out of his head when she'd first shown it to him. Ty had loved it.

But that black dick wasn't here, now was he? So what was a girl to do?

She opened her web browser. "Okay, okay, okay..." she stuck her tongue out and tapped on the icon for her search engine. Uh... how did this, work, anyway? She'd never looked for this kind of thing online before. By the time it was as readily available as it was now she considered herself very much grown out of that kind of thing. She liked the occasional smutty romance novel, but pornography? No thank you.

She needed something tonight though, needed it bad. She typed with one hand, somewhat awkwardly. *Black cock porn.* She blushed just looking at the words. Come *on*, Jennifer, what are you *thinking*? She screwed her eyes shut and hit the search button.

When she opened her eyes again the screen was filled with results, an overwhelming array, almost too much.

She clicked on the first link, flinching inwardly as the screen started to load, the little progress bar filling slowly. The ads loaded first, sidebars and suggested videos popping up all over the little screen. Her eyes went wide and she jabbed the exit button and slapped the phone back down on her bedside table.

No, porn was not for her. Anyway, she doubted that a video would help much. She needed the real thing.

Just then, with a faint whirring sound, her vibrator died.

* * *

-Are U still up, Ty?

-Yeah, I'm here. What's going on, baby?

-I need U...

-Aw, poor baby. I'm sorry; I really can't make it over tonight.

-Are U sure?

-Afraid so...

-But I need your cock... :(

-I'm sorry. I'll make it up to you. But if I don't get this assignment in I'm going to flunk calculus. Probably get kicked off the football team. Probably be expelled, have to go back home and live with my parents... Have to get a job at the local grocery store. I'll be a bagger until I'm sixty. So I really need to get this assignment done.

-Okay okay, I get it. No need to be so hyperbolic. I just miss U...

-I miss you too. I mean it. And I will make it up to you.

-Okay...

-Kisses.

-Kisses, Daddy.

* * *

Tyrone shut the messenger program and opened word processor once more.

He felt a stirring below, and tried to ignore it. He didn't have time for being aroused right now, though it wasn't easy. He never would have expected to find himself having feelings like this about someone like her. She was such a dynamo of sexual energy that sometimes he forgot that she was, when it really came down to it, a middle-aged housewife. And he was a college student, a star football player.

Anyone he knew would probably think he was crazy for preferring Jennifer to all the other girls, closer to his own age that he could easily have been seeing. This is the time to be screwing as many chicks as you can find, they would say, not getting tied down to one person. Especially not if she was a married white woman in her late thirties.

He shook his head and turned his attention back to the book in front of him.

Anyway, he didn't know how much time he was going to have for her this year anyway. Senior year was turning out to be more of a struggle than he'd anticipated. There were plenty of guys he knew who were all too happy to spend their days drinking and fucking around, not a care in the world. They were the ones who didn't care about flunking out, though. Or the ones whose parents were rich enough that they *couldn't* flunk out.

Tyrone wasn't like that. He wanted to make something of himself. He had a sports scholarship, but he doubted a career in the NFL was in the cards for him. He was going to need a real career someday, and if he was going to do that, he'd have to really focus. It had been easy enough for the first few semesters. He'd rocked out a 3.9 without breaking a sweat.

These last two semesters were going to be harder, though.

"Oh *God*, yes! Harder! Harder! Do it to me harder!"

He groaned, his head dropping into his hands. Barry and Becky had been going at it almost non-stop pretty much since the start of the semester. His roommate was one of those twenty year old virgins who suddenly got a girlfriend and realized just what they'd been missing out on, and decided to try and make up for lost time.

That was fine for Barry and all, but it was making Tyrone's semester a thousand times more difficult. It didn't help that he was pretty sure Becky was interested in Tyrone. He had a sneaking suspicion that it was her idea to screw in the next room so that Tyrone would have to listen to them. She was being extra loud for his benefit, he was sure of it.

His phone dinged, and he tried to suppress groan of frustration. It was hard enough to resist Jennifer when she wasn't throwing herself at him. He wanted nothing more than to head out and catch the late bus to her house uptown. He forced himself to stare at the screen, fingers poised over the keys.

Goddamn it. He snatched up the phone and looked at the screen.

It was a text message alright, but not from Jennifer. He felt his eyebrows rise incredulously when he recognized the number. It was from Marquis, the assistant head coach and manager of The Black and White Club, the exclusive interracial swingers club where Tyrone and Jennifer had first met. He opened the text.

-Tyrone. Have a proposition for you. Something I think you'll be interested in. You and your lady. Get back to me.

Tyrone stared down at the message. A proposition, eh? The last proposition Tyrone had gotten from Marquis had been an invitation to the club. It had been the moment which set this whole crazy thing into motion.

He looked at the computer screen, and his homework, then back down at the message. Then back again.

He sighed heavily and started to write.

-What sort of proposition did you have in mind?

Chapter Two

"We're going to attack on two different fronts, essentially. First, we call into question the validity of their so-called experts, which shouldn't be all that difficult considering that none of them has the faintest idea what it is they're talking about. Second, we go after the timeline. *When* did they get the news about the manufacturing flaw, when was it reported, when did they try and put the blame on our client? It paints a clear picture of wrongdoing on their part and... Mr. Brice, am I boring you?"

Percy snapped upright, eyes going wide.

Natasha James was looking at him across the conference room table, her steely dark eyes boring right into him and her mouth set in a firm and disapproving line. She stood with a hand on one slender hip, the other loosely holding a long wooden pointer which she'd been using to indicate information on the projected slide for the benefit of the roomful of lawyers and paralegals. Her grip on the pointer tightened as she eyed him.

Percy stammered. "Uh, um, no, of course not. Not at all. Very compelling stuff. I was just consulting my notes," He'd been up all night studying the case information and, even after a half a dozen cups of strong coffee, he was having trouble remaining entirely conscious. Sleep... ah, sleep would feel so amazing...

Natasha shook her head disdainfully and turned back to the information.

It was a dull case. Big, certainly, but very dull. A conflict between two plastics manufacturing conglomerates, one of whom was represented by Percy's firm. Their clients were being sued over some kind of defective product which had gone to market, a child's toy, he thought it was. Their clients said that it was actually the fault of the larger corporation, while they alleged that the subsidiary corporation was responsible for the product. Percy's clients argued that the toy had only been defective due to a faulty part provided by the larger company and that they were ultimately responsible for the error.

It was tedious stuff.

Percy was used to tedium, however. Corporate law didn't tend to get as exciting as it looked in John Grisham novels, after all. Still, with his lack of sleep and feelings of homesickness, not to mention the general hostility displayed by the staff of the Miami office, he was finding it especially difficult to remain engaged.

Natasha and her underlings had been less than welcoming, to say the least. They all seemed to resent the fact that Jonas had seen fit to provide them with outside assistance. More than that, they seemed entirely subservient to Natasha. They seemed to have sense that she didn't like him, and taken it as their sworn duty to emulate her. It wasn't just that, however. They seemed utterly devoted to her in a way that went beyond the usual supervisor-underling relationship. They gazed reverently at her when she walked passed, fell over one another for the honor of bringing her her morning coffee and generally gave the impression that they worshiped the very ground upon which she walked.

If he could somehow win her over, he had the notion that the rest of them would warm up to him in no time. He certainly hadn't made much progress on that front so far, however. Not that she'd given him much opportunity.

"Perhaps you have something to add, Mr. Brice?" she said, eyeing him with a look somewhere between amusement and condescension.

"Ah..." he flipped uselessly through his notepad, stalling for time. There was hardly anything written down in it, to be entirely honest. "This, um... this Mr. Weber... We've spoken with him?"

The tip of the pointer clacked on the table. "Fred Weber. Yes, the factory supervisor in charge of the manufacture of the item. We've interviewed him extensively. What's you're point?"

"Well, uh... perhaps I just missed it, but it doesn't appear that he was ever questioned about the, eh, what do you call it? The plans."

"The plans? What plans might those be, Mr. Brice?"

A light chuckle, barely suppressed, moved around the table.

Percy frowned. "The plans for the toy itself. It says here that the manufacturing plan updates made on the seventh were approved by Weber, and the productions faults first started showing up around that time. That could be exploited to make our client appear liable."

The chuckling faded. Natasha gave him a very long, very penetrating look. Finally, twisting the grip of the pointer in her hand, she nodded. "That's something we'll look into. Thank you, Mr. Brice." Then her eyes flashed, and she turned to look at her little group of paralegals and junior lawyers. "Who was in charge of the Weber interview?" she snapped.

A man in a beige suit raised a trembling hand. "Uh... I, Uh, I was... Miss James..."

The pointer thwacked down on the table with a loud crack, and Percy jumped. Everybody flinched. The man in beige started sweating, his trembling intensifying.

Natasha's eyes narrowed as she stared him down. "We'll discuss this slip-up further in private, Matthew." Her voice was quiet, and ice cold.

"T-t-thank you, Miss James," Matthew stammered, wilting in his seat.

Percy watched the whole exchange with mounting worry. The lawyer seemed terrified, almost petrified in his seat. Everybody looked away from him, seeming to pretend he was there among them, like they were afraid of being caught up in his indiscretion. The whole thing was quite intimidating to Percy.

What in the world was going on around here?

* * *

Jennifer slept quite poorly after her aborted attempt at self-pleasure.

It just wasn't the same anymore. Sex without Tyrone simply held no appeal any longer. She couldn't satisfy herself, and Percy certainly couldn't satisfy her. She really was owned by black cock now. Nothing else even turned her on anymore.

She sighed heavily, tugging on her stockings and slipping into a pair of burgundy pumps. That wouldn't be a problem if had guaranteed access to it, but that was turning out not to be the case. The whole previous year had been an exercise in restrain and subdued longing, when she'd have much rather it been an orgiastic unending fuck-fest...

Careful, Jennifer, you're starting to sound like some kind of nymphomaniac!

She had to get her mind off things. There had been a text waiting for her when she'd woken. From Tyrone, apologizing for not being able to come by and making some vague promise about some big plan he had coming together. Something that was going to "make up for it" in his words. She was dubious.

Never mind, she was going to go clothes shopping. If that couldn't distract her, nothing would.

It was a beautiful September day, the sun shining and not a cloud in the sky. Everybody was dressed minimally, very typical for Florida. She still wasn't quite used to it, all that skin on display almost all the time. She couldn't help glancing out the window while she idled at the stop light across from the beach. Her eyes went immediately to one man in particular, a tall muscular black man in a little red swim suit that left practically nothing to the imagination. She found herself staring, open mouthed. A slender blonde woman jogged across the sand and looped her arm through his, smiling adoringly up at him. He grinned and reached around behind her, patting her backside gently.

Jennifer felt strange little tickle down below, and her grip on the steering wheel tightened. God, she couldn't escape it, could she?

Honk!

She jumped, glancing back over her shoulder at the car behind her. The driver made an angry gesture at her. She waved him off, putting the car back in drive and heading on her way, turning her attention fully back to the road.

Come on, Jennifer. Get a grip...

The clothing store helped her calm down, but it didn't get her mind entirely off of things. She kept spotting fancy underwear and lacy tops and thinking of wearing them for Tyrone... of his hands sliding the straps off her shoulders and baring herself to him... of his dark hands on her pale round breasts...

She went to the opposite end of the store and looked at shoes, trying not to imagine what it would be like to get screwed in the dressing room. On her way there she passed the infant's section, and had to tear herself away from the adorable little outfits and baby toys. Someday. She went on further, leaving that section behind. She picked up a pair of heels. They would probably make her ass look great, and she knew how Ty felt about her behind...

"Oh my *God*, is that you, Jennifer? I was just *thinking* about you..."

Jennifer whirled around. A tiny little woman was staring at her with a smile of open-mouthed amazement. At first Jennifer didn't recognize the pale and slender woman and looked back blankly. Then it came to her. It had been a long time, almost a year at this point, but she had met the woman before. It had been their very first night in Florida; they'd gone to a party thrown by Percy's boss.

"Matilda? It is Matilda, right? Matilda Harrington?"

Tilly nodded, her hands on her hips. "*Yes*, of *course*. My *God*, Jennifer, it's been far too long. Why have we never had any girl time together? That's strange, isn't it?"

Jennifer blinked, feeling a bit blindsided by the whole exchange. Why should they have spent any time together? They'd hardly met at the party, and had no contact since. The firm wasn't big on family days. There had been a July Fourth barbecue, but she'd declined to attend, having experienced the agony of law firm barbecues more than enough times to know better at this point. "Well, I suppose it is..."

"Of *course* it is, Jennifer. What with all of our shared interests, and all..." she winked, nudging Jennifer and smiling conspiratorially.

"What shared interests might that be...? Oh." That's when she remembered. She'd never put the pieces together before, but hadn't Percy told her that his boss was the one who'd recommended the club to him? Back then she hadn't known just what sort of club it actually was. It made sense now. She thought back to the beautiful tall black man who Matilda had been so attached to. He'd been older than Tyrone, but had something of a similar vibe about him. He must have been Matilda's bull...

Matilda winked again. "That's right; you know what I'm talking about."

Jennifer blushed.

"Oh, don't be shy. Our little secret, my lips are sealed."

"So, um... how did you... you know?"

"Start?"

"Yeah."

Matilda laughed. "It's a long story. Sure you want to hear it?"

Jennifer looked around the store. She wondered if any of those people had any idea of the sort of things which went on right under their noses. She certainly wouldn't have guessed. So much had changed for her in the last year, it was almost unbelievable. She shrugged. "I don't have anything else going on."

Matilda laughed again. "Alright. Come on, there's a cafe next door, I'll buy you a latte."

* * *

She blew foam off the top of her coffee, nursing the enormous cup in her tiny little hands. "I was twenty-two years old when I married Jonas. He was... older. But he was smart and funny and had this energy that I really clicked with. And of course he was rich. Easy to say that doesn't matter, but we both know that it counts for a lot. I wasn't some gold digger, though. I really loved Jonas. There was only one way in which he didn't satisfy me, which was... Well, you know." She giggled softly and bent down to lick the tip of the whipped cream in her cup.

"I know the feeling," Jennifer said wryly, shaking her head. Her own latte looked quite plain next to Matilda's, which had enough cream and sugar and extras to qualify as a desert more than a beverage.

"Fortunately, Jonas had already anticipated my... needs. He'd been a member of the club for years, knew everybody. He took me there on our wedding night, you know."

Jennifer felt her jaw drop. "Your *wedding night*? Are you serious?"

Matilda laughed again. "Of course, silly. Why not? I was his during the day, but after dark I belonged to them. There were six of them, one after the other while Jonas watched from the corner of the room, still in his tuxedo. I had my wedding dress on through the whole thing. You can imagine the dry cleaning bill."

Jennifer wasn't entirely sure if Matilda was being serious or not, but she suspected that it wasn't entirely a joke.

"Marquis took me last, and I knew right away that he was the one for me. We really bonded that night, and it's been the two of us ever since. Well, the *three* of us, really. I love it."

Six in one night! Jennifer had thought she'd been extreme for having sex with three men at once, but apparently she had a long way left to go. Not that she would ever go that far. To be honest, that night, as amazing as it had been, pushed her limits a bit further than she was entirely comfortable with. She was glad she'd done it, and wouldn't take it back for anything, but she didn't think she'd ever do something like that again. "Yes but... had you ever done anything like that before? I mean, that's quite an initiation," she said.

Matilda took a sip of her coffee and shrugged. "Oh, I was always a naughty girl, I suppose. I had quite and adventurous time in high school."

Jennifer just shook her head.

Matilda laughed once more. "My goodness, Jennifer Brice, don't act like such an Old Susan. I know what you're really like." Her eyes twinkled gaily. "Why, I know a great deal about what sort of naughty things you've been up to."

Jennifer arched an eyebrow at that, but didn't ask. To be honest, she didn't want to know.

* * *

Tyrone stepped into the assistant football coach's office. "Okay, okay, I'm here," he said, "What's so important that you couldn't tell me over the phone." He slouched down into the seat across Marquis and only then did he notice that they were not the only two people in the room. A rotund little gentlemen in a smartly cut little bottle green suit stood at the window with his hands clasped behind he back. His hair was snow white, matching his beard and neatly combed. He didn't turn around.

Marquis smiled, his bright white teeth shining. "Tyrone," he said, his deep voice even and calm, "let me introduce you to Reginald G. Mason."

"This really is a charming little school," the old man said, bouncing a little on his toes, his attention still focused out the window at the campus beyond.

"Reggie, this is Tyrone. The boy I was telling you about."

Only now did the old man turn, a warm smile on his face. He looked Tyrone up and down and gave an approving nod. "Lovely to meet you, my lad, truly lovely. I've heard great things."

Tyrone blinked. "You have?"

"Yes, indeed. Oh, don't worry. Nothing incriminating or overly personal. Just... we've been very pleased with your performance."

"We? Who is we, exactly?" Tyrone felt a suspicious concern starting to form. What was really going on here?

Marquis leaned forward. "Reggie is the founder and owner of the Black and White Club. You could call him our benefactor, if you like to think of it that way."

Tyrone frowned. "Okay... so what exactly is it that can I do for our... benefactor? What's your proposal, exactly?"

"Ah yes. Well. My dear wife, darling Penelope, has a birthday coming up shortly. She's getting on in years, just as I am, but she's still a beautiful girl and I am of the opinion that she deserves only the very best. My friend Marquis here informs that you may be that person."

"Oh."

Reginald G. Mason grinned, a marry twinkle in his eye. "It has been some time now since Penny and I were, well, you might say active in the scene. The two of us go back quite a long way, however, and we've a great deal of experience with this. What we need is someone fresh, someone *new*. A real young buck to give her a right good tumble, you see what I mean?"

Marquis leaned forward, his hands clasped. "It's quite an honor to be asked, Tyrone. Mr. Mason has done a great deal for all of us with the founding of his club. He's been extremely generous."

"And I would continue to be so," Reginald added, "I wouldn't ask you to do this for nothing. I'd be delighted to offer a sizable monetary incentive. Oh, not as payment, certainly. Nothing so crass. Simply a token of my appreciation for entertaining an old couple. We would be delighted if you'd accept."

Tyrone looked across the heavy oak desk at the two older men. What were they asking him, really? It sounded an awful lot like they wanted him to be some kind of gigolo, or something. He wasn't sure how he felt about that...

His relationship with Jennifer had come about naturally, based on mutual attraction. They both been at the club for the same reason, more or less, and had entered into the relationship on equal footing, for the most part. This sounded like it was going to be something different entirely.

Reginald seemed to sense his hesitation. He held up a white-gloved hand to forestall any potential objection. "Don't say anything yet, my boy. Take your time, think it over. As for myself, I wouldn't let just anybody into my bedchamber. Not that I don't have complete faith in my friend here," he patted the back of Marquis' chair, "but some things a man must see with his own eyes before he agrees to strike a deal."

"You want me to *audition*?"

Reginald laughed. "I suppose you could say that! My good friend Jonas Harrington is throwing a bit of a soiree this weekend, and I've been so bold as to invite your Mrs. Brice. I thought perhaps the two of you might be interested in providing something of a show. Along with Marquis and good Jonas' wife, of course. I would be most honored to see you in action, my boy. Well, what do you say?"

Tyrone leaned back in his seat, chewing his lower lip and thinking on it. He wasn't sure how he felt about any of this. Still, he'd promised Jennifer that he was working on something after getting that message about a proposal from Marquis, and he felt like he owed her something. It sounded like the sort of thing she might be very much into, anyway, even if it didn't end up leading to anything further on.

He'd have to consider this whole deal with Mason and his wife a good deal more, but a party at some rich lawyer's house and sex with Jennifer? He could handle that.

He tilted his seat back and grinned. "Sounds like a plan," he said.

Reginald G. Mason smiled serenely, and stuck his gloved hands in his pockets. "Excellent."

Chapter Three

Percy frowned at the document in his hands. He read it again, for what must have been the sixth or seventh time. He felt like he was going to go cross-eyed if he kept up at this for much longer. Maybe it was time for a break. He pulled out his phone, glancing up and checking to make sure he was alone, even though he was locked in his hotel room all by himself. No messages. Gosh darn it! He sent Jennifer a quick text.

-Missing you terribly, darling. It seems like it's been weeks instead of days. Have you seen our friend yet? I'm desperate for some new pictures of you "in action." Feeling very lonely here, and could use a pick-me-up if you get a chance.

He looked at the phone, as if expecting a sudden deluge of photos. Of course nothing came. It was early; she was probably still sleeping, or downstairs having coffee and reading the paper. She probably didn't have her phone on her at the moment anyway.

He sighed and went back to his document. Well now, this might be something... He read it again. Was this the tenth time now? But yes, there was definitely something there. Did it warrant showing the thing to Natasha? He dreaded the interaction, but he supposed it couldn't be helped. They were going to have to work together whether she liked it or not, and that was that. He tucked the folder under his arm, then thought better of it. He switched his phone to camera mode and snapped a quick picture of the relevant passage. Better not to risk losing the document in the hallway. He'd just show her the image.

Mentally bracing himself, he headed out and went off to Natasha's room. She was one floor up from him, in 431 if he recalled correctly. He wondered idly as he rode the elevator up if it would be worthwhile to rent out an office building here in Miami instead of taking up all these hotel rooms. Surely the bill would be astronomical by the end of the trial.

Of course, given how many hours were being billed, the hotel costs would only by a drop in the bucket out of the total.

He strode down the hall and lifted his hand, poised to knock on the door of room 431 when he heard something rather odd. It sounded like... no; it *was* a kind of soft whimpering coming from inside. He thought it might be a dog or a puppy for a moment, but no, the sound was definitely human. Then a sharp smacking sound, quite loud, and the whimpering intensified for a moment before fading again.

She must be watching television. Funny, he wouldn't have thought Natasha would be the sort to idle her days away when she could be working. He'd gotten a picture of her in his mind that she was quite the hard-nosed workaholic, but he supposed everybody needed a break once in a while.

He knocked.

There was nothing at first, no sound from within. After a long moment the door swung in, and Natasha looked out at him, an expression of smoldering annoyance on her features. It took him a moment to register the fact, but she was dressing in a somewhat peculiar outfit. All black leather with shining silver buckles and straps, very tight, almost form fitting. She wore a tight black choker and had her hair tied up in a tight bun.

"Mr. Brice. To what do I own the pleasure?" She didn't look especially pleased to Percy, but he didn't dispute the technicality.

"Yes, well, um. I was looking over the Fraser document again, and I thing I've identified some important inconsistencies which we might be able to use to our advantage when the times comes."

"Oh?" She looked intrigued. The Weber incident had bought him at least a slight amount of grudging respect.

"That's right. I, uh. Well, here's the relevant portion." He passed her his smartphone.

She took it, a little dubiously, and turned the screen on. She looked down at the screen for a moment, a look of intense focus on her sternly elegant ebony features. "Mr. Brice," she finally said, "is this some sort of joke? Or perhaps a poor attempt at awkward flirtation. Either way, I'm not sure I entirely appreciate the gesture."

She thrust the phone back at him and he took it, frowning, quite confused. Then he saw what was on the screen. Jennifer had sent him a picture. It just have just come through as he'd passed the phone over. The notification would have been on the main page, and when her thumb had swiped the screen it had opened the text.

It was a picture of Jennifer, and must have been taken by Tyrone during one of their sessions. She was lying on her back with her thighs spread open, naked from the waist down with her hands folded over her breasts in a way that made the wedding ring on her finger stand out quite dramatically. His thick black cock was buried deep in her pussy, nestled between the rosy pink lips, slick with her excitement in a way that was visible even from that distance. There was a caption beneath the photo. *Hey Percy honey, I know how much you love to see your wife getting fucked by this black cock, so here's a picture of me from my session last week with our friend. Enjoy ;)*

He felt all the color drain from his face, and began stammering wordlessly. Finally he tried to choke out a clumsy explanation. "My, ah, wife, she, um... she sent me a..."

"I can see that, Mr. Brice. All too well."

Now the color all rushed back to his cheeks in a bright red blush. "Here," he said, clearing his throat, "this, uh, this is the document."

"Thank you," she said, her tone arch and very cool as she took the phone once again. She read the passage and nodded once. "Hm. You may be right, Mr. Brice. It warrants following up on, at any rate. I'll put someone on it."

He nodded, taking his phone back and clutching it to himself like it was a dangerous animal and might strike if he didn't keep it under control. "Yes, well. Thank you. And, uh, about the other thing, please. I'm terribly sorry, but please just, um, forget you saw it. A complete accident, you understand."

She gave him a strange searching look, his expression impassive. "Was it indeed?" Her eyes flicked downward a little.

The whimpering from earlier hadn't gone away while they'd talked, her standing there with the door open. As a matter of fact, it seemed to have gotten louder. And the more he heard, the more he was convinced that it *wasn't* the television. "Do you, um, is there someone in there with you?"

"Good day, Mr. Brice. If you have any further revelations to share, please do send me an e-mail. No need to make the trip." She shut the door in his face, leaving him standing in the hall, shame-faced and flummoxed.

He went to tuck his phone into his pocket and noticed that his little cock was fully erect in his pants, and bulging out quite absurdly. He blushed anew, and tried to hide it behind his arm as he hurried back down to his own room. He had a lot more work to do today, and he needed to take a closer look at the picture which Jennifer had sent him.

* * *

Jennifer switched her phone off. It was time to stop living digitally. She needed something real. After getting the text from Percy she'd spent some time scrolling through the photos she'd put under the folder marked 'Ty' on her phone trying to find just the right one to send. It had put her in quite a mood, and she was feeling desperate again.

Matilda Harrington had proved to be a great friend. The two of them had hit it off rather splendidly, and had ended up spending much of the day shopping together. Jennifer had shared her woes. Matilda's solution had been for Jennifer to simply find a second man to keep as a sort of backup, but Jennifer wasn't quite ready for that. Then Matilda had offered a suggestion for what she said was "the next best thing."

They'd gone together to a little shop tucked away in the corner of the downtown. It had a large pink sign out front that spelled out in swooping letters the words *For Her Pleasure.*

They'd gone in, and it didn't take Jennifer long to figure out exactly what sort of store it was. Matilda had led her to a display of dildos and vibrators. "Alright, darling, what size are you?" she's said, stroking her chin and studying the boxes, no different than if she'd been shoe shopping.

She started at the small end. Jennifer just blushed and shook her head.

"Bigger?" Matilda asked, grinning and moving to the next size up.

Jennifer shook her head at those too.

"Impressive," Matilda said, "how about this one?"

Jennifer studied it for a moment. It was big, but... if she was trying to find something that would fill her like Ty did... She shook her head.

"Wow." Now she looked genuinely impressed. She went down almost all the way to the end. "Okay, if this doesn't do it we're going to have to go to a specialty store."

"That should be fine."

"My my," Matilda said, lifting the box and studying it up close. "I didn't know you had it in you."

The toy, when combined with her vibrator - now with a fresh set of batteries - had done a great deal to alleviate her suffering. She'd spend the night fucking herself silly with the dildo while she looked at pictures of Ty's cock. It had done the job of getting her off, but it hadn't truly satisfied her the way he did.

Fortunately, that was all going to change tonight. That was the plan, anyway.

Tyrone had messaged her first thing in the morning to invite her to a party. He said that it was being thrown by someone from the club, and that he'd love to take her there for a little fun. She hadn't hesitated to say yes.

About time, Ty!

It was going happening tomorrow night already. God, she had so much to *do*! She decided to treat herself to a little pregame, and went out to the spa. A manicure and pedicure, then home for a nice long soak in the bath. She'd get herself all smooth and soft and relaxed. From the sounds of things, she was in for quite a night.

She'd been going to the Asian spa lately, for no other particular reason than that it was the closest one to her house. The ladies there were all very friendly, if a little linguistically challenged, but she certainly wasn't the type to hold that against them. After all, she couldn't speak Chinese, so their halting English made them much closer to bilingual than she was.

"Welcome, Mrs. Brice, welcome," the madam said, bowing and smiling warmly, "please make yourself comfortable, please. What can we do for you today?"

She sighed, settling into the seat, listening to the soothing burble of vaguely oriental music coming on over the speakers. "Oh, I think a mani and pedi today, Miss Chow."

"Of course, of course. Very happy to oblige. A girl with be with you soon."

"Lovely thank you." She lay back and opened a celebrity magazine. She leafed through it idly as she waited. She read a story about the Kardashians, up to their usual nonsense. She used to think they were so ridiculous, always dating rappers and football players, these big hulking African-American men. She understood it a lot better now. Maybe they were the smart ones after all...

The girl came out, a slender lady with long straight black hair. She greeted Jennifer shyly and washed her hands. "Rub feet?" she offered.

"Oh God, *please*. Thank you so much," Jennifer said with a contented sigh, settling in as the lady removed her shoes and socks and submersed her feet in a warm suds bath. If there was a better feeling in the whole world, she'd never experienced it. Well, except that one thing, of course.

She glanced idly through the movie reviews in the back section of the magazine. Nothing especially interested. It was all comic book films nowadays, not her style at all. It might be a cliché, but she very much preferred a good romance to all that punching and shouting nonsense. Maybe there was something coming out next month. She'd get Percy to take her when he got back, that could be fun.

She noticed belatedly that the foot massage had stopped. She lifted the magazine and looked down. The slender Chinese woman was holding her foot, staring down at her with a difficult to read expression on her face. That's when Jennifer realized, she wasn't looking at her foot, she was looking at her ankle. Specifically, the black queen of spades tattoo. The masseuse looked up, and their eyes met for a brief moment. "Very big," the lady said, and giggled softly, looking away and going back to the massage.

Jennifer blushed crimson and buried her nose back in the magazine.

This was the first time her tattoo had been recognized by somebody outside the club. God, how many people knew? She'd never even heard of the expression a few months ago, now suddenly it seemed that everybody knew about it.

Still, beneath the embarrassment, she felt a strange glow of pride. *That's right,* she thought, *very very big. You have no idea.*

She was very much looking forward to tomorrow.

Chapter Four

Tyrone stared up the long set of steps leading into the mansion.

He'd never seen a place like this before, except in magazines or on television. It looked almost too enormous to be real, like some absurd dollhouse blown up to life size. Jennifer handed the keys to her big black SUV to a valet in a crimson suit who was standing at attention. She came to him, smiling and beautiful.

He held an arm out to her and she looped her own arm through, holding tightly to him as he led her onward.

"This is a hell of a place," he muttered, unsure where to look, his head turning in all directions to take in the sights. "Is this the kind of thing you're used to?"

She laughed. "Hardly. I never saw anything like it until we came to Florida."

"Man, I should have gone to law school."

"Trust me," she said, "not everybody who goes to law school ends up in a place like this."

"Guess not. What's the guy's name again?"

"Harrington. Jonas Harrington."

"You know him?"

"Not really. I mean, I've *met* him, but..."

At the neared the top of the steps she turned to him, planting her hands on her hips and pursing her lips. "I've missed you terribly, you know. You're not allowed to leave me alone for that long ever again."

It hadn't been that long. What was it, eight, maybe nine days? He supposed it had felt like a lot longer for her. He was busy with mountains of coursework and football practice and all the rest of it, while she didn't seem to have a great deal going on in her life except for the occasional social engagement. Privately, he thought she should maybe think about getting a hobby. He smiled back in what he hope was a reassuring sort of way. "Don't worry, baby. Won't happen again."

She punched him playfully on the shoulder and made a pouty face. "It better not. I need you."

He grinned, and he moved in close to her, sliding an arm in around her waist and pulling her close. Her full body was warm and soft against him, like a load of fresh baked French bread right out of the oven. He could feel the curves of her through her slinky party dress. He could feel the outline of her panties through her dress, a thin band around her waist and a little bit down the center. She was wearing a thong. He felt a little shudder move through him. Goddamn he loved her in a thong.

She smiled up at him, giving his waist a little squeeze and holding him tight. Her grin was lopsided and cheeky. "You like the feel of that?" she asked, shifting her hips a little, moving her ass in his hand.

"You know I do, baby. I like what you're wearing too."

"Well, play your cards right, you might get a peek underneath," she teased.

He heard the click of a high heeled shoe on the walkway, and the swish of stockinged thighs rubbing sensuously together. "Are you two lovebirds planning to stand out here all night, or are you going to join the party?"

He looked up. The woman was gorgeous. She was like Jennifer's reversed twin. Where Jennifer was beautifully tall and voluptuous, this woman was slim and perky, a petite little doll next to Jennifer's imposing Amazonian sexuality.

"Matilda Harrington," she said, offering a slender hand.

He took it, his large black hands enveloping her little china doll fingers, and he lifted it to his lips to kiss it softly. "A pleasure," he said, as smoothly as he could manage, hoping for a sort of James Bond type elegance.

She laughed softly. "My goodness, Jennifer, you didn't tell me your friend was such a charmer. I do hope I get a chance to become more intimately antiquated with him..." she eyed him up and down with obvious hunger in her sparkling eyes.

"Tilly!" Jennifer laughed, playfully slapping her hands away.

"Come on then, darlings, both of your come in and join the party. I promise that there's lots fun to be had indoors."

She took them both by the hand and led them on down the path.

"A friend of yours?" Tyrone asked Jennifer.

"Matilda is our host tonight," Jennifer explained, "The two of us have recently become reacquainted. She, ah... helped me with a problem I was having."

Matilda glanced back, smirking, "And how is that going, Jennifer? Satisfactory, I hope?"

"Very much so. Though nothing next to the real thing."

"I'm sure," Matilda said, eyeing Tyrone again. "I hope I get a chance to see it how it... measures up."

Well. She wasn't being exactly subtle. He couldn't say that he exactly minded. She was a sexy little thing, no mistaking that. If he'd understood Mason correctly, he was going to be seeing a good deal more of her tonight. He had a flash of an image through his head of her down on her knees with a big black dick in her mouth. The only thing was, he wasn't sure if he was imagined Marquis' cock, or his own.

Jennifer gave his hand a squeeze and he returned it.

He wondered if she was going to be the jealous type. There was no reason she should be. After all, *she* was the one who was married. Still, you never knew. He was going to have to play it by ear and see how it went, he supposed.

Just outside the entrance Matilda turned to them. She held out both her hands and in them there were several items. In the one hand, masks, little mascaraed ball things that covered around the eyes but not a great deal else. There were two white masks and one black. There were little holes for strings, but there was nothing in them at the moment. Tyrone took the black mask, and Matilda gave him a wink. In her other hand there was an assortment of cords in a variety of colors.

"What's all this?" Jennifer asked curiously, taking a white mask for herself.

"Pink is for cuckolds," Matilda explained, lifting each different color cord as she described what they represented.

"Black for bulls, of course. White is for wives looking for a bull, and silver is for wives who already have one."

"What about these ones?" Tyrone asked, pointing the three gold bands in her hand which she'd not yet explained.

Matilda grinned slyly. "These are for the three of us," she said, handing one to each of them and slipping the third through the holes of her own mask. The shinning cord glimmered in the light as she slipped it onto her face.

"But what does gold mean, exactly?" Jennifer asked.

Matilda's grin widened. "You'll find out."

"So is everybody here a cuckold or a bull?" Tyrone asked. "I don't see a third color."

"Everyone," she confirmed. "This is an exclusive gathering. No vanilla couples on the guest list."

"Sounds like an interesting crowd," Tyrone remarked dryly.

"Oh, I'm sure you'll find it *quite* interesting."

The three of them went together through the doors of the enormous estate.

Tyrone had to make a real effort to keep his jaw from dropping. He hardly even noticed the grandeur and ornate splendor of the massive house, with its dozens of hung oil paintings - some of which he actually recognized from art books he'd read - its marble staircase and roman columns. He paid no mind to the tables buckling under the weight of food, giant gleaming roasts and exotic dishes he couldn't even name, though the smell of them was intoxicating. There was an entire cask of wine that looked like it would have cost hundreds of dollars just for a single bottle and beside that a towering mountain of delicately stacked crystal champagne glasses.

No, despite all of that, Tyrone's focus was entirely upon the people at the party.

He guessed there must be at least a hundred guests wandering through the various rooms of the house, many of them less than fully dressed. An enormous black man who must have been about six and a half feet talk came striding by, a jeweled leash clutched in his massive hand. He looked at

Tyrone as he walked by, bowing his head briefly and rumbling something in what sounded like French. A slender white woman followed after him, dressed in a tiny little party dress that was little more than a nightie. She had a silver collar around her neck attached to the black man's leash. The huge diamond on her wedding ring sparkled brightly.

There were dozens of dozens of white men in smartly tailored suits with pink bands on their masks, conversing in small circles while they sipped wine and chuckled at each other's jokes. He could tell just by looking at them that they were all wealthy. It was an aura that hung about them, a smug confidence in their eyes undiminished by the fact that all their wives were all being serviced by other men.

As for the wives, they were stunning, each of them clearly dressed up to be shown off. Necklines plunged, and skirts rode up high on thighs. They all had spiked heels, some six inches or taller, which did wonders for their tightly covered rumps. They were all bedecked in jewelry, silver and gold and gemstones that caught the light and made them look like a flock of busty blonde magpies about to take flight. Not a single woman was alone, they either moved in groups together or they hung to the arms of their bulls.

As for the bulls, there were a great many of them, though far fewer than either of the other groups, which seemed to put them in high demand. Many had two or three women clustered around them, each fawning for attention. The women with white bands clustered around each available man, and all those with silver bands clung tightly to their man, as if worried that he'd be stolen away from them if left unattended for a moment. The black men were all large, many of them athletic. Some made up for their lack of fitness simply by virtue of their size, great hulking slabs of masculinity. They were all of them smiling, and why not? They'd been brought into the very center of power and influence, turned loose on a crowd of desperate and horny white women who would have otherwise been entirely unattainable to them. They were like a pack of foxes who'd been invited right into the hen-house, and by the rooster no less. And they looked intent on ruffling as many feathers as they could.

Tyrone didn't see anybody else in the entire crowd with a gold band. Not until Marquis came down the stairs.

"Tyrone!" he called, jogging lightly down the steps, a champagne glass in his hand. "Glad you made it, my man, glad you made it." He clasped Tyrone's arm in a firm grip and flashed him a brilliant smile.

Matilda moved to him at once, wrapping her hands around his bulging bicep. "Hey, Daddy," she cooed, gazing up at him with obvious adoration.

He grinned indulgently down at her, leaning in to plant a quick peck on her cheek. "Hi there, pet. You been behaving yourself?"

She shook her head, smirking. "Of course not."

He laughed. "That's my girl. And... you must be Jennifer Brice. We've met before, but it was some time ago."

She smiled, nodding and looking away a little bit. Was she shy? Attracted to him? Tyrone didn't entirely blame her, Marquis was a fine looking guy, anybody could see that. Still... she was his, wasn't she? Sharing her with Percy didn't mean anything, sexually speaking. But competing with Marquis, well... that would be a different matter.

"Tyrone, I was hoping we might be able to talk a little more about the arraignment we've been discussing. There are a few... finer details that still need to be worked out. Assuming you're still interested in going forward, that is."

"Oh, I'm still interested. I haven't made my mind up completely, but..." He slipped his hand down the small of her back, then lower, moving it slowly over the curve of her posterior. He let it slip down between her thighs; up and underneath, pushing her dress in to slide two fingers in a press them against her pussy lips. Through two layers, her thin dress and thinner panties, he felt the soft give of her plump pussy-lips.

She stiffened, standing up to her full six foot height, eyes widening as she squirmed. He grinned, and gave a little more pressure, feeling her lips part just a little bit. He withdrew his hand, leaving her little thong pushed up just a hair into her vagina. She gasped softly, quivering a little.

Marquis' eyes flickered downward, but there was no chance he'd actually seen it from his angle. Tyrone grinned cockily, and the older man's gaze intensified. From somewhere deep inside the house came the sound of a firm slap, a paddle being applied to flesh with no small amount of force. There came a whimper and a laugh and a gentle smattering of applause.

"My my," Matilda said, her lips parting in an enormous smile, "it seems they're starting without us. Come on, let's join the festivities. Our public awaits."

* * *

Jennifer followed Tyrone and the others into the next room, wriggling and trying to tug at the panties pushed inside her without actually doing it. The light inside was dim and flickering, provided entirely by innumerable candles rather than any electricity. There was an odd buzzing at her side and for a moment she thought that she'd accidentally brought her little bullet vibrator along, then she realized it was her phone. Who would be trying to get in touch with her now? Ah, of course.

Percy.

She felt a flash of annoyance. She'd told him that she was going to be out and not to contact her while she was away. She was planning to fill him in at great length and detail afterwards, and didn't need the distraction now. Still, there was a chance it could be an emergency, so she'd better take a look just in case.

She pulled out the phone and glanced down at it as the group went into the far room. She frowned. It was a message from a number she didn't recognize. What did it say?

-Mrs. Brice, you do not know me, but I work with your husband. There's something important which I feel I must discuss with you when you-

She stuffed the phone back in her purse without finishing reading the message. Whatever, she didn't have time to be chatting with Percy's coworkers right now. There were much more important things to attend to in the present moment.

Marquis held the door open while the three of them entered the room. A group of men were gathered around the center of the room, chatting casually and drinking as they watched two women spank each other. They were doing it playfully, still fully clothed, up on a sort of stage area in the center of the room. They ran off, giggling and laughing as the men cheered for them, several mock-begging them to return.

A man stepped up onto the stage. She hadn't seen him in person for quite some time, but she recognized him right away. Jonas Harrington, Matilda's wife, Percy's boss, and the host of the party. He was looking right at her. Well, at all four of them, her and Ty and Marquis and Tilly. He smiled and he lifted his glass, tapping the side of it with a little fork and calling for quiet.

A hush fell over the room right away. Several people turned to look at them. Jennifer felt herself blush and go cold. What was about to happen? Why was everybody looking their way?

"Here they are at last, our gold couples! The very finest our little club has to offer. Here tonight, to offer you a taste of true ambrosia, to witness a spectacle of true magnificence, beauty and carnality. May I present my wife, this gorgeous thing." He held out an arm towards her, smiling and gesturing expansively.

Jennifer leaned over a bit, tugging on Ty's arm. "What's going on here? What exactly is it that you've got planned?" she hissed at him, trying to whisper.

He just grinned and gave her a little squeeze. "Trust me, baby. We're gonna take it to a whole new level."

"What does that *mean*, exactly?"

Jonas continued before Tyrone could elaborate. "And, joining her: a new guest. New, but very very special. I give you this beautiful flower! The wife of one of our very own members who sadly could not be here tonight. When we see him next we'll have to be sure to let him know what the poor fellow missed out on, am I right?" he laughed, and the crowd laughed with him.

Jennifer stared up at the stage with slowly dawning horror. "You... you don't mean...?"

And then Matilda was grabbing hold of her arm and pulling her through the crowd, drawing her up onto the stage. Jennifer stepped up onto the raised area, feeling a bit like a deer when it's caught in a set of bright headlights.

"Don't you want to do this, Jen?" Matilda asked, frowning, her voice was quiet, hardly above a whisper.

"I... I mean, I've never..."

She laughed softly. "You and I both know *that's* not true."

Jennifer blushed. "Yes, well... not in front of so many..."

Matilda wrapped her arms around her. The tiny little woman hardly came up to her collarbone; she had to gaze up at Jennifer, brushing back her hair and smiling. "Just go with it. Let it happen and you'll forget about the crowd in no time, trust me. I'll be right by your side the whole time."

Jennifer was dimly away of Tyrone and Marquis both coming up to the edge of the stage, looking up with eager expressions, yet restraining themselves for the time being.

Matilda lifted herself up on the tips of her toes, and whispered in Jennifer's ear, her breath warm and very faintly moist. "If you want to stop, you tell me. If you don't, then why not just kiss me already?" She opened her mouth, and she pressed it against Jennifer's.

Jennifer was so started that she almost fell over. She stood rigid and stiff, her hands at her sides while Matilda pressed her pert little mouth against hers, her slender hands wandering over Jennifer's body.

It was the first time she'd kissed a girl. At least, if you didn't count that time in middle school with Allison Wheeler on the playground, which she didn't. As it went on, and the seconds ticked away like immense hours, she started to realize that she actually sort of liked it. She felt her body start to relax, start to move more fluidly. She found herself pressing against Matilda's little form, drawing it closer to herself. Her hands moved slowly, timidly, taking hold of Matilda's hips and holding them gently. The soft curve of the other woman's little body was nothing like Tyrone's hard and muscular physique but it was... well... it was very nice, in its own way.

She certainly wasn't ready to renounce men, or anything like that, but... It was nice.

She leaned down, opening her mouth and returning Matilda's kiss fully. She was dimly aware of a sense of growing excitement in the crowd, but it only half registered. Like something happening on the other side of a window, the shades drawn and the curtain pulled across. She was already barely aware of them.

"Do you like this?" Matilda whispered, her mouth so close to Jennifer's that Jennifer could feel the words being formed.

Jennifer nodded, murmuring back softly, "Yes..."

"Touch me. Put your hands on me. Like this..." Matilda reached up and took hold of Jennifer, guiding her hands, placing one on her hip and the other on her backside. "Pull me close against you. Kiss me. Oh God... yes, just like that..."

"I've never..."

"You've never kissed a woman?"

"No..."

"Do you like it? Do you like how I taste, Jennifer? My lips... my tongue..."

Jennifer found that she was breathing hard, her heard beating rapidly inside her chest, drumming a steady beat. She just nodded.

"Take off my clothes..." Matilda took Jennifer's hand again, pushing it up her back, moving it to the little zipper at the top her of dress. "Take it off. Show everyone. Feel me... feel my skin..."

"I thought..." Jennifer felt the tiny little zipper tab between her fingers. She began to pull it slowly down, agonizingly slow. Matilda's dress was tight, her body poured into it almost. She felt the slender woman's form straining against the dress as the zipper descended. "I thought this was about the men..."

"Isn't it?"

"Yes, but... why does it feel like you're seducing me, Tilly?"

Matilda Harrington grinned up at her, her smile cocked to one side of her mouth. She gave her body a little shimmy, and the loosened garment feel in a silky pool around her ankles. She wore no bra beneath, and her perky pink nipples brushed against Jennifer's chest as she moved. She had on black crotchless panties, an intricate lacework of dark silk and lace that framed her charms as neatly as could be. She took Jennifer's hand one more time and she brought it down between her thighs. Jennifer felt the brush of soft lace, and the warm sticky feeling of the other woman's wet lips. "Maybe I am," Matilda said, and hooked her fingers into the wide belt sown into Jennifer's dress.

"Now why would you want to do a thing like that?" Jennifer asked.

"Isn't it obvious?" Matilda said lightly, "You're fucking gorgeous," and she pressed her mouth against Jennifer's once more.

Jonas stood on the far end of the stage still, beaming with pleasure. "Such beautiful ladies. It almost seems a shame to come between them. I do hope you gentlemen are man enough to get their attention," he laughed, grinning down at Marquis and Tyrone, who were clearly starting to get worked up by the sight of their respective lovers embracing one another.

"And before the main event begins, let me just thank you all for coming to our little get-together. On that note, we have some special guests with us tonight," Jonas went on, "My dear friends, Reginald and Penelope Mason. Thank you for joining us," he half bowed to a couple that stood in the center of the crowd, two people older than the rest, who smiled indulgently back at Jonas. "But enough of my blathering!" Jonas said, hopping down off the stage, "Enjoy the show!"

On cue, Tyrone and Marquis both stepped up onto the stage. The grin slipped from Tyrone's face. He looked determined, very serious about the task he was about to undertake. He was focused entirely on her, and it made her knees trembled. She felt herself shiver, her entire body getting warm. Her heart pounded in her chest as he slowly began to disrobe, never for a second taking his eyes off her.

Beside him Marquis was doing the same, though his attention was less exclusively on Matilda than Ty's was on Jennifer. He was playing it up for the crowd. Flexing after he removed his shirt, showing off his sculpted abs and muscular arms for the audience. They murmured and cooed appreciatively.

Jennifer felt her breath catch in her throat as Ty slipped his pants off. Every time she saw him it took her aback just how beautiful he was. His body was like a Renascence sculpture carved from black marble, his features both tender and powerful. And his eyes, his deep brown eyes into which she felt she could fall, tumbling down forever into their depths.

He was naked but for his tight blue boxer-briefs. She found her eyes inescapably drawn to the bulge down there, and she felt herself beginning to salivate.

She was the only person on the stage that was still fully dressed, but not for much longer. Matilda disentangled herself from Jennifer's arms and moved around behind her. Jennifer felt her slim fingers working at the little ivory buttons down the back of Jennifer's dress.

Ty came across the stage, striding purposefully towards her. He reached out and put his hands on her shoulders, grabbing hold of the dress and pulling it down as Matilda undid the buttons. He bared her plain black bra to the audience. Someone whistled admiringly at her full bosom. Ty placed his hands on her, cupping her large breasts in his strong hands. Matilda undid the clasp, and the bra came away. Ty pulled it off her arms and let it fall to the floor.

Although the evening was quite warm, Jennifer began to shiver. She crossed her arms over her chest, holding herself tight. Marquis was coming towards them, his underclothes discarded. His dark skin seemed to gleam like onyx in the candlelight, and his eyes flashed intently as he studied her.

Ty took hold of her wrists and gently removed her hands, exposing her for everyone to see. She felt Matilda's slender arms encircling her waist, pulling her close. She felt the other woman's nipples brush against her bare back. Ty leaned in and kissed her, pinching her nipples, one in each hand, and pulling her close. She felt herself going limp in their arms; it was like she was underwater, suspended between them. Marquis moving in behind Matilda, getting close up against her and grinding from behind.

Ty took hold of Jennifer's hand and moved it slowly downward. He placed it on his cock, letting it rest there, holding him through the cotton of his underpants. Her breathing started to get faster, little gasps. Matilda plunged a little hand into the front of her panties, cupping her pubis tight, her fingers working the soft lips, teasing the clitoris expertly.

She leaned forward and spoke, her breath whispery on Jennifer's shoulder. "It's not my first time," she said, kissing the bare skin, "with a woman..."

The two women sank down to their knees, both together as if it were a rehearsed maneuver. Jennifer dragged down Ty's underthings as she knelt, freeing his by now almost fully erect cock. It sprang out and into her mouth as if guided by a will of its own. Jennifer found that she was no longer in conscious control of her body. She was given over entirely to desire, and acting on instinct and reaction rather than choice.

She took his cock deep in her mouth. He groaned, pushing his fingers into her hair and drawing her closer. She enveloped him, taking it as fully as she could. She heard soft wet sounds beside her and knew that Matilda was doing the same to Marquis.

The two women - both of them married white women, known and respected in the community as fine upstanding pillars of society - sucked the black men's thick fat cocks in front of the crowd of assembled onlookers. Jennifer was glad of her mask, even though she knew it didn't really disguise her much at all, it still made her feel secure in a way. She could do anything, *be* anything. Jennifer had been left at the door, this was a new woman here, nameless and unknown. All they knew of her was that she was a slut for black cock. That was the only thing that mattered anymore.

Matilda's fingers pushed inside her, opening Jennifer's pussy and sliding easily inside. She was so wet; it dripped down the younger woman's fingers, slippery and warm. Jennifer reached one hand up to cup Ty's balls, and moved the other down Matilda's taut belly, then between her thighs. She started to stroke Tilly's exposed pussy lips, feeling them against her fingertips, soft and responsive.

Matilda moaned weakly, then gagged a little as Marquis thrust against her face. Their bodies were pressed together side to side as they both serviced their bulls.

If only Percy were here to see this, Jennifer thought to herself. He would have been ready to explode by now.

She felt a strand of saliva and precum slide down her lower lip, over her chin and onto her breasts. She took her hand from Ty's balls and rubbed it into her skin, moving in little circles over the erect nipples.

Matilda came off Marquis' cock with a gasp, breathing hard and wiping her chin. "Hm, you taste so fucking good, Daddy."

Marquis laughed, a low bass rumble. "You know it, baby."

"Come here," Matilda order, rising and taking her man by the cock, leading him closer. "Come over here, come show Jen what you've got."

Jennifer glanced over, still busy with Ty's cock. Marquis was huge. He wasn't quite as big as her own bull, but they were both so large that there was hardly any point splitting hairs. She felt her eyes widen. Matilda stroked it a little, her slender white fingers squeezing tight at the fat black snake, slick and shiny with her spit.

Matilda giggled mischievously and grabbed hold of a fistful of Jennifer's hair, holding it firmly. She pulled Jennifer back off Ty's cock. "Think she can handle a bit more? I want to see two dicks in this pretty hole. She gave Marquis' cock a tug, pulling him close.

Jennifer looked up at the two enormous black men standing over her. Tyrone glanced at the older man, and the two of them shrugged, as if to say *why not?* They both looked down at her. Marquis looked down and grinned. His eyes glittered like dark stones behind his black mask. "That's a pretty little mouth, baby girl. How about we fill it up for you?"

Ty lifted an eyebrow inquisitively, his fully erect cock gripped in his fist. She stared. *Could* she handle that much at once time? She wasn't sure she'd be able to manage it, no matter how hard she tried. Still... nothing ventured, nothing gained, as the saying went. She leaned her head back and opened her mouth wide.

She didn't get a chance to change her mind. Matilda tightened her grip and shoved forward, propelling Jennifer face-first towards the two men. Marquis' fat black cock shoved into her mouth. It was thick and sweet, salty on her tongue. His skin was oiled and perfumed, a heady musk of something that smelled expensive. Not wanting to be left out, Tyrone moved forward, pushing his own dick into her as well. She felt her eyes water as her mouth was stretched to its maximum capacity. Matilda giggled, pushing her back and forth, maker her get sloppy all over the two turgid cock battling for space between her lips.

The crowd started to cheer, egging the two men on. "Fuck her! Fuck her good, boys! Bend that slut over!"

She felt her cheeks flush crimson. She didn't think she'd ever been in a situation like this before in her life. The sensation was... strange, but intoxicating in a way. She felt somehow simultaneously humiliated and empowered. She was nothing but a fucktoy for them and their cocks, an object to be gaped at in awe by the assembled crowd. But she was the entire focus of the entire room's attention, the object of adoration and admiration. And she felt *so* incredible.

Marquis pulled his wet cock out of her mouth and slapped her face with it, slowly, methodically. Tyrone did the same, then plunged in deep, making her gag on it. Matilda held her firmly in place, making her take it. She teared up as she struggled to endure it.

"God, I'm so fucking *wet*!" Matilda suddenly burst out. "If I don't get fucked right now I'm going to lose my mind!" She stuck her first two fingers deep inside her pussy, brought them out wet and shining, and pushed them into her mouth, sucking them like a lollipop.

Marquis grinned. Matilda leaned forward, her hands on Jennifer's shoulders, and she pushed out her ass. Marquis clasped her hips and entered her from behind, making her gasp and tense, digging her fingers into Jennifer's skin. She kept sucking Tyrone's cock as Matilda got fucked behind her.

She felt her panties getting heavy with her wetness, clinging to her body. A dreadful need began to well up in her, a tingling desire to be penetrated by him. It occurred to her in a dim corner of her mind that today wasn't a safe day, and she certainly hadn't brought any kind of birth control along with her. She doubted that Tyrone had either. Well, nothing had happened so far, she wasn't going to worry about it.

"I want you," she murmured, her voice low and desperate.

"You want this big cock, baby?"

"I want it inside. I want it inside me so bad, Ty, I need it."

Matilda was panting and moaning, gripping Jennifer tight. "Fuck her, big boy, fuck her hard. I want to see you get pounded, Jen, I want to see that pretty pussy of yours with a big fat cock inside it."

It happened as if in a dream. She felt herself being guided down onto all fours, right beside Matilda in the same position. The two men moving behind them, crouching down a little, grabbing their asses, Matilda's little rump and Jennifer's plump booty, and together, moving in perfect synchronization, they were penetrated. Jennifer felt her mouth open and her eyes widen as Ty plunged his cock into her dripping cunt.

The two men were merciless, pounding hard and fast, neither letting up, each seemed determined not to finish before the other. She turned back, and saw Ty, his face screwed up in concentration, grunting under his breath as he pounded her. He reached forward, pushing her face down so that he could really bring his full weight to bear on her, taking her even deeper than before. She stared out at the crowd of faces assembled before her, a sea of masks, pink and white and black and silver bands, all those eyes on her as she was fucked.

"Cum," she moaned, "I need your cum."

They could all hear her, and they began to take up the cry, chanting softly. "Cum! Cum! Cum!" The old man Jonas had introduced was grinning, fondling himself through his pants. His wife was squirming with excitement. "Cream!" she called out, in a clear high voice that sounded almost elegantly regal. "Cream for the Queen of Spades!"

"I *need* it!" Jennifer wailed.

Matilda had been rendered wordless, her eyes rolled back and her tongue out as Marquis dominated her.

"I'm cumming!" Marquis groaned, slamming down on Matilda Harrington's petite little frame, groaning and twitching as he came into her, spilling out between her thighs in thick pearlescent strands.

Tyrone was only a moment behind. He came with a groan, his hands clutching tightly at her hips as he filled her.

Jennifer panted as his cum pumped into her, thick hot strands of it deep into her womb. "Shit!" he hissed, "shit, it's so good!" A strange thought entered her head then, something she couldn't quite explain, and wouldn't understand until sometime later.

It's strange, she thought, *all these people watching me being bred. That's what this is, isn't it? Tyrone is breeding me.*

Chapter Five

Percy gaped at the images appearing on his phone screen. Jennifer had told him about what happened at Jonas' party, but words alone hadn't done the deed justice. Now the pictures were coming in, and they were something else.

The first image was of Jennifer tongue-kissing Jonas' wife Matilda, her hand on the smaller woman's pussy, her eyes shut and her expression one of reverent ecstasy. Percy hadn't even imagined her being with another woman, and the sight of it was so intoxicating that it had given him an instant erection.

The images which came after that, fast and thick, portrayed the increasingly filthy turn of events. Two hulking black men took the white women with what appeared to be a great deal of intensity while a great crowd of masked onlookers observed the scene with congenial interest, as one might appreciate the band at a wedding or the entertainment at a child's birthday party.

In the last photo, which was the one that really sent him over the edge, sexually speaking, was of Jennifer face down on the raised stage, her rump lifted in the air, her mouth open and tongue lolling out as she looked back over her shoulder. The camera angle gave an unobstructed view of her slit, and of the thick bead of milk-white semen which had been deposited there. Like a pearl in the pink folds of an opening mollusk. She looked so beautiful and so lustful, it took his breath away.

He wanted nothing more than to tear his pants off at once and furiously jerk himself off.

This, of course, presented something of an issue, given the time and manner in which the photos were received. They were coming in sent from none other than Jonas Harrington himself, in an attachment reading *Thought You Might Like to See This*. He'd opened the message on his work phone, expecting it to be something relevant to the case he was working on.

He certainly hadn't been expecting to be bombarded by a deluge of explicit images of his own wife being fucked on stage in front of dozens of people. He had opened an email to reply to Jonas, but it remained blank at the moment. He simply hadn't a clue what he might say.

There had been a part of Percy which hadn't quite believed Jennifer when she'd told him about the events which had transpired that night. She hadn't had her phone on her at the time, she said, and she hadn't been able to take any pictures. She'd been somewhat vague, only opening up when he'd pressed her for details, of which those she'd provided had been scant and general. She'd said she was too tired to really go into it at the time, but that she was going to be thinking it over a lot, and would fill him in at length when she felt able. He'd assumed she was exaggerating about what had happened, downplaying it, and so he didn't put too much stock into her vague descriptions of a "public orgy." He could see now why she'd been reticent: it was quite an event which had taken place. No doubt there was a lot to process, and she was no doubt exhausted by the strenuous nature of the event.

Now that he could see the photos he felt an almost intoxicating level of desire. He thought he might rip off all his clothes and fling himself into bed for six hours at least and luxuriate in the images while he played with himself.

Unfortunately, he was in the middle of the afternoon meeting with Natasha James and her entire staff of dedicated workers when he received the message, and they were already looking at him funny.

Had he gone pale? Or blushed? Started breathing heavily? Probably all of the above. He crossed his legs a little, though he was fairly sure there was no way they could detect his arousal given that he was sitting one of the conference room tables and his lap was fully concealed.

He leaned back a bit in his seat, holding the phone close to himself, very very close. No one could see it, could they? He felt a nauseating wave of paranoia. What if someone had already seen? He certainly hadn't been hiding the screen when he'd opened the message. It had been from his boss, after all, and if there was information relevant to the case than he'd likely be sharing it anyway. And after he had opened it, he'd been in such an open-mouthed trance that he hadn't had the presence of mind to hide the screen from anybody. Someone could have seen it easily enough.

And then what would happen?

But he already knew the answer to that question, and the knowledge made his blood run cold. They would tell Natasha, that's what they would do. Of course they would, all of her minions reported everything that went on to her directly with hardly any delay. He glanced first to one side then the other in a way he hoped was surreptitious but knew probably wasn't.

Damn it, he couldn't tell. These were lawyers and paralegals, after all. Keeping a strong poker face in moments of extremity was part of the job, after all. Not the part that he himself had even been particularly good at, but still. Any number of them could have seen, and the longer his phone was out the more chance there was that he'd be discovered.

But he couldn't stop. What he was seeing was too intense, too remarkable. He could hardly believe that *this* was the new normal in his life.

Finally he worked up the resolve to wrench his gaze away from the phone and slap it face-down on the table. He could hardly wait to get away from here, but there was a great deal of meeting to go, and a full day's work beyond that.

He glanced quickly around the room, sure that everyone there had seen the photos and knew his secret. What would that be like? God, he could never show his face in court before. He'd be ruined, a laughingstock if nothing else.

"Mr. Brice?" Natasha's voice seemed colder than before, but perhaps that was just his imagination talking. "You have something to share?"

"Ah... just a communication from Mr. Harrington. I thought it might have something to do with our work, but ah... It wasn't"

"And what exactly *was* it, Mr. Brice?"

"Oh... well, you know. The usual. He was just checking in." He clicked back to his original message, a note to Natasha herself marked *Read at Earliest Convenience*. A few trial strategies he'd been going over in his head and wanted to bounce off his new co-counsel at a later date.

"I see," she said, though she didn't sound at all convinced.

Percy shook his head despairingly. He had to get himself under control, and quickly. He shook his head, looking at the email open on his screen. He hadn't even addressed it to Natasha yet! God, he was unfocused. The photos had rattled him, that was for sure, but he was a professional, and he'd get the job done. He entered her info, *jamesn@firmmail.com* and hit send.

The meeting went on, and he did his best to put aside the images in his mind so that he could concentrate on the task at hand. It proved an exceptionally difficult task. To think, his wife was lying in their bed right now, a young and virile black man's cum still leaking from her pussy...

He'd seen it before, on the morning after she'd seen him, it would leak out into her panties. He found them the next day, Tyrone's spunk dried inside them, tangible proof right there in his hands that another man had taken possession of his wife, had done his marital duties in his absence.

Across the conference room Natasha's smartphone hummed. She took it out with a frown and glanced at it, then sat down to read the message she'd received. Percy was a bit surprised. He thought she was probably reading the email he'd sent her. He'd expected her to study it later, not in the middle of the meeting. Still, he was pleased, as she seemed to be giving it quite a close look, reading intently with her brow furrowed.

One of the paralegals, the one who'd been responsible for the slip-up a few days back which Percy had caught, stood up awkwardly from his seat. He hobbled towards the coffee pot, waddling rather clumsily, wincing as he went. Percy frowned as the man went past him. "Are you alright?" he asked.

The paralegal - what was his name again? Ah yes, Matthew - shook his head dismissively. "Oh, I'm fine. Just, uh... pulled a muscle. Stretching. Yoga, you know."

"Yoga?"

Matthew laughed ruefully, shooting a quick and fearful glance at Natasha, "It's supposed to make you more limber, ironic, I know. Guess I just pushed too far."

"Oh. Sorry about that."

"Yeah," the paralegal said, his face twisting in discomfort as he started to pour himself a cup.

"Matthew." Natasha's voice was cold and quiet, but everyone heard it quite clearly.

Matthew froze. "Ah. Right," he said, and slowly lowered the coffee pot, putting his cup back sadly.

Percy frowned. "What's that about?"

"Ah... nothing. I'm just not thirsty."

Percy shook his head. Something was definitely going on here, but he wasn't going to probe into it too deeply. He had a feeling that he'd rather not know. He turned back to his phone to finished checking his email. The message he'd written to Natasha was still up on his screen. That was funny, usually an email would automatically close after being sent. He hit the exit button, and a warning popped up. *Are you sure you want to exit this message without sending? It will be saved as a draft.*

What? But he'd just sent it! Then his blood ran cold. No. No, he couldn't possibly have done that, there was simply no way. He couldn't have made a mistake of that magnitude, a stupid thoughtless hideous mistake like that just wasn't possible.

He opened the email he'd been planning to send to Jonas as a reply. Right there in the *To* field: *jamesn@firmmail.com.*

No. He couldn't have. No no no no.

He's mixed up the emails, gotten flustered, and sent Natasha the blank reply. But that meant she would have access to the original message as well, the message from Jonas. The phone with all those photos...

What could he do? He felt a clutching desperation rising in him. How to cover this up? He could do something crazy, launch himself across the room and grab the phone out of her hand, or hold a lighter up under the sprinkler to set off the fire alarms, something, anything!

"Could I have the room please?" Natasha said, her voice cool and calm. Everyone stood up without question, packing their things away in their leather briefcases.

Percy felt sick. How could he have made such a stupid blunder? He'd been too distracted, too on edge, to worn out. This whole exercise was driving him mad, and the sight of Jennifer like that had sent him over the edge into a kind of insanity. He started to sweep his papers off the desk.

"Not you, Mr. Brice. I'd like to have a word in private." She didn't look up from her phone, but was still studying it intently.

Percy's heart sank. There went the last bit of hope, snapping like a thread. He slumped into his seat, watching miserably as the room emptied out. Finally, there was no one left but himself and the other lawyer.

She was still looking at her phone, pausing occasionally to jot something down on her legal pad. Percy had horrible flashbacks to being in the principal's office in grade school, though he'd hardly ever been sent there, the few times he had been had made quite an impression. The principal had a horrible way to making you wait, of building up the intensity of the moment by making you sit there and watch him finish filling out paperwork while you squirmed, awaiting your fate.

"Mr. Brice, what are you feelings on interracial intercourse?" her tone was dry, without any trace of either anger or levity.

Percy's throat got dry and seemed to squeeze closed. God, he couldn't breathe, the room was spinning, going dark, tilting out of view. He gripped the edge of the table, trying to steady himself. "I-intercourse?" he squeaked in a strangled voice.

"That's right. Sexual relations between two different races. Say, for example, a white person and a person of color."

"What are my feelings?"

"That's right."

"I..." There were no words in his mind, no thoughts, just a vast and gaping blank void. "I... don't know. Um, live and let live, I suppose, none of my business what two people might do together..." God, he sounded like an *idiot.*

"Do you find me attractive, Mr. Brice?"

What was she talking about? He was confused now. "Well, uh, I never really... I suppose so, yes. You're a very handsome and, uh, charming woman, certainly." Charming might be a stretch, but she certainly had a certain magnetic force of will about her.

She stood up, looking across the table directly at him, her gaze zeroed in on him like a closing vice on his brain. Now that he thought about it, she really was striking, with high delicate cheekbones and bright eyes, her hair back and tight, her skin a gorgeous and arresting black. She was slender, but there was no disguising the full breasts and bottom beneath her suit. She reminded him a little of Jennifer, when he considered it, though her manner was a good deal more intense, and certainly more stern.

"I, uh... I'm not really sure what it is that you're driving at, I've, um..." he stammered, running out of words.

She picked up her long wooden pointer and began to walk slowly around the wide ring of conference room tables, dragging the tip of the pointer on the surface of the tables as she came inexorably closer and closer. "So, you find me attractive. I understand that. Many men do. Men who don't take me seriously. I've developed something of a technique for dealing with such men. Would you like to hear about it?"

Percy's grip on the table tightened. "I, uh, um, I assure you that I, uh, I take you entirely seriously..."

Thwack!

The pointer came cracking down on the surface of the table. Percy jumped. Natasha didn't as much as flinch. Her features were grim and hard. "My method," she went on, "has been very successful. I didn't come to find myself in this position by waiting for men to reward me, Mr. Brice. I claimed it. I worked for it, and I took it. And I will *not* allow you to undermine me with you childish attempts at seduction."

"S-seduction," he said, panic rising in his chest, "I-I've never done, I mean, no such thing, I-"

"Oh really?" she said coldly, and his voice died in his throat. "Showing me the photograph of your wife... *accidentally*," her sneering tone told him what he thought of that, "That was one thing. But this, this is clearly an escalation. I should have taken action then, but I was willing to give you the benefit of the doubt. Now I see that I'm going to have to take matters into my own hand."

"W-wha-what are you talking about?" He shrank back in his chair as she continued her advance towards him. She was like a great panther stalking around the conference room, and he the petrified deer with nowhere left to run.

"This latest series of images, Mr. Brice. Your wife again. And her lover. Showing off for everyone."

And now she stood over him, regal and imposing, towering with the pointer held in both hands, bowed slightly and tense as her grip tightened. What could he say? He searching in a panic for words that might fix things, might set it to right. There was nothing, what could he say? How could he *possibly* explain such a thing?

"At least," she said, her voice cool and soft, "At least she knows her place... serving black cock." She leaned in close, her voice descending in volume as she spoke, until that last word, *cock*, came out in an ice-cold whisper directly into his ear. "Is that what you're trying to tell me, Mr. Brice? That you want to serve me? That you want me to take you? So you've found out about me and my methods. Somehow, I'm not sure. I'm certainly a good deal more discrete about my activities than you and your wife are, but I suppose you've managed to figure it out. Well, you're not the first man I've bent to my will, and if this is what it take to keep my case under firm control, well..."

Her mouth was so close to his ear that he thought she might lick it. Or bite it, more likely.

"That's what I'm going to have to do," she said, icy and cold. "If you are so intent on misbehaving, then I really have no choice but to discipline you very sternly. But, Mr. Brice, I really don't think you know just what you've gotten yourself into."

"I-I don't know what you're talking about. I'm not... I never..."

"Don't play the innocent with me now, Mr. Brice. You knew what you were doing. Sending images like that to me? Using your work phone. Well, you must have known that I could have you fired. Disbarred, even. You've put yourself entirely within my power. Now you're mine to do with as I please. That's just what you wanted, isn't it?" She reached out, and she took hold of him, gripping his chin with her hands, pinching his cheeks and turning him to face her. Her dark eyes were flashing as they bored into him. "You wanted to be my little bitch, didn't you?"

He just stared, entirely at a loss for words.

"Stand up, Mr. Brice, and bend over. Place your hands flat on the table. Don't dare to look at me again. Remember, if you don't do as I say I will ruin you. I don't play, Mr. Brice. I act. If you're having second thoughts now, well. You shouldn't have put your hand in the fire if you weren't ready to be hurt." She swished her pointer stick, brandishing it quite aggressively.

What else could he do? He was, in essence, trapped. He had no allies here, since Jonas had sent the email in the first place he would be in a position of danger as well, so he'd be of no help. He would be more likely to side with Natasha, furious at Percy for letting his secret out. She had all the cards. Obedience was the only option.

He rose hesitantly, shaking a little. What was going to happen? He had a horrible vision of her calling the motel security and having him escorted out, like some sort of pervert sex offender or something. She couldn't do that, could she? He placed his hands down on the table, trembling.

She stood behind him, pacing back and forth, stalking like a great cat in a cage, eager to strike. Her long wooden pointer swished menacingly through the air.

"W-what are you going to do?" he asked.

She stopped pacing, standing directly behind him. "I'm going to teach you an important lesson, Mr. Brice. About showing the proper respect for your superiors." And then, with a sudden *swish* and a *crack* she brought the pointer down hard across his backside.

Percy yelped out loud, flinching as a sudden burst of pain swept over him.

"What was *that*!" he shrieked, tears springing to his eyes.

"That was lesson number one, Mr. Brice. There are nine more lessons to go, and if you keep making noise like that I'm going to have to teach you a few more." The tip of the pointer tapped ominously on the table beside his hand. "Do you need extra education today?"

He shook his head. "N-no..."

"Good. Here's the second lesson."

Swish! Crack!

He bit down hard on his lip, his fingers curling, scrabbling at the tabletop, but he didn't cry out. A tear spilled out and ran down off the tip of his nose, dropping to the conference table beneath him.

"Very good. So you can learn. Keep being a good boy and I might let you off lightly this time."

Swish! Crack!

Percy whimpered pitifully, struggling to hold himself in position.

She patted his flank approvingly. "Very good, Mr. Brice. You're impressing me. Seven more lessons to go. Are you ready?"

"Do I have a choice?" he said, on the verge of sobbing.

"No. You don't. Unless you want to lose your job. Is that what you'd like, Mr. Brice?"

He shook his head.

She stroked his back with the tip of the pointer. "I can't hear you, Mr. Brice."

"N-no. No, I don't want that."

Swish! Crack!

"In future, Mr. Brice, you shall address me as Miss James, or Mistress, do you understand?" Her tone remained calm, conversational almost, as if nothing out of the ordinary was going on. He understood now how she kept her minions so devoted to her, so enthralled and terrified. Why Matthew had been hobbling like that. It all made sense at last.

"I understand..."

Swish! Crack!

"That was the fifth lesson, Mr. Brice. Try again. I understand...?"

"I understand... Miss James."

"Very good, Mr. Brice. Very, very good. I'm pleased that we're making progress. I might just make something of you yet. Now then, we're halfway there."

Swish! Crack!

Chapter Six

Tyrone woke up to the ringing of his phone.

What the *hell*? It was Saturday, his alarm didn't go off on Saturdays. But wait, that wasn't the alarm. Someone was calling him. Who called people anymore when they could just text? He rolled over, patting at his desk for the phone. He finally snatched it up and answered it at the last second before it timed out, without even checking who it was that was calling.

"Hello?" he said, his voice thick with sleep.

"Sleeping away the weekend, Tyrone? That's no way to stay in peak form, you know."

Tyrone groaned. "Coach? Why are you calling me, there's no practice today..."

"No, this isn't about football. It's about the other thing."

"Oh."

"Yeah. We need to meet, Mr. Mason wants to talk."

"Is that right."

"Do I need to remind you what an honor this is, Tyrone?"

"Sure. A real prize. Okay okay, I get it. I'll be good, promise."

"He was impressed, Tyrone. *Very* impressed."

"Cool."

"My office. Half an hour."

"Are you serious?"

"Are *you* serious? If you really want the position, you need to be ready."

He sighed, flopping back down on the bed and staring up at the ceiling, rubbing sleep from his eyes and listening to the hiss of the phone line.

"Tyrone, you there."

"I'm here, Coach. Your office, half an hour. See you then."

"Good boy."

Click.

He ate a quick breakfast, scarfing down a bowl of cereal as quickly as he could manage. Barry came out, yawning and stretching. "What are you doing up do early, dude? Who was calling you?"

"Got a football thing. Need to see the Coach."

Barry just shook his head at that. "Tyrone, Tyrone, Tyrone. It's always football with you. You need to get a girlfriend, my man, that's where it's at. Take from someone who's getting some on the regular: find yourself a chick."

I'm about to have too many to handle, Barry, that's the problem. "I'll think about it."

"You do that, my man, you do that." Barry wandered back to bed, yawning.

Tyrone crossed the campus at a jog. It was already getting warm; the sweet Florida air filled his lungs and woke him up better than any coffee could. The football field looked beautiful in the rosy dawn light, like a gorgeous picture post card, grass trimmed and lines painted on in crisp white strokes. He breathed in deep as he went down to the clubhouse entrance and down the hall to the assistant coach's office.

He started as he came through the door. Marquis wasn't there. Sitting in his chair was a dapper white-haired Caucasian gentleman with a snowy beard and an elegant suit. None other than Reginald G. Mason himself. He began to applaud slowly, clapping his hand delicately together. He was alone.

Tyrone slowed as he stepped through the door.

"Allow me to congratulate you, my boy, on a truly wondrous performance. I must say, I've rarely seen such a beautiful sight. And my darling Penelope had her breath quite taken away by the sight."

"Glad you enjoyed it," Tyrone said slowly, coming in and sitting down across from the older man.

"Indeed. As we are alone, I'll confide in you that you quite outplayed your senior companion. You really are a fantastic bull of a man, Tyrone Jackson, and it was a pleasure to watch. I asked Penelope afterwards what she thought of it and, would you believe it, the woman told me it had made her quite wet with excitement. That's when I knew I'd made the right choice of man for the task." He leaned forward, interlacing his fingers. "Now then, to the particulars. Do you accept? Would you be willing to grand my dearest wife, the light of my life for these last fifty years, a night of pleasure and delights like the one which I witnessed that night? In a far more discrete setting, of course. I would be... personally indebted to you, good sir."

Tyrone took a deep breath. This was all happening so fast... Did he really want to do it? Was this what he was now? A bull for hire? He thought back to the woman. She'd had a certain regal bearing, like a duchess or something. Just at the moment before he came, when he had Jennifer down on all fours in front of him, he had looked out into the crowd and caught her eye. She'd cocked her brow at him, rather daringly. She was a fine looking lady, not the wrinkled granny he'd been afraid of. She was actually, in a mature sort of way, really hot. He imagined her naked in front of him, spreading open her pussy, begging him to fuck her... and he realized that he wanted to do it.

He wanted it bad.

He was going to have to talk with Jennifer about it, he'd see her afterwards to explain, but he was confident that she'd understand. Tyrone grinned, and he leaned forward towards Reginald G. Mason, founder of the Black and White Club. "I'll do it," he said. "With pleasure."

* * *

Percy woke up sore and aching, his bottom still stinging. He groaned. God, so it hadn't been a bad dream after all. It had really happened.

He'd done it, though, he'd made it through. Natasha had had her revenge, or whatever it was, and now things could get back to normal. He was going to be a lot more careful in the future. He staggered out of bed, wincing as he rose. God, it hurt. He couldn't believe that some people did this kind of thing for fun.

Coffee. Coffee and a shower, that's what he needed. He stumbled into the bathroom and fumbled at the knobs. Hot hissing jets of steaming hot water sprayed down on him. He turned his face up into the spray and let it all wash away. Everything was going to be fine; he was his own man again. God, he'd already slept in almost until noon! He couldn't remember the last time he'd done something like that.

Maybe it was time for a bit of a break. He'd take the weekend off. It had been a rough week, he'd logged so many hours on the case that he'd lost track of them. He deserved a little time to himself. Maybe he would drive back home, spend some time with Jennifer, just the two of them. He wasn't sure how he was going to explain about his bruised and aching behind, but he'd figure something out. It had been an altogether strange couple of days, and he needed some normalcy. He'd call her, that's what he'd do. He'd call Jennifer up and they would talk.

That sounded nice.

It was with some reluctance that he shut off the water and stepped out of the shower, probably a good twenty minutes later. He hated to waste all that energy and water, but he'd really needed it today, no question.

He staggered around, feeling on the counter for his glasses. His hand brushed against something unfamiliar, a sort of hard leather case. His briefcase? No, too small for that. He blinked, trying to see. Between him not wearing his spectacles and the fog from his shower filling the room, there was no chance at all of him seeing things properly.

"Looking for these?"

Percy screamed, almost slipping on the bathmat and cracking his head on the toilet. He grabbed hold of the shower curtain for balance, and very nearly ripped it right down. "Who's there!" he shouted in a panic. But he knew. He'd recognized the voice.

Natasha James.

"Here," she said, "you'll want these."

He felt his glasses being pressed into his hands and shoved them on, blinking and wiping at the foggy lenses. She was there, standing very casually inside his hotel bathroom, arms crossed and expression stern. She wore that black leather outfit he'd seen her in the other day when she'd been - he now realized - disciplining Matthew.

"H-how did you get in here?" he stammered.

"That's not important," she said coolly. "The matter at hand is this pitiful little thing you call a dick. Why am I looking at it, Mr. Brice?"

"I don't know!" he wailed, trying to cover himself with his hands, "Why are you in my bathroom?"

"That little thing shouldn't be out on its own, Mr. Brice. I was surprised that your wife allowed you to keep it out like this. I thought about calling her, but decided to take a more direct approach."

"You did?" he asked, not having any sort of clue what he was talking about.

"That's right," she said. "I spoke to your bull about it instead. Tyrone Jackson. A fine young man, very understanding of my concerns. He and your wife Jennifer apparently had a very productive conversation about it this morning, and we've all agreed that this is the best course.

Percy blinked. "What is?"

Natasha reached over and opened up the leather case. Inside was a strange device, a sort of small metal cage about the side of her fist. At first he thought that the shape was... well, no, it couldn't be.

But it was.

"This is a chastity device, Mr. Brice. It's going to help you with your little problem. I don't want to see any more of your pitiful little erections in my boardroom, and I want your mind focused on the task before us, do you understand?"

"I-I-I... you talked with them?"

"Indeed. Your wife was most agreeable to the idea. Your cock is going to be caged, and I will have the only key. If you want to diddle yourself, you are going to have to ask my permission. When you leave us, I will send the key to be kept by your wife. We all agreed that it was high time for this."

"We did?" he squeaked.

For the first time since he'd arrived, Percy saw Natasha James smile. The chastity device in her hands gleamed in the bathroom lights. "Oh, don't worry, Mr. Brice. This is going to make everything so much better. I'm confident that you're going to grow to like it."

She moved one foot back, pressed her elegant red heel against the door, and pushed it shut with a *click*.

* * *

Jennifer lay in bed, staring up at the ceiling. It was almost three o'clock in the afternoon. She was naked, her hair tangled, her limbs and body glistening with a sheen of sweat, and there was cum drying between her thighs.

The shower was running in the next room. Tyrone was washing up.

She had a lot on her mind. She'd had a very peculiar conversation with a co-worker of Percy's, the lady who had sent her a text message on the night of the party. Together, the three of them had come to a bold conclusion. She wasn't totally sure how she felt about it so far, but she would talk with Percy later that night and make sure he was okay with it. She was fairly certain that it was the kind of thing that would very much appeal to him once he'd adjusted to it, and wasn't especially concerned about him not liked the arrangement, which was the only reason she'd agreed to it.

But that wasn't the most important thing on her mind. No, there was something much bigger.

She reached down and felt her belly, cradling it in both hands. *Could it be?* There was no reason to suspect such a thing, no actual evidence or proof, but... She knew that she was fertile, and she was pretty sure that Tyrone was no slouch in that department either. He'd come in her countless times in the last few weeks, never with any protection, never even pulling out.

And now she felt something stirring inside her. Maybe it was just a fantasy, but she thought it was more. A kind of intuition. A woman's knowledge.

"Are you coming back?" she called out.

"Yeah, baby, I'll be right there," he replied, his deep and masculine voice seeming to wrap itself about her like a warm blanket.

She felt a tingle between her thighs were his seed was still cooling. She was going to have to head to the drug store tomorrow, and see about buying a pregnancy test...

Jennifer had a feeling that things were going to get very interesting in the days ahead.

Book Four: The Royal Treatment

Jennifer Brice

Jennifer Brice sat with her hands folded in her lap, watching the thin blue line seem to fade in and out of vision. Was that a second line? Could it be? She crossed her legs. Her throat felt dry.

The discarded plastic pregnancy test wrapper lay twisted on the floor beside the garbage can. She'd tossed it in that direction, but it hadn't quite made it all the way there. She hadn't yet gotten up to retrieve it.

Could she be pregnant?

She thought of the last time, one time out of *many*, that Tyrone Jackson's thick cum had gushed deep inside her, filling her fertile womb with his hot liquid virility. She thought of his face, the picture of contentment, as he withdrew, his huge black cock glistening wet with her sensual fluids. She thought of laying her head back, deep in the afterglow of orgasms which had rippled through her like so many tidal waves, delighting in the feel of his seed within her, and at the possibility which it might lead to.

Now that she stood upon the brink of that possibility, however, she wasn't sure *what* to feel.

She'd wanted this all her life, to have children. It was a dream she'd given up long ago, but never forgotten. Percy, her dear husband, was simply not able to provide the material needed. They'd considered going a clinic, taking advantage of a sperm donor, but not very seriously. That was too clinical for her, too detached and scientific. She knew it was nonsense, but she wasn't sure she could be a mother to the child of a *sperm donor*, those words which left such a poor taste on the tongue. She needed something more raw, more organic and... human.

By the time she'd taken up with the young black man, at her husband's urging no less, she'd largely stopped thinking about having children. She was too old, she thought. Not too old physically, of course. She was in her mid-thirties, but she was fit and healthy and had been told by her doctor that she had the body of someone ten years younger.

But she had settled into her life now, and was no longer sure exactly how a child might fight into it. On the other hand... perhaps it was time; perhaps this was just the thing she needed. That said, she was more than a little apprehensive about what the next nine months might potentially entail.

She looked back down at the pregnancy test in her hands. There was no question. The little blue plus sign was unmistakable.

She was having a baby.

Jennifer swallowed hard. Well then. Well. She couldn't think, she felt like her head was spinning. This was all happening too fast. It was too *crazy* to be real. Shed known this was a possibility, sure but the truth was that she just hadn't taken it seriously. And now it was real.

She stepped out of the bathroom stall and into the pale florescent light of the drug store bathroom. She tossed the test into the trash and washed her hands in the sink, numbly, hardly even registering the action. She looked at herself in the mirror, at her face. Okay, Jen, you did it now, that's for sure.

She walked out, still in a daze, into the pharmacy. The place was quiet, almost tranquil. Soft pop music drifted in through the speakers above. It was mostly empty, the Florida evening outside calm and blue. It was late, what time was it, almost nine o'clock? She hadn't been able to wait. Once the thought had struck her, really gotten stuck in her head, she couldn't just wait at home. The whole day it had been building, like the low thrum of a huge beehive in her ear, and then she just hadn't been able to take it anymore. She'd rushed the store and bought the test, blushing at the raised eyebrow from the teenage cashier, and stuffed it in her purse. It was ten minute drive home, but even that had seemed too much. She hadn't been able to wait, and had come back into the store and rushed for the restrooms.

And the test had been positive.

She wasn't sure if she was happy or terrified. Both, maybe, or neither, she couldn't make sense of the conflicting web of feelings inside herself.

Now she was wandering the aisles, browsing thoughtlessly through the candy bars and aspirin bottles and shampoos and knee braces, touching then, running her hands over the merchandise without really being aware of what she was looking at.

She was pregnant. And she was having a black man's child. There was a tattoo on her ankle, a black spade with the letter Q inside it, marking her for all to see. How had her life come to this moment? It all seemed too much, like the past year had been nothing but a dream, and now she was coming right back to harsh reality.

This is what I am now, she thought. *There's no turning back from this now.*

"Excuse me? Miss?"

She looked up, in a bit of a daze still. A voice, a strange voice, low and rich and dark. She saw a face before her, a man about her age with dark skin, his bald black head gleaming beneath the drugstore light, his gold-rimmed glasses glinting. "Yes?" she answered, after a moment's hesitation.

"I'm sorry," he said, "you just looked like you were... I don't know." He laughed, seeming a little embarrassed now at his presumption. "Are you okay?"

She blinked, her thoughts whirling in her head. Everything seemed to be a confusing tangle. Everything except one pure and overwhelming desire. The desire pushed everything else away, made it all seem so clear and simple. She smiled and brushed her hair back from her face. "I'm fine," she said. "Sorry. You caught me day-dreaming."

He grinned. "Gotcha. Sorry, didn't mean to bother you."

He made a move as if to leave, but her arm, seeming almost of its own volition, was reaching out and brushing against his hand, drawing him back. He looked down at her pale finger whispering against his dark forearm, and when he looked back up, his expression had shifted.

Jennifer smiled. "Oh, it's no bother at all."

* * *

As soon as the lock had slid into place Jennifer pushed him up against the bathroom stall door, breathing hard and pressing her body to him. She groped at his body, kissing him hard and long and deep, panting with need.

He kissed her back, and came up winded. He coughed and straightened his glasses, "Are you, um, are you sure that you want-"

"Take out your cock," Jennifer moaned, feeling at the bulge in the front of his pants.

He coughed again, and hastily unzipped. She reached into his boxer and pulled out his thick dark phallus. It filled her hand, heavy and firm and pulsing with life. She moaned low in her throat as she sank against him, finding his black cock with her lips and taking it fully into her mouth.

"Oh my..." he murmured, moving his hands back and forth from his hips to her shoulders to his pockets. She reached up and grabbed his wrists, moving his hands so that they were pushed deep into her curls of hair.

She sucked him hard, teasing at him with her tongue as she licked and worked him with her mouth. It felt so good and right to have his cock in her. She felt whole, completed, felt her mind going blank as all her worries and fears melted away. There was nothing but this, serving him, pleasuring him, allowing him to take her completely.

"Hm," she moaned, coming up for air, a strand of thin saliva drawing a line between her lower lip and the bulbous head of his manhood, "I love the taste of black cock." She looked up at him. The bathroom lights reflected on his glasses, turning him almost anonymous. He could have been any African American man. His expression was one of stupefied wonder. She grinned, stroking him lightly and licking at the tip of his cock. "You like my mouth?"

He cleared his throat. "Ah, yes, I... it's very good."

She lowered herself, putting her tongue between his thighs, just behind his ball sack, and slowly licking upwards, her tongue curling around his full testicles. She wanted what was inside them... on her face, her breasts, in her mouth, in her ass... and inside her pussy. She wanted his seed in her womb, though another man's had already taken root there. She sucked his balls until they were wet and dripping from her, all the while plying his shaft with slow and steady strokes up and down its turgid length. "Do you want me?"

"What... ah... what do you mean, exactly?" he laughed a little, nervously, and adjusted his glasses.

"Do you wanna fuck me?" she purred, sliding a free hand down her body, over the shapely collarbone and full breasts, the taut tummy and the wide hip, down to the center, the place between her legs already dripping wet with expectation.

"I, uh..."

"You can fuck me," she said, lifting his shirt a little and kissing his stomach, her eyes fluttering and her fingernails sliding gently over the surface of his dark skin. "You can fuck me right here. Bend me over, push up my skirt and pull my panties down... you can stick your big hard black cock in my wet pussy and fuck me. Right. Now." She looked up at him, and he could see by her expression that she was entirely serious.

He swallowed, his throat bobbing. He pulled at his collar a little and laughed, as if trying to escape the overwhelming tension building in the stall between them, the frisson which demanded an immediate and bestial release. "Should I, uh, go buy condoms?" he asked, saying it like it was a joke, like he was trying to lighten the mood.

She shook her head slowly. "Fuck me," she whispered. "Fuck me right now."

He hesitated for one last time, then came at last to his decision. This wasn't an opportunity he was going to pass up.

They fumbled at each other in the cramped confines of the stall. She turned and twisted around, trying not to trip over herself. At first she thought she might bend over and hold the toilet, but that was too low and too dirty. As adventurous and desperate as she was feeling, she wasn't ready to go quite *that* far.

There was a coat hook on the inside of the stall door. She bent at the waist and reached up to hold it, pushing her rump out and bending her head down. He stood behind her, clasping her hips in his large hands as he moved into position.

She felt an incredible tingling sizzle of energy coursing through her as he gingerly lifted her dress, pushing the dark blue cloth up in a thick bundle around her hips. Then she felt his fingers slid under the waistband of her black thong and slowly, the motion made almost reverential by his hesitation, pulling it down.

"Oh my God," he murmured, looking at the plump pink pussy in front of him, "You're so wet..."

"I need you," she moaned, almost to herself, "please, I need this, I need it inside me, please."

He put one hand back on her hip, resting it there casually. Now that she was revealed to him, vulnerable and ready and visibly aching with need, he started to relax at last, to get more comfortable in his role. He gave her rump a firm squeeze. "That's a nice ass, baby," he spoke low, almost under his breath.

She felt her own breathing turning ragged and shivering. She knew that his free hand, the one not holding her, was wrapped around the shaft of his sizable black dick, guiding the head, still slick from her mouth, towards her yearning cunt.

Jennifer gasped when he entered her, her grip tightening on the coat hook as a shudder of overwhelming pleasure swept through her. His cock parted her pale lips, pushing slowly inside her, the thick length slipping easily into the moist depths of her body. He didn't stop pushing deeper until he was entirely inside her, filling her with his whole length.

He moaned softly, holding her ass tight. "Wow..." he said, "*Wow*, you're pussy's good."

"Hm, thank you baby," she moaned, "your cock feels great inside me. It feels *amazing*."

She couldn't wait, and started to slide up and down the length of him, fucking him slowly, working her pussy lips up and down his shaft. Her ass bounced on his hips, and his belt buckle jangled. It felt incredible in her. There was no feeling in the world to compare to black cock.

He didn't make any effort to thrust into her, allowing her to do all the work. She was the one bent over and being fucked, but she felt like she was on top. She increased her pace, bracing herself against the door of the stall as she kept going. The door clattered against the frame as she worked her body against his.

"Do you... do you do this a lot?" he said, his voice a tight groan.

She laughed. "Never before this."

"What did I do to get so lucky?"

She shook her head. "Could you just fuck me, please? I need to be fucked hard right now."

"My pleasure." He seemed to have regained his equilibrium now, taking a firm hold of her hips and pulling her against him. He must have been a good eight inches. Not as big as Tyrone, but certainly bigger than any white man she'd ever seen before. He started to pound it into her, going hard enough to make her gasp at every thrust. Her hand slipped off the coat hook and she stumbled forward, driven face-first against the stall door. He didn't stop, just reached out to grab a fistful of her thick brown hair. He held her face pressed to the door as he fucked her, increasing his pace as he started to get closer to his own pleasure.

The door of the restroom swung open. They heard, though didn't register the sound at first, the clack of high-heel shoes on the tile floor.

The woman paused outside the stall door, hesitating. Jennifer could see the tips of her glossy red shoes and the shadow of her figure lying across the floor.

The man fucking her paused, half inside her and half out. She wanted to scream. She was so *close*! She couldn't stop now. She pushed back onto his cock. "Don't stop," she hissed under her breath.

He coughed, and he kept going. She couldn't see his face, but she thought he must be blushing. It didn't hold him back, however. He thrust hard.

Jennifer couldn't help it: she moaned.

"Oh my God..." the woman outside said. She sounded a good deal older than Jennifer. A fussy busy-body, no doubt. Her shoes clacked as she hurried out of the room.

"We'd better be quick," the man observed, and edge of nervousness creeping into his voice.

Jennifer spun around and pushed him down so that he was sitting on the toilet. She reached down and grasped his cock, slick and wet with her juices, on the verge of orgasm. She straddled him, and plunged him into her. She clasped his shoulders, holding her forehead against his as she fucked him, as hard and fast as she could.

He gasped, and not sixty seconds later his eyes squeezed shut and his mouth fell open. She could feel his hot cum spurting up inside her. She collapsed onto him with a moan, a strand of brown hair swinging down between her eyes.

She smiled at him, and he smiled back, shaking his head in wordless amazement. "This... was not how I was expecting my evening to go," he said.

Jennifer flashed him a grin and stood. She reached down and slipped her panties off, letting her skirt fall back into place. She tossed the black silk thong into his lap. "Souvenir for you," she said, shaking out her hair and turning to go without another word.

"Wait!" he called out, struggling with his pants, belt buckle jangling, "Wait, how will I find you?"

But she was already gone, sweeping out the bathroom door and stepping down the aisle. In the next aisle over the older woman was clattering back towards the bathroom, chattering in an aghast tone about what horrible filth was going on in the bathrooms to the tired-sounding night manager.

Jennifer felt a trickle of warm semen sliding down the inside of her pale white thigh as she stepped out into the balmy Florida evening.

Tyrone Jackson

Tyrone Jackson ran. His feet seemed hardly to touch the ground, kicking up clods of grass and dirt behind him as he flew across the earth. He craned his neck, looking up and back, scanning the darkening sky with desperate searching eyes. The glow of a hundred enormous spotlights filled the night, and the roaring of a thousand voices filled his ears like the howling of a hurricane wind.

Then he saw it, spiraling down like a meteor hurtling to earth. His hand stretched out, reaching to their fullest extent as he raced forward. A few more steps...

The object fell neatly into his outstretched hands, and he clutched it tight to his body, still running as fast as he could.

Then he felt an impact that really did take him off his feet. It was like getting slamming into by a Mack truck. He hit the turf hard, got the wind knocked right out of him.

He lay on his back, gazing up at the lights, washed by the roaring of the crowd turning to cheers of excitement and approval. The football was still clutched in the crook of his arm.

A hand reached down and clasped his forearm. He was pulled up to his feet and slapped on the back, jostling his shoulder pads. "Great catch, Tyrone!"

He blinked, gave his head a shake, and grinned.

It had been a bad throw, a wobbling spiral way off course, too high and loopy for a clean catch. Tyrone had changed direction, racing as fast as he could, slipping past the Linebackers charging at him. He'd caught it at the last moment, completing the pass for a solid thirty yard advancement.

It was late in the game and the score was close. They couldn't afford to lose any ground now. Tyrone's catch had given them a much needed advancement. Now they had a chance.

As the team huddled up, he happened to glance over at the sidelines. The coaches and defense players were all standing by the benches, tensed with anticipation. One stood a little further ahead than the rest, his foot almost resting on the white line that marked the edge of the field. Though night was falling, he wore large reflective sunglasses, catching the stadium lights like scattered diamonds. His large arms were crossed over his chest, but his lips were parted in a dazzling smile of approval. He caught Tyrone's look and gave him a nod. Tyrone nodded back at Marquis, the assistant coach who had become so much more in his own life.

Marquis had a side job. He was the manager of the exclusive high end interracial swingers association called the Black and White club. Tyrone could hardly believe it had been an entire year since he'd been recruited by Marquis. A whole year.

He thought of Jennifer. No, no bad idea! He didn't need an erection fighting for room in his protective cup.

Far beyond Marquis, sitting in the high box seats, the so-called VIP area, there was an older couple. The man had a white beard and wore a bottle green suit. The woman, stately and beautiful in and elegant and regal sort of way, held a pair of spyglasses in her hand, the sort that a couple might bring to the opera house. They looked more than a little out of place up there, with screaming college football fans all around.

They were the founders of the Black and White Club, Reginald Mason and his wife Penelope. Tyrone had a special arrangement with them, that was shortly due to come to fruition. He'd agreed with Mason that he would service the man's wife, after having performed something of an audition. He thought back to that stage, of fucking Jennifer Bryce in front of a room full of rich and powerful cuckolds, white men whose wives could not be satisfied at home. He thought of cumming deep inside her, flooding her with his virile seed.

He felt his cock get hard, fighting against the confines of his protective gear. He shook his head. There was still a game to finish here. He needed to focus up.

He didn't have many games left to play. It was only another few months until graduation. He wasn't sure what future awaited him, but he was fairly sure it wasn't the NFL. He was a good player, but he wasn't sure he was *that* good, or that it was something he wanted. This might be the last season of organized football he ever played. He had to keep his head in the moment.

Marquis' club, Reginald and Penelope... even Jennifer... They could wait until after the game.

* * *

The team came bursting out of the lockers rooms, whooping and cheering and climbing all over one another, aglow with the flush of victory. A crowd of waiting fans were still scattered in the parking lot, shouting and laughing with drunken revelry.

Tyrone slung his duffle-bag over his shoulder. It was a decent walk back to the dorms, but the night was clean and cool, and he felt good. They'd played hard, and scraped by with a tight victory, right down to the clock kinda thing. Anyway, it was Friday and his homework was more or less caught up. He had a weekend pretty much to himself, and he was looking forward to the downtime.

As he walked along the sidewalk, a long black car, gleaming under the blue safety light over the sidewalk, slid up beside him, and stopped.

He paused. His reflection looked back at him in the polished black of the door. The window slowly rolled down. A neatly-bearded man in a bottle green suit leaned forward. He gave Tyrone a nod and a congenial smile.

"Good evening to you, my boy," said none other than Reginald G. Mason himself. "My I congratulate you on a fine game?"

"Yeah, thanks."

The car hummed quietly. The sidewalk was empty.

"Can I offer you a ride?" Mason asked, his tone light. "There's someone here in the car that has been very much looking forward to meeting you."

Tyrone considered it a moment. So, this was happening now, was it? The erection he'd been fighting back out on the field stirred again. Fuck, why not? He stepped down off the curb and opened the door of the car.

The back seat of the car, while not quite as extravagant or ostentatious as a limousine, was far more comfortable and fancy than any normal car. There was a sheet of black glass separating the back from the driver. Reginald gave it a tap as Tyrone took a seat beside him.

An older woman in a silky blue dress sat across from them, one leg crossed delicately over the other. She was watching Tyrone with a cool blue gaze, a look that was both penetrating and full of mysterious depth.

The car pulled smoothly away from the curb, sliding out into the warm night.

Reginald G. Mason reached into a small mini-fridge built into the car and withdrew a tall chilled bottle. He set up three crystal champagne flutes on the little table in the center of the space. The cork popped loudly, and a curling frost of cool air escaped in fine gray tendrils. He began to pour, one glass after the other. The ride was so smooth that the glasses hardly shifted a fraction as they filled with bubbly golden liquid. "A fine game, my boy. Truly fine. I'm no connoisseur of the sport specifically, but I am a great appreciator of all manner of athletics. You did quite well out there, my boy, quite well indeed." He lifted the first glass and offered it to Tyrone.

Tyrone took it with a nod. "Thanks."

A year ago he would have been incredibly nervous in a situation like this. Alone with a rich and powerful white couple in the back of their luxurious car, sipping bubbly champagne, and all the while each one of them knew why he was really there: to fuck the rich and powerful white man's wife better than he ever had or ever could manage himself. You might say there was some unacknowledged tension in the room. All the things he'd experience over the past year, however, had served to prepare him at least somewhat for this sort of thing. He lifted the glass, his hand steady, and he took a drink.

Reginald handed the second glass to his wife, and took the last for himself. He sat back, eyeing Tyrone with obvious interest and appreciation. "My wife is a great admirer or yours, Mr. Jackson."

Tyrone shifted his posture somewhat, turning away from Reginald and focusing instead on Penelope herself. Reginald could watch all he wanted, but he wasn't going to be particularly involved in what took place from here on out. "Is that right?" he asked.

The older woman smiled. Her hair was long and silver, falling sleek and shining over one shoulder. There were fine wrinkles in the corners of her eyes, but they still shone with a lively and energetic light. Her figure beneath the shimmering blue gown was taut and firm. "It is," she said, her voice somewhat soft and delicate.

Tyrone leaned back, spreading his legs and resting one hand tantalizingly, if casually, on the inside of his thigh. "Yeah? And what is it that you admire so much?" He reached down and gave his cock a squeeze. The shape of it could hardly have been less concealed beneath the loose pair of gym shorts he'd put on after the game.

"My goodness," she said, "you are rather forward, aren't you?"

He smiled, and when he spoke his voice was deep and calm. "You haven't answered my question, Mrs. Mason."

Penelope's mouth opened a little as if she were about to speak. Her eyes flicked over to her husband.

"Don't look at him," Tyrone said, still very calm, "Look at me. I know you've seen me fuck. I saw you at Jonas Harrington's party. That's the athleticism you've been thinking about, isn't it? You've been thinking about this." He gave himself another squeeze, and let a lopsided grin creep across his features.

"I..." a fine blush crept over Penelope's cheeks. "I have been thinking about that... yes..."

Reginald cleared his throat. He had clearly intended to keep control of the meeting for a good deal longer than this.

Tyrone wasn't interested. He'd played enough of Mason's games. The interviews, the audition, this ridiculous subterfuge. He'd had enough of it, and now he was going to do his thing, no matter how Mason felt about it. He had Penelope's full attention now, he could see that clearly. Her cheeks were flushed and her breathing had started to speed up just a little, he could see it in the rise and fall of her breasts, squeezed there into that tight blue dress.

"And you liked what you saw?"

She nodded. "Very much, yes. I did..."

Tyrone reached down with both hands. The gym shorts were extremely loose. He slipped one hand in and pulled out his thick cock. "Show me," he said, grasping it at the base.

Reginald G. Mason choked on his champagne, sputtering and coughing as he sat up, pounding his chest with a curled fist.

Penelope's eyebrows lifted fractionally. "Excuse me?" she said, her voice sounding just a little faint.

"Well, you've see what I can do. I did your little audition. Now it's my turn to see what you've got. Show me."

She considered his words for a moment, then nodded. "Well... that sounds only fair."

Reginald regained control of his voice. "Darling, I think perhaps we should wait for a more opportune-"

She held up a pale hand. "Reggie."

He felt silent at once, leaning back and twisting the stem of his wineglass between his fingertips.

She looked at Tyrone for a long moment, her delicate chin raised. Then she nodded. "Would you avert your eyes for a moment?"

He grinned. Very posh. But he did as she'd asked, leaning back in his seat and looking out. The nighttime town slid away behind them, vanishing in a dazzling ocean of golden lights. And beyond that, the sea. A great black velvet carpet churning and roiling in the moonlight.

He heard the long low sound of a zipper being drawn down, and the silky rustle of the blue gown being draw away.

He watched, in the vague and formless reflections on the glass, as the older woman neatly folded the dress and set it beside her on the seat. She cleared her throat lightly, the sign that he was permitted to turn back.

She sat across from him, her pale body clad now only in black lace lingerie that delicately cupped her breasts. It was a single piece that covered her breasts and stomach and bottom, with long black stockings attached by garter belts. The effect was rather intoxicating.

She cocked her head to one side, a light smile playing across her serene features. She was enjoying this. "Well?" she asked, "Do you like this? Have I passed your test?"

He grinned. "Not yet."

"I'm afraid that if you want to see me without any clothing on you are going to have to wait until we're in a more private setting."

"No, this is fine. I like it."

"Thank you."

"Of course."

"So... what is it that you *do* want from me?"

Tyrone leaned back. He was still holding his dick in his fist. He nodded at his cock. "Come say hello."

"Ah..." Her voice sounded hesitant, but her eyes seemed to light up with an eagerness which she was unable to entirely disguise. She rose from her seat, crossing the car gingerly, her glass clutching in one hand.

"I know you've been doing this sort of thing for a long time."

"You've no idea," she remarked dryly, settling down on her knees in front of him.

"How long has it been, though?" he asked, "since you did something like this?"

She looked up for a moment, and her blue eyes sparkled. "Far too long," she said, and leaned forward to take him fully in her mouth.

Reginald G. Mason seemed glued to his seat, his eyes wide. He seemed torn between outrage that the situation had gotten so completely out of his hands and delight at the turn of events. Champagne spilled unnoticed over the edge of his glass as he stared, completely oblivious to the drink dripping onto his shiny black shoes.

That gave Tyrone an idea. He took Penelope's champagne flute form her head. He gave it a little taste. "This is good stuff," he remarked, quite casually. He knew about as much about wine as Reggie did football, but he could bluff. Anyway, it hardly mattered for his purposes.

"Thank you," she remarked lightly, a little smile playing at her lips as she licked his long dark shaft. She seemed rather amused at the turn of events, as if it were an unexpected delight to find herself sucking his cock in the backseat of a moving car.

He took his cock and dripped it into her glass, lifting it wet and dripping over her upraised face. Pearls of crystalline Champagne fell from the tip and landed in her mouth. He shifted his position, inserting it fully into her waiting mouth.

Reggie's glass slipped from his trembling fingers. "Oh my word," he muttered, fumbling to right the thing, sounding quite flustered.

Tyrone repeated the maneuver a few more times.

Penelope laughed. "Are you trying to get me drunk?" she asked. "I'll warn you now that I'm a bit of a lightweight."

He grinned and downed the rest of the glass himself. "Just cock for you then. I take it we have a busy weekend ahead of us?"

She smirked mischievously, and for a moment she seemed no older than a frisky high school student planning to get busy at a party while her parents were out of town. She'd been wanting this for some time now, he could tell.

She was hungry for it.

She gave him one last firm suck before returning to her seat and instructing him once more to avert his eyes. She rustled her way back into her dress and demurely wiped her lips. "I do believe we're nearly at our destination. I'll have to continue this later."

"You certainly will," Reggie said, his tone low and admiring.

Penelope nodded primly to her husband. "I trust you enjoyed the view, Reggie?"

"Always, my darling. Always." He glanced at Tyrone. "There are no objections, I trust, to my continued observations?"

Tyrone shrugged. "I thought that was the idea."

"Indeed."

Tyrone glanced out the window. They were well outside the town now, way out on the outskirts of the city. Fancy beach houses lined the coast, each building more extravagant than the last. They traveled through a heavy wrought-iron gate with gilded golden spikes along the top of the wall.

"Our private beach house," Reginald explained. "We'll have the place very much to ourselves, I assure you."

They pulled up in front of one of the biggest and most exotic homes in the little gated community. It was an older building, but in impeccable condition.

Reginald leaped smartly out, almost before the car had even stopped, and held the door open for the two of them. He seemed newly revitalized, spry and eager with a spring in his step. "Right this way," he said, gesturing to the long stone walk.

"Gladly," Tyrone said, taking a glance at the woman beside him. Penelope smiled back.

"I must tell you, Mr. Jackson," she said, slipping her arm through his as they moved down the lamp-lit pathway, "You're not quite what I expected."

"And what did you expect?"

"Well, as I said, it has been some time."

You're sure you're up for this, though?" he asked, taking her arm gently and holding it as they got closer and closer to the grand spectacle before them.

She gave him a little nudge. "Why, Mr. Jackson, I assure you that I'd not miss out on the opportunity for anything in the world."

Percy Brice

Percy Brice yelped as the lash slapped down across the back of his thighs.

"What now?" he moaned, reaching back and rubbing his stinging rump with a rueful expression on his face and hurt tone in his voice.

Natasha James arched an eyebrow at him, scarcely bothering to look up from her documents as she studied him. "If you need to ask, Mr. Brice, than you may need more discipline. Perhaps you'd like to think on it a moment longer, and tell me what you did wrong?"

He blinked, quite taken aback. "I... well, I don't know, do I?"

Whack! Whack! Whack!

"Not the answer I was looking for, Mr. Brice. You were looking at the screen again. Focus on your work."

Percy sighed. He supposed she was right, to be honest. With no small exertion of willpower, he dragged his gaze away from the projector screen at the head of the conference table. A slideshow that Natasha had put together with the help of his wife Jennifer was playing. It had been looping for some time. Percy had been forbidden to look up at it, but he'd been unable to resist sneaking a few peaks - though he'd paid highly for the violations. He could also see snatches of it occasionally, reflections on phone and tablets screens and in the glasses of the paralegals scattered about the room.

They were all hard at work preparing for the trial, which was only days away now. Natasha had arranged something of an exercise. As a test for her team, and most especially for Percy, she'd put together a presentation consisting of every photo she had of Jennifer Brice fucking black men. They were all projected up on the screen in the big conference room. She alone was allowed to look upon them, the rest of the team was required to bend their focus totally to the work at hand. Anyone found to be in violation was quickly dealt with by Natasha herself.

It had been several weeks now since Percy had entered into his particular arrangement with Natasha James. She was the head of the legal team heading up a difficult and complex lawsuit that had taken up by the Miami office of Percy's law firm. It wasn't long since he'd arrived that he started to notice something... a bit odd... about the way she ran the group. Eventually it came out that the tall and slender African American woman was a powerful dominatrix who had brought her particular skills to bear in the workplace, to great success. Her team respected her like a Goddess, and worked twice as hard as any group of paralegals he'd ever witnessed.

Almost before he'd known what was happening, he'd found himself draw into her web. After she discovered his own predilections, she'd contacted Jennifer, and then Tyrone. The three of them had devised together to put Percy under Natasha's control while he was out of town. She'd taken to the arrangement with great aplomb, exerting her enormous capacity for discipline to take almost complete control of both Percy's sexual life and his work life.

This newest embarrassment was only one in a great series which had been unfolding for some time.

As the days went by, however, and the indignities had piled up, he'd begun to find that he minded them less and less. The infringements upon his freedom had become less and less onerous, and begun in fact to excite him. He'd been in frequent contact with Jennifer, though his calls were supervised by Natasha. She seldom inquired about the specifics of Percy's situation, but she seemed to know a great deal about it, including details that he'd never mentioned. No doubt Natasha was keeping her well informed.

The thought of that brought a blush to his cheeks which he could not suppress.

Percy felt the tickle of Natasha's riding crop stroking gently across his bottom. "Mr. Brice..." she said, her voice a warning sing-song. "Don't let me catch you daydreaming, now. We have a great deal of work to do. You're going to be going up in front of a judge for our client tomorrow, and I want you at your most focused, you understand?"

He swallowed. "Of course, Miss James."

He bent back down over the brief he was preparing. The color of the light on his desk shifted as the image displayed on the wall shifted. He could see the pale pink of flesh tones, and the darker color of ebony skin entwined. His grip tightened on his pen and he wrote another line.

* * *

-Missing you, darling. I'm dreaming of the day when I will be back in your arms. It won't be long now. This case is almost over, one way or the other. I'm tired of Miami... ready to come home.

He hit send and tossed the phone aside. He lay back and stared up at the ceiling. How long had he been living in this hotel room? Almost a month now. God, it was torture. To sleep in his own bed...

The phone dinged. He picked it up. Jennifer had sent a message back.

-I miss U too, Percy. Seems like it's been forever. Can't wait for this to be done.

-Have you been seeing much of our friend? Is he still taking good care of you.

- :)

-That's a yes?

-Yes it is.

-You haven't been sending me pictures.

-I sent them to Natasha.

-Haha, of course. I'll need to beg her to show me.

-U don't mind? I thought U said you enjoyed this?

-No, I don't mind. It's been an experience, certainly.

-That's good. I wouldn't want to do anything U don't want.

Percy reached back and slid the pillow beneath his head, propping himself up. He looked at the message, considering it for a while.

-Hon? You there? She texted.

-I was just thinking. We've come a long way, haven't we? Who would have thought that our lives would take a turn like this?

- :)

-It's just a bit crazy, isn't it?

-Definitely crazy. I think that we might be in for a big change in the future though.

-What kind of change?

-Don't worry about it. We'll talk when U get back. U just have a fun night tonight?

-What's tonight?

-A surprise :)

He was about to text her asking what sort of surprise she was talking about when he heard a knock at the door. It was a firm and assertive knock, not one of those timid little taps from housekeeping. He wondered for a moment if it might be a member of the opposing council, come with some sort of last minute offer. He'd seen that kind of thing before, a failure of nerve on the eve of the trial. Or they could be attempting some sort of power play.

It wasn't the opposition. Quite the contrary, as a matter of fact.

Natasha James herself stood in the doorway. She was dressed in a tight black gown and held a bottle of expensive-looking wine loosely in her hand. In her other hand, slung over her shoulder, she held the straps of her lacquered red high heel shoes. Her stockinged feet stood bare on the soft carpet. She lifted it and arched an eyebrow at him. "A drink, Mr. Brice? Something to steel your courage before battle?"

He wasn't quite sure what to say. This was, to put it lightly, not a side of Miss James which he'd seen before. She was as steely and imposing as ever, but there was an edge of casual ease that he'd never have suspected her capable of. He gawped wordlessly at her, mouth open and eyes wide.

She made a face somewhere between bemusement and annoyance and stepped past him into the room. "I'll take your eloquent silence for ascent, shall I? Good lord, Mr. Brice, I do hope you'll prove a touch more loquacious in the court room tomorrow." She stepped to the table and took two glasses out from where they sat atop the little microwave. She put the bottle to her teeth and bit down hard on the cork. Without so much as smudging her perfect violet lipstick she pulled the cork out with a *pop* and spat it to the floor.

"Sorry," he said, shaking his head and shutting the hotel room door. "I just... I didn't expect you here, is all."

"Well now," she said, one hand on her hip and a glass of dark wine in her dark hand, "one must learn to adapt to the unexpected in this profession, mustn't one?"

"I suppose so. I'm not working right now, though, am I? I was trying to relax. Calm my nerves before the big day, you know?" There was, perhaps, a slight note of reproach in his voice as he stepped across the room and took the cup from her hand. He lifted it a little, giving her a slight salute before he brought it to his lips for a sip.

She poured herself a glass and lifted it to her lips, never once breaking eye contact with him. She drank slowly, then set the glass back down with a sort clink. "That's the difference between you and me, Mr. Brice."

"What is?"

"I'm *always* working."

"Really."

"Yes."

"How were you working this afternoon?" he asked, feeling the warmth of the wine rising to his head. Perhaps it was the drink, or perhaps he'd simply been thrown off balance by her sudden and unexpected appearance, but he felt a surge of boldness. He would never otherwise have dared to ask such a question of her.

To his great surprise, she actually seemed amused at his gentle rebellion, in her impassive way. "Indeed I was, Mr. Brice. There is more to the work than simply putting one's head down, after all. It is about the entire energy and mindfulness of the team which must be considered."

She stepped closer, bottle in hand, and she refilled his glass. Her eyes had the hypnotic power of a serpent's gaze. He found himself locked in them, totally entranced in those cool brown depths.

"So..." he cleared his throat, feeling an uncomfortable twinge low in his stomach, "Is *this* work as well then?"

A wicked little grin twinged at the corner of her lips. "It certainly is, Mr. Brice. This is entirely work related."

Slowly, sinuously, she reached for him. He felt his body freeze as she touched his skin. Her skin, which he had never felt before, never would have *dared* to touch, was as soft as if she'd just stepped out of a sensuous milk bath. The tip of her delicate finger trailed slowly up the length of his arm, starting at the wrist and winding up to his upper bicep.

"W-what are you doing?" he choked, feeling like his throat was closing as he struggled to get the words out. This turn of events was, to say the least, unexpected.

"Why, I'm going to help you relax, Mr. Brice." Her finger tilted forward, pushing the sharp red nail against his arm, making him give a little wince of pain and leaving a pink crescent in his skin. "In my own way."

He swallowed hard. "What did you have in mind?"

"Something Mrs. Brice and I have been discussing for quite some time, actually. We believe that this would be a good time to make our acquiescence... a little more physical."

"You... you can't mean?"

"What?" she asked, jutting her chin out imperiously. She stepped even closer, and it was impressed upon him again just how much taller she was than he. "What can't I mean?"

"Y-you want me to fuck you, is that what you're saying?"

She laughed. It was a beautiful and ruinous sound, sharp and mocking. "Oh, Mr. *Brice*, how could you *think* such a thing?"

He realized he'd made a mistake, gone too far. He stammered. "I-I'm sorry, I didn't-"

She reached out, her hand snapping to his chin, pinching it, drawing his face close, cheeks squeezed between her powerful fingers. "Do you really think that I'd ever let a toad like you fuck me, Mr. Brice? Do you think that I'd ever let a white man fuck *me*?"

"N-n-no, of course not, I just, I mean, I meant-"

She held a finger to his lips, silencing him instantly. "Don't speak, Mr. Brice, you'll only get yourself in more trouble. You've misunderstood me, but you're not... entirely wrong. One of us is going to get fucked tonight... but it will certainly not be me."

She uncrooked her finger and the red shoes fell to the carpet. He saw now that she'd been holding something else in her hand all along, a red object the same color as the shoes, attached to a black strap.

It was a cock. A sizable dildo in marbled latex, maybe seven inches long and about as thick around as the base of a large carrot. It was attached to a black strap. It took a moment, but it did eventually click in his mind what this meant. It was a strap-on dildo. And she was planning to fuck him with it.

He felt a warm and rising panicked embarrassment flood through him, and a voice in his head immediately started shouting out protests and denials which his tongue would not shape. Whatever protests his brain might be considering, however, the rest of his body had other ideas. He felt himself getting hard, his stubby little cock turning firm in his tight white underpants.

"Is... is that...?"

She just nodded.

"You can't be serious."

Natasha sighed. "Mr. Brice, I would think you know me well enough now to know that I am rarely other than serious."

"Yes, but, I mean, I've never..."

"But you will, Mr. Brice. Don't be afraid, you won't be alone."

His throat tightened. Surly she didn't mean herself. The presence of Natasha James, of all people, would hardly come as a comfort.

By way of an answer, she took her smart phone from her purse and plugged in a long cable. She stepped away, moving to the television across the room. "You may have taken the time to acquaint yourself with some of the more advanced features of the hotel, though I suspect you haven't. You may not be aware, for instance, that each and every one of the executive suites, such as this one, is equipped with a fully functionally video conference unit."

"I, uh... no, I wasn't." Oh *God*, what was she planning? He felt his whole body tensing, tight as a drawn bowstring.

Natasha plugged in her phone and pressed a few buttons on the remote. She stood with a hand on one hip and an expression of grim satisfaction. The screen turned on, blank and dark for the moment. "Can you hear me, Mrs. Brice?"

Percy felt a chill go through him. Jennifer? It couldn't be... why, he'd been talking to her just a moment ago and she hadn't said anything about... Wait a minute. Yes, she had said something, hadn't she? The *surprise* she'd mentioned. This was it, wasn't it? She knew all about what was going on, what was about to happen.

"I hear you fine, Tasha." Jennifer's voice. She sounded excited, giddy almost. There was laughter in her voice. When had the two of them become so familiar? He'd never heard anyone refer to her as anything other than Miss James.

"I'm going to leave the screen off in here, Jennifer. Can you see us?"

"I sure can!" she giggled, "Hello honey!"

Percy clutched at himself. "Uh, hi, Jen..."

"You can see the bed, Jennifer?"

"Yes I can."

Natasha set her phone down on the night stand. "Very good. Mr. Brice, I'm going to ask you to take your pants down and bend over the edge of the bed."

He felt himself pale. "B-bend over?"

"Indeed." Natasha seemed hardly to be paying any attention to him. She'd move aside a little, out of the sight of the camera, he thought. He knew from experience that he had better not be caught staring at her, but the glimpse he got in his peripheral vision made it clear what was happening: she'd moved her dress up a little, and was strapping on the dildo over her clothes. With it in place, she let the dress drop back down, draping it over the hard protrusion.

"You'd better do what she says, honey," Jennifer said, her voice shaky with delight.

He nodded, moving towards the bed, his hands trembling with nervous excitement as he fumbled with his belt and zipper. He stood at the edge of his hotel bed, looking down at the floral pattern there. Slowly, hesitantly, he lowered both his pants and underwear. They fell to his ankles with a jangle, and he bend down.

Percy could only imagine the sight his wife was getting right now, his pasty white skin, his big ass sticking out. It made his ears prickle with embarrassment, and a fierce heat rose in his cheeks. At the same time, he felt keenly aroused. He could scarcely recall the last time he'd felt this turned on.

His breathing started to come fast and hot as Natasha moved into position behind him.

"Face forward, Mr. Brice. Good boy."

He heard the jangle of buckles and straps, and he could only imagine what it must look like, the startling scarlet cock attached to her, straps cinched up across her chocolate thigh. He heard then a popped cap and the slow and sticky sound of a thick liquid being poured out and rubbed beneath her hand. He shuddered with ecstatic delight as he pictures her standing behind him, stroking the hard cock with her lube-slick fist.

She moved closer behind him, so close he could feel the heat of her, the brush of her smooth thigh against the back of his leg. He felt the press of the head of the dildo at his puckered bottom, and he bit down on his lower lip.

Miles and miles away, lying in their bed, in their house, his wife started to breathe hard. He knew the sound. She was touching herself while she watched the dark skinned woman take hold of his hips, and slowly sink her strap-on inside her husband's body.

Percy groaned, struggling to hold himself in position as she entered him.

"That's very good, Mr. Brice," Natasha James murmured soothingly as she began to fuck him with long and assured strokes. "Now then, aren't you feeling more relaxed already?"

Jennifer Brice

Jennifer flopped back in bed, her hand slowly moving inside her panties. She moaned softly, gripping the bed sheets, gritting her teeth.

On the computer screen across the room her husband was bent over with his pale ass in the air, yelping and groaning as the statuesque black dominatrix drove her strap-on cock deeper inside him.

She imagined Tyrone fucking her as she watched, tried to call back every memory she had of his massive black cock splitting her open and filling her. She thought of his hands on her skin, his lips on her neck and ears, his tongue in her mouth. She wanted him, wanted him bad.

The woman on the screen, Natasha, threw Percy down on the bed. She climbed on top of him and buried her fingers in his thinning hair, shoving his face down into the pillow as she mounted him. She straddled his body, shifting her hips with a steady and powerful rhythm, dominating him completely. She wanted was he was getting, and yet here she was desperately rubbing her clit and biting back her moans, alone in the house, alone in the cold bed while her husband got fucked.

It wasn't *fair.*

She felt like she had when she was a teenager, stuck in her room at home listening to the distant creaking of the bed springs while her parents had sex in their room upstairs. She'd been a little grossed out, of course. They were her mom and dad, after all, and weren't supposed to be having sex. Yuck.

At the same time, however, she'd been a little jealous. She used to climb out of bed in the middle of the night and put her ear to the heat vent in the floor and listen, holding her breath and trying to quiet the thumping beating of her heart as she struggled to hear her mother's faint tinny moans echoing through the vent. She would imagine what it was like to be fucked by a man.

She'd seen pictures once, in a dirty magazine somebody had left on the playground at school. She imagined lying on her back and spreading her legs, reaching down to spread open her pussy lips. She tried to imagine what it might be light to feel a man, his body hot and strong, laying down between her thighs as he put his thing in her. It was difficult to imagine what the sensation might be like.

She'd experimented, trying to approximate the sensation. She would use the soft rubber handle of her hairbrush and hump her pillows and old stuffed animals. None of it seemed right, they had been to unresponsive, to inert and cold, the brush handle so small and thin that she could hardly feel it.

Then, in high school, it had finally happened. She'd been dating him for a few weeks... Bobby Thompson. It was a lot like any of her other, earlier, high school relationships, all furtive touches and shy kisses, only bordering on sexual. They went out to the drive-in theater together and watched a movie, she didn't even remember what it was. To be honest, neither of them had been paying much attention to the screen. They were too busy making out and touching each other. Afterwards he drove her home, but he didn't take the usual way. She'd waited, frozen in her seat, not wanting to say anything, consumed with an overwhelming feeling of excitement and fear. Could it really be happening? Was this it? She didn't want to say anything, lest it dispel the moment.

Bobby had pulled up to a quiet bluff over the town, way out in the darkness. He'd cleared his throat, leaned back in his seat. "Well," he'd said, "it sure is a pretty night, isn't it?"

That was the first time she'd ever seen a cock. He had taken it out and shown in to her, and she'd showed him hers in return. She remembered feeling a twinge of disappointment. It had been so small, hardly more than a finger. She'd expected it to be big, monstrous, overwhelming, something almost terrifying. She had expected something powerful and domineering, something she would have no choice but to surrender to. Bobby Thompson's little pink cock, however, looked like it could hardly measure up to the handle of her hairbrush.

She made the best of it. She'd touched it, rubbed it a little, even let him try and put it inside her. They'd climbed into the backseat, very awkwardly, all elbows and knees. Finally she'd been lying down and he'd pushed up her skirt and gotten between her legs. He'd reached down and put it inside her. She'd heard about condoms in health class, but it hadn't seemed the time to mention wanting to put one on. He'd started flopping around, his expression squeezed and pinched. Not sixty seconds later he'd made a face like he'd just been punched in the stomach and groaned. A moment later he'd slipped back, flopping back against the far door. "Oh my *God*," he'd said with a cocky grin, "did I rock your world, baby?"

She blinked at him, more confused than anything else. Had it started yet? Wasn't it supposed to hurt? She'd been wincing and bracing herself, expecting pain. She reached down and felt something thick and sticky on her thighs. It was silky creamy pale when she lifted her hand, and she realized that it was his cum.

So, that was sex.

It wasn't the best experience she had in high school, but it wasn't the worst either, sad to say. By the time she met Percy she'd had sex with maybe half a dozen boys, none of them any more impressive than Bobby had been, to be entirely honest. She'd gotten used to it, and no longer felt disappointed at their little dicks or lack of stamina. It was something she simply accepted as natural.

She'd never lost the vague sensation of yearning, however, the itch in the back of her mind that kept telling her there must be more to it than this, must be something better. Boy after boy, however, all with the same result, and it was difficult to think that her fantasies could possibly be in any way realistic. Percy had been the worst of them all, sexually speaking. He was very dear to her, and she loved him deeply, but he'd always been crap in bed. She'd tried not to mind, told herself that it didn't matter. Love was what was important, not sex.

But then she'd met Tyrone.

The first time he fucked her it had been like all her dreams were coming true. Sex really could be good, she really *could* be pleasured by a man. It had been like night and day, like somebody had thrown a switch.

There was no going back now. She didn't think she could bear to have Percy's little thing inside her again, not after what she'd experienced. It would have been a joke, would have been ridiculous. That was why she'd agreed to Natasha's plan.

The other woman was something of an enigma to Jennifer. She was a strong and powerful confident black woman, so what did she want with Jennifer's doughy little white husband? It didn't entirely make sense of Jennifer, but it certainly seemed to make Percy happy.

On the screen across the room he was squealing and moaning, begging for her to fuck him, his ass quivering with every impact. She had a fistful of his shirt all balled up in her hand, and was riding him relentlessly.

Jennifer couldn't help but be turned on by the sight, even if it wasn't exactly her thing. Something about seeing the way she took charge reminded her of Tyrone, and that turned her on. She slipped a finger inside, feeling her soft wet pussy with the tip of her middle finger. A little quiver ran up her spine.

She lay back and tried to enjoy herself, but she just couldn't help feeling like she was a kid in her bedroom fucking her hairbrush again.

She needed Tyrone's cock, there was no getting around it. She needed it now.

She wiped her finger on the bed sheet and picked up her phone.

-Please come fuck me, baby... I need U :(

There was no reply. She waited, watching the screen.

-Are you there, Ty?

Nothing. It didn't look like the messages were going through. He must have his phone off, or not with him. She sighed heavily and tried to content herself with watching the video feed on the screen.

* * *

Jennifer almost wasn't aware of getting dressed and walking outside. Before she even knew that she'd made up her mind she was behind the wheel of the car and pulling out of the driveway.

She'd watched all the way to the end of the video conference. Percy had been passed out on the bed, his ass sticky with lube and his mouth open. Natasha had winked at the camera and given her strap-on a little shake before switching off the video. And Jennifer had been alone again. Not that she hadn't been alone in the first place, but as least she'd been able to pretend. The entire time she'd wanted to run over to the computer microphone and scream into it, "Percy, I'm pregnant! What the hell are we going to do!"

But she hadn't. The words weren't far from her mind the whole time, but she'd kept them inside. She couldn't tell him like this. It had to be face to face. Tyrone too. She needed to have them in the room with her, that was the only way. But neither of them were *with* her. Why weren't they with her? She wished sometimes she could keep them both on a leash, tied up in the back to be used whenever she needed them. Well... maybe Percy. Tyrone could keep *her* on the leash if he wanted, as long as he didn't let go of it.

So, there she'd been, sitting in her bedroom, squirming with unrealized sexual energy, a huge secret burning a hole in her mind. No one to talk to, no one to fuck. *If I stay here*, she'd thought to herself, *I'll go crazy*.

So, before she even knew what she was doing, Jennifer got up from the bed and dressed herself and went out to the car and drove off into the warm evening.

She didn't even know where she was going when she'd started driving. Well... that wasn't entire true. She'd *known*, she just hadn't been willing to admit it to herself. But here she was, pulling up on the side of the road and getting out of the car.

There it was, right in front of her. *The Black and White Club.* The little inauspicious sign, the light over the door. You would hardly even notice the place if you didn't know it was there. But Jennifer knew. She knew very definitely. She'd done things in that club that she would never forget.

What did she want to do there tonight, though? Why had she come? To tell the truth, she wasn't altogether sure. Not sex, she didn't think. Her hookup at the drug store had satisfied her need for anonymous sex, at least for the moment. The next time she opened her legs it was going to be for Tyrone, and no one else. She wanted to be here, though, she knew that much.

She went to the door and the doorman let her in with a familiar smile. "No husband tonight?" he asked, reclining against his post and grinning.

"Not tonight."

"Very good, ma'am," he offered, with a little tip of his cap.

It was cool and dark inside the club. Delicate jazz music floated in over the speaker system. She felt herself immediately begin to relax. Something about the place felt comfortable, safe and secure. She felt like she belonged here.

This is where she'd met Tyrone.

It was a particularly busy night at the club. There were dozens of couples clustered around at all the tables, and groups of young black men in snappy suits sauntering casually up and down the room, like prowling wolves on the hunt, flashing their dark eyes and bright smiles.

She glanced around the room, searching in vain for a place to sit down. It seemed that every table was occupied, ever seat at the bar across the room taken. The beaded curtains at the far door danced and jangled as a steady traffic came and went to and from the private rooms upstairs.

"Excuse me, but, are you looking for a seat?" a soft voice spoke, seemingly right next to her elbow.

She jumped a little, and turned around. A young white couple was sitting at one of the tables, looking rather skittish and nervous. The man, a clean-shaven fellow with close-cropped dark hair, was tapping his fingertips nervously on the surface of the table. He seemed skittish and jumpy, always licking his lips and glancing around. He seemed to be on the verge of laughter. The woman, a pretty little blonde thing in a blue sundress and pearls, looked just about as nervous as her husband. The diamond on her hand glittered in the low lights.

The woman blinked her big brown doe eyes up at Jennifer. "You can sit with us, if you like."

Jennifer glanced around once more. It didn't seem likely that she would get a better offer. "Thank you, that's very kind," she said, and took the third chair across from the young couple.

They sat together for a moment, Jennifer daydream about the past, the young couple anticipating the future with nervous energy.

"You come here often?" the man asked, tapping his foot on the floor.

"Not so often, no..."

"But you have been here before?"

"It's our first time," the young woman explained, blushing pink.

"That's right," her husband took over. "We were invited by a friend of mine. He used to be a regular, I guess. Him and his wife split up though, or something."

The young woman shook her head "Such a shame."

"Anyway, he told us about it, and it sounded like just the thing. We've always wanted to try something like this. You remember in college, Mandy? What we did in college?"

She smiled shyly. "Of course I do."

The man turned back to Jennifer, grinning, "We used to hook up with other guys. They'd come back to the dorm room and I'd film them on my smart phone. We up the videos online. Had quite a few fans, actually. We could have gone pro!" he laughed. "Never did it with a black man, though. Not a lot of brothers at our school, I guess. I don't know. Anyway, it seemed like it might be fun." He was babbling a little, like the ceaseless chatter was the only thing keeping his nerves at bay. "It's been a long time, though. How long has it been, hon?"

"Three years."

"Three years, that's right. We've been out of the game awhile. This is our first time trying something like this since we got married. I don't know, kind of makes it extra special, somehow. Extra exciting. I don't know why that is. Anyway, we're new here; don't really know our way around yet. I don't suppose they offer guided tours here, unfortunately!" He laughed again. "Do you just... start? I don't know."

Jennifer smiled. God, only out of college for three years. They must be, what, twenty-five at the most? Just babies, really. She could hardly remember being that young, tried to imagine herself and Percy in a place like this at their age. God, what a sight that would have been. She almost laughed herself at the thought of it.

"That's about it," she said. "I think you'll find that they're very welcoming here."

The young woman blushed. "Oh good," she said, beaming happily.

Especially looking like that. You are a nice little thing, aren't you? I'm surprise nobody's claimed you already. Jennifer grinned.

The young man took a deep breath. "Look, I'll just... I'll get us some drinks. We'll see what happens? Alright, hon?"

The young woman nodded. "Alright, I'd like a drink." She turned to Jennifer. "Can we...?"

Jennifer shook her head. "No, that's alright. I'll leave you two alone. Don't want to get in the way."

"Okay." The young woman smiled brightly, if a little nervously. "Any advice?"

Jennifer smiled back. "Just let it happen. Do what comes naturally. You'll know when it's right." She spotted a tall young black man standing across the room who seemed to have just noticed them and was eyeing the young woman with obvious and undisguised interest. Jennifer nodded in his direction. "I think, if you like, you might consider speaking with the gentlemen over there."

The young woman followed her nod. A broad grin spread across her face. "I think I might just do that, thank you."

Jennifer rose from her seat. "Happy to help."

Tyrone Jackson

Tyrone marveled as he stepped across the threshold of the Mason's beach house. The name seemed quite inadequate to describe the stunning structure. It was more grand by far than most homes he's seen, easily rivaling Jonas Harrington's enormous mansion for opulence, if not size.

Reginald led Tyrone and his wife inside the house, taking a moment to stand back and marvel at his own building. He glanced at Tyrone, a twinkle of pride in his eyes as he twirled his cane absently. "You like the place?" he asked.

Tyrone felt his gaze shift from the building to the woman coming in silently behind him. "Not half as much as I like her," he said with a grin.

She smiled and bowed her head in mock-deference while Reginald chortled. "Well said, my boy, very well said. A fine pair you two make indeed, a very fine pair." He rapped his cane firmly on the hardwood floor. "Now then, a few simple ground rules. First, as to the house and its accommodations, please consider it your own. It's well stocked with food and wine both, and I urge you to surrender yourself entirely to whatever culinary pleasures you desire. You may have any room you like, and feel free to take advantage of the spa and the beach front. As for Penelope, you may feel free to take advantage of her as well!" he roared with laughter, then turned serious a moment, "Within reason, of course. I'm afraid I must insist that you wear a prophylactic when making love to her. A simple precaution, I'm sure you understand."

Tyrone felt a twinge of disappointment. He didn't care for condoms in the least... But he supposed that he'd have to put up with them for the weekend. He'd suffered through far worse. And anyway, he was starting to feel more and more interested in Penelope Mason the more time he spent in her company. The older woman had an aura of understated eroticism which he'd not noticed at first, but was now finding harder and harder to ignore. She seemed to exude a subtle sexuality.

He wanted her.

"I must also insist that I be present at any such couplings. We have the entire weekend ahead of us, and I trust that all three of us shall have an invigorating and expansive time in each other's company." He lifted his cane and gave it another emphatic rap on the floor. "Let the Bacchanalia begin, my friend, my darling wife, and may we all three of us drink deep from the well of human pleasure tonight."

"Hear, hear," Penelope said softly.

"Sounds good to me," Tyrone agreed, eyeing her up and down.

"Well then," said Reginald G. Mason, "let the fun begin!"

They fucked twice that night, though it wasn't exactly what Tyrone had been hoping for. The sex was very proper and choreographed, with Reginald insisting upon certain positions and tempos, even going so far as to swoop in and arrange his wife into the posture most pleasing to him from where he saw watching and pleasuring himself.

Tyrone found it quite frustrating, so much so that he could hardly appreciate the woman he was making love. He felt more like a prop, a doll in Mason's playhouse. The sex was clearly meant as a display for Mason to admire, rather than being something for either of the actually participants to enjoy. Add to that the condoms, which chafed both figuratively and in a more literal sense, and he was starting to find the whole experience rather less pleasant than he'd hoped.

Still, he couldn't say that it was entirely unsatisfactory. The food was incredible, and the house was absolutely stunning. He had free reign of the place, when he wasn't being summoned for another session of showy lovemaking.

Mason drank heavily, downing cup after cup of outrageously expensive wine. Penelope indulged more sparingly, taking a sip for every few gulps her husband downed. She went through the whole thing with an air about of almost of indulgence. When Mason had first proposed the coupling to Tyrone he'd made it sound like it was a special gift for his wife. Now that they were here, however, it appeared to be the other way around.

She never once said a word against him, nor did she seem in any way to bristle under the constant barrage of instruction. She went through the whole thing with a sense of detached and absent pleasure, as if what were happening were nice enough, though of no great concern to her.

Tyrone found her calm a little bit maddening. The longer the evening went on, the more taken he felt himself becoming with her. There was something enchanting and beguiling about her manner, something that made him desperately interested. He wanted to see the real her, to crack open the shell that her husband had built around her and let the real woman out. Mason, however, didn't appear to have any interest in letting such a thing take place.

They were all sitting in the living room after the second horribly staged session. Mason was drinking, of course, and regaling them both with stories of his exploits in the early days of the club. Of things that he'd seen and done clearly meant to astonish and amaze his listeners. The more he talked, however, the more slurred and confused his words became. Finally, halfway through a story about watching a visiting African Prince with a cock like an elephant's fucking a four foot ten eighteen year high school student, his chin dropped to his chest, and he began to snore.

Tyrone watched, waiting to see if the sleep would take. After a solid four minute he hadn't made so much as a twitch. Reginald G. Mason, it was clear, was asleep for the night.

Penelope rose with a ghost of a smile on her lips. "I do apologize about my husband. He does so love to go on."

Tyrone shrugged. He would have worded it a bit more strongly than that, himself, but... "Are all those stories true?" he asked.

Penelope laughed softly. "Oh, more or less."

"Even the one's about you?"

Her eyes sparkled, twinkling with a subdued mischief. "Oh, those one's most especially."

"Sounds like you've had some experiences."

"Oh, I certainly have. That's all in the past now. We've far more subdued than that now, as I'm sure you've gathered. You found a room, I trust?"

"Yeah, thanks."

She nodded curiously. "Then I will bid you a good night."

"Good night, Penelope."

She gave him an odd look that he couldn't quite decipher, then she swept away upstairs.

He waited for a long moment, sipping the last of his wine, then he shook his head and went off to bed. The room he'd chosen was on the first floor, with a great wide window looking out at the ocean. Even after having spent so long in Florida at school, he still found himself just a little bit entranced by the sight of the sea.

He lay in bed, suddenly restless, tossing and turning and staring at the ceiling. Even though he'd cum twice already today, he still felt pent up, almost bursting. The sex had been so halting and demonstrative, it almost hadn't counted. He rose with a sigh and went out the sliding door. He walked down the beach, feeling the sand beneath his feet. It was still warm with the fading heat of the day.

He walked down to the water and stood with his feet in the surf, watching the way the moon played upon the shifting tides.

What was he *doing* out here? The whole thing seemed like such a waste now. He wished he were back in his dorm. Or, better yet, with Jennifer. She hadn't been talking to him much lately. It had only been a few days, but he was beginning to miss her. The arrangement with Mason had seemed like it might be a laugh, and Marquis had been so insistent about what an honor it was for him, but now that he was here...

It was only another day. He could put up with a couple unsatisfactory tumbles if it meant being wined and dined in this luxurious house.

He turned to go back inside, and then he saw her.

Penelope Mason stood at the door, her long white night gown dancing in the breeze. Her long gray hair, which she'd been wearing up the entire time, was no loose and flowing in the wind. She looked like a pale ghost, almost, coming slowly down the beach towards him, her feet lighting gently on the sand. The moon was so bright that he could see her clearly, even now in the depths of the night.

He stood, his hands in his pockets, and he watched her approach.

"I saw you out here," she said as she got closer, her voice soft and calm.

"I just wanted to look at the ocean, I guess."

She stepped beside him, sliding her arm into his. He turned, and they looked together out at the water. "Beautiful," she said softly.

"Yes it is," he said. But he wasn't looking at the sea anymore.

She made a face of mock-reproach in his direction. "Come now. I'm too old to be charmed by that sort of flattery, you know."

"Maybe I'm not trying to flatter you."

She sighed, shifting deeper into his arms, wrapping her small and delicate hands around his forearm and bicep. "It has been... a very long time."

"A long time since what?"

She smiled sadly. "Since I've been along with a man like this. Alone on the moonlit shore of the beautiful ocean. With someone... someone as fine as yourself."

"Mason, he doesn't... let you out to play anymore?"

She shook her head. "Not for a good long while now. He's a good man, and he's been a good husband to me for a long time. Only... things have changed. We're neither of us the same anymore. He's become... more controlling, squeezing tighter and tighter. I'm not sure he even realizes it. But... the tighter he squeezes the more I feel myself slipping away. This is all I've wanted... just this. The club was always his passion, making a place that he could own and control.... But I just wanted this."

Then she turned and she looked into his eyes. She seemed to him very beautiful and, in some ineffable way, terribly sad. He gathered her to him, wrapping his strong arms about her gossamer form, and he held her close.

She laid her head against his chest, her eyes shut. She pressed her ear to his breast, listening to the thump of his heart beating. "You are... a very beautiful man, Tyrone Jackson."

He grinned. "You too, Penelope Mason. A beautiful woman, I mean."

She laughed. Her slim hands were touching his chest, hesitantly, slowly sliding in under his shirt to touch his naked skin. The feel of her skin against his own was electric. Very much unlike the way he felt with Jennifer, but enticing in its own way. He bent his head down and he lifted hers, his fingers gently cupping her fine chin. He leaned in and he kissed her, his broad lips pressing warm against her little mouth.

She opened to him, moaning softly as her little tongue slipped out and caressed his own, her hands clasping more firmly about his midsection.

They sank together down to the warm sand, embracing closely, sinking into on another, no longer performing or showing off for anyone, their bodies answering to the yearning call which drew them together.

Tyrone caressed the side of her face.

She snuggled up to him, kissing gently, her lips brushing his. She had a needful hunger to her, but was no rushing, was not falling head-over-heels with passion. She was measured, calm, taking her time with him.

She looked up at the sky, and he looked with her. The stars above seemed like a million diamonds scattered across an inky velvet expanse that went on endlessly.

"I was seventeen the first time I had sex with a black man."

"Yeah?"

"That's right. It was so long ago, but... it almost feels like yesterday, somehow. It was in the mid-seventies, but it still felt like the sixties to me. We were all hippie free-love flower children, me and my friends. His name was Leroy, and he was in a band, and he was *beautiful.* Looked a lot like you, actually. We made love in a field, wildflowers all around us like a firework. We were naked and I ran into the flowers and he chased me and when he caught me he made love to me. I was a virgin then... not after he was through with me. It was... a kind of magic. One of those perfect moments which you spend the rest of your life hunting after, trying to recapture some small fraction of the feeling again."

"Is that what we're doing?" he asked, kissing her cheek softly, nibbling at her ear.

She smiled. "It doesn't bother you? That I'm so much older? Had so many experiences before this one?"

He grinned. "No. Not one bit."

Then he moved on top of her, and it was like they entered into a shared dream. They undressed each other slowly, working ivory buttons and brass zippers by the pale starlight, and all the while the ocean murmured its comforting song or waves upon sand.

They lay naked on the beach, her on her back and him above her. He moved into position, then hesitated. "Should I... do you want me to put a condom on?"

She looked up at him, biting her lower lip, and for a moment he saw that timid little virgin dashing about the field, some spark of her fanned to life in the older woman's breast. She did not speak, but shook her head, and reached down to put him inside.

He groaned as he slipped inside, raw and naked, his thick black cock parting her pink and rosy lips. She still felt tight. And wet. She clutched to him, sand clinging to her back, her nightgown pushed up around her hips and dancing in the wind. She held him close as he started to move.

He was slow at first, gentle. There was a voice in the back of his head telling him to be easy on her, not to take things too far.

Her fingernails bit into his shoulder blades. "Fuck me," she moaned in his ear, her breath hissing, "Fuck me hard, Tyrone. Don't hold back."

He did as he was instructed, shifting his weight down and pounding home a deep hard thrust. She gasped, throwing her head back, writhing in the sand and groaning in delicious agony. Her hands moved gently down to his hips, holding him firmly, pulling him towards her, into her, deeper and deeper inside.

"Oh my God, Oh my *God*, she started to moan, her fingers tightening, sliding even further down to hold his buttocks, guiding his strokes, pulling him, her throaty moans rich with yearning and desire.

Tyrone's foot shifted in the surface of the beach, his toes sliding into the sand. She was so soft and wet inside, he felt like he could lose himself in her, abandoned himself right here on the beach and drift with her up into the scattered star-field above.

"Cum in me... Cum in me, my darling... I need it... it's been so long."

He lifted his head, looking into her eyes, cupping her cheek with one hand. "Are you sure?"

She nodded, her eyes squeezing momentarily tight as a jolt of pleasure swept through her. "Yes... yes, I need it... I need your cum in me. Harder... do it harder. Fuck me."

He redoubled his pace, driving his cock into her slippery warm hole again and again. He grasped her hands in his own, entwining his fingers with hers pushing them down into the giving sand, pinning her beneath him as he fucked.

Finally, with a deep and satisfying moan, he came. He could feel his whole body release as the thick warm cum spurted out into her wanting body. She seemed to wrap herself around him, enveloping him tightly.

He rested his head on the sand beside her, breathing hard, struggling to catch his breath. She stroked his back, her hands cool and soft to the touch. "Just stay like this a moment," she murmured in his ear, "Just stay in me awhile longer."

He needed no encouragement. He brought her mouth to his own and kissed her, softly and deeply, tenderly. He could feel his cum sliding out of her, slipping out into the sand beneath them.

Above the stars seemed to wheel and gleam in the endless ink-black sky.

Percy Brice

He woke up sticky and sore and aching. He moaned.

It had been a dream; it had to have been a dream. Surely he hadn't consented to let Natasha James fuck him with a strap-on dildo, *surely* not.

The aching in his thighs and the sweet sore empty feeling in his backside, however, said differently. He rolled over with a groan.

"Oh God, yes, Miss James, yes! Please, fuck my fat white ass harder, *please*!"

He blinked. A voice penetrated the retreating fog of sleep. Was it... his voice? Goodness, surely he hadn't ever said anything like that. No, it must be someone else.

"Fuck me! Fuck me harder! Please, I need you cock!" He heard the harsh sound of a paddle slapping against flesh and the wet squishing sexual sounds of rough penetration. He sat up slowly, and he let out a yelp that was almost a scream.

Natasha James was standing at the foot of the bed, looking down at him with a cool dark gaze. She was slowly pulling on a long pair of black leather gloves. She stood with one foot up on the edge of the bed, spreading her thighs wide and assertive and almost aggressive. She wore black leather, her hair pulled back in a tight bun.

Percy flopped back down, breathing hard, his hand on his heart. He was fully awake now. "My God," he panted, "you scared me! What are you doing here?"

"What am *I* doing here, Mr. Brice?" she asked, her voice tight and grim.

He sat up, shaking his head and blinking as he looked around the room. The place was a mess, furniture upturned, soiled tissues and ripped clothing tossed all about, the sheets in a tangle, half on the floor. Wine glasses and empties bottles lay all about. A large bottle of sexual lubricant was open on its side on the nightstand, drooling thick clear liquid. The television screen was playing back what he could only assume was the video feed of the previous night's activities.

He could see himself, bend over on the floor, ass pushed high in the air. Natasha James stood over him, like a great ebony sex god, grabbing his hips tight and ramming her cock again and again into his asshole while he whimpered and begged for more. He blushed at once and had to look away, though he could hardly filter out the sounds of his own animal moans and her tight grimacing snarls.

"My goodness." he said, looking about the place.

"Indeed," she said lightly. "I seem to recall leaving you with instruction to tidy the place up. You did promise at the time, as I remember."

He blushed deeper. He didn't doubt it, though he himself had no such memory. He remembered very little of the night before. How much had he had to drink? God, what had he *done*?

"More importantly," Natasha went on, "I do believe you are expected in court approximately one hour from now."

Percy blanched. He froze for a moment, then burst into motion all at once, scrambling about the place, trying to run in all directions at once. He had to comb his hair, had to find his clothes, had to *shower*. God, he needed to *go!*

He fumbled out of bed, tangling in the sheets and flopping on his face right in front of her. She moved slightly, pushing her tall shining leather boot under his chin and snorting derisively. "Goodness, Mr. Brice, you really must pull yourself together. We're all counting on you." She turned then and strode out of the room, her hips shifting sinuously as she walked out. She cast a final look back over her shoulder, her smoky eyes cool and mysterious. "I'll see you in court."

The door shut behind her with a hard click, and he rose to his knees.

On the television screen across the room he was moving into a similar position, a slender dark hand lifting his chin and another guiding the thick red dildo between his lips. He winced as he watched himself clumsily and haltingly deep-throat the big cock, pushing his face so far down that his pale and flushed cheeks brushed Natasha's mocha brown thigh.

"Suck my cock, Mr. Brice, suck it deep. Tell me how much you love being my little slut-whore."

He wasn't sure he if was glad to have no memory of the moment or disappointing. He fumbled for the remote and switched the television off, allowing himself to breathe a sigh of slight relief as the images blinked out, leaving nothing but the reflection of his chaotic hotel room in its place.

He didn't have any time to collect himself, he had to get *going*. He yanked the blankets off himself as he rose. He heard a clanking sound, and he looked down with a frown. There was... something, *attached* to him. He rubbed the last of the sleep from his eyes and reached down. It was a device clasped onto his penis and testicles, a sort of metal cage type thing that fully encased his balls and shaft. There was a little hole at the front where he could see pink, but everything else was encased totally in the device.

He paled. A vague memory swam slowly back. He recalled Natasha standing over him as he lay on the bed, his wife Jennifer panting with lust as she watched over the video conference screen. "This should keep your little thing out of my sight." He recalled her voice, contemptuous and absolutely masterful as she reached down and turned a little golden key in the little golden lock. He reached down. The lock was still there. No sign of the key.

He was... he was... in chastity. He recalled agreeing to it, at Jennifer's urging. Now that he was awake, however... well, he wasn't so sure.

He cast about desperately for the key, feeling on the night stand and dresser in vain. There was no sign of it. Of course there wasn't. Natasha had it for sure. He sighed and shook his head. What had he gotten himself into here?

He had no more time today to worry about it, however. He hurried into the bathroom. The device didn't exactly make it easier to pee, but he managed it. He studied it closer while he took a brief shower. It was tight and unyielding. He wondered what it would be like to get an erection while he was wearing it. He doubted the experience would be especially comfortable, though he supposed that was part of the point.

It hung heavily between his thighs as he got out, the lock clattering slightly against the cage as he rose. In a way he almost liked the extra weight there. He wondered if this was a bit how men like Marquis and Tyrone felt, with those huge monstrous cocks dangling between their legs all the time.

When he slipped his white briefs on he took just a moment to admire the slight extra bulge that the chastity device afforded him in the mirror. Nobody would know from the outside what was really going on down there...

He dressed quickly and tried to tidy the most egregiously sexual evidence of the previous night's activities. It was hopeless. He was just going to have hang a do not disturb sign on the door. God, what would housekeeping think of him if they saw? He'd been here almost a month now and gotten to know several members of the hotel staff. He dreaded to think about how they would look at him if they knew, how they might *talk* about him. He shuddered.

Someone came up behind him as he was fastening the notice to the outside door knob. He jumped a little. It was Trisha, one of the paralegals. He jumped a little when she tapped him on the shoulder. She looked him up and down briefly, a sly smile playing at her lips. Or was it his imagination.

He groaned inwardly. God, what if the whole team knew what had happened? That would be just like Natasha. For all he knew she'd been linking the whole staff in on the video conference. For all he knew they'd all been watching his humiliation. He felt something stir down below and tried desperately to redirect his thoughts.

"Ah hm, uh... yes?"

Trisha's grin grew a bit more pronounced. "Miss James sent me, I've brought a car around to take you to the courthouse. You're ready to go?"

Percy cleared his throat and lifted his briefcase. He took a deep breath and, with a truly herculean effort, he swept it all from his mind, allowing only the particulars of the case to remain. He had a job to do, and a client to represent. He wasn't going to let the firm down, he wasn't going to let Jonas Harrington down, he wasn't going to let himself down, and he *certainly* wasn't going to let Miss Natasha James down. He squared his shoulders and nodded to Trisha. He spoke in the deepest and most confident voice he could muster, which admittedly wasn't much, but you use what you have. "I'm ready."

* * *

The conference room was a chaotic hubbub of cheering and jubilation. Percy found himself being pounded on the back, having his hand shaken, even kissed once on the cheek by a cute little paralegal, which of course made him blush terribly.

They had never even made it into the courtroom. Percy had been standing just outside the door, about to take a deep breath and head inside, when a man in a fine gray suit had called out to him. The represented the opposing party, he said, and he'd like to have a word, if he could. Percy had looked about in vain for Natasha, but she'd already been inside. There was no one to help, no backup. He'd stepped into a spare room with the other lawyer. Another man was waiting there, a heavy set man with a drawn face and a heavy frown. The president of the company which had brought the suit.

They wanted a deal. They'd flinched, and now they wanted out of it before going any further. They were prepared to accept a cool million dollars for their trouble, a good deal less than the fifty-five million in damages they were now asking for.

The lawyer had grinned and held out his hand. "Well," he'd asked, "what do you say, my good man?"

Percy had narrowed his eyes and sat down, ignoring the offered hand. He opened his briefcase and took out his notes.

"Just a moment," he said coolly. "Let me just let you know what you're really going up against here." He laid out what was in essence the opening argument he'd been prepared to give before the judge. It was a strong case, and he delivered it with a savage conviction that he'd never before experienced in a setting like this.

Five minutes later, he closed the briefcase. The other lawyer's smile seemed a good deal more strained than it had a moment before, and the old man's face had gone pale.

Percy had leaned back in his chair. "That's about the size of it, gentlemen. The fact of the matter is, I wouldn't want to bring a case like this to court. Why... it could end up looking very bad for you lot. Bring a few things to light that you might rather keep hidden. Of course... that's your call, isn't it?"

Ten minutes later, he shook the lawyer's hand and left the room.

There would be no trial. The prosecution, regretfully, withdrew their suit. The judge hadn't been happy, but Natasha had been. Her mask of calm had been, for just one single split second, broken. She stared at him, open-mouthed, eyebrows lifted in quite shock. A second later her placid mask slid back into place, as if nothing had ever happened.

That night, the whole team assembled in the conference room at the hotel, and Percy regaled them with an exact account of what had taken place.

It was a victory. Not the sort of courtroom showdown that John Grisham might write about, but it *was* the way things tended to actually happen in the real world. If you things when your way, of course. It was a big win for Jonas Harrington's firm, and for all of them in the Miami branch who had pulled it off. Natasha and Percy both were going to come out of this looking particularly good, and they both knew it.

"Mr. Brice, I honestly have to say that I'm impressed." Natasha was shaking her head slowly at the head of the room. "I didn't think you had it in you."

He laughed. "To be honest, I wasn't sure I did! As soon as I got in that room the adrenaline just kicked in. I would have been lost if not for all the data and information we put together. It might have been decided behind closed doors, but this was a team victory. I couldn't have done it without you."

The whole room sent up a ragged cheer. Someone popped a bottle of champagne. A general merriment bubbled through the room, an intoxicating and thrilling burble of mirth and relief. They had been driven hard for the past four weeks. Natasha had driven them like a slave-driver - sometimes all-too-literally. A handful of paralegals had the welts still to show for it, even Percy had picked up a few. But now it was over.

They'd done it. They'd won.

Natasha stood up, raising a hand for silence. The entire room went dead quiet, all eyes turning to her. They gazed with a kind of awed enthrallment, a sort of rapture. They looked at her with worship in their eyes. To his surprise, Percy found that he felt much the same, despite the metal chastity device strapped to his body. Or, rather, perhaps it was *because* of the device. That, and all the rest.

She stood there, her features stony and stern. She looked like a black goddess, hands on her hips, her business suit sharp and crisp. Her chocolate black skin seemed to glow in the conference room light, as if she were an otherworldly being descended amongst them, blessing them with her luminous presence.

"Good work, everyone." The tiniest of smiles cracked her lips. Another cheer went up, rising to the ceiling.

Her hand rose again. "I especially have to congratulate my co-council, Percy Brice." She turned to him. "When you first arrived, Mr. Brice, I have to confess that I was less than pleased to see you. I didn't think we needed you. I thought you'd been sent down to meddle, that you were nothing but a pencil pusher. Over the last few weeks, however, and this morning most of all, you've proved just how wrong I was. I have to thank you now, and... I'm going to say something now that I don't say very often: I owe you an apology."

A low murmur of disbelief rippled through the room. None of them had *ever* seen Natasha James humble herself in this manner. *Never.* It was a sight that was hardly to be believed.

Percy smiled. "Thank you, Miss James, but I can't take complete credit. If not for you, things in that meeting would have turned out very differently."

"Nonetheless. I want to offer you something, in gratitude, and to make up for my attitude to you when you first arrived. Whatever you'd like, ask... and it's yours." She leaned forward a little, placing her hands on the table, and she slowly sat down. Her staff stared at her in staggered disbelief. Could *this* be Natasha James, the iron bitch? The cruel dominatrix who *always* got her way? Who never gave up control, not matter how little, not even for a moment? Could she have really just said *that*?

Percy looked at her, long and hard. Slowly, he felt a smile spread across his lips. "Ah," he said, slowly and thoughtfully. "Anything...?"

She didn't speak, just nodded. A single deliberate nod.

Percy leaned forward. He felt a weight of his chastity device against the the chair beneath him. All day long he'd been riding the surge of his unexpected coup. Now, his confidence had never been higher, and he was prepared to take a risk. To do something he never would have been able to bring himself to do before.

"Alright then," he said. Then he leaned back in his chair and spread his hands out wide. "I want to taste your pussy. Right here, in front of everybody. That's it, that's what I want."

And audible gasp passed through the room. Something almost approaching panic began to spread through the assembled paralegals. Nobody, *nobody* had ever made a request like that of the Mistress. She had never been exposed to them in any way, no matter how much she had demanded of them. It seemed unthinkable.

Natasha James' features, however, didn't as much as twitch. She stared at Percy with that same cool and mysterious look in her eyes as always.

He squirmed, wondering if he might have gone too far. There were some lines which could not be crossed, no matter how big a victory you might have won.

Then she stood up. Still looking him in the eyes, she stepped up onto the long conference room table.

You could have heard a pin drop in that room as she began, very slowly, to walk down the long length of the table. Her stockings swished lightly against each other with every step. Percy found he could no longer meet her gaze. He looked down at his hands, turning his wedding ring on his finger and swallowing hard. He heard the footsteps stop right in front of him.

Natasha's glossy red high-heels were right there in front of him. Slowly, he looked up at her. She was looking back down at him, her features impassive, but her lips slightly parted. A strand of dark hair hung down between her eyes. Slowly, agonizingly slowly, she reached down and wrapped her fingers around the hem of her tight pencil skirt.

Percy felt his breath catch in his throat as he watched, stunned.

She lifted the skirt, just a fraction of an inch, then another. Her hands drew the tight dark fabric upward. It slid smoothly over her stockings, rasping ever so softly. Then it cleared the edge of her stocking, slipping over the top of the black frill. He could see the straps going up to where they hooked onto her garter belt. She kept lifting the skirt. Finally, with a sort of soft pop, she pulled it up over her hips.

He swallowed hard. She was wearing white cotton panties; they stood out shockingly bright against her dark thighs.

He could feel the whole room watching, every eye laser focused on the woman standing above him. He could feel it, but he could not look. He could not have looked away no matter what happened. The room could have caught fire, and he would still be frozen there, gazing up into those dark eyes.

She nodded her head brusquely down at him. "Stand up, Mr. Brice."

He did as she instructed, stumbling a little as he got up out of his chair, clutching at the edge of the table for support. He stood, and found himself very nearly level with the panties, staring right at them. He couldn't tell where to look, up at her face or at the panties.

Was this really happening? *Could* it be? Was he about to see Natasha James' pussy? He could hardly believe it, hardly endure the quiver of anticipation writhing in his gut. He felt his cock starting to strain against the device.

As if sensing his growing discomfort at his imprisonment, she smiled. It was a thin and wicked smile. She tugged playfully at the waistband of her panties with one finger, teasing at them. "I must admit, Mr. Brice, I'm surprise."

"O-oh?" he had to force the word out through numb lips.

"Indeed." She reached into the little pocket of her suit and took out a small golden key. "I would have thought you might ask for this. I don't give offers like this often, you know, and it might be some time before you have another chance. Are you... sure you wouldn't like to reconsider your request?" She cocked an eyebrow playfully.

Percy swallowed hard. Was he sure? He licked his lips, he tried to think. His mind was racing. His cock ached in its cage, getting harder by the second. He could feel himself squeezed by the tight and unyielding grip.

Slowly, he nodded.

"You would? You want to ask for this key?" she purred, lifting the little golden thing to her lips and biting gently on it.

"No," he said. "I'm sure. I'm not changing my request."

She smiled, and, for the first time, it seemed almost genuine. Her tongue slipped out, sliding over the little gold key. Then, with a slight shrug, she dropped it into her coat pocket. "Suite yourself, Mr. Brice." She reached down then with both hands, hooking her thumbs under the waistband of her panties and pulling them down off her hips.

They fell with a whisper, dropping to the conference table, tangled about her ankles. She stepped lightly out of them, lifting the panties on the tip of her shoe. She moved it deftly towards Percy, draping it over his upturned face.

He blushed, reaching up to pull them off and holding them clutched in his hands. They were still warm with her heat, ever faintly musky. He swallowed again and he looked up, holding the panties in both hands.

Her pussy was right there in front of him. It was breathtakingly beautiful, smooth and brown, shaved hairless and ripe as a peach. There was the faintest trace of moisture in the cleft between the two dark lips, and a pale hint of pink.

The whole room seemed gasp, all as one, and then fell deathly silent.

She shifted her weight forward, pushing her hips towards him. "Well, Mr. Brice? This *is* what you wanted, isn't it? Are you man enough to take it?"

He was frozen, faintly aware that he'd begun to twist the white cotton panties slightly in his hands.

She laughed. "My timid little cuckold. It's right here in front of you, don't you want it? Don't you want to taste your mistress' sweet pussy?" She reached down with one hand, sliding it softly over herself. Her middle finger slipped between the puffy dark lips, parting them ever so slightly. She brought it away, and there was a crystal clear drop on the tip of her finger. She held it out, and smeared it over his mouth.

Percy licked his lips, and a trembled shuddered through him. He was tasting her pussy. Right now, the tangy flavor of her was on his tongue. Still he could not bring himself to take the final step.

She laughed again, throwing her head back. She reached out and shoved her fingers deep into his thinning hair, and she grasped him tight. "I swear," she said, turning to address the room, "some men are just useless, aren't they?" Then she pulled him close with a none-too-gentle tug, and buried him face-first in her crotch.

The power of it at once seemed to overwhelm him. He felt his eyes go wide as her pussy pressed up against his mouth and chin. His lips were pinched tight shut at first. She moved her hips, gyrating slightly, sliding herself over him, opening her own lips so that the wet pink folds of her smeared across his face.

Slowly, timidly, he opened his mouth and dared to poke out the tip of his tongue.

A moan escaped deep in his throat. She pulled him deeper, tightening her grasp on him. His hands reached up, fluttering, to paw at her legs and thighs. Her knees were bent slightly, shifting herself forward to more fully draw him towards her.

He opened his mouth more fully, tasting her deeply, letting his tongue slip out. The tangy sweet taste of her flooded his mouth. He licked her deep, drawing his tongue slowly up from bottom to top. She quivered slightly, unable to completely maintain her icy facade as a tingle of pleasure rose up her spine.

"Hm... that's very good, Mr. Brice. Very good." She laughed. "Tell me something, would you?" she gasped softly, interrupting herself for a moment. She bent low, caressing his head. "How does your cock feel, trapping in there?" she spoke low and under her breath, only to him. "Is it starting to ache? Starting to *hurt*?"

He wanted to grit his teeth, though obviously the fact that his tongue was out made that bit difficult. She wasn't wrong, his dick was starting to feel *quite* uncomfortable, squeezed in its little cage.

"I loved caging up that wimpy little white cock," she moaned, her voice hardly raised over a whisper as she moaned and rode his face. The hard heels of her red shoes clacked on the top of the table as she shifted her weight. "You have no idea how much pleasure it gave me. That little dick belongs to be now. Not to you, not even to Jennifer. It's *mine*. I hope you enjoy this, little cuckold, because this is the last time you're going to get this close to a pussy for a long time. You're *never* going to fuck your wife again. I talked to her last night, after you passed out on the bed with your ass still open from my fucking. She sold your cock to me, Mr. Brice. And why not?" She yanked his hair again, shoving him deeper between her folds. "She has no use for a puny thing like that."

He groaned. Her juices were running down his chin down, dripping down her thighs and falling to the conference room table, making a shining pool between her lacquered shoes.

"And just in case you're thinking you might be getting away now, remember this:" she leaned in close now, "I'm coming with you when you leave Miami." She patted his cheek, with an almost affectionate gentleness. "I think we're going to be having a lot of fun in the future, you and I."

* * *

Percy snapped his briefcase shut and clicked the lock. He looked around the room once more and gave a sigh. So, this was it, then. After almost a month here, he was finally going home. It was strange, he'd started to become attached to the place, almost. Certainly a lot had happened here.

But she was coming back with him, wasn't she? Natasha James, in his town. In his house, maybe? She and Jennifer seemed to have become quite close, remarkably. He wondered how things would be when he got back... What would she think of it then?

His phone chirped, almost as if in answer to his thoughts. He reached down and looked at the message. From Jennifer.

-Hey honey, just wanted to say travel safe. I love U. Please come home soon. We need to talk about something.

He swallowed. Well, that was ominous. What in the world could she want to discuss? Certainly enough things had happened to him while he was away. He wondered how eventful her time had been. No doubt she'd been busy...

He picked up his case and, after one last check around the room, he headed out the door, down the elevator, and right to the front desk to check out. It was time to leave Miami behind.

Tyrone Jackson

He woke in bed, with only the faintest memory of how he'd gotten there. He looked down. Penelope Mason was snuggled in the crook of his arm, her silver hair swept across her face as she slept on.

Ah, of course. He remembered now. He remembered making love on the beach. Not just once, but several times. Him lying on his back while she rode him, her head thrown back and the stars shining above her while she clawed at his chest and screaming with the force of her orgasm. He remembered carrying her into his bedroom, still laughing and kissing her, and he remembered the final slow fuck under the covers before they'd both collapsed into a panting heap and fallen instantly to sleep.

How could he have forgotten?

He reached down and stroked her hair, lacing his fingers through the soft silver curls, watching the way it fell across her fine features. She was a majestic creature, Penelope. He'd seen a glimmer of it before, but it was only last night that he'd come to fully realize just how impressive she really was. She had the dignity and beauty and bearing of a European countess. And, once unleashed from her husband's controlling instructions, she was real tiger in the sheets. She certainly knew her way around a cock. He didn't think he'd ever been driven so hard, or matched point for point the way she'd done.

He loved Jennifer, and she was an incredible lay, but Penelope had something she didn't: experience. Penelope had been servicing black cocks for decades now, and she knew what she was doing. For the first time, Tyrone had felt himself outmatched. At first he'd driven himself almost absurdly hard, trying to keep up. Eventually, however, he allowed himself to surrender. She wasn't dominant or controlling, but she knew what she liked and she knew how to tell him, and she knew how to make him feel good.

He'd cum at least three times during the night. To be entirely honest, he was rather spent.

The sunlight was filtering in through the half-closed shades, spilling in long golden shafts through the dusty air of the beach house. He settled back, sliding deep into the soft bed, and he allowed himself to doze off once more.

As sleep crept back over him, he found himself wondering, idly, just how much of the previous night's activities Reginald G. Mason had slept through, and how he might react if he were to learn what he'd missed out on.

* * *

As it turned out, Mason had slept quite sounded through the entire night's activities, and woken with a rather crushing hangover. He was nursing his head and wincing at every loud noise when the three of them sat down for breakfast.

It was quite a staggering feast, more food by far than they'd possibly be able to manage. Tyrone wondered where it had come from. The whole table had been prepared when he'd come in, and her certainly didn't think either of the Masons had done it. He supposed they had service staff on call somewhere.

"Ah... not as young as I used to be," Mason groaned, grinning ruefully and massaging his temples. "Ought to have known better than to press it so far." He jabbed his fork in Tyrone's direction. "Let my sorry fate be a lesson to you, my boy. Enjoy your revels while you have the strength for them, because eventually it starts to wane."

Tyrone nodded agreeably, taking a large bite of what he thought must be a crepe. He shifting his seat back and the chair leg scrapped audibly on the floor. Reginald winced in pain.

"The two of you were quite a sight though, I must say that. Don't regret a moment of it, despite the headache," he said, brightening up at the memory. "Quite the stallion, isn't he, darling? Just like I told you."

Penelope nodded serenely. "Oh, certainly. Quite lovely."

"Yes!" Reginald chuckled, "A fine performance, very fine indeed. Reminds you of old times, doesn't it, darling?"

"Very much." She smiled, an odd secretive little smile. Tyrone couldn't help but wonder just how much she'd gotten up to, over the years, that Reginald didn't know about. He suspected that there might be quite a lot that had escaped his noticed.

They ate the rest of the meal largely in silence, and odd something hanging in the air between them.

That afternoon, Tyrone left them, making his excuses for what he had to go earlier than expected. Reginald seemed disappointed, but he was still nursing his hangover, and didn't put up much of a fight. Penelope said nothing, only nodding, that same calm and serene expression on her delicate face.

She caught him just at the door as he was heading out. "Tyrone," she said, and he paused. She came to him, like a swirl of gossamer silk dancing in the wind, and she put her hand on his arm.

He looked at her, and he felt a tug.

"Why are you leaving?" she asked, her voice plain and direct. "I'm not asking you to stay, I'm just... curious."

He shook his head. "I'm not exactly sure, to be entirely honest. Part of me wants to stay."

"And the other part?"

"I'm not part of your world, Penelope. And I never will be. I'm just not cut out for this."

She nodded silently. "I think I understand. Be well. Perhaps we'll be again someday."

"Maybe."

But he knew that they wouldn't. He would never cross paths with Penelope Mason again, and they both knew it. They would, however, always have that night, that time beneath the stars on the sandy beach in the warm Florida night.

She kissed him gently on the cheek and gave his hand a light squeeze.

He squeezed back and he went out the door. It was time for him to go home.

Fifteen minutes later, as the bus heading back towards the dorms rocked and swayed, he got a text message from Jennifer.

-Ty, I need U. Please come to the house, we need to talk about something important.

Well then. This should be interesting.

Jennifer Brice

Jennifer was pacing back and forth, wringing her hands and biting her lip.

It had been a strange week. She'd kept to herself, mostly, not talking much to either Percy or Tyrone. Ever since the drug store and her anonymous encounter there, she had been on her own. The weight of the news she carried was heavy on her, like a stone around her neck. How would they react? What would they say? Would they be happy? Horrified? Angry? She really couldn't say.

Hell, she really could say for sure how *she* felt about it! She had a feeling that she wouldn't really know for sure until she had them both in the room and was looking them right in the eyes. Her husband and her lover both.

She'd been without them too long, and now she needed them both. Right here, right now.

She looked at the clock again, for the hundredth time in the last twenty minutes. Percy was due back at any moment. Tyrone was on his way. They would be here soon, and she was going to tell them. But how the *fuck* was she supposed to do that?

Hey, guys, how's it going? Oh, by the way, Ty, I'm having your baby.

She hadn't been this nervous before in her entire life. Not that she could remember, anyway. She needed a drink, something to steady her nerves. She made it all the way to the liqueur cabinet and was just about to pour herself a nice stiff drink when the realization hit her: you can't drink when you're pregnant.

She put the bottle back with a sigh. It was probably too early to matter, but she couldn't say for sure. She couldn't say much of *anything* for sure. She was going to have to start doing some research, that was definite.

She heard a key turn in the front door lock. She breathed heavily, trying to calm her nerves. It was going to be alright. Somehow.

She was walking into the room when the door swung open and Percy stepped inside, his suit rumpled and his briefcase clattering against the frame. He sighed when he saw her, and smiled with obvious relief. "Hey, Jen." He stepped inside and put his case gently down beside the door.

Tyrone came in behind him, poking his head in, then following.

Percy grinned. "We ran into each other outside," he explained, "came up the walk together."

"Oh," she said, swallowing hard, "that's lucky." Nothing for it then, she'd have to tell them both together. Maybe that was best. She could get it out of the way all at once.

"Hello, Jennifer," Tyrone said, his voice smooth and soft and deep. She felt it having a calming effect on her right away. She felt herself already starting to relax, though only a little bit.

He came to her, and he embraced her. She felt herself sink against his chest, wrapped in his strong arms. He kissed her softly on the top of the head, his full lips brushing over her brown hair. "I've missed you," she murmured, breathing in deep of his strong sweet scent.

"Missed you too," he whispered back, stroking her head with his powerful and gentle hand.

Eventually, though she found herself not wanting to, she had to break the embrace. Percy gave her a quick squeeze and a peck on the cheek. "Hey, hon."

She kissed him back, pressing her lips to one cheek then the other. She smiled warmly at him. "Hello, darling."

She felt better now that they were both her. She felt supported, buoyed by their presence. But of course the hard part was still to come.

"Please," she said, holding her hand out and gesturing them further into the house, "come sit down."

They followed her together, walking into the living room. Percy sat in his chair with a sigh, rubbing at his sore neck and groaning. Tyrone leaned back, his legs spread assertively, one hand resting casually on his crotch.

Jennifer stood in front of them, her hands clasped behind her back.

"Percy... Ty..." she looked at her husband, then at her lover. It was all going to be okay, just keep telling yourself that it's all going to be okay. She took a deep breath and cleared her throat. *Here goes nothing.* "I have something to tell you."

Book Five: The Owned Hotwife

Part One - Jennifer Brice

Jennifer fidgeted, sitting on her hands and looking down at her shoes.

Tyrone and Percy stared at her, their faces blank and uncomprehending for a long and drawn out moment. The words seemed to hang in the air, visible almost, like a great flashing red neon sign that read *I'm Pregnant* in huge lit-up lettering.

Percy blew out a long slow breath, putting his hands slowly up under his chin.

Tyrone leaned back against the couch cushion, his expression inscrutable.

"Well..." she said, "what do you think?"

Neither of them said anything. Finally, Tyrone stood up. He took two steps across the room and looked down at her, her beautiful young black lover, the father of the mixed-race baby growing now inside her belly.

She looked up at him, feeling awed by him all over again. It didn't matter that it was her house, or that she was so much older and more privileged, she felt herself naturally submitting to him as she looked up. There was something about him that she craved. His mastery.

He touched her cheek with his hand and lifted her chin so that their eyes met. Her husband Percy seemed to fade into the background of the room, pale and colorless, as she stared into the dark brown eyes of her black lover.

"Are you really pregnant?" Tyrone asked, his voice deep and soft.

Jennifer swallowed, and slowly nodded.

"Show me," he said.

"H-how?" she murmured.

"Show me," he said again, and slipped the strap of her shirt down off her shoulder.

Now she understood. She began to undo the buttons of her blouse, her eyes never leaving his as she started to remove her clothing. She dropped her blouse to the floor, then slipped her skirt off. She sat there looking up at him, and she put her hands on her belly, caressing it, holding it. Surely it was only her imagination, but she thought she could already feel it swelling, filling with his child.

He groaned, and then he reached into his pants and pulled out his cock. "Suck it," he ordered.

She obeyed eagerly, cramming the massive black dick in her mouth. She saw her husband out of the corner of her mouth, squirming uncomfortably in his chair, a stricken expression on his face as he watched his wife sucking another man's cock, another man's child growing inside her.

Jennifer thought of Percy's limp little white cock, hardly able to believe that she'd ever been able to tolerate having it inside her, or even near her. It seemed pitifully inadequate to her now, little better than a bad joke. She cared for him, but she'd lost her ability to respect him as a man. He had become sexless in her eyes.

She couldn't ever go back to that, not ever. Black cock was the only dick she was ever going to take again, and that was the way it would be. She could feel her pussy getting wet, her slit moistening slowly, getting slippery and creamy. She didn't care that Percy was watching, didn't care that he was probably getting hard.

He was never going to fuck her again, she'd decided it, and this moment only crystallized it in her mind.

She looked at him, and their eyes met. She shook her head slightly. *No. Not you. Never again.* She turned back and focused her attention once again where it truly belonged: Tyrone's black cock.

Her black lover grasped a fistful of her hair and drew her head further down on him. "Don't look at him," he said sternly, "shut your eyes and suck."

She did so, closing her eyes and surrendering herself to his use, reveling in his power over her, in her body's need for his guidance.

He groaned, tightening his grip on her head. He held her firmly and started to drive his hips back and forth, fucking her face without any care to her struggles or soft gagging, using her without mercy.

She was his now, utterly and completely. He had colonized her body, and everybody knew it. She could hear Percy moaning and twisting in his seat, but he didn't try to rise or make a move. He knew better than to fight over her anymore; he'd accepted the fact that she was now owned by another.

Tyrone pushed her back, his fat black cock slipping wet from her mouth. It hung heavy and dark between his thighs, thick and beautiful. She gasped, reaching up to wipe the spit hanging from her lower lip, but he caught her hand before she could. His grip closed around her wrist and drew her up to her feet, then twisted her around and bent her over on the chair.

He grasped both her hands behind her back and forced her head down so that she was bent over the armrest of the seat. He murmured appreciatively as he pushed his hand between her thighs. "Look at that wet pussy. That white girl pussy soaking wet for me..." he said, and pushed a finger inside her.

Jennifer Brice gasped, flushing with sudden embarrassment. Why she should feel embarrassed now, after all she had done, she couldn't say. Some reactions couldn't be controlled.

"You want this black cock in that pregnant hole, don't you, babe?"

Percy groaned, she couldn't tell if in ecstasy or despair, and she didn't much care right now.

"Yes, master," she panted, "please, please fuck me. Fuck my pregnant cunt. Breed me, master."

He grabbed her by one hip and he put the head of his cock to her labia, sliding it against the slippery folds for just a moment.

She bit her lower lip, wincing with anticipatory dread and delight. This moment, this moment right here was what she had come to live for. The first moment of pained surrender, the moment when she gave herself up to his use, when he took utter possession of her. It hurt, it hurt every time.

He was *too* big for her, that was the simple truth of it. How did she keep taking this, why did she *love* it so much? It shouldn't work; much less make her feel so good. Being stretched, opened in a way that should be beyond the limits of her body to endure. And yet she craved it.

She was a slut.

Her eyes snapped open at the thought. And, just then, he shoved himself into her. She yelled out, her fingernails digging into her palm and her toes curling as he filled her cunt. Her little pink pussy stretched to accommodate that massive cock ramming into her. Her mouth opened in a silent cry of agonized pleasure.

She was a slut for black cock. She would suffer anything to be used by him. Throughout all of this, she had never allowed herself to think that, never admitted the real truth of the matter. She wasn't *normal.* Normal women wouldn't fuck another man in front of their husband, would they? Normal woman wouldn't push themselves to the verge of their body's ability to tolerate in order to serve as a man's sexual plaything, would they?

Or... maybe she wasn't so different. Maybe other women were like her, maybe *all* women were, deep down. Ready to be enslaved to the cocks of their black masters, just waiting for the moment they could allow themselves to accept the truth, acknowledge their real selves.

Jennifer knew now what she was, she accepted it, and in that acceptance she felt a kind of peace, a contentment.

This was her place, her *destiny*, to be taken by black men, to give herself to them freely so that they might use her.

Tyrone pushed her face down as he hammered her cunt, pounding it again and again with long strokes that forced little grunts and moans and sighs of pleasure from her lips. She could feel herself given over entirely to him, her pussy soaking and creamy with the issue of her lust. Her juices rolled down the insides of her pale thighs, frothed white and soft at the base of his cock.

She thought of what was happening inside her: his seed taking root. A black child in her belly. *His* child.

He'd bred her, made her belong to him. It kept going through her head, again and again repeating.

"I'm yours," she murmured, "yours..."

He grunted hard and thrust once more, then let out a gasp as he cum spurted out, filling her inside with his hot cream.

A smile curled slowly across her lips. "Yours," she said again.

He reached forward and stroked her hair, like he was petting an obedient dog. "That's right," he said, "mine."

He drew back, and his cock slipped out, falling hard back against his thighs like a slab of meat. She slithered down to the floor, feeling both filled and emptied out at the same time, as if she'd been hollowed of everything that had been her and had it all replaced with what was *him*.

She licked drowsily at his fat cock, slurping up every last drop of his beautiful cum.

* * *

"You're really pregnant?" her husband Percy asked nervously as they lay in bed.

"I'm really pregnant," she said, only half paying attention to him as she turned a page of her paperback novel. He seemed dim to her now, distant almost. Was he upset? Concerned? Worried? She didn't entirely care, she realized. What was happening to her?

"And... it's his?"

She looked at him. "Well it certainly wasn't anything you did with that little thing of yours, honey."

He colored, blushing bright red, and he swallowed. "Right. Of course."

She shut her book and put it on the nightstand. "Don't be worried, Percy. This is what we wanted, remember? We always wanted children, right from the very beginning, didn't we? That hasn't changed, hasn't it?"

He shook his head slowly, and reached out to stroke her arm. "No. No, it hasn't changed."

She took his hand and gave it a squeeze, then placed it back on his side of the bed. "Good. This is no different than getting a sperm donor, really, and we always said we might try that. I want you to be okay with this, Percy. You're my husband. You're going to be raising the baby with me, after all. They're going to be part of *our* family. Tyrone is... well, he's everything to me, but he's not a part of that. He's separate. That's my other life." *My new life,* she thought, but didn't say so.

"I understand," he said, "I'm happy, really I am. I'm excited. It's wonderful news. This is everything we always wanted."

"It is," she said, and gave him a tight smile. "I have to thank you again, Percy. If you hadn't brought me to the club that night... none of this ever would have happened."

He laughed a little. "It's a bit wild, isn't it? Man..." he shook his head disbelievingly, "what a ride it's been."

She laughed too. "You can say that again. No regrets?"

He looked up and he met her eyes. He seemed to consider the question, *really* consider it. "No," he said finally, after thinking on it for a good while, "none at all."

She leaned over and gave him a soft peck on the cheek. "Good." *It was too late to change now, anyway.* She was changed forever, and she couldn't go back even if she wanted to.

He leaned closer to her, moving as if to kiss her, his pale lips pushing out and his hand sliding down to touch her thigh.

"Hm," she grimaced, turning her head away and removing his hand. "I don't think so. This isn't yours anymore, Percy. Remember that."

He leaned back, blanching slightly. "Right. Sorry. Lost my head."

"If you want to play with that little thing of yours you can go do it in the bathroom," she said, pointing to the door on the other side of the bedroom. She leaned back and picked her book up again. “Anyway, I didn't think you were allowed to do any of that sort of thing anymore. Isn't she keeping a leash on you? I don't imagine you'd want me to tell her that you just tried that.”

“No, no! Of course not,” he said, squirming a little.

She grinned. She could tell how hard he was even without seeing it. To an outsider this arrangement might seem unfair to him, demeaning and horrible. She couldn't think how she might ever be able to explain it to somebody from the outside world.

On the other hand, in their life before Percy hadn't been able to get a hard-on no matter how much or how hard he tried. This was better for him too, and the evidence was right there in his pants.

Jennifer Brice snuggled down under the covers as she read. While her eyes went slowly across the page she gave her thighs a little squeeze. She thought that she could still feel Tyrone's cum inside her. She was never going back.

No, this was better for everybody, that was for certain. She'd never go back.

Percy Brice

Natasha James walked slowly around the sofa, a long leather riding crop held loosely in her dark fingers. Her expression was stern and cool as she circled Percy, occasionally flicking out the riding crop to give him a swat across the backs of his exposed thighs.

He yelped as she gave him a harder than usual smack, and twisted against his restraints.

Percy Brice was trussed up in his own living room, bent over on the sofa in a complex series of rope restraints. His wrists were tied together, as were his ankles, and the bound hands and feet were then secured by a strong line to the sofa itself. He wore a leather collar with heavy jangling metal rings that clattered when he moved – as much as he was *able* to move, at any rate.

A dog's leash was hooked onto the collar. Natasha had clipped it onto him, as soon as she'd arrived – having sent work ahead of her that he should present himself unclothed and collared, wearing the leather band she'd given him after their last encounter.

Percy had almost refused the order. *Almost.* He felt a keen and almost painful shame verging on dread – though he couldn't deny being almost unutterably excited by the whole thing. He knew what would have been in store for him had he not done as instructed, however. As embarrassing as his current situation was – and as *painful* as it could be – it was nothing compared to what Natasha had shown herself capable of.

"Good piggy," she said softly, and stroked his upturned backside with the flat top of the riding crop. "Good little soft pink piggy..."

He felt a strange mixture of sensations at those words. Something between lust and adoration and excruciating shame.

He was utterly exposed, utterly demeaned and owned. It should have been unbearable, intolerable. He was a wealthy and successful lawyer, after all, and there was no reason why he should have to submit to this manner of indignity.

But one look at Natasha James was all it took to bring him quivering to his knees. She was quite the most imposing and – his wife excepted – beautiful woman whom he had ever laid eyes upon. She was tall, stately and statuesque with flashing dark eyes and gleaming ebony skin like chocolate and coffee. Today she wore a tight leather skirt and a severe dark blazer unbuttoned low to display her ample mocha cleavage. He wasn't entirely sure why she had chosen him, as she had, to be her special plaything.

Her entire department at the Miami was in sexual thrall to her, he knew that well enough. She could have played with anybody she wanted, bend them to her will. And yet she chose to be here. It had all been arranged between the three of them, his wife and her bull and his new dominatrix master: Percy belonged to Natasha.

His little cock ached agonizingly, desperate to be touched. It had been so long since he'd had sexual release. It quivered erect between his pale thighs, dribbling precum at a prestigious rate so that it ran down his balls and dripped onto the couch.

Natasha had arrived in the city not long after Percy had returned from Miami. Several weeks had passed since then. Since he'd heard the news about Jennifer and Tyrone...

He'd not been allowed release since then, and it was beginning to drive him almost mad.

"Please, Mistress," he moaned pitifully, "*please...*"

Swat!

The riding crop slapped down hard on his backside, making him jerk up with a groan.

Natasha's eyes flashed. "Did I ask you to oink, little fat piggy? Did I tell you I wanted to hear you speak?"

"N-no, Mistress... It's just-"

Swat!

She made a low sound in her throat somewhere between a purr and a growl. "And yet you still feel that you've the right to speak to me?"

"*Please*," he whimpered, speaking as fast as he could to get the words out before she could strike him again, "I need it, please, I need to *cum...*"

Swat! Swat! Swat!

"How *dare* you, piggy!" she snarled, "Bad enough that you're disobeying me by speaking, and now you have the temerity to ask for that? No one here wants to touch your wimpy little white cock, and nobody wants to see that pitiful little puddle that you call cum. You're worthless, piggy."

She knelt down beside him, and placed a hand flat on his backside. She was wearing black latex gloves. The material brushed softly over his skin.

"You couldn't even impregnate your own wife with that thing, even if you had been able to get it up. You're a eunuch, piggy. It's best that you start thinking of yourself that way." And, as she said that, she slipped her middle finger into his clenched anus.

He moaned, twisting against his bonds. "Please, mistress, I-"

"*Shh!*" she shushed him, almost violently, and pushed her finger in past the first knuckle, "You don't speak to me." She reached forward and slipped something over his head. It was only as the thick rubber ball entered his mouth that he recognized it for what it was: a ball gag.

He moaned around it, almost immediately feeling the uncontrollable buildup of drool in his mouth.

"I don't want to hear about this pitiful little cock ever again, piggy." She pushed a second finger into his butt, then gave his dangling balls a slap with her other hand.

He yelped painfully into the gag, twisting his hips in a feeble and useless effort to escape.

She gave him another hard slap, batting them like a cat playing with a dangling string. "I don't want to see it, I don't want to look at it and I *certainly* don't want to touch it." She stood up and fingered his ass roughly from a standing position, her bare leg brushing against his side as she towered over him.

He shuddered. It hurt to be penetrated so roughly in his unprepared hole, but sensation of her fingertips brushing against his prostate deep inside sent waves of pleasure coursing through him. The two sensations, pain and pleasure, discomfort and enjoyment, mingled confusingly in his mind, twisting together and interweaving themselves.

She fucked his bottom with her hand for some time, working up to three fingers, almost splaying him open. He could hear his ass making hungry gaping sounds, and his ears prickled with embarrassment and his lower half ached with the pain and his spin tingled with ecstasy. Finally she gave him a kind of reprieve, and slipped a thick butt-plug into his ass. “We'll just leave that in there awhile, shall we?” she said coldly, and pulled her glove off with a rubbery snapping sound.

He relaxed just a little, panting and drooling pitifully around his gag. He could feel the huge plug stretching him, opening his hole. He dared not raise his eyes to look at the tall beautiful black woman dominating him, much as he wanted to. He watched her legs and her feet as she slowly started to prowl around the sofa once more.

“I think we're going to need to have a serious talk about our relationship, piggy,” she said softly, paddling his buttocks gently, almost playfully, with her hand. “I'm not entirely sure that you understand your place.”

She sat down on the arm rest of the sofa, right in front of him, her legs spread slightly. He couldn't see anything in the dim shadowy realm beneath her skirt, but he knew what was there, what beauty and pleasure lay hidden in the musky dark.

“Out there, in the world, we are equals. Both lawyers, both working for Mr. Jonas Harrington's law firm. You may stand beside me and address me as Miss James, as if you were more than a worthless little piggy. Perhaps this is what's confusing you. Perhaps I've allowed you to become too familiar.”

She slapped the back of his head, then pushed him down so that his face was against the sofa, and she put a foot on the top of his head. He felt the sharp stiletto point of her leather boot pressing against his skin.

"Maybe in future I should require you to genuflect at all times, to crawl before me down the halls of the office like the piggy you are, leashed and gagged and naked for all your underlings and peers to laugh at and be disgusted by, would you like that, piggy?"

"*Naoph,*" he mumbled, trying to speak around the gag and through the sofa cushion.

"No, I didn't think you would. And it may yet come to that. In the meanwhile, however, I think I'm going to need to provide you with a more permanent reminder of who your proper owner really is. Did you enjoy wearing your chastity, piggy?" She lifted his chin and pulled the gag roughly out.

He panted weakly, gazing up at her. "No, Mistress," he finally managed after catching his breath.

A slow smile curved across her red-painted lips. "Good. You weren't meant to. It was meant to remind you that you're nothing but a disgusting little white piggy fucktoy, and that your pleasure means nothing. Tell me what you are, piggy."

He swallowed, a fresh wave of same rising in him. "I... I'm a piggy. I'm a pitiful little fucktoy, Mistress."

"Very good," she cooed, patting his balding head gently, almost affectionately. "That's exactly right. And... does a little fucktoy like you deserve to orgasm?"

"N-no, Mistress."

"That's right. So put it out of your mind, piggy. I'm going to put you in chastity, and I'm going to keep you that way. I'm going to keep it tight, until that little thing you dare to call a penis is properly trained. Every time you get one of your little erections, it's going to hurt you. It's going to *ache*, until your little worm is too scared to ever come up again. I don't ever want to see your cock get hard again, do you understand? You're my eunuch, piggy. Cocks are for real men."

She bent down, clutching his face in her hand and squeezing his cheeks as she forced him to look up at her. He groaned.

"Tell me something, piggy," she said, her black skin perfect and beautiful and filling his vision, "what does a real man look like."

"B-black..." he mumbled, "black men are the only real men."

"Yes," she purred, "and why is that?"

"They have big cocks," he said.

"And they have *seed.* Real seed. The kind that can get your wife pregnant, not like you have in your little balls. How does it feel, piggy, knowing that a big black stud, a *real man*, fucked a baby into your wife?"

He swallowed and looked down, breathing hard, his mouth open, the words trapped in his throat.

A flash of displeasure crossed her features at his delay, and she reached suddenly forward to wrap her hands tight around his dangling balls. She gave him a hard squeeze and a jerk, enough to drive the wind out of him and drop him shuddering and trembling face down on the sofa. "How does it *feel*, piggy?" she snapped.

"It feels good!" he wailed, "It feels so good to know that she's being fucked by a superior man! That she's carrying his baby! I love it! He's so much better than me and she loves his cock! She won't touch me anymore, and I love it!" Tears of pain rolled down his fat cheeks as he sobbed, gasping for breath.

Natasha smiled slowly. "That's a good piggy," she murmured, "now we're making progress."

She rose. A moment later, he felt the cold touch of metal at his groin, then the painful click of the chastity device snapping into place around his cock. He winced and moaned as she tightened it, until finally it was painfully tight, squeezing down his erection.

"I'll tighten that more when you get soft like a good piggy," she said, and paddled his rump. "Now then," she said, stretching her neck, "it's time for you to service me."

He heard the whisper of her panties falling to the floor. The sofa groaned as she settled her wait in it in front of him. He dared to glance up as she began slowly to roll her skirt up her smooth black thighs. Her smooth shaven pussy was right before him, soft and brown and musky and desperately inviting.

He knew that this wasn't going to be easy. Natasha James didn't cum easily, and she would demand at least one orgasm before she let him go. He might be down there with his mouth on her, his tongue circling her clit, for as long as an hour. Probably more. He could already feel the sweet ache moving through him.

Percy's eyes flicked to one side.

Jennifer, his wife, sat on the chair on the other side of the room, watching them both with a strange and gleaming look in her eye as she watched her husband be demeaned and dominated by the powerful young black woman. She had one hand in her pants, making slow circles. Her belly was already beginning to show, swelling under her tight shirt with her black lover's child.

Natasha grabbed his head roughly and jerked his mouth against her cunt, and she put him to work.

Tyrone Jackson

Tyrone jogged into the locker room, breathing hard and sweating. He slumped onto the bench. The other players slapped his shoulders as they walked past.

"Nice play, man."

"Great job, Ty."

"Good season, dude."

He nodded and smiled back at them, but didn't say anything in reply. A thousand thoughts swirled through his head, a dizzying number of questions to which he had no good answers.

The last game of the football season was over. His last season ever, it seemed. He'd be graduating in the spring with his business degree. He'd never planned to go out for the pros, though a couple people had encouraged him to give it a shot. He didn't want to spend his whole life chasing that dragon, not after seeing the way the system chewed up players and spat them back out again. He didn't have any job prospects lined up, but he figured he had an okay shot. His grades were solid and he felt like he had a good head for it.

But of course it was more than just skill that mattered. Connections were just as important. Maybe Percy Brice and the Black and White Club could help him out there.

He grinned at the thought and shook his head, feeling a kind of amazement at how things had been going down since he'd let the team's assistant manager Marquis talk him into joining the club.

Was he really going to have a kid? It seemed almost impossible to believe, surreal and strange in a way that baffled him any time he thought on it too long. What was he going to do? Just watch from the sidelines as they brought up his child? Fade away and forget that it had ever happened? Or... and this was a thought he had to force himself not to consider too closely... he could just take Jennifer away. She'd come with him, he knew she was. He could take her and they could start their life somewhere else, away from all this, away from her husband, just the two of them.

Did he want that? He wasn't sure. He... cared for her. She ignited his passion in a way no woman ever had before. And he knew if he told her to follow him that she'd do it. At first, anyway...

It was all too crazy to think about. He didn't know what kind of money she had, but he'd little enough himself. Certainly not enough to support both of them and a kid. And he didn't know Percy well, but he didn't think he wanted to do that to the guy.

As he sat there, thinking back on the way his life had been transformed over the past few years, he came to a decision that he hadn't even realized he'd been weighing. He got up from the bench and pulled his gear off, then peeled his sweaty uniform over his head.

He walked naked to the showers. He could feel this thick dark cock swaying, brushing against his thighs.

He loved his cock. Loved fucking with it, especially white women like Jennifer. He was proud of it, proud of the way his teammates would still do double takes when they saw him in the shower, the little white boys trying not to stare while their eyes bugged out. He had a monster, and he knew it.

But maybe it was time to take back possession of the gift he'd been given.

He stepped into the steaming hot watched and turned his face up into the searing stream, and he let it wash all his thoughts away.

* * *

"You looked good out there, kid." Marquis grinned, the wide white smile spreading across his dark face. His large reflective sunglasses gleamed, and in them Tyrone could see his reflection staring back at him, seated uncomfortably in the little chair on the other side of the assistant coach's desk. "We're going to have a hell of a time trying to find somebody to take your place when you graduate."

"Thanks, sir," he nodded, "Thanks for saying so."

"No problem. But you didn't come in here to get your pole greased. What's on your mind?"

Tyrone licked his lower lip. "I... I think I'm done, sir."

Marquis sat back and steepled his fingertips, gazing over them at Tyrone. "You're not talking about the team, are you?"

He shook his head. "No sir."

"The Club."

"That's right."

Marquis drummed his fingertips lightly on the desk. "Well... that's another matter."

"I just don't think it's for me."

"I disagree. I think Mrs... Brice would too." He hooked a finger between the lenses of his glasses and drew them down to the tip of his nose so he could eye Tyrone over the tops of the frames. "I think you could have a bright future with us, Tyrone. Be a shame to throw that away."

"Maybe. But I think it's time."

"Not falling for her, are you Jackson?"

"Excuse me?"

"Brice. Not thinking about... running off with her, or anything, would you?"

Tyrone blushed.

Marquis frowned and pushed his glasses back up. His silvery gaze seemed to bore into Tyrone, laser focused and powerful. "That would reflect very badly on the club, Jackson. Men bring their wives there to get fucked, not stolen out from under them."

"I'm not going to do anything," he muttered.

"Of course not. You're smarter than that, Jackson... Anyway. We'll miss seeing you around the club. Be just as hard replacing you there as it's going to be here." He flashed Tyrone his wide smile, though it didn't seem especially friendly to Tyrone this time. "You're hanging me out to dry, here, Jackson."

"Sorry, sir..."

Marquis waved him off. "Ah, don't worry about it. Fresh blood. That's all. Always good to change things up. We'll be alright, and I dare say you will. Let me know when you start putting in job applications, I might be able to pull a few strings for you, maybe have a word with Mr. Mason. He was quite pleased with your performance a couple weeks back. *Quite* pleased."

Tyrone swallowed. "Glad to hear it." He wondered how pleased the founder of the Black and White Club would be if he knew the truth about how far Tyrone and his wife had eventually gone, right under his nose outside the beach house while he slept. He'd have to hope that Penelope Mason didn't suddenly decide to tell her husband. Might cause... trouble.

He needed to get out from under all this, start fresh. This was the right call, he decided. He'd gotten in too deep with the club, and it was time to cut ties.

Marquis leaned forward. He held a hand out, opened an offered to Tyrone. Tyrone took it and the two black men shared a firm handshake. "Been a pleasure, Jackson," the older man said.

"Yeah," Ty murmured, "you too."

* * *

Tyrone knocked gently on the door of his dorm room. He'd been waiting in the hall for almost an hour, looking at the red scarf dangling from the doorknob – his roommate's *do not disturb* sign. His girlfriend Becky was over, and the two of them were no doubt going at it like wild rabbits, as usual.

One of these days he was going to hide that damned scarf – not that it would be likely to stop them. Probably just result in him blundering in on them and Becky coming onto him again. That was the last thing he needed: *more* drama. His life was crazy enough without Barry going nuts on him. Becky – a sizable white girl – had already made it *quite* clear that she was more than willing to trade up from her tweedy black boyfriend for a studlier model, though Tyrone didn't have the heart to tell his roommate that.

"You guys done in there? It's almost midnight, dude, I gotta get some sleep."

The door opened as if on cue and the chubby girl came out into the hall in what she no doubt thought was a sultry maneuver, fluttering her eyelashes at Tyrone and swaying her hips a little so that her enormous pale breasts swayed from side to side. "Hey there, big boy," she said, biting her lower lip and looking him up and down. "I think I wore him out." She stretched luxuriantly, "of course, I could still go another few rounds," she said, then tried to laugh it off as if she weren't blatantly hitting on him.

The girl was thirsty, there was no denying that.

Tyrone brushed past her. "Sorry," he said, "maybe another time."

She scoffed, "Your loss, Ty."

"Goodnight, Becky," and he shut the door.

Barry was already sleeping, his blanket drawn over his mostly naked body – thank God. He snored softly, one arm thrown over his eyes. There was a used condom hanging over the edge of the trash can, glistening softly.

Tyrone shook his head and flopped down in his own bed. The springs squeaked beneath him.

Barry stirred. "Oh, shit... sorry man," he said sleepily, "didn't mean to nod off."

"No problem."

His roommate grinned. "She really wore me out, if you know what I mean. That girl can *ride*, bro."

"I'm sure," Tyrone said, and rolled his eyes in the darkness.

Barry sighed heavily. "Man... it's crazy. I always *dreamed* of having a girlfriend, right? A sexy white girl with a fat ass, man, that's the fantasy. Can't believe how good it is. That bitch is a total ho for black dick, brother, know what I'm saying?"

Tyrone snorted. "Yeah, I kind got that."

"Man," his roommate breathed out a long slow breath, drawing the blankets up and over himself a little better. Their dorm wasn't cold, but it did get cool here in the Florida winter. "What a thing, brother. What a thing."

Tyrone stared up at the ceiling. "Hey Barry?" he said, and already regretted it.

"What's up?"

"Ah, nothing, forget it."

"Come on, brother, open up. You know I got your back."

"Just... what would you do if she... you know. Got pregnant?"

There was a long silence in the little dorm room. Barry whistled, then laughed a little. "Man, that's a heavy one. I mean, she's, like... she's keen, you know? Never wants to wear condoms, never wants me to pull out. I gotta frickin' fight her to use protection. Thought it was supposed to be the other way around. And I been tempted man, been *really* tempted to bust that nut up inside, you know? But... I don't need that, man. That kinda complication."

"Yeah?"

"Course not. I mean, look at me! I'm just a kid, you know? I can't be having kids of my own. No matter how much I wanna knock that ho up. Gotta hold back, right?"

"I guess so," he said, and winced. He'd never been able to hold back even a little, and neither had Jennifer. They'd hardly even discussed the idea of using protection in their torrential outpouring of lust.

"Anyway, Becky's... don't get me wrong; she's a hot piece of ass, but... I mean. Not really looking to settle down long term, right? I mean, white girls are just for fun. My mom would kill me if I brought some cracker ho back home with me."

"Yeah," Tyrone admitted, "mine too."

"Anyway, I'm gonna try not to think about it. Shit, man, you gonna make me *worry*. I'm stressed enough about finals, I don't need that on me."

"Sorry."

"Whatever, brother, no big thing." Barry rolled over and he settled his head into the pillow. A few minutes later, he was sleeping.

Tyrone lay awake a while longer, staring up at the darkened ceiling above him. *White girls are just for fun.* That was true, he knew it was. Especially married ones who were ten years older than him.

His phone rattled in his pocket and he dug down to take it out. The screen glared brightly at him as he switched it on, and he winced. There was a text from Jennifer.

-When can you come fuck me, master? I need your cum in my pregnant white pussy...

He stared at the message for a long time. He should ignore it, should start to pull back, get out of her orbit, at least long enough to clear his head.

It was too late for that though. He could no more say no than he'd been able to stop himself from fucking her raw all those times. He texted back:

-Soon, baby. You'll get your cock soon. I'll be there tomorrow.

He should have known better. He couldn't escape that easily.

Part Two - Jennifer Brice

Jennifer sat at the bar, watching the light and shadow dance in the corners of the room. A dozen couples – most interracial, some otherwise – were scattered about the club. The barman came up to her, his outfit crisp and neat, his dark features arranged in a mask of calm. "Would madam like to look over the wine list?"

She grinned ruefully and shifted back a little from the bar so that he could see the huge swell of her enormous belly. "I'm afraid not," she said. She was wearing a cute top and a little skirt that showed off her legs. Might as well enjoy it while she could. Her ankles were already starting to swell just a little.

"Ah. Terribly sorry, madam, my apologies."

"Not at all. I'll just have a water, if that's alright."

"Of course," he said, and retreated with a slight bow.

She sighed and caressed the curve of her full body. Every day for the past six months she'd been getting bigger and bigger and bigger. She felt like an overfilled balloon now, like she might pop at any moment. And she'd still three months to go! She could hardly believe it.

The truth was, however, she *liked* the feeling. She enjoyed the sensation of her body changing, her breasts and belly expanding, all of it. She was changing so that she could bring *his* child into the world, and that made all the discomfort and pain and exhaustion worth it. She could hardly wait to meet her black baby.

There had been an unexpected side-effect of the pregnancy that she'd discovered after the end of the uncomfortable first trimester and which hadn't slacked off in the slightest all through the second: she was unbelievably horny. Her hormones were going wild, and she could hardly stand how turned on she was nearly all the time.

She had been fucking Tyrone almost daily for the past three months, to the extent that she was starting to push against the bounds of his own impressive virility. She would ride him for hours, taking one load after the other, always ready for another after the first, then the second, then the third.

It was like being pregnant had rewired something inside her brain. She could hardly contain herself when she was around him. She'd even gone so far as to sneak into his dorm room a half a dozen times – a heavily pregnant woman, about forty years old, sneaking into a college dorm, imagine that! – and she'd fucked him there in his bed.

She'd fucked him at her house, in her car, outside, anywhere she could get her hands on him. Black cock seemed to be the only thing she could think about anymore, and not just Tyrone's either. She couldn't keep her eyes off them when she passed them in the street or at the supermarket. Just one look and she was soaking her panties, imagining what it would be like to fuck them, and she'd go running to find and fuck Ty.

It had finally gotten so bad that he'd told her he need a break, just for a couple weeks while he prepped for his finals. She'd agreed – reluctantly.

So now she found herself back at the Black and White Club, the place where it had all begun for her, where her life had been changed forever.

The waited gave her a glass of ice water and she took it gratefully, sipping it carefully. The ice clinked against the glass when she set it down.

"*Damn,* girl, you are looking ready to pop!"

She glanced up. A young black man sat across the bar, grinning at her as he lounged on the edge of his seat, his long legs spread a little and his body leaned slight towards her. His skin was a caramel brown, his eyes an exotic green. He had short curly hair and an expression of confident ease. He wore tight leather pants and a loose shirt open down the middle to reveal a good portion of his toned chest.

"Not quite yet," she said, "still another three months to go."

His eyebrows went up a little, and he slid two stools down so that he was sitting just beside her. He held one hand out. "D'Shawn Green," he said smoothly.

"Jennifer." She shook his hand and, though she tried to resist it, she couldn't help feeling a little thrill of excitement run through her. Immediately she wanted to touch his chest, run her fingertips over the smooth dark skin, feel the coiled masculine power of the muscles beneath.

"Daddy here tonight?" D'Shawn asked, nodding pointedly at her swollen belly.

She cocked an eyebrow at him and grinned a little. "Nope."

"Aw, that *is* a shame," he said, stretching languidly, appearing quite casual and at ease. "He a brother?"

She nodded.

"Somebody you met here?" he asked, his own eyebrows lifting.

She nodded again.

"Interesting. He give you that too?" he said, and reached out to take her hand again. He drew it slowly towards himself and touched the gold band on her ring finger. His thumb slid slowly over the smooth surface of her wedding ring.

"Nope," she said, and her smile widened.

"Well well," he said, and leaned back against the bar. "Guess I find that a little curious."

"Oh?" she rested her elbow on the counter and studied him, "what's curious about it?"

"Well. You're here, but not here to drink. So I guess that means you're here to see somebody. But there's nobody here. So that tells me that you haven't met the person you wanna see yet. So maybe... I'm that person."

"You might be," she said, still trying to hold herself in check. It was difficult to play hard-to-get when she was already aching for his touch after only just meeting him.

"What kind of company you looking for this evening?" he asked, smiling easily, his tongue moving over his full bottom lip.

"Only one way to find out," she said, and she turned towards him, her legs parting just a little. Her skirt rested over her thighs, revealing the shadowy gap between her legs. She glanced down, then back up at him. *Let's see how bold you really are*, she thought to herself.

D'Shawn, as it turned out, was *extremely* bold. Without a moment's hesitation he placed his hand on her thigh.

She shuddered, her body quivering at the sensation of his touch. She looked down, marveling all over again at the way his dark skin looked contrasted against her pale white thigh.

He began to slide it slowly inward, moving it beneath her skirt. He looked up at her, his startling green eyes locking onto hers. His smile widened when he discovered her secret: she didn't have any panties on under her skirt.

She swallowed hard as his finger brushed against the tuft of hair down there, then lower. He drew his knuckle slowly down between her lips, parting them ever so slightly. She bit her lip. Hard.

"You wet, girl." He said, his voice low but still conversational and calm. It was as if he were remarking upon the weather. *A rainy day downtown.* She shivered again and clutched her thighs together, involuntarily trapping his hand between her legs. His finger teased her opening, playing with the folds of her pussy lips and making her tingle all over at the feeling.

She moaned softly, and held the counter for support.

What are you doing, Jennifer? She was letting a stranger finger her in front of a whole crowd of strangers. Nobody was paying too much attention, but D'Shawn was making no efforts whatsoever to hide was he was doing from the room. He was using her boldly and openly, making her his own personal plaything in front of everybody.

And she was letting him.

Not just letting him, she was loving it. She reached down and held him by the wrist, pulling his hand a little closer. He grinned and curled his middle finger out to slip it between her juicy lip, sliding it oh so easily inside her. She quivered at the sensation. He started to move it casually in and out, making little wet sounds beneath the bar.

"You a good girl, Jennifer?"

"Yes sir," she murmured, her eyes closing as she drew in a sharp breath of gasping pleasure.

"You wanna make my big black cock feel good, don't you? That's why you came here. You came to get fucked."

She nodded, her fingers tightening, the nails scratching on the surface of the bar.

"You a thirsty girl, Jennifer. It's that baby. Now you had a taste of black you just need more and more, that right?"

"That's right," she moaned, "I need it."

"Well... might be I could help." He grinned, and put a second finger into her. Her hips started to rock ever so slightly on the bar stool as she moved against him. She could feel her juices spilling out, coating the top of the leather stool beneath her thighs.

The wet noises she was making were impossible to disguise anymore. The barman, being the discrete gentleman that he was, turned away and busied himself at the far end of the bar. "Please," she moaned, "*please* can we go find a room? I need to get fucked, please."

D'Shawn just smiled. "Nah," he said, "I'm good here."

She blinked at him. "W-what? You... don't want me?"

He laughed and slapped the bar. "Shit, girl, I didn't say that! Of course I want you. I just said I'm good here."

She blinked, the realization slowly dawning. "You mean... right here? In front of everybody?"

He turned and made a little show of scanning the crowd. "Everybody? Ain't nobody here but you and me, the way I see it. At least nobody you need to worry about. Only thing you need to think about is right here," he said, and grabbed his crotch.

Her gaze followed his head, and found the bulge there. Immediately, the last of her resolve melted away. The moment she took in the shape of him, huge and bulging inside his pants, she knew that she would do anything to have it, even if it meant doing it right here at the bar.

D'Shawn slowly unzipped his pants, then he put his hands up on the bar. "You want something," he said, as if it weren't any concern of his what she did, "you help yourself." Then he called over the bartender and ordered a drink.

Jennifer looked slowly around the room. She locked eyes with a younger white woman sitting in the corner with her husband. The other woman smiled at her and gave a little nod, then crossed her legs and settled in to enjoy the show.

Jennifer couldn't help smiling back. She was going to do this. Oh God, she was really going to do this, wasn't she?

She slipped off the stool. There was a shiny patch where she'd left a wet mark on the black leather. She got down onto her knees and reached into D'Shawn's pants, then drew out his thick hard black cock. It was beautiful, and utterly irresistible.

She sucked his cock hungrily. D'Shawn drank his wine, murmuring his approval occasionally and stroking her hair while she gagged on him.

Her mind went blank down there, emptying of everything that wasn't him and his dick. This was where she belonged, it was her place. She was a slave to black cock, and that was how her life was going to be from now on, there was no denying it anymore.

She caressed her pregnant belly as she choked on his dick, hungry for his seed within her womb.

She couldn't say how long it was, but eventually he drew her up and pushed her against the bar, though he was, of course, careful of her belly. She stood there, clutching it with both hands as he stepped behind her and slowly lifted her skirt.

"Hm... that's a tasty ass, baby," he said in her ear, cupping her bottom with both hands. He gave it a firm squeeze, then reached down to grab his cock and slap it up against her sopping pussy.

She moaned and leaned forward slightly, hyper-conscious of that fact that she was being watched now by no less than a dozen people, with more turning their gazes upon her every minute.

She pushed back onto him, her whole body tensing with the delicious feeling of taking his cock into her. She felt her pussy squeezing hard on his thick black member, and he let out a grunt of pleasure that she was sure he'd tried to hold in. She smiled. That was her favorite thing: pulling those expressions of pleasure out of them, when they were unable to deny just how good her pussy was.

He settled back against the bar-stool and he took a long drink. "You just keep working that cock, baby," he said, and slapped her still clothed rump none-too-gently with the flat of his hand.

There was no outward evidence of their activity, at least not definitive proof. He'd only pulled himself out through his fly, and his body against hers covered up what was revealed by her hiked-up skirt. Their motions against the bar, however, and her moaning and the wet sounds of her pussy on him left little doubt as to what they were doing.

She turned her face down to look at the bar, her cheeks flushed with embarrassment as she worked herself up and down his long shaft, grinding and twisting her hips as she fucked him. The Jennifer of even a year ago would never have done this and, even if she somehow had, she'd have restricted herself to only the slightest and most tentative of rocking motions, trying to maintain some facade of deniability.

Now, however, she gave herself over completely. She was a slut for black cock, and it didn't really matter anymore who knew it. Let the whole world see, for all she cared, but that wasn't going to stop her giving this black dick the ride of its life.

She felt her swollen belly rocking against the bar, and she reached down once more to hold it in her hands.

His hands found hers, both of them slipping around her sides to cradle her belly. "Hm, I love this, baby... Love fucking your big pregnant body."

"Yes sir," she moaned, and thrust back on him again.

She fucked him there at the bar, watched by everybody in the club. Finally, with a groan and a grimace, he rammed fully in and shot his load, cum spurting deep inside her pussy.

"Fuck, baby, that was good," he said, slumping back on the stool. He reached a slightly shaking hand out to pick up his drink and he finished it in one long swallow.

She smiled at him, and reached back to flip her skirt down. She step away, her thighs trembling. She could feel his hot load within her, a thick drop of cum slowly sliding down to her lips.

"You gonna give me your number, baby?"

She smiled and shook her head. "I don't know about that."

"Come on. Am I gonna see you again or what?"

She put her purse over her shoulder and started towards the door. "Just keep coming by the club," she tossed back over her shoulder with a wink and a laugh, "I'll be around."

* * *

Jennifer sat in the stands, looking down at the lines of young people filing slowly into the huge outdoor amphitheater, all dressed in blacks gowns with those funny flat tasseled hats. She craned her neck, trying to get a glimpse of their faces as they came in.

She was sitting way in the back, no surprise there: all the proud parents of the graduating class had taken the better seats. She was just an onlooker, and outside here.

What was she even doing here? She didn't have a place here; this wasn't a part of Tyrone's life that included her. She reached down and held her full belly.

She felt a yearning for him, a sense of... she wasn't sure exactly what it was. He was, in many ways, her first love. Her first *passionate* and sexual love, at any rate. She loved Percy, of course, but there were days when they felt little closer than siblings of even cousins. It was a strange sensation for which she had no proper words.

Jennifer had no clear way to process the feelings which she was experiencing. There weren't any self-help books that pertained to the subject, no talk shows which she might turn to for advice. She couldn't even talk to her old friends about this, certainly not her family.

Her parents knew she was pregnant. She told them that she'd gotten a sperm donor, which was close enough to truth that she didn't feel any guilt withholding the full reality of the situation.

She still wasn't sure if she loved Tyrone, that was the problem. She loved what he did to her, loved how he made her feel. He was beautiful and powerful and majestically sexual, but she couldn't say if there was more to it than that. She didn't think he loved her either, not in a deep or passionate way, not beyond the sex.

And that was alright. Their relationship had never been founded on love. It was about the attraction of it, the intense physical need which they'd felt for one another. But that was all.

He had his whole life ahead of her. Looking down at the graduates still filing in, she was struck with just how *young* they all seemed to her. Ty was so mature that she forgot sometimes that he was still only in his early twenties.

She had to let him go.

She caressed her belly, smiling as she felt movement inside, a gentle kicking. The baby had never been meant for *them*, it had always been hers. A gift from him to her, something that she'd always wanted and her husband had been unable to provide. She didn't want him to feel burdened by the thought of it. It was best that they just... drift apart, go their own ways.

They had touched each other's lives in an inescapable manner, in a way that she thought would change them both forever. But everything had to end sometimes. A new chapter had to begin.

She reached down and she touched her leg, just above the ankle on her calf. The little white Q inside the black spade. The sign that she was forever marked, forever claimed. You could see it faintly through her dark stockings, but wouldn't be able to make it out clearly unless you looked closely.

Then she saw him, and her heart leap despite herself. She wanted to raise her hand and wave, but resisted the impulse, biting down on her lower lip.

No. It was better to let go...

By the time Tyrone Jackson had filed in and taken his seat she was already gone.

Percy Brice

"Hurry *up*, Percy! There's no *time* for this!"

"Yes, yes, I'm *coming*, I'm *coming!*" Percy glanced once more into the little nursery room they'd set up for the baby. Everything looked perfect: the pale blue walls, the little rose pink bassinet, the pile of toys and big soft stuffed animals, the mobile slowly rotating where it hung from the ceiling. He'd been laboring over it from weeks now, coming up every day after work to put in one more thing or adjust the position of something.

He felt a tear in the corner of his eye. God, he was going to have a baby! He'd given up the idea years ago, and now it was really going to happen... and he could hardly wait.

The fact that the child wasn't biologically his didn't really seem to matter anymore. He didn't even think about it, to be honest. He didn't care whose DNA the child had or what they looked like, this was going to be his child. He was going to be a father!

Natasha appeared in the doorway, frowning deeply. "Percy!" she snapped again. "Jennifer's waiting for us at the hospital right now. Come *on!* This isn't the time to lollygag."

"Right, of course, I'm coming," he said, and switched off the nursery room light.

It was a strange and quiet ride to the hospital with his dominatrix. For once, she had nothing to say. Natasha James, the hardest and coldest woman he'd ever known, seemed now almost giddy with excitement in a way he'd never seen or thought possible. Her fingers drummed on the wheel as she drove, and she kept smiling a strange little smile of pure uncomplicated happiness.

"You're excited, aren't you?" he asked, grinning a little himself.

She shot him a look, but didn't deny it.

"I can't believe it's really happening... this has been the longest nine months of my life," he said, and rocked his head back against the seat-rest.

She cocked an eyebrow in his direction. "Were you worried?"

"Yeah," he admitted, laughing a little, "I was."

"I thought I'd kept you too busy to worry," she said with a smirk.

He shifted a little in his seat. He was firmly in chastity right now, as he usually was these days. It had started to get so that he felt almost naked without it, as if he were missing something essential, like walking out of the house with no socks beneath his shoes.

Natasha had molded him in the past few months, transformed him entirely. He was hers now, eager to the point of desperation to please her, and he'd never been happier. Jennifer had Tyrone, and the others from the Club she'd started to see, but he no longer felt even the merest shadow of envy of conflict on that score.

He hardly knew what he'd do now if Jennifer wanted him to have sex with her. It would have felt *wrong*. Her pussy was too good for him, it always had been and he'd been fooling himself to ever think otherwise. Any pussy was too good for his wimpy little thing. Being used by Natasha satisfied him utterly, and he wouldn't have it any other way.

She pulled up in front of the hospital. He popped open the door and rushed out, Jennifer's overnight bags slung one over his shoulder and the other in his hand.

"Hey Percy," she called across the seat, her voice uncharacteristically soft, "tell her good luck for me. And let me know how it goes, alright?"

"I will," he said, beaming back at his Dom for a moment before turning away.

"And Percy!"

He looked back once more and saw the softness completely melted away, that cold look of command firmly back in place on her dark and regal features. He knew that look, and knew what it entailed. He shivered with excitement. "Yes?"

"I'm giving you some time off to take care of Jennifer, but she'll be giving me constant reports. I know you aren't going to disappoint me. If you do, you're going to be in for a punishment like you can't imagine when I see you again."

"Love you too," he said – an uncharacteristically bold response for him, one that might just get him in trouble if she remembered it by the time they saw each other again – and he rushed into the hospital.

It took him fifteen minutes to find his way to the birthing unit. He babbled at a nurse for a moment before she finally directed him to his wife's room. Jennifer was already straining and gasping inside.

"Percy!" she said when she saw him poke his head through the curtain. "You made it, *finally*."

"Sorry," he said, and lifted the bags for proof. "Had to swing by the house and grab these."

"Oh good, thanks sweetie, thank you," she said, huffing a little, looking a bit pink.

"Sure thing," he said, and slipped into the seat beside her. He picked up her hand and gave it a squeeze. "You doing okay, honey?"

She grimaced, shrugged, then laughed. "It's, uh, well, it's not easy. Almost there, though, almost made it."

"You're doing amazing, honey. This is the home stretch. You're practically there."

"Yeah," she said, hissing in her breath, "but this is going to be the hardest part, I think."

The curtain opened and a tall man with round glasses and a white coat and clipboard came. He took in Percy's presence and gave a little nod. "Ah, Mr. Brice. You're just in time." He blushed a little.

Percy frowned. "Hm? How do you mean?"

The doctor sighed and sat down beside the bed. "You're wife is doing great, Mr. Brice. But, ah... things are developing a little more slowly than we like to see."

Jennifer frowned. "What do you mean?"

"I'll, uh, I'll cut to the chase, shall I?"

"Please do," she said, narrowing her eyes. Percy knew the expression well, and didn't blame the doctor one bit for quaking in his shoes.

"We need to kick things into the next gear, if you take my meaning. We've, ah, we've found that the best way to kick things off is for the, um, the husband to... Well, for him to have sex with you. It stimulates the body, helps get the process going."

"Sex?" Jennifer said, looking deeply incredulous.

"Sex?" Percy squeaked, and felt himself going pale.

The doctor nodded, pursing his lips. "Sex. Just, you know, nothing fancy. Just the usual thing. That'll help us get started. I'd recommend it. Strongly. Just to make sure that we don't run into any complications."

"You can't be serious," she said.

The doctor laughed. "I certainly am. It's a common enough practice, I'm sure you heard about it in your birthing classes."

"They did mention it," Percy said, blushing at the memory. Jennifer shot him a glower.

"I'll leave you to it then," the doctor said. "Just shut the door, I'll see to it that the nurses don't disturb you while you're... busy. Best of luck. And nice meet you, Mr. Brice," he said, reaching over Jennifer's massively swollen belly to shake Percy's hand. Percy returned the handshake in a kind of daze.

Then the doctor left, giving Jennifer a little nod on his way out. He shut the curtain behind him.

Jennifer slammed her head onto the pillow. "Oh my *God*, this cannot be happening!"

"We'll figure something out, honey," he said, and gave her hand a nervous little bad.

She looked up at him, exasperated, "Oh? And how are we going to do that? Even if you wanted to, Percy, and even if *I* wanted you to, you're not exactly equipped for it! I doubt I'd even feel you in there anymore. Besides," she said, and reached down to shove her hand between his legs. She gave his chastity device a little rattle, "you seem a bit tied up at the moment. It's not like I can just go out there and pick up some sexy black doctor in the hallway, is it? I can hardly stand up right now!"

He gave her hand another reassuring squeeze and gently extracted himself. He didn't even feel a moment of shame or outrage at the insult to his masculine prowess. She was right, of course, and there was no reason to argue the obvious point. "Don't worry," he said, and pulled out his cell phone. "I'll take care of it."

"How?" she wailed.

He just grinned, and turned the phone on. "Just leave it to me, sweetie."

* * *

Percy breathed a huge sigh of relief when he saw the glass door of the hospital swinging open. *About time.* He'd been starting to get worried. He got up and cross the lobby. "This way," he said, "her room is just back here."

Tyrone Jackson nodded at him, his hands deep in his pockets. "Sure thing," he said, and he followed.

Percy explained the situation on the way there. It had seemed to him that there was a growing distance between Tyrone and Jennifer. He was around less often, and she more frequently saw different black men to satisfy her needs. But the connection was clearly still strong. He'd responded to Percy's text immediately, only asking for the hospital address. Fifteen minutes later here he was.

A nurse game them a strange look as they entered Jennifer's room. Percy ignored it, and tugged the curtain shut.

Jennifer looked up at Tyrone for a long moment, her face a little red, breathing hard and clutching her enormous belly. Slowly, a smile spread across her lips. "Well..." she said, "this *is* a nice surprise."

Tyrone shrugged, shuffling one foot. "Percy said you needed help. So here I am."

"My knight in shining armor," Jennifer said, without any apparent sense of irony, and she reached her open hands out to him.

He went to her and they embraced tightly. Then he caught her chin in his hand and turned her face to his. For a long moment they stared into one another's eyes, and then he leaned in and planted a slow and sensual kiss on her lips.

Percy felt a tightness down below as he started to strain against his chastity device.

She moaned softly. "Hm... I feel better already."

"Then you're going to love this," Tyrone said, and pulled his shirt off.

She bit her lower lip, then laughed a bit and pulled her hospital gown off. "Sorry about the bed," she said, scooting forward a little bit, "be kind of a squeeze."

"That's fine," he said, and unbuttoned his jeans.

"I remember that tattoo..." she said gently, nodded at his exposed chest. Beneath the crest of his team were the letters JB inked in black. *Jennifer Brice.* Percy felt a twinge. She really did belong to him. His symbol on her calf, her initials on his chest. They were linked.

"Yeah," he said, and touched it with the tips of his fingers. "Something to remember you by."

She smiled, a little sadly, Percy thought, and nodded.

Jennifer lay on her said on the edge of the bed, fully naked. Tyrone slipped in behind her, and put his hand on her hip. Percy's breath caught in his throat as he looked at her lying there, full and voluptuous, the skin of her tummy stretched tight with this man's child. Her breasts were enormous and her belly huge; her entire body seemed engorged and sexual. "Start slow," she said, "if that's okay... and we'll see where it goes from there."

"Sure thing, baby," he murmured, and kissed the back of her neck.

His black hand slid down over her pale belly, holding it firm and close as he pressed against her from behind.

She moaned, and lifted one leg just a little bit, shifting her bottom back to give him a better angle. He lowered one hand and put himself against her opening, then held her again as he slowly shifted forward. She groaned and shut her eyes tight, shuddering already with pleasure. "Yes..." she whispered, "that's where I need you, Ty... right there inside me."

Percy cleared his throat. "Would you, ah... would you like me to leave?"

She shook her head, not opening her eyes, "No, no you can stay. If it's alright with you, Ty?"

The black man shrugged.

Jennifer patted the seat of the little hospital stool in front of her. "Come here," she said, "I want to hold your hand... this is a family moment."

He came and he sat in front of her. He took her hand and held it gently in both of his own, caressing her palm.

The hospital bed creaked slightly as Tyrone started to shift back and forth.

"Oh, my boys... my boys... this is just what I needed... thank you for coming, Ty, thank you so much."

"Of course, baby," he whispered, already starting to breathe harder as he got into the rhythm of things, "anything for you."

"And Percy... thank you for getting him for me. I knew I could count on you, sweetie..."

He smiled, and he tightened his hold on her hand.

Tyrone gave a deep slow push, and she whimpered, grabbing hold of the armrest of the bed with her free hand, her knuckles going white as she gripped it.

"Oh God!" she groaned, "Oh God, yes! Yes, right there! Make me cum, Ty, please..."

He reached around to cup her swollen breast, the pink bud of her nipple bright between his chocolate-brown fingers. He rolled the nipple gently, then gave it a little tug. A bead of white milk appeared at the tip, gathered there for a second, then rolled down over his dark knuckle.

She moaned and whimpered and she pushed her hips back against him, grinding on the cock buried deep within her. "You make me cum so good, Ty... you always make me cum."

He grunted, and tightened his grip on her hip, his dark fingers digging into her pale skin as he rocked her back and forth, using her like a sex toy almost, pleasuring himself with her body. Jennifer's eyes squeezed tight in ecstasy.

Then, all of a sudden, they snapped open, and stared right into Percy's. Her hand caught his and squeezed tight, fingernails digging into his skin. Her mouth opened in a perfect O and she gasped with pleasure. "I'm cumming!" she panted, hardly able to get the words out, "Oh *fuck*, I'm cumming!"

She and Percy's eyes were locked together as her orgasm rippled through her, shaking her right to the core. He felt his cock getting painfully erect inside its cage, but he didn't care; he welcomed the pain.

Tyrone groaned, and he came deep inside Jennifer's pussy, and rolled back with a sigh.

Jennifer waited just a moment longer, riding the high crest of her orgasm, then she squeezed Percy's hand again and spoke, her voice extremely calm, but tightly urgent all the same. "Percy," she said, "get the doctor. It's coming."

* * *

Twelve hours later, Jennifer Brice delivered a beautiful baby boy. He had dark mocha skin, lighter than his father's but certainly a good deal darker than his mother's. She named him Tyler Brice. Ty for short, after his father.

Percy thought to himself, as he held the little bundle in his arms, that he had never seen anything so beautiful in his life.

Tyrone Jackson

Tyrone watched the lights of the city streaming by, gold and white and red and blue, flicking across the windows of the car.

"Florida, man," said Jack Thompson, "what a rush."

"Yeah," Tyrone agreed. "Sure is."

"You ever been down here before?"

"Yep."

"Oh yeah?" Jack asked, glancing over and giving him a look.

"I went to school here."

"No shit?"

"Yeah."

"So... it's been, what, four or five years since you graduated?"

Tyrone thought about it for just a moment. "Four," he said.

Four years since he'd last seen this city. Four years since he'd last seen Jennifer. They'd intended to keep in touch, but she'd been so busy with the baby, and he'd been so busy with his new job up in Georgia that they'd fallen out of the habit. Then, when things had finally calmed down for him, he realized that it had been almost a year. At that point, it had seemed... awkward. What was the point? Their paths had diverged.

He'd taken his business degree and joined the little Atlanta brokerage pretty much right out of school. Jack had come on board about a year later, and they'd developed a good working relationship. So it was that, now that the firm was growing, the two of them had been chosen to go together down to Florida to discuss a big deal. It was a huge step for the company, one that was bound to change things in a big way for everybody. The fact that he'd been entrusted with making the deal said a lot about Tyrone's place in the company.

He'd done well for himself. A good word from a certain Mr. Mason had helped him get his food in the door, but he'd done it all on his own after that, proved himself a skilled and canny businessman. Everything was working out.

Now here he was, back in Florida. It was like turning back the clock, somehow, seeing this city... it was a strange feeling.

The meetings had gone better than anybody had dared to hope they might, so Jack and Tyrone had spent the evening out celebrating. It looked like they'd both be the new golden boys when they got back to Atlanta after this. He watched the lights go by, feeling the gentle buzz of the drinks he'd had humming in his head, and Tyrone allowed himself a little smile.

Everything was working out okay for him.

Then the car turned down a familiar street, and all of a sudden there they were, driving slowly down a road he knew all-too-well. He sat up. "Wait," he said, "hold up."

Jack pulled over smoothly. "What's up?"

"I just... I saw someplace I used to know."

"An old haunt?" Jack said with a grin.

"Something like that. Let me out, would ya?"

"You serious?"

"Yeah, just let me out, I'm gonna drop in for a minute. I'll catch a cab back to the hotel, okay?"

Jack leaned forward and looked dubiously up and down the street. "You sure, man? I can come with if you want?"

"No. Thanks, but... this is something I wanna do on my own."

"Okay then," Jack said, and put it in park. "See you in the morning, then."

"You got it. Thanks, Jack."

Jack flashed him a grin and shot a finger-pistol in his direction. "Are you kidding? After today, thank *you*."

"Ha. Right, you too."

And then he was out in the warm summer air of the quiet Florida street. He stood there for a moment, his hands in his pockets, and he waited until he heard Jack pull out behind him and start to drive away.

He wanted to be well and truly alone for this. It had the feeling to him almost of being a kind of pilgrimage, a sacred moment. But *why?* Why was he doing this? It was stupid; he should just go back to the hotel now and forget about it.

His feet didn't listen to his head, however, and they carried him on past the little plaque and to the door. *The Black and White Club*, read the plaque.

He knocked on the door, his heart in his throat. *Just go home, Ty*, he told himself again.

The little window-slit opened. "How can I help you?" came a muffled but deferential voice from within.

"I just wanted to come in for a minute," he said, rather lamely, he thought.

"Invitation only," the voice said, a bit less friendly now.

"I'm a friend of Mr. Mason's," he said.

There was a pause, then the door swung open. Tyrone looked both ways down the empty sidewalk. He hesitated for just one more moment, then he walked inside the club.

* * *

Tyrone got a drink at the bar. For a time he just sat there, watching the people come and go. He observed black studs and wives paring off, husbands looking on with expression of jealousy or ecstasy or some combination of the two, and all the rest.

He bought a drink and he drank slowly, meditatively.

It had all started here. As a matter of fact, he'd been sitting on this very stool at the time, just drinking and facing the wall when Jennifer Brice had approached him. She'd been so timid and strangely innocent then. So... supplicant.

He grinned slightly at the memory, shaking his head. He turned back and he looked at the table where she'd been sitting when they had first made eye contact. It was empty now, the unused chair facing out as if somebody had just pushed it back and risen from it. He wondered if the seat would be still warm with the heat of their body, whoever they were. He wondered who they were and what they had come here to find.

And he wondered if they had found it.

He finished his drink and set the empty glass back on the counter. A watery ring gleamed on the polished surface. He drew his finger through it, tracing lines on the varnished hardwood.

"You want anything else?" the bartender asked, coming over and casually wiping about the ring with an unthinking sweep of the cloth he kept folded over one arm.

"No," Tyrone said, "I'm good, thanks." He turned and started towards the door. What had he been expecting to find here, anyway? Maybe he shouldn't have come...

He'd meant to walk towards the door but somehow found himself instead turning towards the red curtain which hung over the entrance to the upstairs. His feet seemed to lead him there of their own volition, like he'd wandered into a trance almost. He walked slowly through the curtain and then up the stairs.

The feeling of the air changed, taking on a dense and complex shift. There was an ineffable and powerful sense of sexuality in the air, a musky headiness far stronger and more intoxicating than the drink he'd had at the bar.

He walked randomly down the long hall, though his feet seemed to know where they wanted to go.

There was a small crowd gathered outside one of the many doors of the wall, a sort of reverent silence among the onlookers. And, from within the room, the sounds of sex.

The grunting, the panting, the creaking of bed-springs and the moaning, the wet noises of lubricated skin on skin. Tyrone felt a tingle of arousal coursing through him. He stood at the edge of the crowd, craning his neck to try and get a look inside, though the crush was too deep, the crowd too thick.

"Oh, *fuck!*" he heard a woman's voice, and it struck him as oddly familiar, though it was difficult to say for sure, as it sounded strangely muffled, like there was a ball-gag in her mouth or a hand over her lips. The tingle of arousal great stronger.

"What's going on?" he asked someone at the edge of the crowd, a young guy about his own age dressed in a polo shirt and crisp khaki trousers.

"J's putting on a hell of a show, man."

"J?" he asked.

"Yeah," he said, and lifted an eyebrow. "You new here? Everybody in the club knows J. She's like, the ultimate white slut. She's got three black guys in there right now and she's giving them a run for their money." He looked Tyrone up and down. "You wanna get in there and help out?"

He just shook his head. "Not tonight, thanks."

And yet, despite his refusal, Tyrone still found himself moving deeper into the crowd, finally nudging his way through the doorway so that he could take in the sight before him.

A tall white woman, he thought she was in her mid-forties – though she looked amazing for her age, was in the center of the room, almost completely naked and down on all fours. She wore a tight black leather collar and a garter belt and stockings. Her soft brown hair swayed as her head bobbed back and forth on the huge cock shoved in her mouth, and her full rump rocked sensually on the two cocks inserted into her holes, one in her pussy from beneath and one being pounded down into her ass from above.

Three pairs of black hands clasped her tight body, the dark skin sharply contrasting with her pale skin. Her face was turned away from him, busied at the crotch of the standing man as he fucked her mouth.

The crowd was murmuring with silent admiration and arousal. There was a sensation of sexual anticipation among the onlookers, like an orgy might break out at any moment. They were all feeding off of this one woman's voracious and incredible sexual energy. It seemed to radiate out of her as powerfully as the rays of the sun, suffusing everyone who saw it with an overwhelming lust.

Tyrone felt his cock getting hard in his pants, straining against the cloth as it grew erect.

He watched for a while. He saw a slender white woman's hand brush timidly against the front of his pants, but couldn't see who in the crowd had groped him. He saw several people kissing now, black hands sliding into panties, white hands clasping black cocks inside pants.

"God, she's amazing..." he heard somebody murmur.

"A true queen of spades," another said.

And all the while the woman in the room kept fucking, taking all comers. Tyrone was about to turn to go when one of the men screwing her grabbed hold of her stockings and ripped them off. He slapped her flank and grinned as he plunged his huge thick black cock deeper into her.

Tyrone stared across the room. There was a small black tattoo on the woman's calf: a little spade with the shape of a Q inside it. Then, as if sensing him, the woman turned her head and, for just one moment, their eyes locked. Those familiar green eyes.

He smiled, and she grinned back, then took the huge cock back down her throat, her attention returning to the men fucking her.

A moment later when she looked back into the crowd, she didn't see him. He was already gone.

As Tyrone walked back down the stairs he could feel the immense energy of the room behind him, the powerful sexual radiance pouring out in an endless flood. He nodded to himself as he went back out through the swaying red curtain and across the bar to the door of the Black and White Club.

That man who'd spoken had been right. She was indeed a true Queen of Spades.

ALSO BY THIS AUTHOR

Erotic Fiction:

The Hotwife Island Series:

Hotwife Island

Hotwife in Bondage

Hotwive's Ball

The Southern Belle Series:

Balling the Southern Belle

Taking the Southern Belle

Erotic Novels:

As Black As Midnight

Snowbunny's Paradise

Printed in Great Britain
by Amazon

21145564R00212